What Readers Are Saying

"Luminous, visionary, powerful and passionate, this novel is at once a profound analysis of the ills of today's world, a teaching of deep clarity and understanding, and an empowering call to action, all in the absorbing, beautifully written tradition of Native American story telling."

Deborah Joy, PhD, Berkeley, California

"This is beautiful and important and good. It let me know—in a new way—that I am not alone. It is a gift. It says words out loud that have existed, silent, inside of me for . . . well, forever."

Valerie Klokow, Hartford, Connecticut

"*Going to Water* is far more than just a good read; it is both transformational and transcendental. There is a new and wondrous richness in the use of language which readers will find sublime and which will transport them into unexplored dimensions of emotion and understanding."

Martin Scanlon, Bonny Doon, California

"I love this book. There is so much here that feels like it's right at the heart of everything. It educates me and makes me wonder. It respects my intelligence and my heart, touching something huge. I have never read anything that felt quite this free from conventional limitations, and I think that is just what is needed. I hope that many, many people read this book and learn from it as I have."

Ashley Crawford, Santa Cruz, California

"*Going to Water* is in touch with a reality more real than many will ever know. Herein lies the salve to heal some of the world's wounds. A recommended read for anyone needing the nourishment of beauty, authenticity, justice, and love."

Carolye Kuchta, Vancouver, BC, Canada

"This book finds me where I wander in the whirl of this time, and puts one hand on my back, a friend in the madness. It guides me to the places where I feel my significance in the world expand and change in its potential."

Alison McGregor, Santa Cruz, California.

"The story is as familiar as an old dream dreamt since time began, and then in turn, it reveals my own heart and understanding of what I have never known. It's more than a book . . ."

Laura Dickie, Aptos, California

"Stan Rushworth weaves a prophetic tale that spans time and realities like a literary ballet."

Kristi Moya, Montecello, New Mexico

"I became 'the fly on the wall' in places I'd always wondered about, at the blood-soaked valley of the Little Bighorn, and meeting personally with Adolph Hitler in an informal gathering at the Berghof. The novel puts you there hand in hand with the famous and infamous, entwined in a colorful tale reflecting the age-old battle between good and evil."

Joseph Napolitano, Aptos, California

"*Going to Water* is a novel so full of the truth of United States history that it is amazing and very touching. This is a stark and loving look at what we must soon come to terms with, and is a beautiful read."

Ayla Raven Eagle, St Ignatius, Montana

"Simultaneously microscopic and telescopic in its view, the story of Little Rain compels us to take a serious plunge into the emotional currents that drive human action and therefore create consequence. Reading this novel is akin to entering into a dream state, a place where we can not only learn to see in a new way, but use that new sight as a way to hold history differently in our minds and hearts. *Going to Water* is a testimony to the fact that Indigenous cultures are ever-present in constantly shifting forms, just as water shifts from ice to vapor and back to water."

Jacqueline Ramos, San Francisco, California

"The sweep of the discussion is epic, like a dream structured in a series of parables, the warmth and humanity of the narrator carrying it along. I love the answer to the question, 'Where do you put the hatred'—that life is given by accepting the support and love of family and friends—It clarifies the hope."

Kellogg Fleming, Corralitos, California

"I was negotiating seeing and blindness, loneliness and companionship, strength and weakness, a journey of self-learning that demanded I take a stand on my values. And what I appreciated most was that I could always go to the poetic language, carrying me through a forest, the song of a bird, a familiar sun-bathed field, allowing memories the opportunity to discover what is real, again."

Saul Ramos, San Jose, California

"Stan Rushworth has a style, grace, and ease of presentation that is natural, simultaneously informative and uplifting, with elements of stream-of-consciousness and magical realism. I was deeply moved by this book on many levels, and the more I read, the more deeply I craved to belong to the kind of community the novel presents. This is simply a masterpiece."

Stefan Malacek, PhD, Tillamook, Oregon

"At a time when so many people are feeling powerless and overwhelmed, their dreams impossible to attain and their lives and visions rendered invisible, Stan Rushworth offers, in this sweeping moral fable, *Going to Water*, an antidote to despair as powerfully efficacious as those Beginning Rain administers from her magical pouch, when she time-travels to a series of shameful and catastrophic episodes in human history, confronts the instigators of particular evils with the effects of the destructiveness they have unleashed, and helps them to see their limits and offers them different choices.

Going to Water is a polemic of the heart, a 'telling [of] the plain truth in a world spun on lies' for people 'isolated in their own tragedies . . . who cannot see the larger pattern,' who need 'not so much to be cured from their ailments but healed in the mind and heart and memory.'

For, 'without truth there can be no reconciliation. Without truth, there is no revelation, and without that, well, nothing furthers. It's a simple thing.'

Going to Water is unashamedly didactic in its intent and execution, as are all the great moral fables, and teaching stories, whose primary purpose is to instruct, guide, strengthen and inspire right action in their listeners.

But what makes the reading of this novel an experience of delight as well as one of learning and which balances the lengthy passages of overt exposition is its compelling and powerful narrative where evil is confronted and overcome and sometimes overcomes, where the reader is swept into a multi-layered cosmology peopled with such unforgettable characters as Will Rogers, Pol Pot, the witch, Eva Braun, Goebbels, the Apache, Grandfather and Grandmother, Little Rain, Sweet Hunter, husband of that consummate time traveller and powerful medicine woman, Agana, Beginning Rain - and their lovely son Unole.

'Through story and song and names' Stan Rushworth demonstrates that it is possible to remember and hold both the dreadful and unforgivable events of history that have wounded so deeply the vanquished and vanquishers, and at the same time 'to grasp in our hands . . . [with a] kind of gracious, tenacious knowing,' the redemptive 'obligations of love and understanding . . . seeing the balance in the midst of numberless choices of perception.'

Going to Water is also a hymn to the wisdom of the Indigenous peoples of America, a testimony to their resilience in the face of dreadful losses, and a call to us all to remember: 'we [are] the same people, the same clan,' and that the stories 'all fit together, like a puzzle in time and space [and] must be taken apart to be rebuilt in the right way.'

'It's all there for the remembering', *Going to Water* tells us. 'Don't forget anything, and hold it gently inside of you, because it's still moving. It's all still moving, and when you remember everything, you get a say in where it goes.'

Going to Water helps us to remember."

Dr. Terry Whitebeach, Orielton, Tasmania

GOING TO WATER

THE JOURNAL OF BEGINNING RAIN

A Historical Novel
by
Stan Rushworth

*for Jessica,
In thanks for
your focus and
fine work ?*

Stan

Talking Leaves Press

Stan Rushworth
P.O. Box 1091
Freedom, California, 95019
www.talkingleavespress.com

Edited by Victoria Devereaux
Cover Photograph by Justin Maxon
Cover design, interior design, and production by Joan Keyes,
    Dovetail Publishing Services

A Glossary has been provided on page 383 to briefly describe
the historical events and people in the story.

ISBN 978-0-9910372-0-9

DISCLAIMER
This is a work of fiction.
While some of the characters in this story are historical and public figures, with some of their lines spoken out of the pages of history and public record, their motives, statements, reasons for the
actions in their lives, and their personal philosophies, are solely
the products of the author's imagination and reflections. All the
conversations and meetings exist only in this story. In addition,
the author has fictionalized certain historical events for the sake
of the story, and does not claim to represent them as fact.
This is a work of fiction.

For all my family,
and all my relations

"*The ideal of a single civilization for everyone implicit in the cult of progress and technique, impoverishes and mutilates us. Every view of the world that becomes extinct, every culture that disappears, diminishes a possibility of life.*"

—Octavio Paz

"*We must love the world,
and we must sing that love song in the morning light.
That is what I know,
and that is all I know.*"

—Dr. Darryl Babe Wilson (*Iss/Aw'te*)

GOING TO WATER

The Journal of Beginning Rain

PROLOGUE

When I first met her, she was standing alone by a small frozen pond at the edge of her town, long before America. She met my eyes without fear, searching my insides, and she knew why I was there. We sat in silence for days, listening to the world around us, and we walked in the snow-patched woods together, and then on the eighth morning, still in darkness, I woke in unexplained dread in her family house, and as I crawled through the cold toward her sleeping-robes, I could hear her parents crying, entreating her to stay with them, to not die. She lay curled in a weak ball on her robe, and the light from a small burning torch her father held showed her grey pallid face. Tears fell out of her half-closed eyes and dried on her face and nose, then they stopped altogether. As the sun rose, she did not change her position. Her mother pushed warm corn meal into her mouth, but it fell out of her open lips onto the robe, and she was motionless and limp. All day long she remained this way, and others in the house prayed in her direction and gave her room, moving their robes away to let the family tend to her. They went about their day silently. Her father knelt next to me where I sat by her, looking to me with pleading eyes, but I could only nod in acknowledgement,

1

as helpless as he was. Her mother did not look at me, but she put water and food before me, as I sat and watched her child. But I could not eat. As night fell, her skin grew paler, and she looked as though she would die soon, her breath a faint whisper in my ear when I put my face next to hers, listening. I touched her throughout the day, and she was cold, her skin indented where my fingertips or palms gently rested on her.

When night fell and the other family members had returned, eaten, and gone to sleep, the girl had still not moved, and her breath was even fainter. I said all the prayers I knew to protect her, brought in all the forces I knew to call for help and strength and seeing, but she still did not move, and a deep sadness and fear began to rise up in me. I did not know what to do, where to go in myself, and I felt powerless to help her, but I could not leave her. I could not stand and go to the doctors and tell them I too was helpless. It was not a matter of pride or refusal to accept my impotence, but of something that nagged at me, a sense of incompletion and an insurmountable compassion for this girl who had come into my life, another who carried my name. And she brought me into my weakness, it's true, into confronting that all I had been taught was useless to help her. She was gone from us, and she was still going, drifting, and it was not out of her own desire to be in the next world, no moving forward, no illness of the body saying it was time to move on and be thankful for all she'd been given in her six short years. No, it was a burden put on her from somewhere else, a weight, a huge stone on her spirit, on her desire to live, and she was leaving because she did not know what to do with this burden, and she was without any adult reasoning I might conjure or speculate that might somehow help. As a child falling into this kind of tortured being, in between life and death, she tore my heart out and put it in my hands, and it would have been in her hands too, if they hadn't been spread lifelessly on the dark fur under her body, the dark fur her pale face lay etched against in soft firelight. I cried long and deep until my stomach ached, and then my tears left and I too was empty. With no direction and no purpose, and no cure, I slowly curled up next to her on the soft fur and rested my hot forehead against her small skull and cold skin. I went to sleep with her, and lying there beside her, I fell deeply into her world, where I saw what I could have seen through no other way, and I began to understand. I saw the dreams of this magical child, found the beginnings of what must be done, and knew what I had to say.

GOING TO WATER

1

People think it's an impossible mission, but I regard it my duty. They don't understand how time works, is the problem, how it is a vast sea, a swimming thing, and that every moment is touching every moment there ever was or ever will be. As for us, the Indigenous, they say it's all over and done, that we've been effectively destroyed, eradicated. The last of our elders are dying off now, reaching toward a hundred years of life lived hanging on by a thread, no young ones stepping up to take over. There's no time, is how the young ones see it, so busy making a living, driving here and there, paying this bill or that trying to feed the kids, or if they're kids themselves, trying to figure out what it all means, what their place in the big scheme is. But it isn't over, not by a long way, because we're still here fighting. If it were over, why would this persistent enemy in the shiny blue Italian suit keep dogging me so, no matter where I go? He still knows our power, that's why, and it makes him tremble. He fairly shakes in fear, hatred, and frustration because he cannot root us out from what he thinks should be his world.

When I go to George Armstrong Custer as he lies dying on that smoky blood-stained hilltop, and when I talk to him and he sees me, sees what he's done, something happens. When his eyes find life just before they cloud over yellow on that purple evening, the whole world shifts. Truth comes alive then and fires out into the sky like a flock of escaping bush wrens, sudden and fierce yet delicate too. I don't know where that truth goes, but I know it goes somewhere, and that it reaches someone, something. I see it in the faces of those tired warriors watching, waiting for me to finish with Custer. They know. They haven't forgotten where power lies because they're still living in the time when it was everywhere, known by everyone. They stop and let their carbines and bows and knives hang at their sides. One kneels, his palm touching the ground to take part in something he doesn't exactly follow, but he knows that something necessary is happening. Dying horses whimper in pain, close and far, steam rises from the pools of blood, eyes stare aghast into the purpling light, but beauty grows over the field like spring flowers.

Is it about forgiveness? Who can forgive Custer or John Chivington, or any of us for our own depredations, or any of them, for the world they brought from another continent, the world backing them up that pushed them forward to get what was wanted, the world that followed in prairie schooners, on horseback, walking? No, it's not about forgiveness, but something else. It's about seeing, because the blinding has been so effective it's turned history itself into billowing clouds of impossibility. It's impossible that we survive and move healthy into the supposedly modern age. Impossible that we still see the world the way we have for millennia. Impossible that we still be at all. What's true is that those clouds of forgetfulness and impossibility are white canvas blowing in the breeze above steady churning wagon wheels you cannot hear, but that grind your present world, in your imagination, like stones in a flour mill called inevitable progress. You can only see the drifting quality of the long trains and women with bright gingham dresses wafting in the breeze. You can only see the forward inevitable motion of it all, the progress, the destiny, the loveliness next to tragic inevitability made oh so small by all that goodness and promise, the tragic inevitable and natural disappearance of us, the old ones, the anachronisms. You cannot hear us, our voices, our crying, but can only see the drifting white canvas like thick fog on civilization's early morning.

So no, it's not about forgiveness but something else. You see, if Custer sees, then it makes it possible for everyone between him and me to see. Everyone doesn't have to see everything. I mean, it's not necessary, but now they can see, because Custer himself has opened a door for them through his own vision of himself and his life, his own knowing. Damn the historians anyway, who work for the miners of yesterday and today. Damn them all. They're the mental miners perpetuating only what they want to remember, not what actually was. No. I can't care about them now; only eventually when everyone collects into being the same under the same sun and then I truly care for them too, victims of their own imaginations. It's really about the people, like it's always been. It's about their seeing, because they're the ones who can turn this wagon train aside before it goes like lemmings into the seas of Norway. The masses are the people who drove it. That's where it started after all, with the millions of people, and it has not altered its course in four hundred years. It's only collected more wagons, from all around the world, wagons full of gold, gingham, silver, uranium, women, coal, children, and minds, minds of all colors from all places.

But this week, to bring it home, the Apache flew his arms and eyes around in the parking lot of the movie theater on Thursday in a rage, saying he didn't "give a shit" these days. "They don't care," he snarled. "They just don't care, or they'd learn about us. And maybe then, themselves." He's right, of course, but who started that uncaring, and how does it continue? Now they're born anesthetized, big white syringes pumping "numb juice" into unknowing brains and fresh hearts. The beautiful living spirits who walked through their houses to smile into their babies' following eyes got quickly replaced by cartoon dinosaurs and furry monster puppets. Even now the trees try to speak to them by the time they can walk, but the glowing minds can only reach so far because of everything constricted around them. The children climb up into the low branches and feel the wonder, but they cannot hear the trees' calling voices or look across an oak-dotted canyon to see the old women who still chatter under the giant tree at their mortars, chiding, smiling, and beckoning. The constriction begins so early it gets in the way of seeing what must be seen, and this is where I work, where my mission lies, in the invisible realms of the mind, not only of children, but of all people who walk across these island nations in their hard boots, their insulating rubber soles, their Guccis and cowboy boots. You see, I know all these many minds work under the power of the "mind inside of nature," as the Tairona call it, and I know that anything is possible. Even if it does not happen, if my mission fails, I must still attempt it, because I know what is real under all this fantasy. I do know, despite what some of my people claim is impossible. It's a matter of dignity, I tell them, and this they fully understand since dignity is where they are born and where they live, and hopefully, where they will die. It's the dignity I work for, no matter how they might laugh at me and call me a crazed fool, on an excited evening under bright stars, the invisible new moon, and a blazing fire.

GOING TO WATER

2

My name is Agana, Beginning Rain, and no one knows when I was born. That's because I'm like the Cloud People, who evolved from nowhere. We have always existed, and when conditions were right, we came into being. The truth is I've been around a long time, and I'm no one to mess with. I am a tall, strong, smart woman, and on good days, fearless enough to get the job done. I will match wits with anyone, and I can back up the tongue they say is smart with fists, feet, knives or guns. I can slice someone apart with a gaze or bring a person down onto the soft earth in peace and gentleness, whatever needs to happen. Someone called me beautiful the other day, and it surprised me because I don't often think of human things that way, although stars are undoubtedly beautiful, and the sunrise, and each precious breath. But when I bent to wash my hair later that day, I gazed into the still pond anyway, and my open black hair hung its tips into the cool water as I kneeled over its surface, and the eyes that sparkled back up at me had a brief moment of looking like stars, so I thought about what that woman said and took its meaning into consideration. Beauty is a powerful thing in this world, after all. It can hide people, keep others from seeing what's beneath, intentions, darkness lying in there ready to pounce. It seduces too, promising things, drawing another person or being into a sphere of influence, like the flash of a lure to a hungry trout. Like Custer. They say he was beautiful too, but me, I only remember the crimson of his blood and the blood of those he touched, like a scythe he was across our lands.

Because of that memory, I had to go there, you see, just before he died. I stepped between all those steel-tipped arrows and dying creatures to where he lay dying, close-cropped golden hair matted with sweat and horse blood and human blood and fear. Everything was getting quiet like it does after a battle, the surreal quiet and drone of death stepping away in the mind, from the mind. The warriors' hands were shaking, quivering as the fighting power fell from them, all of it over now, another reality slipping into place, the kind of knowing that each warrior will learn to live with, learn to carry, whether it's in his nightmares, dreams of glory, or knowledge of being part of a history that will last forever. It's in the smell of urine and blood, in his fear, in his having won the battle, in the strength he lets slide off as another way of living enters him and changes him forever.

The warriors saw me approach Custer, and they backed away. My flint knife was not for killing, and they could see its medicine, centuries old. One man dropped to his knees, placed his palm on the earth and sang softly, watching, helping us all. A pale blue mist rose from the ground, and silence encompassed the general and me. He was afraid when he saw the knife, fear peeling his eyes back so the whites shone brightly up at me.

"You're safe," I said. "Soon to be dead, but safe. And you will not die at my hand." He took a breath. The fear did not leave his eyes, but it wasn't of me anymore. It was of himself, of what he would see of his life in the next moments, meeting his own heaven and hell because this was the world he knew and made for himself and everyone else. Heaven and Hell, that simple scourge brought into our land. I saw his journey flit across his eyes, then I let four small drops of dark liquid from my pouch fall into his mouth, and slung it back across my chest. "I want you to live a little longer, so you have time to think. You must look at all the killing you have done, at the way you have seen us, at the cowardice you displayed in killing so many innocents." He stared at me, wanting to be hard, but he could not. "Now your arrogance has finally killed you and your men, and your terrorizing my people is finished, and you have to listen."

He tried to speak, but his voice was cut short by the approach of three Cheyenne and Hunkpapa fighters. I looked at them quickly, and they stopped a respectful distance away. They had never seen me before, but they knew me, knew who I was. Our people are like that. They could see what I was doing, so they watched, standing very still. The warrior with his palms on the ground continued singing very softly into the earth.

"Do you see it now?" I asked, but Custer stared straight ahead, refusing in his stubbornness, though he was no longer afraid of the men. I reached down and sliced a small tuft of his hair with the flint knife. "Gold," I thought. That's what it's all about, Custer leading the geologists into Sioux territory despite government promises, as usual the promise falling prey to the need of those who break it, predation justified by need. I held the hair in front of Custer's eyes. "Here's your gold," I said, not to be cruel, but to be real with him, no pity and no mercy. I led his eyes to the ground, and he followed my hand forward and downward until my fingers touched the earth. I scooped a small hole in the soil, then covered it, and Custer's eyes stayed on the tiny dark mound.

"Maybe Earth will take you back to the truth now," I said, very softly, for I wanted him to listen to his own voices. We all listened, the warriors and me, and Custer, and the sky began to change around us all, dreadful dark then light, light then dreadful dark, moving above the softly circling blue mist. "It is up to you now. This is your chance, so don't be as stupid in your dying as you have been in your life. Take your chance."

Custer stared and breathed, and his eyes turned to the darkening purple sky, then back to the damp earth, while the herbs opened his heart to his mind, and he breathed on. The warriors watched, asking themselves if this man deserved the chance he was getting to see himself, maybe to make amends as he died, but they knew enough of life and death to know this was not their decision. Each of them had fallen to the cruelty that had too long spread across their vast holy prairies a plague, and each had to make their own amends in whatever way they could. Few were spared the corruption within this great change come upon them. For them to deny this fighter, this man, this scourge, this hero of the enemy his own moment in the growing darkness, would be to deny themselves the same possibility.

Then Custer looked directly at me where I remained kneeling above him, and his eyes finally, finally, fell open. There were no tears, but there was a moment of their glazing over when I knew he was seeing his wife's eyes in mine, and I let this happen with a rueful smile, tender and hard at once, for I would never be fooled by such things. And though he was cruel and deranged, it may be that he loved too. I have been seen as many things, beautiful and kind and cruel and ugly, and as long as that vision serves Earth, I will let it be. I know any vision changes when I don't hold to it, and change it did, quickly, and then I became all those Indian women who fell under his sword, and his eyes stayed on mine, straight into me unflinching, widening, his soul breaking open, and I stared back into him. It did not take long, for the medicine is quick in its purpose, and he was a child beneath me, lying against the contorted limbs of his dead comrades.

"Why are you helping me?" he asked, struggling for an answer, trying to move, but he could not.

"It has nothing to do with you," I said. "This seeing is just what is possible for us all, and you are at the center of something horrible and large and strange, at this moment, and it must be done like this for everyone."

And then he turned and died, looking down at Earth, a strange smile pulling at the corners of his mouth, not a satisfied smile, but something of other-worldly irony and sadness. I stood slowly and walked down the hill to vanish among the people and the electric purple night.

The warriors knew not to touch him, not to cut him, but to leave him lying where he was. It was done now, and the white newspapers would say the worst about our mutilations no matter what was done or not done, no matter what soldiers who knew better might see in the following days, as the populace was lost in their craziness and lust for war and gold at this point. What happened that day was a powerful center of a huge churning movement in history, a beginning to what would follow for the next hundred years, and what we accomplished together held a secret that would perhaps only fully come to fruit in still another hundred years. Who knows, maybe what we accomplished that day helped to prevent even more ravages than history has held before our dismayed eyes.

GOING TO WATER

3

I called her Little Rain, with her soft face in the shape of a pale heart, and she always looked at me as though she knew what I was attempting, but despite our closeness in the world of dreams, I did not really know. I do know that after Custer's death and seeing, something was different. When I returned and fell into her in the night, our foreheads gently touching, it was different. There was a softness to some of the pictures of huge steel walls, textures she would never know in her life or touch with her fingertips, but textures that lived in her imagination. The softness was enough that a child could reach out, and where it was touched, it would hesitate then fall away to reveal something beautiful behind, a vastness of landscape, perhaps, or a hawk's body curving through a pale golden sky. And where her heart inhabited her dreams, it moved in the direction of the landscape, the sky of the soaring bird, the bright blue stream snaking through grey granite towering stones, and she breathed then. She shuddered next to me in the darkness and took in her breath sharply and something changed inside her.

On the next morning she woke and looked into my eyes, beckoning. With my help, and by grasping my arm in her small fierce fingers, she tottered to her feet on the grey robes, then gestured to the outside. She led me, all while clinging to me to maintain her balance, straight into the woods, and her strength seemed to return as we found our way through the small meadows and streams. Then without pause, she followed a certain tiny stream up a gentle slope where there was no path until we came to an almost perfectly round pond beneath an overhanging ledge. A giant sycamore reached its arms out over us from high above, the dark iris of the pond staring skyward through nearly leafless branches. She stopped, let go of my hand, stared upward at the grey morning sky, then turned to look at me briefly before facing the pond again. Then she suddenly raised her hands skyward in an abrupt motion, opening her palms, and strode into the slowly circling water. She walked to the center, to the eye of the pond, and lowered her hands, resting her palms downward on the surface, which quickly returned to its gentleness after her having walked through it. The black water encircled her waist, and she looked downward into its depth silently, eyes wide open. She went to the water, and the water took her in, and I watched from the edge, crisp leaves crackling beneath my bare feet softly.

GOING TO WATER

4

The Apache went under the knife today, more bypasses than you can shake a stick at. One doctor pegged it from his smoking, another from something else long-standing in the blood, but what they don't know is the anatomy of the broken heart. Is he a victim? Yes and no. He's no one to pity, that's for sure, yet pain has gone deep into his heart, and it's inherited, his legacy. Why? Alongside a million reasons, it's because he's invisible. He is his people, and he is invisible. He is his history, and he has never been able to live as the man he is. No matter how bad he gets with people, how selfish, arrogant and pushy he seems in his struggle to live, or how kind he is in finally finding his balance, he is always all of us.

This is what they don't get. We cannot be divided even when we live the division to the maximum degree possible. Even when we're crazed. We cannot really be split apart because it's the same as trying to tear one part of the sun from another on a hot day. But we try to become what's surrounding us because that's what's happening. Or we try to adjust, and in that adjustment we go spinning off the wheel. You can see the attempts everywhere, Indians stealing from each other on Casino reservations, Indian gangs killing each other for the white powders, a twisted irony. We fall together because we are together. Even the rich Indian tribal leader or casino magnate or congressman tumbles headlong alongside the most down and out street bum scrounging a dollar for a bottle of wine. The nature of the fall is just different, more internal. It's the Indian college professor who shoots himself in the parking lot, right in the lonely heart.

The heart. That's what it is. It's all about the heart binding us over all these centuries, the heart that rises up out of the land and binds us together, and when we're stretched thin by our hatred of each other, our disdain for the Indian scouts working for "them," past and present, and when we dive into unknown waters of the spirit through drugs and alcohol, trying to numb the pain and grief, escape the confusion and frustration and the sense that it can never be made right, this is when the heart tries to stretch beyond what it is capable of. It tries to make it right, to love, to deal with it all, but it can't because it's stretched from Pine Ridge to Fresno, Guatemala to Alaska, and the sinew begins to ache with every pump, the spirit calling up all the adrenalin to keep it firing, but it just tires. It just gets worn out, beat down, and in those moments when the woman goes back to bed on a Monday morning instead of going to work, the weight of it all comes tumbling like soft deep water pressuring her back into attempted and impossible dreams. Bed-covers smelling like sweat cover the eyes, and the heart gives up. It collects its pain then and stores it, and as the mind reflects under the moisture of that suffering, it sees everything overwhelming it, from the pain the children take into themselves to the panic in the body politic as it plays out on the radio, in the classrooms and churches, in the music, everywhere in what they arrogantly call the "greatest experiment in the history of civilization." The Indian knows the price for this experiment, and this is why the Apache will lie thin in his bed listening to the almond wood burn in the stove. He will sing his songs in a faltering voice at first, but he will keep on singing.

And he will come around again. He's tough, and I will use him again. This I know. He is an ally, and I will need him because I do have enemies. He knows where and how to fight, and because of this I am never alone.

GOING TO WATER

5

Some say I have an attitude. Maybe so. It's that I'm unafraid to say what I see or to jump into the middle of things not knowing where they'll go, even despite all the mistakes I've made, all the times I've been just plain dumb. I just can't find another choice. I am afraid, deathly afraid sometimes, at the distances between all of us. I'm afraid of how thick it is, this pallor and wall, and the fear pisses me off, so I get pissed at all the things that scare me. When I'm angry enough, I jump in, no matter how cool I might look or think I look. "Calm the voice," I say. "Don't offend." But I am offended, so desperately offended that I cannot contain myself. I wait in those corporate meetings where I sometimes work, waiting for someone to speak in false compassion about all those people who will be affected by that day's decisions, and the words are sometimes there, "the people," but they ring hollow alongside the bottom line of the paycheck, or the financial viability of whatever is proposed, and it's so obvious that it parades across the room in a green suit made of giant hundred dollar bills, the living spirit of Mephistopheles in a Halloween Dollar costume prancing through the room. But no one sees this spirit, like the children no longer hear the trees singing, because he is the conductor, spider webs emanating from his green fingertips to control the tongues of those speaking, clever words rolling out of the mouths to voice concern, care, logic, sensibility. I look around the room aghast, bitching deep inside myself, but controlled, on the back legs of my chair, eyes bugged out in dismay, heart chattering in fear, and then I speak. This is why they say I have an attitude. I am defending the human race, defending Earth herself, defending all that lives.

GOING TO WATER

6

The truth is I'm really nobody, and that's my protection, which makes it ironic that I have enemies. But I do. I saw the big one recently on a trip to Italy, lurking behind a white marble column like a dark figure out of Shakespeare, studying me to see just who I was. I was listening to my friend Will Rogers talk to the dictator Il Duce, assuring him that he was not going to be one of the recipients of Will's by then famously scathing interviews with politicians. When Will was asked to run for the president of the United States he said he couldn't lie well enough to handle the job. That reputation carried on ahead of him. Not that the dictator had anything to fear, but he did think most highly of himself, and like all such men a certain insecurity hovered about him like an unseen knife threatening to cut off all the international esteem he had built through his carefully benevolent acts to the Italian people. And people around the world listened to Will, a plain talking Cherokee man. But Will himself later said in an interview, "I'm pretty high on that wop," and then went on to add, "Dictatorship is the best form of government. The thing is you've got to have the right dictator." Ah yes, classic Utopia. At that point, Benito (he said I could call him that, being quite the charmer and ladies' man) had done right by the common man, one of Will's concerns about the lack of that in American politics, and Il Duce had done that through the sheer force of his personality. He cut through all the red tape and got things done. A chicken in every pot, a car in front of every house was his aim. Social reform for the good of all, like a good king, a soldier king, a sharp-looking, sharp-dressing manifestation of the risen Christ everyone in the Christian world seems to keep hoping will appear, by and by. If he isn't in long flowing robes, well then, put him in a military uniform. As long as he delivers the promised land, follow him to the ends of the earth, and since Italy couldn't be much more Catholic and much more the granddaughter of old Rome, what works on all those subterranean fronts is what goes.

Some people said Will's comments showed his political weakness, kind of an intellectual or spiritual flaw, though the word "spiritual" wasn't used much outside of séance circles or churches at that time. They said Will was feeding into the Fascist frenzy, that dictatorship in any form was flat wrong despite the notion that as Americans they'd been doing whatever Congress told them to do for a very long time. But to them Congress was representative of the will of the people, regardless of it being largely made up of families who sent their kids to the best universities and social clubs, where they'd been hobnobbing together in their secret societies and coming-out parties since before the term oligarchy came into being. Well, maybe that's so, and if it is the will of the people, the working people, then I'm more scared than I thought I was before this notion ran across the landscape of my imagination like a wild burro. I asked Will about his comments in the magazine, and we talked about it on the flights around Europe after meeting Il Duce, and it seemed he was far more thoughtful about it than he was made out to be. He looked out the window of the plane when I asked him, not saying anything before he looked back into my eyes, and in those moments, I saw he didn't know. He really didn't know, and the world he had in the palm of his hand, according to those who might envy his influence, his mind, his humor, and his sheer talent and humanity, seemed far beyond his understanding, some object out of reach like in an unsatisfying dream or unrequited love. When he said he only knew what he read in the papers, he meant it. He really meant it, and that's why I was head over heels in love with him. I loved that man with all my heart and still do, but he was well and truly married just like me when I knew him and traveled with him, and I would never have challenged that for either one of us. He was my hero because countless Indian families talked about him, the Indian everyone in the world knew as a real man, not some wooden statue, the man who saw through the pomp and vanity of the affairs of state and put it like he saw it.

Yes, I loved him, but even if he or I hadn't been married, I still would never have been with him in that way of a man and a woman. That's just plain against the rules. You can't slip into another's time to win the heart, dabble to satisfy your own life and emotional needs, and then live in your primary time as well. It's a matter of right and wrong action, and you have to have that under strict and complete control. You must know yourself and your limitations, and it's finally, ultimately, about a bigger kind of loving. When Will would look into my eyes with all the trust in the world and show me the places where he was lost and confused and small, I could never betray that trust by trying to fill the shoes only his wife could fill. I knew what it meant to be his friend. This isn't about morals, but about right action. The teachings are very clear, and living outside of them is catastrophic.

This brings me to the enemy behind the marble column. He was watching me from the moment I entered the huge room where we met the dictator, his dark eyes never leaving me. On one hand it seemed like his job was security, since there was obviously a man assigned to watching all of us, and maybe he just drew the straw with my name on it back in that cold grey planning room. But no, he was something else, a churchman turned soldier, looking into the mystical with a sharp knife in his boot, and he was a creased-trouser, button down tunic kind of soldier with a tight ass and mean eyes, and he saw my difference. He couldn't put a name to it, not yet, but he knew something was up because he worked in the mysteries of the soul, so like all those protectors of the suites of power, his response and impulse was to destroy that which he did not understand. It's an old story. Ask Cochise's multilingual son, the educated Chiricahua who died of mysterious food poisoning on a negoti-ating trip to Washington, his beautiful homeland the point of Washington's focus. Power is a ruthless thing that does not reflect upon itself. It only looks at how it can maintain itself into eternity. I knew I would have to watch my back while in Rome, and I suspected that his roots were international as well, so the whole trip took on another magnitude with those dark eyes behind the white column, a column that had surely known many such moments during the rise and fall and continuation of the empire. But like I said, I really am nobody, so I hunkered down inside my nobody and followed Will through the building under a mask of obedience, a face that power just loves, and that it attributes to its own fragile beauty.

Power is what this is all about, finally. It's not morality, not really. Sometimes people who know my mission call me a moralist, but they're missing the point. It's not about good and evil because those terms are imports, outside my cultural frame of reference. No, good and evil are not relative, but relatives within the fear machine, little brothers and sisters running havoc all over the world completely out of control, creating panic and wars and destruction so gruesome it's like the last time gruesomeness will ever be, so it conjures itself up and up way beyond belief. It has to express itself, is what I'm saying. And what is in my frame of reference is right and wrong action, which is not the same thing. Right action is measured instantly most times, and sometimes it takes awhile to bear fruit, but in the waiting time, there's no harm done.

There may be frustration for it to come round maybe, but no fracturing in the meantime, and no picture of what'll come, no ideology. It's measured in the eyes of the people and creatures involved, in the color of the evening and the feel of the air, and in these things it's tangible, much less abstract than even the most exquisitely wrought policies of eventual redemption. It's pragmatic, as they say, something that works for the people immediately. Okay, someone might say that was exactly what the little Italian Benito did, make things work for the people, and he created a satisfaction that turned into a belief in him, the man, with the ardency of a faith, but it was a dream of something even more beautiful coming down the line that seduced the minds of the people, a promise he made and kept expanding, and this is what made it a form of the millennial religions, the "by and by" crowds, and the proof of this is where Il Duce went with it, off the edge of decency and respect. The seed for his fall and thirst for ultimate power was always there in the religion he was raised in, because power is at its center, be it modern and secular in form or outright old-time kneeling, but it's not right action. It's one man's or one church's picture foisted on another. It's control in the name of the by and by. Just look at history; take just one look because that's all it takes. Is outcome a measure of intention, or what? Where's the right action when brutality comes along to make a belief stick on another person like a scar?

This is where the enemy lies in wait, where control and autonomy meet, to say it in the simplest form, though it is not always this easy to see, not always the white goose on the dark road. But in Rome, with only that one quick glance I could see the watcher's program, like Custer's eyes when they held all us Indigenous into being something even less than animals. It's blindness and scorn and compartments that kill, a shape of the mind, a geometric thing, like a rack of cookie cutters or a box with cubicles in it, a huge form that surrounds the man with purpose and direction, like the spinning electrons of an electromagnetic field around a heat-seeking missile's guidance module. It's like a humming computer tracking the target and the nuclear missile both, computing for the point of impact, destruction of the unknown the goal it has in its glistening silicon and neatly soldered mind. But the enemy is organic at the core too, shifting and changing, not always obvious, often devious, nothing alien or foreign, nothing to stereotype or identify so easily or glibly. One must be very careful to navigate safely in this world. One must be able to be no one and everyone at once. One must be the right kind of invisible.

GOING TO WATER

7

I'm telling this story on paper in the beginning of the twenty-first century, so it's laid out in this language, this English, and in this style because this is how I talk in this time. It's how people talk today, a little less than the mushed-down syllables and mumbles I can't get onto paper, the "Whassup?" of California and the "Howzit?" of Hawaii, said so fast it's almost British, the mouth closed, lips protecting bad teeth from the cold wind, or what? How did we get here with language? How is it those girls in the Munich airport wonder how come I know they're from L.A. just by listening to their vowels tumble all over one another like an orgy of California bronzed blondes? No, I know, I shouldn't talk like that, but what do you do in the face of it all?

This story is now, but it's very old too, and I'm telling it now because of the urgency today, in this time, the intensity of how sharp thinking has been submerged by buying and selling of souls and furniture alike, all within a great whirl of castigation and promises of freedom and happiness. Among many forms, it's fast food and plastic bottles, what the crusty old German social critic sees as "Consumer Fascism," as he looks across the big pond from his bucolic Bavarian farmhouse. He remembers the Nazis of his past, and their promises, their Volkswagens, "the people's car." Today the inhabitants of Turtle Island are at war in the oil-producing countries, and nobody doubts or talks about why they are there, for oil and new markets, as inevitably dwindling resources run up against the appetite of the industrial surge of the last hundred years, a giant burp in evolution; supposed evolution, that is. It's that thing about time again. A close friend of mine once told me that "There are only two or three human stories, and they go on repeating themselves as fiercely as if they'd never happened before," as we swept off on our separate rivers, me thinking at the time that everything was brand new, being young in the way I saw things, even for one like me. As another kind of youth, like glistening metal teenagers, the machines today act as though they will be forever, and that they are the natural product of their humans getting smarter and smarter, so they call it progress and evolution and put the label of "natural" on the plastic bottle selling the Mother's blood, water itself, "natural" water. Machines do this, and humans comply in smiles. International companies, like the empires of the Aztec and Maya and Inca and Romans did with blood, buy up the water of places half way around the known globe from their seats of power, and sell it back to the people from whom they take it, at the same time giving it an exotic label to those far away who buy it in fancy restaurants. Is this urgent? Is there something to talk about here, or am I wrong? Is this evolution or digression? Is it regression? Is it the digestion of all we should have learned by now from our many mistakes, or is it a huge flatulence in the face of true time? Am I made crude by my utter dismay?

Here's the problem for me as one who moves in time and space: Last week, and I shake my head to use the term because it was over eighty years ago, that Roman soldier in a silk suit behind the marble column was visible, on the outside where I could see him. Today he is able to move freely on the inside of people even more effectively than the witches of old could, until they were seen, because of the modern blindness that all the fear and loathing manufactures in the flesh and blood and bone of humanity. In the old days, the proverbial days, before all the ambient noise of this age drowned out the signals of dark magic, a good curer could see the work of the witch, could see dark and light, right and wrong action, or the aberrant sorcerer plying his trade toward his own ends. The witch might fly through the night as an owl and enter the dream of his victim, and a person simply resting outside watching the night walk across the sky dome could see that witch's curve against a bright, starlit sky plainly, a silhouette above the hogan or longhouse. The watcher might tell the story then of what he saw, and people would listen, and they would go to the healing woman for help, and the next night she would scan the sky herself, and talk to the injured spirit of the victim, giving it back its will to live. The people would go to the sorcerer and throw him out of the village, and his raven would turn against him to ally with the people, chasing him off into the desert. This is what I have seen with my own eyes, what I have learned from the old men and women, and what I have listened to since I was a child.

I'm talking about what we see with our eyes, but a lot of it is sound, too, because time and sound are closely entwined, and because of this, listening is a key too. Therefore, words are a key, because words are ultimately sound before they are meaning. They arise through meaning, but their impulse is out of something deeper, so it takes a lot of the mind, the thinking, to listen in the best way, to listen to the words emerge, spring up, even out of oneself. When listening to another, it requires even closer listening because the meaning is already there from another world, humming in the tissue of the sound, formed out of that other being's life and the lives of all of his kind that came before him. People in modern time may think it cliché or only symbolic that in other times many beings talk with humans and other beings not of their own kind, animals and plants and spirit beings. In today's world, this ability is very lost, which is much to our disadvantage. Some even call it a stereotype of Indigenous life, but today a young Apache girl dances on the grass beyond the ball field, talking to the wind, and when recess is over, her teacher asks her what she was doing. "Talking to the wind," she says, smiling, matter of fact. In a hastily convened conference, the teacher tells the parents she is worried that their child is schizophrenic. She does not think to ask the child what the wind said. It might have been of value to the teacher, but there is no question because she is certain the wind cannot talk, nor can hummingbirds or trees or skunks. Skunks can get their point across, but they cannot voice their feelings about how they are seen or what they smell on the coming breeze. "Ah yes," thinks the teacher, "The earth is our mother," and this becomes a symbol of taking care of the earth, recycling plastic and metal and paper and driving a hybrid car. Never mind that all cars are hybrids, coagulations of earth and fire and water and thoughts called science and convenience. But to this young Apache girl, Earth is her mother because she is composed of all the earth is; she cannot be separated by a symbol or a metaphor or an idea. She reaches into damp soil like she runs her fingers through her hair, like she talks to Wind. It's just who she is.

This ability is what today's enemy seeks to destroy, and he's doing a very fine job of it, I must say. Even in Mussolini's time, I could recognize the witch and his dark silk suit, much like when he took the shape of the owl or coyote or raven, but today he takes even more shapes, even the shape of me in all this noise and glistening metal surrounding me, and sometimes when I look in the mirror I cannot tell which of my dreams he attempts to invade, or what shape he intends. I must listen; I must continually listen and watch and ask for help, for I am not alone. I am not alone, and I can never forget this. If I did, I might not make my way home, and that would be a horrible fate, a fate he wants for me.

8

It was the latter part of the twentieth century, the Indian wars went on and on, and I was on a high mesa trying to stop colossal wickedness and stupidity. A young Indian woman on her knees begged for her life, an equally young Indian man standing behind her. She prayed and talked to her absent children as though they were actually there looking on in horror at their mother's terror.

"Be strong. Don't fall into this craziness. Don't fall into it." She repeated the words to them over and over, speaking into the cold air. The sand before her was her children's flesh, their eyes, their ears.

"You should've thought of them before you snitched," the young man behind her said. His braids fell across his face as he leaned down to talk to her. He tossed them back over his shoulder with his free hand, pistol gleaming in the twilight.

"I'm not a traitor," she insisted in her dismay, eyes wide. "I'm not." "Please, please don't kill me. Please don't kill me. My children, my children," she kept saying over and over in rising panic.

"You beg now, don't you?" the man said bitterly, his words poison. "Now that you're caught."

I came from behind them and spoke quietly. "Don't do this," I said, and the man turned to stare at me. He had no idea who I was, and he hadn't heard my approach. I could see him searching quickly. Was I an agent too? No, he could see I could not be an agent because of my extreme age, but he didn't know me. He saw only an old Indian woman. He was much further into the new ways than the warriors who killed Custer, who knew me with only a glance. This man had forgotten how to see. It had been programmed out of him. This was why he could follow the orders to kill this woman, all on what someone else said, all on fear, not on what it was known by him that she did, not by how his heart should know the young mother kneeling on the sand before him. He was the executioner, not the decider, the decider who would never see her real blood flow. That man would stay smug in his tower of gangster righteousness and cowardice. Divided functions and divided people made responsibility for life impossible in them both.

"If you do this," I said, "It will go on for a very long time, and it will destroy you. It will destroy all of you and your dream. All of us."

"What do you know?" the man said, the man who was a boy. "Who are you?" He thrust his smooth chin forward and challenged me, but there was fear in his eyes. He reached a hand to push me, but it stopped before he touched my body. The hand stopped not by my action, nor even his, but by something inside him he did not understand. The pistol quivered, but he still held it in the direction of the kneeling woman.

"This is wrong," I said sharply into his startled eyes, then stepped past him to the woman, and she saw me with the first gaze. She too had forgotten how to see, but seeing was closer to the surface for her, and being so close to her death brought her quickly to the truth. It brought an older way back to her. I kneeled in front of her and spoke up into the boy's face.

"You're angry, but it's not her. It's not her at all. It's everything that has happened, and you have to see this. Yes, maybe it's the white man, or what you call the white man, or those within his ranks who manufacture the killing and everything else that robs us of life, but it's not her anymore than it's you. And today it's not about the white man. It's about you."

"What the fuck…" he waved the silver pistol at me, feigning rage.

"You won't kill me, so don't threaten me," I said. "Think about your orders, and don't do this. It will come back on all of you. It will discredit you and your children and all others you're with for a very long time, and it is exactly what your enemy wants. You are being manipulated."

"But…"

"They will be able to say 'See, they are no more than savages,' and they will be right. They will be right because they know what savagery is, very well. They know it. And now you are proving them right."

"Shut the fuck up, old woman. Or I'll kill you too."

"No. You can't and you won't and I'll be gone by the time you do this, or by the time you take responsibility for all our lives and don't do it. I'll be gone when you wake up and let her go."

He lowered the gun, and the young woman fell forward in the yellow dirt, her shoulders shaking with sobs and the quiet prayers and begging, begging not so much for herself as for a better life for her children, because she was seeing it all laid out before her now. She could see her history.

"This woman is Crazy Horse," I said, "and you are working for someone who is afraid of his true power, that same power she carries. That shadow man, the controller, refuses to see what true power is. You are caught like those before you got caught in the divided camps, and you are not thinking. You are not using the mind you have been given, run by your lifetime of sorrow and fear. Division is destruction for us in every way. We have survived only because of our unity, even with all our differences, so don't forget this truth. This is what they took from us. They even wrote down that they would do this, and what is worse than what they took, is what we gave away, and that's the same thing we need now, our unity. And this is how we treat each other? This woman is Crazy Horse and you are the soldier holding the spear to his ribs, and now you have the choice of what to do.

"You're talking crazy talk," the boy said, but his voice feathered down softly in its aggression, his knowing and surety slipping away, beginning to listen. Then the fear came again and the cold edge followed. "You're fucking crazy." It took his whole lifetime to make him this way.

"Who are you listening to? Are you listening to me or to yourself, or to the Mafia movie you have been shoved into? Is this the old way, to execute a woman with a bullet in the top of the head? Is this our way? Do we maintain our lives and our pride and our dignity on this yellow mesa this way? Through execution?" I turned to spit like the old woman he saw before him, and my hair drifted silver across my face in a rising breeze. Yellow dust brushed across the boy's boots and the young woman's hands where they pressed into the earth.

"But she turned against her own, against us," he spat.

"Do you know this without a shred of doubt? Did you see it? And even if she did, is this the right or smart way to deal with it? Do you, as the young man you are, have the right to take this young mother's life for this accusation? What is this you are doing? Is it an example to keep the people in line? If so, then you are a fool, and those who told you to do it are also fools, if not the enemy themselves. You turn against your own in this killing more than she ever could have. It is you who turn on your own. You become the enemy. Go into the mountains, and talk to the old people. They know, and you know this."

He lowered the pistol then and stared at me, beginnings of darkness putting shadows between us, but light flit through his eyes for the first time, and when the woman's prayer rose in cadence his shoulders rose as if to not let him hear her, a shield to cover his ears and heart, to protect himself, and he turned away from her because he could not stand the pain his righteousness had hidden from him.

I stepped back from the girl and touched her cheek with my fingertips. I wanted to stay but could not. I could not interrupt what would happen any more than I already had because I do not make the decisions. I can only say what I see, and others will do what they will. I wish it were otherwise, I truly do, but then it would not be what we eventually found over thousands of years that worked so well, and I would be the dictator of what is right. I would be both the decider and the young man with the chrome pistol, and the whole world would be the face of my own desire, and I do not know enough for that. No one does. That is not my mission.

But what was happening here now was becoming good. The young man began to see, and the girl's pleas to him and to her Creator and to her children began to penetrate his hatred, getting through to the truth his heart knew. I thought my work was done, or that I'd gone as far as I could, so I turned and walked away. The girl did not look up at me, and as I moved into the twilight the boy nodded slightly, moisture on the edges of his eyes. The world was theirs now, our future and past, the legacy and story that would heal or divide years and people, generation after generation.

The evening's first stars spoke down to me, beginning night's song, and the trail opened as I moved out of the couple's range. I could still feel them but could not see them, and a hint and surge of possibility carried satisfaction into my mind and belly softly. I breathed out into the night, then in again, drawing the high mesa air into my lungs, the pale light shifting down and down as my steps lengthened toward the leap outward into timelessness.

Then I saw him, a flash of shining silk suit and a brush of wings, changing, a shadow moving at the speed of light past me toward the young people posed in the decisions of their lives, our lives. There was a glint of silver, a chain and a cross, a metallic sound and the whimper of a stolen animal heart rushing by, and it was urgent and fearsome and vengeful. I felt a lunging in my heart as I spun around, but I already knew it was too late as the weight of the universe faltered, increased, hesitated, and crashed down around my ears with the sound of a single gunshot. It was done, and fear rushed through me like an icy wind.

GOING TO WATER

9

We slept again, and this time I regretted I'd returned at all, in any shape. Little Rain was deathly still, and in the middle of the night I had to pull my forehead away from her, our touch electric and cold together. Strange shapes permeated our imagination, creatures made of iron and cables running across a dry brown and rock-strewn plain, dirty chrome creatures that spoke in tones like old stones tossed together in a hollow log, sharp and offending. When I woke, my brow was tight and sweaty, and her eyes were squeezed shut. Though her body was completely still, her whole being was agitated and tense somehow in its lifelessness, strange contradictions swimming between us. I crossed my arms over my heart and lungs and sang protection songs in my mind, and when early morning sun streamed through the door, she woke with a start, staring directly into my eyes, and I saw her fear. It bounced into me and echoed through the halls of my own fear, and suddenly the young woman on the mesa filled me, her eyes and her voice praying in terror, and the shot rang out, clearly, and Little Rain's eyes widened, and I saw she'd heard it before, that it was an echo in her too, and she pleaded with me in panic and silence, mouth open as though to say something, but there was no sound at all. She could say nothing, and I knew I could never come to her this way again, not like this, because she had dreamed it and I had to work the solution.

"I understand now, I really do. I thought it might be like this, but I didn't really know, and now I do." I held her shoulders and poured my words into her eyes, "It's all new to me too," quietly shouting to her and to myself and to everyone who could hear this story this cold morning. "I'm sorry. I'm so very sorry."

There was a silent moment, like the silence before Creation, then she reached out and pressed her small hands against my chest, grasping my dress and pulling me closer, and her eyes sprang tears that smelled like rain and earth pouring from the center of her tiny body, and we held each other for a long, long time.

GOING TO WATER

10

Wind swirled the tops of the giant green eucalyptus groves in huge green circles this morning. The sky was grey behind low and dark incoming rain clouds. The valley roared with the trees, and when the rain came it did not lessen my pain, did not lessen the loss, and when Will put his big hand on my shoulder I could not look up into his eyes.

"You going to be okay?" he asked, and when I shook my head he sat down and circled me with his arms, nothing more to say. The rain slapped against the window in wind-driven rhythms, sporadic, heavy, increasing and lessening, and he held me tightly, staring out into the wet grey world alongside me.

This is the feeling that started my journey a long time ago, this very same emptiness and sorrow. This is why I've become a traveler. Maybe back then I thought I could escape the loneliness by running through time, just like I ran from the night on the mesa into these warm arms, but that ancient long-ago running was an illusion, only the beginning. It was the beginning of seeing why I had to travel like this now, not for myself but for the elders and the children. Those are the needs

I eventually learned to see, but not before the depth of the transgressions had opened before my own spirit, and I fell in, all the way down into the lost place where there is nothing that works, nothing that means anything. My own descent was what brought me to jump on this train of time and seeing. I was originally born into a time of enormous possibility, of love and confidence and promise, and I watched it all fall away, or felt it fall away with every fiber of my being, not so much in the world around me, because I couldn't fully see that world yet, but inside myself, where I touched another world. I had stood on a cold morning mountain, ecstatic in the pine smell of dawn, the crisp beauty of the day spread out in a desert valley, and I turned to the seven directions, the two poles of the open eastern gate, the south, the west, the north, into the universe, and into the center of Earth, clear through her and out into the vast sky again. That was my birth. And by evening, I had come to listen to a young girl cry from a great distance, a sound like quail in dry brush, and I felt my own shoulders shaking, and looked down into hands wet with unnamed sadness, unfounded tears, unfounded because I had not yet understood the magnitude of the aberration that grew around me as I grew. I only lived it, felt it, breathed it. That breath was my childhood, gone, lying in a whisper by the mountain path cold and pale.

By the time I was in my teens, my transformation had begun, and it started with the dreams. There were dreams of power, and dreams of being without power, dreams that reflected my life and dreams that were whirlpools to another time and place. Some terrified me, some comforted, some cajoled, and some demanded. I remembered them all, then and now.

"I'll get you something," Will said, and he left me staring but calmer, remembering I was safe with him. But the young mother on the mesa was dead, so I was not safe. The gunshot sliced through many women, and through my skull. It was echoing. They took a woman's life, one who would bring more children into the world. They halted the progression of life itself, at the same time crossing the fire of the children she'd left behind, the greatest violation. Now the lives of all those people the children touch will bear that scar. Everyone will feel that searing disappointment and terror passing through their own lives and it will be all that much harder to get back on track. But these men had lost respect for all women by now, had forgotten whose wombs they emerged from. They were already transformed into kings in their own minds, great warrior kings who'd lost their knowledge in a long drawn-out process they'd succumbed to. They had become their own bitter lost empire. There would be no remorse spoken of for what they'd done, as arguments would play out across the country for years on what was done that night. They'd forgotten their own histories, who they were and therefore who they must become again. I can see this now, how the killers were victims too, yet still killers. But I could not see it then, not when I was young.

"Drink this." Will handed me a white painted cup full with bright hot tea that burned in my chest each step of the way down, until it glowed like a coal in the center of my belly. I could feel it reach out through my skin like long fingers trying to stabilize my torso, trying to place me and hold me so I would not topple and spin away into my own darkness. I recognized it and nodded to it and to Will.

"Thank you."

He nodded. He understood because he too traversed two contradictory worlds within his own time, and he spent his life trying to get people to do the simplest thing, to think about how they'd arrived where they were. He once said a pioneer was someone who, when he wanted more land, "would go out and kill an Indian to get it, then come home and complain about the price of the bullet." He said that, and this sentence went all out across the country and into the broader world on the scratchy radios of his time, and nobody shot him or denied it, so it either meant nothing to them or they knew it was true. And that's the seed of the huge national depression we see everywhere, the mania that continues today, that fact. The pioneers and their offspring knew their own moral failing. That's what threw my young breathless enthusiasm for life alongside the path so empty and forlorn, and that's what still eats away at the flesh of young people all across this land, though they might not find the words for it. At the beginning of the twenty-first century the nation that holds the land of my birth has the most powerful army the world has ever known, has the most amount of people in prison the world has ever known for violent crimes against each other, and the most amount of people on pills to keep them quivering just above that state of spirit called clinical depression, and at the same time they call it the freest country the world has ever known. I'm no logician, but my head is swimming with all these thoughts. I shake it from side to side because these facts are only data, only things floating on a more meaningful depth of knowing, on the surface of the deep water. They are only pieces of information. They are not the core of the living plant, the life beneath the information, the part the witch beast is steadily gnawing at, invisibly. Invisibility, yes, that's his key. He works on blindness, and to depress. That young man on the mesa did not see him that night when he flew into his heart in a flurry of sudden fear, lifted that shiny pistol up through the evening air again with his very own hands and tricked him with his own rage into pulling the cold trigger. He and all those who were instruments of that abomination killed their own spirits with the shot that penetrated a bright and loving young mother's brain, then the beast tossed them aside into eternal chaos and insanity. Their sadness and hatred was and is our downfall. It is also our inheritance and our loss, and the manner of a strange redemption, if we would only listen. And we share this with everyone. Everyone. This is the surprising part, the hard part for everyone. It is not ours alone.

"You're seeing how it's all divided again, aren't you," Will asked, and I nodded as he continued. "Yep, that's the big one. Always was and always will be til folks figure it out. It's been working on us a long time. Too long, if you ask me. But then, that's what keeps it going. Seems like no one can figure out how to reverse it, this dividing up."

I couldn't tell him about the casinos on the reservations, couldn't jump that far forward, but I knew I didn't have to. He'd seen it in the oil lands in Oklahoma, the oil murders, the competition amongst us, and when we were unified, the use of many things like blood-quantum to both deny and confer mineral rights to whomever the powers that be wanted to have or have not, dividing the tribes on the inside, all done from the outside. Who took that power? The nation did, all under the blinking starry-eyed gaze of its constitution and lady justice standing there with her shirt-sleeves rolled up like she was posing for a Rosie the Riveter poster. Who gave them that power? No one did, unless we count those of us who gave up our ways and went their way just because that stink of progress seemed so horribly inevitable. That was in the nineteen twenties and thirties, and it continued around coal and all the other minerals and working human bodies, all over the Americas uninterrupted, and in the twenty-first century it's in the dollars falling out of the mouths of slot-machines to career across the floor willy-nilly, people on their hands and knees chasing them, kicking each other aside. "You're only a quarter-blood. You don't deserve any of this money," and they kick them out of the tribe, shoot them on today's yellow mesa, toss them into a ditch along the road outside any hot valley casino town. They become their own enemies, enemies to their own people.

But there are those who fight it there too, really fight. They hold together, feed their own, educate their own, learn the lessons from the past, and move back into the old ways, and sometimes they even influence those people with casino dollars and flashy tokens. These people are the ones I hold to, the ones like Will but more in the background, not the stars but the ones who quietly took me to the old sources when I was dry and empty. These are the barely visible ones in this world of intense chimeras of power, the ones who lifted me so unobtrusively I hardly knew they were there. Acquisition is not their god, but survival is, the survival of everyone.

"Is that tea working on you yet?" Will asked, bending down to look into my eyes. He'd spared me direct eye contact until now, knowing I needed time to let my mind spin back into its own knowing, sorting thoughts and feelings. His dark eyes drew mine into them easily because I was willing now. I remembered waking up one morning realizing I was not alone, not separate, and that I never could be, and his eyes took me to that soft morning gratefully once again.

GOING TO WATER

11

The black mud smelled like cool blood. The sadness I'd been nurturing got me out where that damned beast could sense me, and sure enough, he tracked me to the end of the valley, tree top to tree top and then swooped down on me. I dove for the coyote bush and scrambled through the rabbit trails just in time, the beginning darkness hiding me, but I could smell his acrid breath and hear his excited breathing. Rain flew in arcs from his dark wings and I pressed my face against the slippery earth in hiding, cold and shaking as much with anger at myself as from fear of him. My depression gave way to full heart-racing realization of the danger I was putting myself in, so I gathered power from the woods around me quickly.

"Beautiful Earth, come into me now. Come into me now," I chanted silently.

I quickly knew he could not kill me because my strength began coming back with that prayer, surging up through me from the thick wet soil clinging to my skin and clothes. But it had been close, and I could hear his thoughts.

"Where are you? Don't you know you can't hide from me?"

I said nothing aloud or in silence to reply, but only listened for his position. He could feel my power building and knew his brief window of opportunity had already disappeared, but he couldn't stop his lust, his urgency. He parted the coyote brush with his wings and beak, eyes flashing, talons shredding the branches and tossing them through the air. A distant great horned owl called to its mate in alarm then was silent. All the valley was watching in the purple-black light.

My muscles sucked in the rainwater, the mud, the oily smell of the brush and the fresh pungency of rain. I breathed it in, pulsing with it, pulling the strong wet air into the center of my thighs, calves, feet, arms and chest. Then I stood slowly, no longer weak, sadness replaced by fury and by knowing, fury at the predator for his very existence and dogged insistence, and fury at myself for allowing myself to fall so low into despair, knowing this indulgence is too dangerous at this point in the battle, for a constant battle is what it is.

My head rose above the low brush and I saw him just as he turned to see me. Our eyes met and I saw the fear in his, then the quick hatred and arrogance, the pretense at knowing. He was smug, curling his lips back now as he became a man to see, leaving the bird in the shadows behind him. As a man, he attempted to dominate me, no longer possible as a beast because it took too much of his power to maintain that form against me. It was good for moving through space quickly, but not for a real meeting. For that he would have to become himself, visible, and ultimately, his most assailable self.

"Old woman, you will be mine," he snarled, but he could not see anything aside from my burning eyes, and as I took form to him in the darkness, rising from the tossing bushes and rain, I became young and strong and beautiful, skin glistening and resilient, and he recoiled, turning his face to the side, his eyes fixed on me. This had happened before. Beauty is his enemy, true beauty, and though he is transfixed by it, he cannot maintain himself in its presence. The great owl in the distance called the change it saw to its mate, and the wind diminished the man-beast now, shrunk him down into his true cunning and trickery. The owl could see his fear, and the wind could feel it. He reached a hand toward me as if to curse me, to grasp my throat and choke me, but the wind gusted through the coyote bush and around him, lifting him away in a swirl of impotence, and he disappeared into the night sky. The owl called again and peace began to fall upon the valley.

GOING TO WATER

12

This morning I was telling a friend some of these stories, and he said I had to include the humor in it all, in the whole shift of things and where it is in the twenty-first century. Ah yes, this is the challenge because in the bigger story the humor is only dark and dry, a coping mechanism, a pervading sense of the ludicrous or the absurd. Maybe it's nihilistic humor, and maybe it's a strange slapstick too. For example, we wonder how the English were able to conquer us, calling themselves the pinnacle of civilization, creating and foisting the ideas that led to Manifest Destiny, the superior destiny of the white race, all while wearing those silly collars, being afraid of nudity and sex in the light, and enslaving their children. I can't even think about the lack of bathing and the mind-numbing perfumes, or the brilliant sewer systems of London, nightly filled buckets of shit and piss tossed out the window the next morning onto the sidewalks. That's why they wore big wide-brimmed hats, leather capes and tall boots! With even these tidbits of thought, tips of the iceberg, where is the sense of universal justice or evolution in this continental change? Is balance hiding somewhere in this absurdity? I was reminded of this on a recent visit to England in the late eighteenth century, the very time in which the English and Americans were amassing the wherewithal to expand west of the Mississippi, at the beginnings of their machine age, what they call the Industrial Revolution.

I went into a lead mine up in Yorkshire to find a lost child for a family of ancient English healers, and found him there digging away with many of his brothers, small children used because of the cramped quarters of the mine. The long cylinder of stone through which we walked hunched down to half our height, smelled of tallow, and young boys held wooden candle holders with dripping flames in their teeth as they leaned forward picking away in side shafts barely wider than their shoulders. The air tightened my lungs and the cold stone smelled metallic and dripped icy water down on us. Lead was thrown into small wagons and pulled out of the long shaft by even smaller children, and a four year old boy pumped a bellows to push the tallow smoke toward the mouth of the mine, a black hole in the lush green mountainside. White sheep grazed on the slope above the depths and dry-stone fences traversed the hills like they had for centuries. In the nearby town, the mine owners sat on embroidered chairs, sipped rare brandies and talked of the riches to be had in the colonies, secure in their superiority, in their civilization. John Locke's ideas would promote private property in the primitive colonies where no one person owned land, but where the land owned us. Maybe his ideas were extraordinary and fresh to the English commoners, but they spelled death to us, who were owned by the land and free upon it. I smelled the perfume and sweat in the folds of the English clothes and thought of the Taino wondering at the odor drifting across the bay from out at sea even before they sighted Columbus's ships. An old Taino man told me on a starlit evening, hidden from the conquistadors in the folds of his jungle, that he knew they were coming, and his surprise was that something that smelled so bad could actually be alive and so potent, but then he said, "Death is potent." He crouched in the mud and grinned across the darkness at me, but fear consumed his eyes and formed the shining teeth of his laughter.

Over two hundred years after the trip to Yorkshire to find the child, I visited the very same mine with friends, folk musicians chronicling the history of sorrow, courage and struggle in the British Isles over centuries. Their children, ages six and ten, sat poised upright in the bow of a small narrow metal boat, as we clanged our way through the hard rock tube to the center of the mountain, floating on the dark water that had seeped down through the last century. The kids laughed, unafraid as we moved deeper and deeper, while we adults shuddered each time the boat banged against the rock wall, jarring us in our seats, our yellow hard hats often scraping the carved round top of the tunnel. A sixteen year old schoolboy filled with sardonic comments was our guide, telling us the history I'd seen in the flesh, and the kids listened intently, but they still laughed at the echoing sounds of metal on rock, water lapping underneath. It was a journey to the center of the earth for them, yet they listened in their acute intelligence to the boy's jokes, looking up at him where he sat facing us from the bow, his face glowing barely visible in the dim light of tiny electric bulbs, like outdoor Christmas lights, strung along the high sides of the tunnel.

"Now we're coming to the smallest beach in the world," he heralded with mock pride, and the kids leaned forward to see. "You'll never see a beach this small anywhere else." We arrived at it and the boy stopped the boat. A spot of rocky sand eighteen inches across stared up at us open-mouthed, the opening of a side tunnel the same width and height reaching the length of a child's body into the mountain. "This is where the little ones worked, it being too small for a grown man," the boy said crisply and plainly, like a punch line, and the kids grew completely silent and still. The small light at the tiny tunnel's end shone on all our faces like a dull yellow eye, then we moved on, deeper and deeper in silence, and it seemed a long while before the jokes came to our guide again, a long while before the kids laughed again. In that silence, something unnamable and precious grew between us all, and our laughter, when it finally and gratefully came back to us, had the taste of metal and time.

GOING TO WATER

13

The crazy wind blew harsh across the land again and claimed three this time, three of the same mixed family up in Minnesota, in the summer of 2011. The mother, a white woman, took her own life out of loneliness, fear and sadness, and her sorrow passed into the son, like it always had, all his short life long. But this time he turned his anger on the father instead of himself, picked up a pistol and shot this gentle Cheyenne man in the head. When the police came he shot at them too, then killed himself with a final shot to his own head. This is the simple story. The longer tale is centuries old, a huge weight on the soul of the people crushing reason and compassion into dust and scattering it before the community's dismayed eyes.

All of my life, save certain violent and insane times during war, I have gone into the spirit world when a friend or companion has died, helping them on their way. It's been a two way street, usually, and when my prayers for following light and courage come into fruit, the spirit comes to me in a dream or vision, telling me what's going on. "It's just like we imagined,"

Ricky said from the other side, "beautiful and grand, and I'm not afraid. It's okay, all okay." And when I told his mother this the next day, she found instant comfort in her mind that lasted a year, until he came to her in a dream too, telling her not to worry, then she knew still another layer of comfort, and she passed this on to me in a long-distance telephone call. Ricky's spirit circled around us in this way. Another time, a woman I helped die had her daughter give me an old family crucifix and words of thanks for my helping her on the journey. When she died, I was far away, but we spent time with each other in the ether and it was good. There have been many times like this, where the boundaries melted, like with time, where time and space interchange and everything is fluid and good and timeless and we can find our ways together.

So when the mother leapt into her own void and hanged herself, and I found out, I began to talk to her to help open doors. I knew her well. I talked for a long while with the father about his own grieving, and he said he was trying to help the son "move on" in the most positive way. I am telling this story only because of his compassion, born in his desire to understand how everything works to serve life, even in death. He would want me to understand, and to say what I saw. He'd been a conscientious objector during the early years of Vietnam, a man of conviction and bravery in his values, a man who always provided for his family. His wife's death drove him to try to understand their forty years together, but taking care for his son was foremost in his mind. He saw and felt his pain and wanted to help him with it. And he saw the anger at him too, because it was he who had told her early one foggy morning that he could no longer let her fears define his life, control his every move in life, and this refusal initiated an impending split, with her running into the arms of a younger man and incurring the disapproval of relatives. She had always been a wild soul, driven into wild loneliness by alcoholic parents who put her in front of the television and drank themselves away. She learned to "channel surf," as she put it, to live in seven different stories at once, riding the remote control like a wild horse charging across the plains, and normal single or even double channeled life did not satisfy her, did not challenge her, but this is what she lived now with her family, only one or two channels. Even so, the other channels in her mind did not stop, even though her husband was so solid and predictable and loving, but the channels spun off into their own realms, becoming stories based on an elemental childhood fear of rejection, and they ate at her. "Does he really love me?" "Will he always be there?" "Am I a good enough mother?" She was physically voracious, tall and beautiful with long black hair, and demanding of love, and her man was strong for a very long time, but he ran out of gas with aging and not tending to his own spirit. He grew fat around the middle, full in the jowls, and his black eyes grew dull. He could not rejuvenate himself as the mountain for the family anymore, and he told her so. He was spent. His spirit was tired, his heart giving out, and he knew it. The doctors told him he had to change or die. But it all came crashing down in a way he could not have imagined. One night, when the younger man she'd found and run to fell asleep out of his own exhaustion, having nothing more as cause than a long fishing trip, she tilted suddenly and deeply into her ancient fear and hanged herself in the living room while he slept huddled deep in their bedcovers. Only weeks before, she'd discovered she had ovarian cancer, perhaps the final seed of doubt about her life and value as a woman.

Days later the son blamed the father for his mother's sorrow and death, and he shot him in the temple point blank to prove his point. He had told his father, one reasonable day before, that his mother didn't hang herself on purpose, that she'd just gotten caught in a moment of insanity, and did what she would never intend to do to them all. Did he do the same thing the next day? Get caught in his own moment of insanity? Maybe he only wanted to try on her feeling, like putting on a jacket to see what it felt like, but couldn't get out of it. Or was he trying to make his father not "move on" from the sorrow, but to stop and feel the depth of his grief, to share that inconsolable grief, to lie with him in his elemental depression, his fear, his terror? The father would want us to understand his own murder, to have compassion for the son who killed him. He would want us to feel both their desires for life and let the rest go. But what is the rest? And should the survivors let it go? What does it even mean to "let it go?" Where in this universe does "it" careen off to?

When I was told of my friend's death and the suicide of his son, I went into the spirit world like I always had upon a close death, especially since he and I had so recently talked our ways through the mother's life and death. But when I opened that door, instead of finding a vast pool of living darkness, light and motion, I found only a static block, a wall of something like synthetic black stone that I could not define, impenetrable, dense and unfamiliar, fearsome in a cold nameless way. I was afraid, and I immediately protected myself, put up shields of light and pulled away. I gave offerings to them all, saw them briefly staring at each other with incomprehension and tension, bright eyes wide and staring across a chasm at each other, like in a moment before war, the millisecond between when the trigger is pulled and the hammer falls, when time halts completely and everyone sees. No one can move but everyone sees, and in this infinitesimal moment an enormous fact engulfs them, the fact of what they've begun and can never change.

Did the beast have a hand in all this destruction? I could not see his wings, could not feel his cold breath nor hear the rustle of his silk suit, but I knew this horror and tragedy was of his world, not of him personally, but of his sources and his brew and momentum, though he was nowhere present in person. He didn't have to be. He was not needed because the son had formed his own reflection of the witch beast, dipped into the pool and drew out his own ammunition, out of his own blood. This is where we are in all this grief. This is how out-of-control it has gotten.

Do we call it darkness? Yes, in one manner of speaking it is. Do we call it evil? In another manner of speaking we may. Is it unassailable? No, it is not, but it is too much to enter into and change as one person, one spirit, one traveler. It is too consuming. And this is why I do this work, this traveling and touching down here and there over time in minds that have changed and will change the world. True seeing is not done alone, and is virtually impossible by only one person, so there must be understanding across the ages, a gradual shifting of possibility in many minds. But we are in a difficult time here in these centuries, and on this day of trying to help my friends' spirits, I could only back away and pray, leaving them to their own devices. After all, we must all know our limitations, and mine are huge and daunting in the face of such terror.

GOING TO WATER

14

I came home yesterday to a silvery dawn, really home to the place of my origin, and I thought about how strange it is that a home once so full and expansive to me, even limitless, is now valuable because of what it lacks, because of what is missing from it, even more than what it actually is. What is missing are all the things that live in what is called modern times, the mechanical things and structures, the kinds of roadways and their oily smells, the stiff synthetic clothes, closets to hold them, all the stuff and confusion in the lives of the people who will someday live on this very soil on which I now take my much-needed rest. They are not here in the time and place of my origins, and the silence of their absence allows me to be filled with awe at my exquisite and ordinary life.

My young son, Wind, met me at the singing tree and we sang our song, calling all the spirits who had protected all of us in our time apart, both he and I, and his father. His sparkling eyes asked me as many questions as there are stars and gave me huge room at the same time. There would be time enough. My heart jumped to see and feel him, to feel his small arms around my neck and the strength of his love pouring out of every part of his squirming body. Our song reached into the Universe through the air he is named after, Unole, down into the earth at the base of this tree who had sung with us since his birth, only ten years ago. He tapped the rhythm on his clapper stick, a gift from one of the singers from the west, a huge man, a giant smiling bear who grinned in silence as he handed it down, looking straight into Unole's upturned face.

As always upon returning, I went into the ceremony lodge with three others, one of us in each of the four lateral directions, the great sky cords holding Earth in her place in the Universe. Before the door closed and dropped us into darkness, I saw the leader's hair spread out in the light of the opening, her shoulders drooping toward the red-hot stones, and time flew all around me in a swirl, finally settling into one solid time long before now, thousands of years ago. The herbs tossed on the stones curled ancient smoke into my open nostrils, the same herbs used forever, and the deerskin door fell behind the leader, leaving us in darkness. Only a faint red glow came from four of the stones, the four in the cardinal directions. The center stone was a deep hot blackness between them, holding them together and keeping them separate at the same time, and at the same time it was a hole out of which everything came and into which everything went, before it spun up through all the other surrounding stones to carry us where we needed to go. The songs began with the drum leading, each song progressing in intensity, the gentle protecting songs lifting into the spirit-calling songs, and soon we were surrounded by the ancestors, dancing through our songs, minds, and prayers. The afternoon took us home, to our deepest home, took us all the way back to where nothing mattered but way back then, and how we are connected to that place right now, to how we are that place now, timeless. Nothing mattered but the children down the hill, the waterfall behind the village, the animals filling the forest, night folding around the round dark houses, and our families gathered around the fire in the evening. There was nothing else.

I was tired, raw from all the traveling, hungry for sustenance and freedom from all the conflict of the future, so Earth flew up through me like always, her minerals scratching their ways through my skin into the blood and heart of me. Earth lifted my mind to nothing but Unole, my man Sweet Hunter, and all those here, and the future slipped away on a prayer song. The darkness, silence and heat gave and gave, and I lay motionless soaking it in. This ceremony was promised to us, promised to last forever, and it's still true, as it must always be.

Later in the evening we sat around the fire listening to stories of bravery, cleverness, and intelligence, to riddles for the children and reminders for the adults. Summer is over now, and the crisp evenings of autumn hold the hills close together, trees beginning to huddle toward one another for warmth, touching their rustling shoulders. Leaves swirl through the branches gracefully, gingerly, proud of their flight and beautiful colors. Unole curled up against me and listened to his father's story of talking to the deer we had eaten that night, of how the deer gave her life, telling us she could no longer bear young, so she would feed us now, and we should all be grateful, reminding us in her death song. The Corn Mother told her story too, and ended with her own gratitude and the sparkling dark eyes of the elder women. It's always the same stories, binding us all to one another and the world around us. And those who stray from the path got a story tonight too, as always, always funny and looking foolish in the way they think they can outsmart Earth and the ways of things, always getting their fingers burnt, villages swallowed, children lost, and pride embarrassed. I tended the low fire alongside everyone else, reaching from my side of it to place a branch just where it began to cool, and I thought about this life here and all its extraordinary sophistication, all the obligations of love and understanding the children must learn, all the stories adults must remember to keep the balance, to keep seeing the balance in the midst of numberless choices of perception, and our smallness in the face of everything that carries us.

When the fire had gone out and the children were put in their beds in the round low houses, Sweet Hunter took me to his hides outside in the glen, in his own kind of gratitude, running his hands down the muscles of my thighs, up across my belly and breasts, and across my lips. He smiled and watched me smiling at him, and he looked down at my body as though it were the first thing he'd ever seen, in wonder, like he was born as a fully grown man and I was the first thing he ever saw, and I breathed in his form of worship, if I dare say it that way. More than worship, it's a marveling I see in his eyes, a deep pleasure for all of life itself found in his vision of my body, in my curves and textures, my resilience and strength as I move next to him, naked in the cool evening, feeling his flesh coil all around me. I relish his vision and give my power to him, coiling and uncoiling my muscles with a grin. Our touch is gentle and strong, his hands smooth and powerful, and tonight I opened to him in hushed private laughter at the phenomenal joy of it all, at being home and at the life I have here. The moon had risen, striking through the trees to light his moist shoulder and my leg as it stretched out, shining out from under the thick brown furs. When he entered me, tears rolled down my cheeks, and I was laughing too, crying and laughing, and he kissed my tears, drinking me as I drank him, and then we slept a quiet sleep, dreaming nothing different from what we lived in that moment. I was home then, fully home, in ceremony and in love, in the spirit and the flesh, the best combination there is.

GOING TO WATER

15

I was trained to the seeing. Maybe I always had it, that and the listening. That's what some of the people say, but the truth is that while other kids were off playing stick ball, hunting or pretending to hunt, or grinding corn or nuts into flour, I sat in the grass by the really old people, the ones who could barely speak because of their advanced age and frailty. I'd listen carefully, painstakingly, as they looked skyward with glazed watery eyes in older languages designed to talk with all the powers surrounding us, the very spirits of our creation. Often the elders would talk as though I wasn't even there, seemingly lost in a reverie, but even one glance or an old brown hand reached out in my direc-tion told me it was all for me, not a removed reverie but a joining thing, something I should reach into like put-ting my hand into a clear rushing stream. It had to be, for I was often the only child there. And one gesture would be all I'd need to know the power of the story, and strangely, it might not even be the story itself or the language but the mood it put me in invisibly, or what I saw in the world around me while listening.

The old ones would transform me, shape my world into something different, something even more grand and awe-inspiring than the world we were already given. I learned to know the grass with those old people, to see every tiny red or black or striped bug between the blades, and to know their borders and worlds, their orderliness in the parts of the field they inhabited. A tiny red spider had his territory in a range beginning just a breath up from the black loam out of which his blade of grass rose, ending halfway up the blade, and he never altered in this dance of his life's position. He never touched the rich soil nor extended past his invisible border. He didn't have to. Everything he needed was in an area less than a fingernail's length. He slept in a tiny round home he spun and attached to the back of the blade, along its arching spine that kept his home dry and cool, and his bright vermillion life had infinite meaning as I watched him, face down in the grass, and heard his story. He knew his place, and all others honored this. And beneath him were the darker creatures of the black soil, churning through its depths in caverns they carved by devouring Earth herself, and above the tiny red creature were the long-legged hoppers and the striped leaf-tip eaters, each with his own meaning and position, not in any ladder of more or less importance, but in a manner of operation that works. And I could smell it all too, smell the wind changing in the seasons, or long before rain or storms, or the whirling winds' dry pungency, and all of this I got simply sitting by the old ones and listening to how their voices gave me all my senses, and to how that listening magnified these senses beyond my wildest dreams into tools I had only heard whispers of. This is where it began, or where they began it in me, and it just kept on going.

As I grew, I would dance through the surrounding forests or out in the open meadows smelling the rich acrid soils, the bright sharp pines, the spicy grasses, the winds, everything that came to me in an unsoiled world. But it wasn't always easy or strictly beautiful, for I learned the smell of death too, and of violence, of ignorance, and of change in people and therefore the world. A handsome young man filled with a strange feeling when a girl he courted went off with another man, and I saw him being consumed by this feeling, this jealousy turning ugly and violent. At first I didn't recognize the feeling he carried, as I'd only heard of it before then, not felt and seen it like I had seen the grasses and animals, but my grandmother watched him and told me clearly that this feeling could not work among the people or for him, that it was too different than what we knew between us as right for men and women, and she told me in no uncertain terms, nodding and pointing with sharp eyes, telling me to go to him one evening at the edge of the fire, to sit with him. She told me to listen to him, so I did, though his manner infected me too, and I complained to grandmother petulantly, my face twisted in annoyance at her. But she pointed, and the man told me about his violence, his desire to beat the other man, and he said he feared the feeling because it threatened to control him. He was shocked when I described his face to him, mouth turned down in a scowl, eyes dark and dull. I asked him what he saw a number of times when he looked at the girl, and he finally stared for a long time and saw that the girl was happy on the other side of the fire, sitting over there with her chosen one. "Do you believe this is her choice?" I asked him, and his love for her surged up through him and quieted his fear. "Yes, it is," he said, watching her, and he began to free himself. He saw that her freedom of choice was his own freedom. It's not that jealousy was unknown to the people, not at all, but it was new to me that day, and to him, and he needed to talk and see with another set of eyes to quell the confusing violence. He only needed to see himself and her, and to listen more deeply, to question rather than act.

Shortly after that, a beautiful young woman became angry at her inability to keep pace with her partner's quick humor, his cleverness, and she began thinking her mind was too slow, so she blamed herself, and eventually her man too, and their children became frightened in the shadow of constant blame. She began shaming them when they had done nothing shameful, as she spun circles in her own pain. "What's wrong with you?" she'd demand, and they couldn't answer. I asked grandmother about it, having seen how the woman "crossed the children's fire" in her confusion, and I could say nothing because I didn't understand it. In the woman, I saw the change only in the color of her eyes and the change of her smell, a sharper sweat than usual, acridness coming from under her arms, like the bitter pitch of a poisonous plant, so the grandmother talked to her, listened to her, and the woman remembered through her own talking that minds are always different in their own ways. She saw the slowness of the grandmother's wisdom, found by facing her own mistakes, and saw herself speaking fifty years from now, remembering this day. Her man was quick and facile, and she was sure and solid, and she'd forgotten this simple difference that had attracted them only a short number of years before. It's easy to forget simple things like this, and through my training it became my job to see the changes in people, in the surroundings, in the weather, how it all affects us, how we become the rain and the fog and the sultry heat of summer and the biting cold of fall nights, and to train others my age and younger to see the nature of changes, and to talk to the grandmothers and grandfathers, and to dance in the meadows with the children, in order to pass on what had been given to me. This had been going on for a very long time, and it worked well, and I was now part of a long chain of people providing in this way. It was satisfying, and it was my obligation, and I was happy.

GOING TO WATER

16

And then one night I had the first dream of my own that brought me fully out into the long traveling. In this dream, I saw and began to know what they call the future, and I didn't like it. It frightened me. I had been spending a lot of time in the deep woods with the old couple. They flew through the treetops at night protecting the town, and the town was large, with thousands of people, so their nights were long and their job huge. The old man was squat and strong, a human tree trunk who could lift a grown man into the air like he was a two-year old child, and sometimes men went to him for just that, for the experience and the memory of being tossed into the air and caught by their fathers, treasuring that moment of exhilaration and freedom and trust, flying free yet knowing their father's strong hands and arms would gather under their small arms and carry them back to the ground. Fully grown men would bring food, skins, hunting weapons, whatever they were good at providing as gifts to the powerful man who would toss them back into childhood as easily as he would lift a bow. They didn't know all his powers, and maybe if they had they would have been afraid, but that's only surmise, because even then not everybody understood the powers of the will and the spirit and the body. He was thick in all ways, dense as a night forest, with a wide chest and thighs made of pure muscle, forearms and heavy wrists wrapped in sinewy muscle, yet he moved like water, liquid in the night, like mercury, like a shooting star falling through the night, and he was dark, like that same night the moment after the shooting star vanishes, only his eyes holding the memory of the star's quick flight across the mind. And he was funny, poking the ribs when seriousness took over, or breaking wind at just the right time, when a man might be confessing his innermost mistakes. He would laugh uproariously when he tossed a man skyward, and the older the man, the louder and deeper his laughter. He was contrary, as they say, backwards in many things, irreverent, and yet he was so full of love that he always shone like the morning sun, dark yet bright, steady yet always moving, a fire darting through people's lives, ageless and powerful and beautiful, and I loved him with all my heart, my Grandfather Tree.

Grandmother was equally powerful, but she was more like a smile, a very clear and shining smile. She was small and strong, with the sharp nose and high cheekbones of the northern people who had come down long before, her skin reddish in the sun, like fall maple leaves. Her hair was like her skin, auburn, and her temperament flashed like the evening sun, so grandfather walked softly around her, quieter than with anyone, yet there were still times when he would turn his fire in her direction, when her tongue got too sharp. They tested each other constantly, and loved each other deep in the forest away from the village, for they were too wild and free to be part of the families with all their kinship obligations, rules, and observance of etiquette, all the things that kept our ancient society in fine order. This couple was everything the order of the village was not, the antithesis of order and civility, yet their entire existence was for the good of those with whom they could not intermingle. They had their own kinds of obligations and rules that were intimately and forever tied to the townspeople. They were the other sides of decorum, fierce in their confrontations with the forces they fought on the borders of civilization. As I grew to know them, I wondered aloud at the choices they had made to become these kinds of protectors.

"There is no choice," Grandfather said one windy night in reply to my question. "When you see what needs to be done, and that there is no one else to do it, you just do it. It's simple." I admired his clarity. He always knew where he stood.

Grandmother poked the fire and chuckled sharply. "Yes, he never thought about choice because he is so noble," she laughed, "so giving and selfless," she said, tossing her head back, long auburn hair catching the red firelight. Then she stared hard. "Tell her the truth," she demanded.

"That is the truth," Grandfather said, but he paused, looking down before he went on. "It's not that simple," he offered quietly, a bit sheepish for a man that strong. "You have the things you want, you know, and as the powers of perception and abilities grow, you want to do this and that with them."

"Hmm. Yes, tell her the truth, not what you finally accepted only because Uncle sat you down and made you see it."

At the mention of Uncle, Grandfather blanched and listened more deeply, then continued. "So you do those things, finding out about your power by hunting, traveling, being with women, and nothing works out because you're outside your strength with only those things, outside what you can really do. Everything is less than what you're supposed to be doing, so you eventually have to go back." He paused again, scratched his belly with a big hand while looking up into the night sky, then got quiet for a very long time before he spoke.

"And then there is Uncle," he sighed and went on, settling into what was a long speech from a man too restless to talk for long.

"I was young in my power when Uncle told me the story about the original witch, and that story brewed in me a long time before I knew what it meant. That's the way Uncle and his stories worked, like impregnating someone, and there's a long period of the baby growing inside, and eventually it has to come out and live its own life, and with living its own life your life is no longer the same, never the same. Something is born, staring at you wherever you go, and it's all different." He scratched some more, thinking and scratching that great broad chest. He ran his palms down his arms from the shoulders to the fingertips, stretching toward the fire, and night birds called to each other from behind us in the east, calling across to the west of our camp, their sounds arcing across the life path. His black hair reflected starlight straight back into the sky.

"Uncle said that before the young man was a witch, he was taken to the forest to shoot a rabbit by his grandfather, according to custom. He'd gotten good at the bow, so it was time. They waited a long while in a meadow, then a big buck rabbit appeared. The young man took careful aim, looking at the animal's steady black eyes across the short distance, then released the arrow, and it struck the rabbit in the heart. With a startled look, it fell dead almost instantly. The boy and his grandfather walked to the dead rabbit and the grandfather took it in his hands. He felt it for a moment, then he placed it in the boy's hands. 'Feel its death, its life and now its death,' he said, looking and waiting. 'This is your doing, and it can never change.' The young man knew what was expected of him, so he felt the death, put on a humble face, and circled tobacco over the rabbit's limp body with one hand, thanking it. The grandfather watched with approval, yet something bothered him, something in the boy's eyes. Inside, hidden from the grandfather, but not entirely invisible, the boy was exulting at his power over life itself, in this first kill. He was not ashamed or humbled, but was gleeful, just a small amount. It's not that one shouldn't feel the strength of that act of killing, but there is a right way, and a choice to be made."

Grandfather Tree shook his head sadly as he came to this part of the history, frustration building on his thick brows until it burst out in anger, and he shook his mighty fists at the night, his great shaggy head turning all around him as though he were looking for that witch boy so he could turn him upside down and inside out, thrash him within an inch of his life and bellow down into his face the horror of what he was doing.

"Uncle said everything gradually began to change then for the boy, and he started going into the forest alone and killing animals, and his exultance grew with each killing. But he held it from his grandfather, and he put on a face of calm humility as he came back to the village with his prey. And the people were happy with what he provided them.

"But his gradual change built up, out in the secret parts of the forest, where he danced around his kills and touched their blood like it was a lover, and he talked to himself of his skills, which kept improving. Soon he could shoot a deer through the heart from a longer distance than he'd ever heard of, and he was proud, too proud, and still he kept his pride hidden. He told himself that he fed the people, even though he knew better."

Grandfather grew more upset as he told me the story. He sprang to his feet and circled the fire, picked up a large stone and flung it into the forest where it crashed and bounced into the darkness, and the night birds were silent. Everything was silent and still, and even Grandmother said nothing. She knew the enormity of the young man's decisions, the depth of his aberration, and she remembered her own fear despite her obstinate, consummate strength and determination, her power and explosive abilities, and the eternal connections to all that is good, to all the good spirits she'd spent her life cultivating. Despite all this, the story kindled her knowing fear and wariness.

"And then his secret life took a turn, and it sped upon him like a panther attacking from behind. His spirit and mind spun around to see it loom above him, reach out its paw and toss him, speeding him away from any chance of saving himself. But still he had a choice, even at that last moment. Though his pride pretended that he didn't, he still had a choice. But he accepted the will of what he had created, the will of the panther that was nothing but his own selfish desire. And from then on, his eyes glowed with his own creation, his private world, and he looked down on the people when he brought them food, making demands upon them with his demeanor."

Grandfather fell silent then, and he caved in upon his sadness, curled into himself, arms wrapped around his trunk, his chin tucked into his chest, and his hair hung around his face making it invisible, and his breath grew silent. It was as though he was dying or disappearing or becoming a stone there by the fire, something to be talked about in the future as people looked at the dark human-like shape resting there. But he was only gathering himself.

"The people accepted his food," he said plainly, having arrived at the conclusion, "but when they ate it they eventually began to be sick. That's the way it works. We cannot eat food killed like this and given like this without consequences. Some consequences are simple, some very complicated, but they were so long in coming, the parents did not recognize why their children got strange illnesses the old herbs would not cure. And they did not know why some children turned away from them, turned away because that's what the boy began for them. That's what happened," he said, "the turning away," returning slowly from his sadness to his everyday passion.

He looked up at me then with a glint in his eye. "And that's why we came, me and your Grandmother, and those long before us, and now you, the feisty girl. That's what Uncle told both of us, and he said that young man was 'a complete idiot,' and he shook his head like he always did when he saw stupidity." Grandfather imitated Uncle's slow side to side shaking head then, and laughed quietly into the firelight, but without humor.

The next morning after eating, in very early light, Grandmother continued on the origins of these things in our lives. "The same thing happened far in the south, a long time ago, when Corn was brought to the people. Smart men and women watched the different corn grasses grow, and they had visions and dreams of marrying corns, so they put them together, married their tiny blossoms, and after a time of blending pollen and flowers with warm wind and gentle hands, the small clusters of seeds got bigger and bigger, until they eventually formed the yellow corn, the blue corn, the many-colored clusters we eat today. The corn-makers' visions were gifts from Earth and Sky, from how things are and how they change and come to be, and eating Corn made people strong. And when there was little meat, they survived on Corn, like this we just ate."

She ran her finger along the bottom of a polished brown gourd in front of her and held a smear of morning gruel on her finger tip, where it shone gold and wet in the sun. She smiled and stared at it, sitting on her knees, back straight, long auburn hair falling to her waist. She raised her arm high in the air and turned it, to where the sunlight brightened every side of the glistening corn meal, then she slowly brought it down to her open mouth, slipped it in and sucked with a grin forming on her lips. "Delicious," she said calmly, "so good that some strange people turned it into a god," stretching the word "strange" all long and lilting. Grandmother was mischievous in almost everything she did, a heyoka, as the plains people call them, so she reached into the gourd with an elaborate gesture of pomp and ritual, bringing a huge dollop of meal out into the air. "More God," she said. "I eat more God." She licked the corn off her finger in a lascivious manner, eyes sparkling, like sex in the first light of morning. Her voice deepened and she spoke in sonorous tones. "In fact, I am God's partner, the source of this food, as I created it out of my own vision, and you must now worship me as you worship the God I have created for you." She laughed uproariously, shoulders shaking.

"Agana, I do not make light of our creation and all the ways that support us, of anyone's Creator, but of these fools, those who fool us into believing Corn, or any gift, is their doing. I tell you this because what happened then is terrible, because bringing all our experience and learning into only one human source is very dangerous indeed. Those strange people, not the watchers of the grasses, but ones who came later, created a priesthood, a group within themselves that took the power from the people and brought it to themselves. They began forming pictures of themselves on stones and telling the people stories about what is real and what is not. They sucked the lifeblood from the people and made them believe it was only through feeding them that the people would survive."

Grandmother's teeth clenched as she talked, and the delight in her mockery flew away as the enormity of the story grew. Like Grandfather, her anger built and built, but unlike him, she did not take it into herself. She let it burst out in the brightness of fresh daylight, and the trees stood back and listened as her voice rose and filled the meadow. Flowers quaked in the wind of her anger, and grasses bent from her fury.

"Eventually, they killed people to offer their blood to the gods they'd created, and the people they killed were those who saw through the lies they'd been brought up to believe. This had gone on for a long time by this point, but many people born into it did not forget the gift of their birth and the beauty of their lives, despite the power of the priests, because the truth is simply the truth, and it never goes completely away, even in the most powerful deceit." She was not shouting, but her lips curled up in scorn, and her teeth and eyes flashed, and her hair flamed out from her livid face. My body shook as I listened, though the sun was warm on our chests. She saw my fear and caught my eye carefully then, coming down and down with me into her gentleness again, and I remembered who she was and what she was capable of. I found my comfort with her, in her eyes as they became the color of dark clay.

"So, many people left," she smiled. "They walked out quietly in the middle of the night and headed north, to where they'd heard stories from travelers about different kinds of people who did not slaughter their own, where there were no priests or kings." She smiled a broad smile, reached over to hold my hand in both of hers, and finished. "And those people who escaped came all this way here, over many years. They brought us Corn, and the memory of their kingdoms and priesthoods. Both the food and the stories have stood us well over generations, as we have sustained ourselves on the food and studiously listened to their memory."

I wondered if there had been something similar deep in our own people's past, something that made our ancestors leave the woods of the north to walk into the hills and valleys where we now lived. I asked

Grandmother, and she listened deeply to echoes in her mind before answering. "Yes, it happened, but it was so long ago we don't remember when it was, only that it was. And there was no place to run to, so the people rose up against the priests and killed them, led by a courageous leader. It did not last for many generations this time because maybe the people remembered through the story of the Corn people. Exactly when these things happened is a mystery to us, like our very origins, and like the choices we make in the face of true power and false power, but it doesn't matter. All we know is that it's our job to watch for the sorcerer's grab for imbalance, hard as it is to understand why he does so. Maybe his strange desire is something that comes through people like a comet comes through our sky on a long, great cycle so huge we cannot see it. Maybe it flies in a shape we don't know, so we cannot predict its choices in time or place or person. We know the comet is always there, moving, but we cannot say what it will do. Some things we cannot answer, and that's as it should be. Even then, granddaughter, we must always think about consequences. I'm sure you agree, and this is why I trust in you and love you so very much. You have a very beautiful mind, and you are only now beginning to realize what it can do for you, and for all of us. You begin to know the power of thought."

She smiled into my eyes for a very long time then, uncharacteristically, for she was usually fluid and quick, darting here and there in vigilance or in agitation, but now she settled into me, like the blue sky itself was pouring through her into me.

"You're a good one, all right," she said, patting my arm. "Now let's go find that old man of mine and go fishing."

I laughed because I knew very well what that meant. They would take me to a beautiful spot along a sparkling stream, give me a spear lifted from its secret spot, and leave me on my own to stare, waiting for the succulent brown trout to appear. Tree and Grandmother would put their fingers to their lips, wide-eyed in playful admonition toward silence, and back away, then turn to rush into the forest together hand in hand, disappearing to leave me in silence. Then, from a distance, I would hear their squeals of delight snaking through the leaves they rolled upon, and their joy always brought a smile to my lips so broad and sudden that even the long brown trout I hunted were startled out of their studious watching, enough to copy my grin.

17

The two dreams were so real in both instances that I could not tell if I was really here or not. I lost my sense of real time and didn't know. It's like this sometimes, and I feel like I'm slipping down a muddy arroyo toward a vast swallowing lake, and I don't have any idea where I am in this world.

In the first dream, I was standing on a hillside downslope from the pine-covered ridge of the volcano Unzen in Japan. In my climb up the ancient trail, artfully placed stone steps worn by centuries of sandaled feet carried me higher in the most difficult parts, and bird sounds darted all around me like the butterflies and dragonflies of all kinds surrounding me. Bamboo rustled in a light breeze, and people dotted vegetable fields below, getting ready to take breaks from the hot sun. Tea Plants and Mulberry trees expanded across the slopes radiating outward from the trail, and wild silk moths dotted their leaves, having escaped the confines of centuries-old harvesting areas. I stopped to study the magnificent prisms of their wings and bright orange-yellow colors, eye-shaped circles staring up from each artfully crafted wing in perfect symmetry, the moths crawling from place to place, steadily eating and breathing, for they do both at once, efficient as they are, but they cannot fly even with all that beauty. It's a seeming quirk of nature that puzzles my mind, yet the beauty prevails over their inability to use the tools they are given, wings that look as though they could carry the moth to heaven and back, over and over. But they cannot fly.

As I stood contemplating the creatures, the air suddenly shuddered, and even those voracious moths stopped, motionless, strangely frozen solid in the midday August heat, and now they became an even deeper contradiction of nature, with flightless wings and completely still. The birds silenced themselves too, landing without chatter instantly, as if shot from the sky but staring, as frozen as the moths. I looked around me but could see no source of the sudden change. I was alone, and I'd never seen this place before, yet I strangely knew it well, in a way dreams often provide. I looked down at the fields below, and saw sun-leathered faces all peering skyward in the stillness. Then a wind came circling around the shoulders of the mountain, stinking electric and unholy, and I turned toward dream magic in order to survive, to lift away. Something horrible was happening, and I didn't know what it was. I flew upward, pulled my body up in fear and deep trepidation to the edge of the mountain, and the wind swirling around it like water around a boulder was hot and relentless, steady, a tremendous force, but I rose through it like one can only do in a dream. Like a meteor's passage across the night sky, I rose to the shoulder and looked beyond, the mountain my huge protector staring in the same direction I was, toward the valley and city beyond. Then there was the sound and the horrible sight of it.

A giant yellow cloud rose from the city below me, bright orange at the base, the colors of the silk moths, and the wind tore trees from their roots and scattered them like straw. The cloud roared and rose so high it looked as though it would reach the sun itself, become the sun, explode the sun. Something terrible had been unearthed, and screams were borne on the wind, screams of old people, women, young people, children, animals, and the smell of burning flesh stung my nostrils and seared my memory. I had never before known such a thing, and I reeled in its intensity. An old woman tumbled through the air, passing by me inextricably in slow motion, the terrible wind going much faster than her, horror consuming her face as she disappeared from being. Within the roar, I heard the voices of a couple arguing about a move in a parlor chess game only a moment before the blast, as though their words were living in a capsule of safety, words flying through the heat alone forever, a polite but firm argument oblivious to the enormity of what was happening or what had just happened to them, words like flying body parts separated from cohesive meaning and all reason. The cloud rose and rose into the sky, a moth now liberated by humans from its bondage by humans, becoming a monstrous thing, nature turned backwards upon itself, and the smell of poison radiated over the land, killing all in its wake, either instantly or in long lingering moments, moments I later saw would in fact become months, years, and countless generations.

In this blast I saw how time works, how it stretches out longer than we can imagine, and how even those who would learn to forgive the act of this bomb, forgive both themselves and others on both sides of the war that built it, would never be the same. A choice had been made, and this dream plunged me into that choice made centuries after my original time. My spirit was shattered, my heart exploded, my brain irradiated, and in that chaos a steady resolve was born. There must be a way to stop this, or if not to stop it, to turn it away like a herd of stampeding elk, from ever happening again. There must be a way. A vow began to curl upward from my stomach, through my heart, and into my shimmering mind.

GOING TO WATER

18

The second dream attached to the first like a baby to its mother, like an infant strapped to the back of a Mayan woman working her onion fields high on the green slopes of Volcano Atitlan, or a little one clinging to the brown and black patterns of its mother's dusty shirt on a long flat road in Africa, where she carries two blue plastic pails to get water from a distant well. This second dream is evidence of how the child clings to the mother in adversity, how it grows from the life the mother lives, somehow surviving, a glint in its eye no matter what confronts it. It's how things grow out of other things, some wonderful, and some that fill the human spirit with dismay. It's evidence of how the agricultural fields of California grow out of the slopes and valleys of Nagasaki, and how they intertwine.

The images pieced themselves into my reality without order or sequence, a hospital bed and a joke to an elderly nurse about how I, who look so vastly different from my Filipino friend, was his sister. The nurse was Filipino herself, wearing a pale orange gown patterned with barely visible white butterflies that flew gently as she moved around the room arranging her tools. She raised her old eyebrows my way and stared before finally smiling, recognizing that our bond was of the heart and spirit, not blood, though blood too would soon enough be our bond. Tubes and monitors surrounded us, beeping sounds and soft voices mingling with intercom requests for this doctor or that to go here or there. My friend Johnny's humor, the intrepid face of his courage, kept his wife and me alive as he faced an impending death from cancer.

In another dream moment, weaving through the hospital scene, I saw him standing on a bridge over a serpentine river moving through wide fields of strawberries and lettuce and broccoli, hands in the pockets of his Levis as he watched his people's lives unfold. He lived in and worked the fields and orchards that feed America and beyond, and he wrote the stories of the people in poems, stories of the workers, stories of hard labor, pesticides and chemicals surrounding their lives in misty dawn shrouds of transparent white. He chronicled their drinking, fighting, loving, their incest, feasts in harvest celebration, their poverty, pride and triumph.

In the dream, Johnny died after a month of illness, during which time we held eagle feathers, dusted our combined world with pollen and tobacco offered for new beginnings, for possibilities of the mind and heart, and for who we are in the realms we so inadequately call spirit. The word is inadequate in this time, this century, an impoverished and captive sound, less than what it should be only because the possibilities that lie buried under it are so huge. Instead of one word, it should be a huge library of sound running polished hallways everywhere in all directions, and each hallway should be filled with everything and everyone we have ever known. It should be filled with song, with smiles and laughter and tears, with the sound of sunrise and the whisper of sunset, and the driving heat of the day. It should glisten and move and promise freedom, and it should deliver that promise of freedom, in love, with every second of experience, for this is the world out of which we emerge.

"I can feel the wind," Johnny said, holding the beaded white feather firmly in his right hand, eyes half-closed, "and I can hear it." As solid as Grandfather Tree, he sat broad and strong on a black leather couch, the sounds of children splashing in a turquoise pool in the distance outside, calling out to each other in play while he listened to the wind under the eagle's wings.

When he died, his wife Angeline held him in her arms with all the love in the world, and the Hunkpapa medicine woman dabbed the continuously flowing blood away from his nose and mouth, the blood that would bind us all in his beauty and strength. His family surrounded him, brothers, children, a sister, and in their quiet midst I haltingly sang our song of calling all spirits to be with him on his journey, following the quiet voice of the medicine woman. The song had filled the room so fully even before it became sound that it was hard for me to find the words, to ride them and give them to my voice. Like Johnny was growing to be, the words were everywhere, coming out of everywhere, because every morning at the quiet time, the time when the world around us is waiting and silent and letting us be, just at the first beginnings of light, he and I had been in that song together, and this goes on and on still. It never stops, and it never should. It's connection, release, a salute and a prayer, all at once, and it goes everywhere.

The explosion that took Johnny's life is one we all live with, harsh truth be told, the promise of smiling "little Tommy Atom" to bring peace to the world through the notion that "progress is our most important product," and that fear and destruction bring peace to people. Inside all who live in these centuries of the machine age is the residue of Earth tossed willy-nilly into the sky without regard to consequence, and as I move through this time I feel and suffer from the displacement of minerals, bone, chemicals and liquids too, the blood of humans infused with parts of the earth better left alone, un-isolated. I know these things in my own body simply from passing through, where chemicals reside in the tissue around my heart and invite the electrical charges I need for pumping my blood to obey their own mindless commands. They are not meant to live there; they have their own place among the other tissues of the soil, within the mountains and under the strata between the surface and the center of the earth, and when they are put into the streams and rivers in order to mine gold and other single parts of the world, they flow into our bellies and veins and flesh. And they scream to get back to the earth, to get out of us, and their screaming is our demise.

In the face of the insanity we live in this age, Johnny showed me in this dream of his dying that he was not bitter or angry about his time. For him, love and dignity won over politics and dispute and power and wealth, although this was not a simple thing. Despite his knowing the source of his early death, for he was still a young and vital man, he did not feel sorry for himself, nor did he wail, blame anyone, or complain about any of it. Rather, he looked upon his two beautiful sons now growing into young men and he smiled. He kissed Angeline's hand, coming out of a coma-like state to fight with the limitations of his body to reach for her hand and press it to his lips, in love and gratitude, making sure she knew, for the coma had come upon him suddenly. They had been caught together in the daily web of hospital visits, long walks down the hallways to get hydrated and to get chemo, when it suddenly hit him and he was gone, whirled into the beginnings of the world beyond, the world of origins and mystery. But he came back for awhile, and he breathed and waited for his family to surround him, giving his love and patience to them, healing them with his quiet breathing, listening to their stories about their lives with him, stories crossing childhood's many years, cowboy outfits and cap-shooting six-guns, laughter and wonder, and when his breathing slowed and finally left, his oldest brother's strong and tear-filled shout filled the room with ultimate, crucial truth, the truth he knew as a veteran of war: "Let it go, Johnny. You fought the good fight." I looked out the window, and an early Monarch butterfly circled a tall bamboo stem in the cement hospital courtyard, bright black and orange swirling upward in yellow light.

This is how the dream lives with me now, because in all the years I've known this man in his time he has sought to "do the right thing," seeing a huge swath of time, and his life is evidence of what I am capable of too. These are his words, words about beauty, words and actions that outlive the contradictions we all have come to live, the contradictions that develop on deeper and deeper levels the more we fear the very world we have created, strangely, out of an elemental fear of the world itself, the primitive world before now. But control of the world is not the answer, while self-control just might be. The beast who chases me dashes across the night sky on his own fear, runs crazily from his eventual demise, refusing to see himself in a world of balance. The bomb over Nagasaki was conceived in fear and then used to inculcate fear and power, dangerous allies to make friends with, for they will seek their own perpetuity and run from change and from their own deaths. They will seek to make themselves be the sole mode of controlling the world and the people and creatures within it. In preponderance, fear tilts the very axis of Earth herself, and in this state of imbalance, the sorcerer thrives, for illusion is his lifeblood, illusion and forgetting what is deeply true, no matter how far we run from it.

These two dreams, which were really one dream bound together in two parts, lifted me out of my time and threw me somewhere else for the first time in my life. They carried me into another time that would eventually become my own, one that would be a frightening time for my people centuries later. The first dream was of the horrific mechanical symptom of human aberration and the spread of a deep and powerful disease, an abomination of life, and the second dream contained the precise antidote to that disease and elemental disturbance. The second dream was of a hero and an inspiration, a straightforward, hard-working man of vision, and a true friend I would someday have the honor to meet again.

GOING TO WATER

19

It was almost a day's walk to Little Rain's village, so I was ready to rest after a steady trek up tree-covered hills and down through open valleys. Her town lay near a stream, spread out neatly, surrounded by woods on a gentle slope to the south and a steeper bank to the north. Late afternoon sun cradled gentle plumes of smoke rising from the first fires of dinner, and children played around the stream, calling to each other and chasing in the light, which would soon shift as the sun dipped into the branches of the western trees. On the far end of the village, I could see Rain's still posture at her edge of the woods, and I could feel her filling with its creatures, with their sounds and motions, with their quick and quiet eyes. It made me smile to see her stillness in this way, her absorbing the world before her, because now I knew the momentous quality of what it provided her, the solace and relief it gave from that other world that invaded her without consent, without choice or control, out of nothing she or her people had done or could imagine being done. I loved her then, standing on the hillside above the town, and that love was simple and huge. She became my child in that moment, in the distance against the sketched woods of an old painting, a small form sitting vibrant in between centuries without knowing, having no words to put to what she saw and knew in herself. She was not my blood kin, but she was my blood. She was in it, of it, and we ran through the shapes and sounds and smells of it together, so she was my daughter and my sister at once, and I smiled in this knowing, for it began to form in my mind that perhaps she knew more about all of this than she could articulate, but she knew nonetheless. Maybe she did. Yes, it is true that she was lost, truly lost and very near death from the sadness when it came pouring down upon her, up through her, yet at the same time, our connection was an indication, even a harbinger of something I did not understand, something I could not articulate any better than she could, and in this something began to grow.

After catching my breath, I stepped slowly down the zigzag trail toward the town. Halfway down, I stopped still and looked up from the small brown stones dotting the path to look in Little Rain's direction. As I looked, she turned and gazed straight up to where I stood. Though she was too far away to see her face, I thought I saw her smile, but I knew it could only be my desire, my imagination playing tricks on me. She raised her right hand high in the air and held it there, and I returned the greeting, clutching the long brown and white owl feather I'd found for her on the way, holding it high in the air, where its soft tip pushed its way into my two dreams and began the prayer found in understanding and its sister, abject humility.

GOING TO WATER

20

It was very early one morning only days after the two dreams, when I finally fell into the new time solidly and physically, like morning dew falling from one flower to the next. The yellow cup of a small finger-sized trumpet blossom fills until it can hold no more, then the weight of the water tilts it over suddenly. The water falls quickly down through crisp air into the open mouth of a blossom below, filling it instantly with a shudder. It's done that quickly, gravity pulling my body into the twentieth century for the first time head over heels.

I lay in the rough dirt of a plowed brown field on a flat valley floor, distant cottonwood trees arching over what I thought must be a small creek. I'd never seen this kind of disturbance done to the ground before, and when I rolled over on the rough clods to look into the sky, I saw wires strung from tall poles alongside the field's edge, and four blackbirds launched off the black lines into a hot blue-grey sky, circled me, and disappeared in the distance. There were no other birds, and I was startled at such a thing as only two pair together in a vast sky. Where were the flocks that blocked the sun like living and sky-dancing clouds of birds? Where was everyone else?

There was a buzzing sound, like a wasp in a sudden straight line digging into the earth just beyond me and to the side, and a puff of earth splitting away, rising and falling. The wasp carried the smell of metal, and then there was an explosion following on its heels, the sound of a gunshot. I was being shot at, once, twice, three times, and I pressed into the furrows and scanned the cottonwoods. Halfway up a tall tree, a young man, yet a child, sat cradled in the neck of the tree taking careful aim with his .22 long rifle, then squeezing the trigger. I raised an arm to wave him off, but he fired again. Why, I could not imagine. There was no reason to it, no explaining. I was simply there, and he had a gun. It seemed that simple. I could not see his intentions from so far away, but there was an emptiness where his spirit should have been, where even from that distance it should have shone around him, but there was only dullness. I became afraid, for I hadn't seen this senselessness and vacancy before, not even from the witch boy, not even from him, whose presence was voracious, not deadened. Face in the rough dirt, I crawled along the furrow until it became inches deeper, then I found a smooth round stone, looked into the position of my attacker and hurled the stone with all my strength, remembering what Grandfather Tree had told me about seeing the spot I wanted it to strike. I aimed for the branches just above the boy, and my aim was true. The stone carried itself on the motionless blue-grey sky alongside my will and shattered the silent leaves above him, and he scrambled quickly down the white trunk and disappeared down the creek bed in panic. I rolled over and looked upward into the vast sky and breathed heavily, and the sound of my quick breath and frightened heart was all I heard. Where had I landed? I lay there until evening darkened the sky, watching red trails of sunset light high in the sky, crisscrossing lines between me and the stars. As I calmed, a very dull yet steadily humming roar filled the air around me in what should have been silence, and I listened to its undifferentiated noise, like an ambiance but hectic and frenetic, something quick and encompassing in its frenzy. When purple sky settled in, I rose and walked through the sounds toward an orange glow beyond the black silhouettes of the cottonwoods, listening for some kind of meaning in the cacophony of signals assaulting me, but I found none. There was nothing I could grasp in my fist and look directly into.

It was a small town, full with young people, paved streets, huge old maple trees in full green summer leaf, and music reached out from seemingly every corner. People stared at me in my deerskin and boots, smiling ingratiatingly, and I wondered what they thought because few connected for more than a split moment, and no one lingered in my returning smile. It was like walking through a dream, but my body was heavy as living stone, real and vital, flexible and strong. I had a spring in my step, and there was no lifting away as in a dream, no floating from thing to thing, no suddenly being where I might focus and then arrive with no steps in between. It was real, no dream world, but another world I remembered. It was the world of Johnny's hospital, Il Duce's guardian witch, and the bomb exploding over Nagasaki, but it was in another corner of the twenty-first century's urgency, and it was my first real time here.

I heard drumming, and in the near distance I saw a tall young man with an eagle feather in his dark brown felt hat, greeting people as they passed by on the street. I walked toward him, and when I got there he smiled and looked away, motioning me in. There was a colored drawing beside an open door, of a man in a white cowboy hat looking upward, a feather, a prayer circle and a cactus plant on a desert landscape. There was a drawing on a stone from the very old people in the south. There were many written words, some big and some small, and I had not yet come to understand them, but they seemed to be promises of some kind. They felt this way. It was all new to me, and I hadn't yet found the ability to suddenly grasp all the tools of my time, but I would learn that skill quickly. That would be simply another level of arriving, of allowing myself to fully arrive without any resistance. In this way the language would pour into me alongside everything else I'd need.

I strode inside, scanning the large room, where I saw the drum, three men and one woman drumming, the man in the white hat standing with his back to the others, and a table where a smiling young girl in dark braids and Indigenous dress took paper from the many people that began to fill the room. The young girl

102

confused me because her dress came from many people, some from the Great Plains, some from the eastern
woodlands, and some from the southern countries far
below us. I wondered who her people were. I thought
maybe she didn't know, and was searching for them.

The man in the white hat seemed to be the leader,
so I walked up behind him and respectfully waited
for him to sense my presence, at a polite distance. He
did not seem to know I was there. Eventually, the
young girl came and told him the people were ready,
and by her deference, I knew she thought him a great
leader or medicine person, and she then introduced
him to the people as the "shaman." I did not know
the word, even though their language was slowly
beginning to penetrate my mind, and I remembered
pieces of it through the dreams that brought me here,
dreams in which I fully understood all that was said.
He was shocked as he turned and saw me standing by
him, and I thought he must have been in some kind
of trance or prayer, but nothing of the sort emanated
from him. He was only alone and inside himself, as
far as I could tell. He glanced at me in curiosity as he
stepped before the crowd.

With his white hat firmly on his head, he raised
the eagle feather above him, and I stood as it went
up, yet few others in the room did so. He asked them
to stand, so they did, though uneasily, and then he
prayed, while I kept waiting for him to take his hat
off. I thought that if the prayer was to be sent, it must
come upward through his open mind, and if it were
heard, it must come downward through his open

heart, but the thick white felt and wide brim obscured both directions, hiding him, hiding his eyes, and the prayer was something I did not understand, a seeming ritual disguising something else very personal within him, yet the people deferred to him, held themselves back in some kind of awe, and I was confused, watching and waiting for something grand to happen, but it did not. The prayer finished, and the people mingled in confusion and deep expectation.

Afterwards, as I watched people sign papers and shake hands with the young girl, the leader walked over to me, but he was hesitant, withdrawn somewhere, yet still bound by some rule or dictate within himself to approach me. When he got to me, he seemed disturbed by my smell, by the richness of the deerskin and soil and wood smoke, perhaps, but I could not tell, for he suppressed his repulsion and turned it into something else. He looked me up and down quickly, pausing at my breasts, as though I could not see him evaluating me as a beautiful young woman only, not as a being, then his gaze rested on my eyes. His eyes were dark brown and wavering, once he let them be seen under the hat brim, coming in and out of focus, and he never really arrived or allowed himself to be seen directly, but came at me from one side and then another, all while holding very still. Something like sexual desire, or his peculiar form of it, rose in him and he spoke to me.

"Are you interested in becoming a shaman?" He emphasized the last word, wrapping it in mystery and potency.

I looked at him silently because I had not yet attained speaking in his language. Then I replied in my own language, and startled, he took a step back. But while my words were a shock, they were also a challenge to him, and he chose to ride the challenge. He came at me only as a man then, but not even fully that. Even his male stance was an illusion. I thought he was not a man, not even a boy, yet his age should have made him a man. I could not find just what he was.

"Medicine. You know, medicine," he said. He spoke slowly with his voice slightly raised, as though I could not hear well. The English opened to me at this moment because I saw how important these words were in this world, to him and those around him, and the enormity of my physical presence here now became consuming to me. I had to surrender to all of it because I was fully here physically. I had to dive in and let it all pour through my heart, mind, and body. I could not be only partially here. Because my body was so solidly leading me now, there was no room for distance or translation. What had begun as imagination, dream, and another knowing and thinking, now became my reality, and it was a confusing reality of images with only partial substance of mirrored reflections and electronic dreams.

The leader saw me understand his words, and he smiled slightly, though his lips did not lend themselves easily to the motion. It was more of an effort, something forced as a capacity he knew he needed to have in order to have influence over the people. It seemed not his nature, but he did it anyway, and it was almost a comical thing to behold but for his intentions, which seemed not good, yet were too weak to fear overtly. He asked me again if I would like to become a shaman, and stared into me, daring enough to take a step forward toward me. With that step he entered my place in the world without shame, clear through my boundaries of respect. He reached out and touched my shoulder, and in this touch and the gaze that came with it, I saw several important things. First, he did not know I was with a man already. He could not tell this, though it inhabits my whole being. He could not see the presence of my man surrounding me. Second, his desire was confused with his fear. He was afraid of me, yet he sought to bury the fear with an imagined sexual power over me. He wanted me to submit to him, and his return promise was that he would make me a medicine woman, a shaman, give me his brand of holiness in trade for my body, which would be my spirit. Third, when I watched this unfold, looking at him, his eyes clouded into something that must have worked with the women of this time, and it was a mask, a reflection like the drawing on the paper outside the room, the paper with the promises and the upward turned face, as though looking into the universe itself in its grandness. But I looked directly at him, and his vision of me bounced back against his dark pupils, shaded by the broad-brimmed hat, and the reflection that shone there was of himself, white hat and all, with its brightly beaded headband of turquoise, orange, and yellow, medicine colors. I was not present to him, though he stared into my eyes. I saw the image on his eyes, the picture his eyes should see, and it was not me. It was his own face bouncing back from my eyes, and I was amazed at this. I'd never seen this before, never in our world, where we see each other clearly almost all the time, even in our mistakes, for good or ill. I quickly realized I would be spending a lot of time in a world where I would be virtually invisible, a projection on the part of my viewer, and I began to think that this was part of the problem, that this was another arrow in the witch boy's complicated quiver. It turns out I was right, and the consequences were enormous, far beyond what I could have imagined. I reflected on all the faces walking the street outside, and I remembered. I remembered the vacant spirit around the boy with the rifle who greeted me. I thought of this, then I understood the man standing in front of me, and my anger began to burn.

He was waiting for my answer to his question of whether I wanted to become a shaman, like him, I supposed, and I became furious and consumed with the preposterousness of where I was. I realized he was selling an image of medicine, as he called it, ancient ways of healers, the ways of the southern elders, and I was suddenly torn between laughter and hatred, but I could go into neither place in myself, for I saw he was caught too, ensnared in a trap of his own making, his deeper memory caught by crisscrossing wires and shiny things covering that deep pool where he might know himself. Cars drove by on the street outside, exhaust smells wafting into the room alongside the scent of giant maples and summer sweat and the ever-present metal. I was here in the twenty-first century, for the first time for certain, and I could only stare in dismay.

But I could not resist my anger, finally, which sometimes swells out of me like Grandpa Tree's anger, and I fought the urge to slap him with my open palm. I looked at the medicine man with my real eyes, with the eyes from my time, burning through the images he worked around me and on top of me so laboriously and with such purpose, and my gaze shattered all he stood for and all he stood behind. I shattered his place of hiding simply by seeing him. He stumbled backward suddenly on the force of my stare, almost falling flat on his back, but his girl in deerskin grabbed him, trying to steady him, but she was frail and light and he was thick and heavy. I took a step toward him but stopped. He gathered himself from falling, clawing at the girl's shoulder to find his balance, almost caving her in, but she struggled and held up finally, his knees buckling too but holding finally, then he turned and ran toward the back of the room, where he flung open a black painted door with a crescent moon on it and disappeared, his girl in deerskin and bouncing quills following on his heels. I turned and left the room swiftly, amazed to see that few of the people had even noticed what had happened, but then I wondered, in the face of all this, what could they see anyway?

As I turned, I thought that this man was not the witch, not the man in the Italian silk suit, nor did he work for him directly. He was a distant product, who probably never even knew the source of his own pain and fear. I record this meeting with him here only to remember my first visit, and to remember my realization of how deeply subtle the power of the witch and his obfuscation had become by this time, so subtle it seemed the whole town had succumbed to its numbing power. I longed then to see the sparkling eyes of children, for I thought they surely must still be fresh, alive and full with potential to counter this prevailing entanglement of feelings, this torpor and disintegration of the heart's seeing, this blanket of blindness over the whole town. Surely they would be able to help change this direction with their dreams, their wonder, and with their awe.

I ran into the street and looked everywhere frantically, but I could find no children. It was late, and only adults milled about in the hot valley night. I ran into a park, into the middle of an empty ball field and stared up into the face of the moon. Tears poured down my face, and the salt filled my mouth, open and crying. The moon stared back, its mouth round in a circle of concern, surprise, and consternation. It waited a full breath, recognized me, then began grinning in my face like a wonder-struck child. I was not alone after all, and I knew there would be help. Moon spoke to me then, and my tears turned toward laughter because they had to, but it was not an easy thing.

GOING TO WATER

21

I remember it as tumbling through time out of control. I had walked out of the town crying, feeling lost and angry, until I reached the creek and cottonwood trees. I climbed down into the creek bed, slipping down steep slopes of dry dirt in the dark, and I nestled into the fold of two giant white trunks standing so close together they formed a nook of safety for me. I curled up on the ground and stared down into the small running creek with my eyes in slits, and a small coyote stole out of a broadly spreading tangle of wild grape vines on the other side to look at me, his hind legs trembling in readiness to bolt away. But we softened together, and he helped me come back, breathe, and realize I would be all right. I needed sleep, and I fell away in gratitude as he coiled himself on the ground to watch over me.

When I woke in the middle of the night, Coyote was still there, eyes glistening brightly in the darkness, and when I began to tumble head over heels through time, he only watched, watched until I disappeared from his world.

I went everywhere, or so it seemed. There were great ships with white sails and the people watching them arrive from hilltops on the eastern shores. I watched it all, frightened at the enormity of what was impending, and I was with the people, sometimes holding hands simply watching, shivering, and sometimes I trudged through bitter ice and cold snow carrying a child westward, seeing the people spread out in lines in a driving white storm. Then I stood in ceremony in the southwest as five young men rode out to meet the incoming blue-coated army, to hold them off long enough for the Sunrise Ceremony to be complete for the women. Another time I watched a medicine woman hold her strong quivering hands to the sky and tell the fighters where the enemy was and when they would come, and I saw her disappear with the fighters into the rough arroyos and sage while we hid in the boulders silently nursing our hunger and hushing the children. I went everywhere, even to the couches of England, where I saw the first Indigenous brought back to be viewed by the royalty, straight-backed and beautiful men and women gazing upon the English and visiting European noblemen and women without fear, with curiosity, and I watched them too as they slowly realized how they were being seen, that they would eventually be enslaved or used to enslave others. I even listened to the conversations among the noblemen of principle and honor as they told the slavers and merchants that here was a nation of people who deserved their own dignity, that no man could own another. I watched their arguments be stifled by history and held down by the practicality of greed and acquisition, the notion of eventual conquest and submission, a strange bowing to a twisted notion of evolution. I even stood next to a Spanish king as he signed the law against slavery, only a few decades after first contact, as he put his pen to parchment, and I tumbled through the Caribbean islands and the whole of the Americas for five hundred years to watch those papers crumble into dust or be used as kindling to start the campfires that would soon come to dot our entire landscape in its bright orange glow. I careened through all of this, through events, through people's teepees and dining halls, through intimate scenes and great halls of government, through private murders and moments of deep desperate love, and through it all I felt every emotion I could imagine a human being feeling. It was as though my DNA had burst open and flooded me with the entire memory of humankind, and I lay spread before it, spread out and wondering.

But everything has its place, and the strange and resolving thing about that night was that although it filled me with the same fear as the terrible dreams, and poured the desperation of my tears under the moon through me over and over, it also gave me the longest view I'd ever had, like hunting from across a vast plain, where you see the prey and the prey sees you, and you talk to each other, hopefully finding some kind of peace with each other for what is to come. A dance is begun, and if it is a deer, you begin to thank it beforehand for its life, and it softens. If it is an enemy, you sing your ferociousness, and at the same time you tell it silently that you come to it with an open mind and open heart, because in this position you can see best. You can react quickly. You can listen well, smell the wind, and sense what is coming your way. You prepare for your own death and come to peace with it, hoping you've put your house in order, and from here you can fight with all you are. It works best this way because there is nothing between you and what you must do.

So the long view calmed me and fired me at the same time, and the sense of being out of control no longer bothered me. I knew it was a learning, and I could feel Grandfather and Grandmother somehow on the other side of it. I saw Will and the Apache that night too, as I somersaulted through parts of their lives, and other allies who would come my way when the time was right. The desperation I felt at the beginning subsided when I began feeling the threads surrounding me, touching me from everywhere, and there was no emptiness that stayed. It all began to smell like my home, and it became something about cleaning house then, something about work, about a job to be done. I saw Grandfather's glinting smile then, and I understood the first edges of answers to my questions of him, of how he came to his position, of why he did what he did. I saw Grandmother smiling, and her smile was the welcoming avenue back home, an avenue I now knew I could take any time I needed it. I had only to imagine her. On the line of thought visible in her sparkling eyes, I would be returned to my rightful place, my place of rejuvenation and even solace, for solace had quickly become like fresh meat to my hungry spirit. All it had taken was an honest look at history and where we are headed, to need that food piled before me like a mountain, hot and steaming.

GOING TO WATER

22

The man in the blue Italian silk suit led me up a long winding white marble staircase to a huge room overlooking the plaza. He thought we should get to know each other while the others talked since I was new to this group. Priceless art stared silently down at us as we slowly climbed the cool stone steps to the room, which was also decorated with paintings in gold-covered wooden frames, intricately and painstakingly carved by artisans from everywhere the church reached its long fingers into the world. He walked to a broad set of ornate double doors that opened onto a small balcony with a commanding view of Rome, and on this day, an almost empty plaza. The move to the doors was purposeful, as though walking in the leaders' footsteps would incur awe in me, since this path and those doors, and that balcony, were just like those next door that had been used for centuries to look down upon the upturned and adoring faces of the people below. But he did not open the doors. He could not, as it was not his place, so instead he stood back a full pace and stared, remembering all the generations he'd stood in the shadows listening to the roar of the crowds. I watched his pensive sharp face, his cool good looks, and the glint in his eyes.

He did not recognize me because he was so full with the power of the place, but I knew him. I remembered his gaze from behind the tall marble column when I'd been in this country before on the trip with Will to visit Il Duce. I was surprised he did not see me, but I was much older-looking now, dressed in a beige suit with coifed hair becoming a foreign diplomat's private aid, and perhaps my dignified bearing and credentials impressed him. I was obviously a very mature woman with some influence, and he knew the power of aids, attendants, and security next to those with the titles, with the faces the world sees. He motioned me to sit at a long polished table with an elegant gesture of his arm, a combination of deference and command, playing with both expertly. As I sat, others walked softly into the room and took their seats at his nod and welcoming gesture. He was formally gracious, but he seemed annoyed that others had interrupted us so quickly, for he was obviously looking forward to our interchange. I was new and fresh to him. Servants brought tea as the others settled themselves, and the smell of Darjeeling drifted through the room mixed with the faint residue of frankincense that permeated every corner of the vast palace. The smell was a sweet mixture, a rich mixture, and it turned my stomach slightly as I studied the other faces discreetly and smiled at each one. Power was the name of the game at this table, sweetness the ruse, and riches the surroundings. It was all long in the making, at least by their standards, and it was very deep in the mind. By my reckoning, it had been going on far too long and was far too deeply rooted.

"So what do you think of these German defectors?" he finally asked, "for that is what they are indeed, defectors, and are they not a problem?" It was a question that needed no answer, but still, he was testing, truly asking for a response so he might assess the lay of the land. Hundreds of thousands of German Catholics had quit paying their tithes to the Church, which were paid alongside state taxes and collected by the state. They refused in a small way on the basis of economic hardship, still reeling from the worldwide recession of 2008, and they were simply out of money, but most recently and most importantly, they refused in protest of clergy abusing children. On top of the acts themselves, they were outraged that the Church had hidden the perpetrators. They were furious, in fact, and utterly disconcerted, which led them to march in the streets and refuse their tithes. This conference had been called to discuss how the Church could present the problem to the world community, and we in the room were the helpers of the politicians, the quiet and invisible advisors, those who dispensed advice and revealed positions gleaned from others like us, ideas found and discussed just before the bishop's bath, or while shaving, or in the truth just past a sufficient number of glasses of fine Scotch whiskey late in the night, when the mind needs to be unburdened and truth lays itself out through the air of the quiet room.

"This is a matter of many millions of dollars, and perhaps even billions," the portly man from Spain offered. "Is it not?" He sipped his tea, stared at it a moment, then waved to a young manservant standing at the door and asked, "Would you get me a glass of sherry?" The servant glanced at the leader, who sat at the head of the table and assented with a slight and knowing smile, as though he'd seen this request before many times from Spain. The servant moved off silently.

The leader agreed. "Yes, much money is at stake, but the more important thing is the obedience."

A younger woman sitting across from me looked over the top of her glasses and nodded. "When you agree to be a member of the Church, you cannot back out because of economics or personal choice. You enter into a covenant with God when you agree to the Church's rules and decisions."

The leader smiled and gently stroked the blue silk of his left sleeve with his right hand, but he seemed unconscious of the action, as deliberate as it was. Something was tightly held in him, very tightly, something threatening to himself and everyone in the room, but no one else noticed it, at least not apparently. For all his confidence here in a quintessential seat of power, he was strangely afraid. I smiled inside at this irony, for if anyone should be afraid, it should be me, or perhaps the other Indigenous in the room, but I was confident the leader would not show his true self with all these people present. Since he did not recognize me, there was no need to worry, so I waited.

The conversation went around the room like a board game, each aid following the next in asserting the Church's power, until it got to another person from the Americas, who seemed very uneasy with the whole situation. Finally he spoke, an Indigenous man in late middle age, a physically strong man, though small in stature. His expensive suit fit him perfectly, yet he seemed out of place in it, out of place and time. His deep brown eyes carried pain centuries long, and next to the pain lay his conversion and his love, for someone good within the church had gotten to his heart, had truly loved him in the midst of all that sorrow, and this love set him on the path to where he sat now.

"But the Church is denying the Sacraments to people," he pointed out, "and many will see this as sacrilege itself." As he spoke, it was obvious that he was highly educated in a fine university, albeit religious in focus. "In fact, isn't it sacrilege by canonical definition?" His words carried the power of history and his eyes looked to the leader's response without trepidation. He was objective, yet not. His passion was shimmering, close to the whole surface of his being.

"Ah yes, but you are young," the leader said, "and new to this counsel, so let me explain." He folded his careful hands in front of him on the golden oak table, leaned forward and spoke. "The final truth of this matter is much as our astute colleague has indicated," he said, nodding toward the young woman in glasses, who was pleased at the recognition. "When one joins the Church, one submits to the Church as the arbiter to God. One agrees that the Church is the sole representative of God as well, his manifestation of perfection on earth. We are His house, and by definition we are perfect. If one then denies this relationship, this contract with the divine, if you will, one spurns God himself. Those who spurn God are not worthy of the Sacraments, simply put. Would we perform a sacred marriage ceremony for a professed atheist? Of course not. It is merely a matter of logic, really."

The leader paused, contemplating the effect of his words on the group, and specifically on the Indigenous man, who sat unmoving, waiting for further explanation, his hands also folded on the table in front of him, a small mirror to the leader.

"Further, it is important to note that we will continue to offer confession, but only to those on their deathbeds. After all, redemption may be found through realization of one's sin, and we must provide for that possibility." He smiled ingratiatingly, his eyes cool and examining his words' effect on each and every person at the table, one by one. "Don't you all find this reasonable?" He waited a moment, and added, "Perhaps it goes without saying that we will not conduct ceremonial funerals for those who have not renounced their position of refusing tithes. They must go to God following the choices they have made in this life, and they must suffer the consequences."

The Indigenous man's lips trembled, but he said nothing. Perhaps he was used to silencing himself, yet was still not comfortable with it. I began to observe that his personal religion within this church and this holy empire was something different than the others', that it had an older attachment, a link to another way of seeing, and he struggled with that link, trying to bring who he was into this century, trying to focus all of himself into something less than himself, trying to fit. I could not watch in silence any longer.

"If I understand this correctly," I said, "the refusal to pay the nine percent tax, for a tax is what it is, collected through the German state, is for two reasons. One is personal hardship, as judged by the parishioner, and the other, certainly the most important, is rage at the sexual abuse and the Church's mishandling of it?" I formed it as a question, though it was a statement.

The leader unfolded his hands and pulled at his blue cuff as he turned to face me. "That is correct, technically speaking, but for your rather harsh choice of words. However, these are not the real issues."

"What are the real issues?" I asked directly on the heels of his response, quickly enough for him to see my words as a challenge.

"The lay people are not to judge the Church's decisions on how to attend to internal matters like this," he fired back, "nor are they to decide if or when or how much they will tithe. The Church fully attends to their needs, and for this they must support the Church as it sees fit, as the Church defines. If they do not suit our needs, we will not suit theirs. As I said before, it's quite simple, and I don't understand your confusion, Mrs.?"

I ignored his request for my name, which he had forgotten, though we'd been formally introduced in the ornate entry hall below. My name had echoed against the walls with some resonance, but his preoccupation with this crisis stifled what I assumed would normally be a highly refined and precise mind.

I replied quietly, but it was no longer easy to do. "So the Church will define both the parishioners' needs and its own, and the flock will decide nothing within the Church about its public affairs, yet the people themselves are the backbone of the Church?" These were children's lives we were talking about in controlled tones, cool as the blue silk of the leader's perfect suit. It became tortuous.

"That's correct, but you have one thing backwards, and that is that the people are the backbone of the Church. In fact it is the opposite. We in the Church are the people's backbone. They are not ours. Without the order in their lives that we provide, they would follow their human instincts into chaos. Surely you know the fundamental flaws of humanity." He paused, raising his eyebrows at me, then stumbled inside himself for a moment, and in that moment he descended into an unknown place, inexplicably, as though it was unknown even to himself, at least partially. "Perhaps your being from America has confused your logic and thereby your tongue." With these last words he dropped a telling step down into himself. He became something more like what I'd seen lurking by the column in the meeting with Il Duce. He pointed at me with his blunt manicured finger, pumping his arm at the elbow in challenge. "Why don't you enlighten us about this situation?" His eyes began a subtle transformation, and the sleeve of his shirt protruded from the jacket cuff, shiny white against silky blue. He pulled it back into order, but the civility eroded from his eyes, and the room silenced itself. Faces masked over into waiting and watching, and even the passion of the Indigenous man retreated, as though he were watching the flogging of a terrified acolyte in a California Mission, but was helpless to stop it.

I continued, despite the fact that the situation could evolve into anything, including something extraordinary and unknown, but I was confident the leader's need for secrecy would protect me. "The Church assumes it has power over the man or woman's soul with this action, but it has no right to do that. People must exercise their faith in freedom because each individual's relation to the Creator is their own. That's the easy part to understand. The hard part is the children. Parents must protect their children. This is a law of Nature. One must never cross the children's fire. That is the ultimate sin."

"You speak blasphemy," he burst out, pounding both fists onto the heavy table, which took his fury with a solid echoless thud. It was an ancient tree that monks had turned into a long thick slab centuries before, and it was unimpressed with the leader's anger or his physical power. It accepted the single deliberate thrust, took it in, and lay silently, the hands of all the emissaries resting on its broad golden belly in nervous control.

"No, it is logic," I went on, calming even more now, slicing away at the power he threw at me, presenting cool reason to all at the table. "The Church's job, if it is to heal and provide an avenue to faith in life itself, must provide what the people need, as they need it. If the Church and its representatives violate the people's children, and protect the priests who desecrate children's spirits, then the people must rise up and speak out, and the Church must change." I spoke firmly, looking directly at the leader, who now leaned back and studied me from another place in himself. He sought calm but could not find it anywhere but in a stony façade. His former fascination with me became a livid thing that ran across his face both wildly and intensely controlled. He labored under the gaze of all the representatives, all the studying eyes of those with influence and silence. His studying me made the others study him, study the both of us, and he was not used to this position, not at this point in his evolution or career, so he chafed. But he rose to the situation, no slouch in realms of power and deceit, and calmed himself.

"Don't tell me you're one of those throwback Liberation Theology advocates from the colonies," he scoffed. "Not at your age, and with your obvious sophistication. We took care of their kind quite awhile ago, and their origins as well, those priests who from the beginning maintained that the Indians under their spiritual care were already living as the Christ taught." He leaned back in his chair and chuckled. "What an absurd notion, especially about primitives," he said, squarely facing me, then glanced around at the others for assent, but they only watched. The heavy Spaniard fingered the now empty sherry glass in front of him, then motioned to the silent attendant for more, tapping the glass with his fingernail quietly, like the sound of a distant cricket.

"No, I'm no-one," I said, "but I'm a woman who knows that children are sacred, not the priests who defile them, and that the spiritual is not for sale, but that this is exactly what the Church is doing, selling salvation while children's souls lay scattered to the wind. You violate your own prophet. To deny the Sacraments because of money and your lack of atonement for criminal behavior shows you for what you really are." My anger and resolve took a breath, and I spoke to everyone else, avoiding the leader's eyes. When I met the Indigenous man's eyes, I tried to tell him it would be all right, that he must be himself even here, for not everyone at the table was like the leader, not everyone did the beast's bidding, not here and not in the Church where it spread across the world, and yet here in the room with us now was this tremendous force within the Church that must be dealt with. Perhaps he knew this, or he wouldn't be here, but he was at the top now, all the way up through the halls of hierarchy, perched on a giddy branch that swayed in the wind of the public eye, and he could see the frailty of it now, the power and its frailty.

"Don't become the money-changers," I said simply to the others. "You have enough money already. If you run out of money for your charities, sell one of these priceless paintings to a rich industrialist or the Russian mafia," I prodded, smiling, but no-one smiled back, and the young woman with the glasses started forward so sharply that the glasses slid through her perspiration to the very tip of her nose. She pushed them back, but the gold-rim glasses slid again. She was now nearly as angry as the leader, but she was not dangerous, only mindless and arrogant. The leader grasped the edges of the old oak with both hands, eyes on fire. "And remember the children," I said quietly, "because they are at the center of this."

"How dare you!" he shouted, raising his voice towards its real force for the first time, and the others reeled back in their chairs. The Spaniard downed his sherry like it was a shot of bourbon in a late night Madrid bar, eyes glistening, staring at the leader with something like suspicions confirmed and terror at the same time, face contorted with both emotions.

"How dare I? How dare you?" I retorted, still calm, but forceful and demanding. "Your savior died for his principles, and you defile his memory with your taxes, with your control of the people, and with the crimes you try to hide. Don't you know you are supposed to be the keepers of the sacred, the keepers of the medicine for the people, and that medicine can never be for sale? Don't you know this? Don't you remember? Don't you remember that the children are everything? Everything sacred?" I looked to the Indigenous man as I asked the final question, and he did remember. He did know, but still he said nothing. Generations of acquiescence swam through his brown eyes and twisted his university tongue in confusion. What could he say or think here? What was allowed? The Spaniard locked onto my eyes like a strange drunken sailor, and if we'd been in a bar, he'd have looped his arm over my shoulder in confidence, calling me his true "sister" in faith, but he only stared, pleading with his eyes, asking me if I knew what I was doing. I did by now.

I had come here with a purpose, and it was high time to reveal it. I'd heard what was happening, listened to the outraged German people on the news, and heard the hollow pro and con comments worldwide. It was an opportunity and a necessity, so I talked to respected friends in the New York diocese, people who knew me and trusted me. I found that their emissary was ill, so I offered my services and they accepted, and the plane ride was the next thing, with plenty of time to reflect on all of it while the jet roared over the Atlantic. I thought of Atlan to the south, the great body of water to the east of the Maya, and I remembered the "shaman" in the hot valley town of my first entry. It all fit together, like a puzzle in time and space, and I saw one more time that it must be taken apart to be rebuilt the right way, and this begins in the thought. The pieces are in the wrong places, with arrogance where humility should be, pride where knowledge should be, and the characters, the people, are upside down too. Those who should be simply forking manure piles are ruling nations. And it's too often true the other way around as well. Very kind and wise people travel through life without recognition, and this is a great loss for everyone. It's not that they should be put high on a ladder, but just that recognition of them gives strength to everyone who comes in contact with them, and this influences many. It ripples outward through a people, and it makes living a better thing, a better thinking. I thought about all of this while the jet soared above white sheep's back clouds, so now I couldn't look back, not once I saw who was in control in this room, no matter the consequences, not here, nor back on the homeland, for it was all one place. I had to keep pressing forward, unrelenting.

I heard a fierce scratching sound and turned to face the leader. His hands were under the table. "No one talks to me this way," he began to say in his controlled language, but it ended in a snarl. The scratching stretched everyone's imagination, and they looked around frantically, but it was coming from the leader's end of the table. "I know you," he snarled again. "I know you now." But amazingly, he found his sophisticated grammar again, and calmed momentarily in it, the sound of tearing wood subsiding. Faces calmed, though everyone struggled with the electric hatred coming from this handsome man in the blue silk suit. They struggled with something they could not see, something horrible and alien to their thoughts and experience, so they sought to place normality on top of everything.

"We must be civil above all else," the woman pushed her glasses up yet again but spoke meekly, with feigned authority on the edge of her own growing madness. She was from a very rich country and represented billions of dollars for the Church, and she clung to that, but it was nothing in the face of what she was seeing. She unraveled thread by thread, still barely clinging to her reality.

"I know you too," I shot back to the leader. "You were with the dictator back then, the same as you are now. You made the deal between him and the Church back then, a covenant of silence in the face of brutality and assassination, in exchange for the Church's independence, and for money." I spoke knowing that the others would think my words a metaphor. "You killed many then, and you would do the same now to protect your seat of power. Your position of demanding obedience is only one step from direct killing, and you have no remorse. You care nothing for the souls of the faithful, nothing for the children whose spirits you kill forever. You care only for your power over them. You are about bodies, bodies and money and stolen souls." The people at the table recoiled from my words, but the Spaniard nodded. He was drunk now and adrenalized enough by the confrontation. He knew the prices paid in dictatorships, no matter what they called themselves, no matter what face they put on in the morning before they had their pictures taken and their songs of universal love and freedom sung.

The scratching and tearing rose in intensity and the huge table vibrated, the leader's forearms under the table pulling towards his chest, his claws tearing into the wood invisible to the others' eyes. The Indigenous man's mouth fell open as his imagination fell into what he was seeing, unbelieving, and the leader's suit bulged along the biceps and shoulders. The leader's face churned red then dark, mouth turned down in a sneer, and his head tilted forward, eyes glaring straight ahead, then at me.

"You are a monster," I declared, "by your own choice, and you destroy everyone, all those who stand against you and all those who follow you." I spoke like I was giving a lecture or performing a monologue in a Shakespearean play, the simple lines rolling out of me of their own volition, with passion, purpose, and resolve, my voice steady and sonorous. I watched the language and admired its beauty, as it was not my own, but it could have been had not my destiny been something else, somewhere else. But the truth is always beautiful, no matter the tongue, and the truth is what carried at that table, the long table that remembered the forest of its birth and watched this unfolding.

The leader glared and his eyes narrowed, and he growled in fury, but still he wore the suit, and when he pulled his hands out from under the table and slammed them down on its polished surface again, the claws were just disappearing back into being polished fingernails again, and in that brief millisecond he was revealed. The manservant dropped his platter, turned and ran from the room. The Spaniard shouted, "I knew it! I knew it!" The Indigenous man crossed himself over and over as he scrambled to his feet and fled along with the others, squeezing himself through the door alongside the young woman, whose glasses lay quivering on the table alongside her overturned white teacup. Soon it was only the leader and me and the staggering Spaniard, who bent over in readiness with fists clenched. I sat watching all this speed and commotion, muscles poised, then rose to leave in calm readiness, my hand clenched tightly around the black handle of the fiber knife in my beige suit pocket.

"You will pay for this," the leader glared. "You will pay dearly for this."

I stared at him, defiant and ready.

"We already have," I said quietly, staring into his eyes. I backed to the door, pushed the drunken Spaniard through the opulent gold jamb, and closed it solidly behind me. "We already have," I repeated to the Spaniard, whose eyes suddenly sprang tears five hundred years in the making, and more.

23

Pre-dawn lavender light flowed down the mountain-top above Will's ranch toward the open black sea. The horses chuffed in the morning chill and greeted me, nuzzling their steaming grey breath into my hands. An apple to Cowboy and an apple to Rosie brought me the horses' enigmatic smiles, gifts bestowed in this agreement between humans and the once-wild, free animal. Out of the shadows, Will rode hard into soft purple light, his hat glistening and the smell of horse sweat flooding over me like dust as he reined to a stop. I laughed.

"I heard you out here," I said over the mare's heavy breathing. "I hope you don't mind."

"For you, never," Will touched his rumpled hat brim with a jovial nod. "Where've you been this time?" He swung his leg back over the black horse's rump easily and stood before me, grabbing my shoulder with one strong arm, giving me a squeeze and letting go with a broad smile. Rosie and Cowboy nosed my pockets until all the apples were surrendered, the black mare waiting behind the other two horses, staring at me from her dark sockets, and when she finally got the apple she wanted, she tossed her head and flashed her eyes. Quickly, the dawn spilled over us, and life was as it should be. It was easy.

"Let's go to the tack room," Will urged, turning as he spoke, and I followed. In a warm stall next to the room, he unsaddled the mare and rubbed her down silently. I watched as she took his hands, the towel, and the brush in stride, knowing this ritual all her life. I smiled as she looked over her shoulder in approval with a softly chiding horse's love, always giving permission, always blessing the cowboy with her presence like a haughty but kindly queen.

I built a small fire in the pot-belly while Will put away the saddle and bridle, glancing out over the corral to the sea beyond, which was now turning even more purple, with a brighter blue thin line beginning to stretch across the horizon on a cloudless morning. Soon the sky and the sea merged, with only the horizon splitting the blue into partitions, one vast expanse above, one shimmering expanse below. The last stars blinked out and the stove crackled red, welcoming the enamel coffee pot clanking down on its lid.

"So where've you been?" Will resumed.

"The Vatican, Mayan land; all over," I offered as a start. Will nodded as though he understood all of what I did, and why. In his huge way, he did understand. He knew me like no one else, not even my Sweet Hunter, because Will knew the distance we all had to go in this century, when the whole world seemed ready to explode. He felt the urgency. He traveled from China to Russia and to all of Europe trying to make sense of it all, listening to people over a cup of coffee, people who would just as soon shoot one another in the forehead without a shred of mercy, if they got close enough to take a bead.

"What happened?" he asked. I was silent before I spoke, and when the words came out, they erupted like hot stones out of the volcano Fuego. I described the parts about the scene in the Vatican that I could tell him, about the children, and he nodded again. He thought of me as his "poet." That's what he called me, the storyteller and weaver of yarns to teach the children, so I was free to say a lot of what I'd seen without him thinking I was crazy, without stretching his mind beyond its limits of credulity. The witch's claws were political metaphors to him, I guessed, but sometimes he looked at me like he really knew it all, knew just exactly what I was about, where I traveled and what I saw. Those moments were like lucid dreams, and they passed, but in them we saw each other for ten thousand years in the same faces. Who knows what had passed in our blood over all that time? Certainly neither of us knew exactly, but we had our suspicions. And all we cared about was this beautiful knowing that we were the same people, the same clan, the same purpose made human in different ways.

"Yes, it's a hard thing," he said, pausing, then looking down at the worn old floor. "When it comes to the kids like that, it's a very hard thing."

When he finally looked up again, I gazed back into his eyes out of a few moments in my own imagination, and I saw how the scene at the Vatican connected to

Will's life and dreams. There were tears on his cheeks. We searched each other's spirits, and we sought and found our peaceful moment, in the warm tack room with the smell of fresh jungle coffee in a blue tin pot, and all the while the world churned its way onward. The anger grew out there despite all Will's efforts to change people in some small way, to alter the course toward something better with humor and honest reflection.

"I want to talk with this man Hitler," he said, surprising me, "and a friend is arranging it for our next trip. I want you to come with me. This man troubles me. People work hard to make peace and he tears up the papers with a shrug. He wants something else, and a strange kind of fellow he must be."

I poured the coffee for both of us, blew hard over the surface of my cup and sipped it loudly. I saw things Will didn't yet know would happen. Dachau, the beginning of the camps, and Auschwitz, a certain culmination of something neither Will nor I nor anyone else would ever understand, but Will wanted to talk to that maker of death himself. He wanted to see what he could find there, and this is why I loved and trusted him so much. He knew everything begins and ends in the thought.

"What puzzles me is how so many folks is following him. That's what gets me wondering. I know the common folks are poor and all, but..." His brow furrowed, and he looked deep into me, as if searching for an answer, as though he could see all the images scattered in my memory, all the Indian children lying curled up on lonely bunks in boarding schools waiting to die of sadness, all across the United States and Canada. He looked so deeply into me, so intensely, I thought he might see them all, even the neatly ordered bunks with the skeletal faces staring out through big dark eyes under shaven skulls. Could he see the connections? The millions dying under Stalin and Mao and Pol Pot? The Mayan Kings? What could he see? I thought, "Everything. He sees everything, because he is reaching out and holding me in his arms, so he must see everything right now." The coffee steam rose between us, drifted directly through our sorrow and confusion, and he let me go, lightly touching my cheek with his strong roper's hand, and I smiled and touched him back, my good brother.

When we entered the ranch house, Betty looked at us and smiled. "You two solving the world's problems again?"

We both returned her smile, and Will shook his head, "Way too much to do on an empty stomach." She turned away with a glint in her eye, and went through the kitchen door. Will shook his head again and smiled. He'd always said Betty was the best thing that ever happened in his life, and each time I met her I learned another reason why he felt that way, because he wasn't just saying it; it was a fact at the base of his whole being.

The kitchen door swung open again and she strode through with a plate of hot bacon and eggs, biscuits and gravy. Orange juice from the big oranges grown just down the valley was already on the table, so we said a prayer and dove in.

"You know, it's not just because of the breakfast," Will said to both of us, and we all knew just what he was talking about. She smiled with a nod. She was that way. You never had to fill in the blanks. She knew what you were thinking, and if she didn't, she'd ask, if she felt you didn't need it private. She was strong, intuitive, a twentieth century white woman's version of my Grandmother in the woods, only she wasn't a medicine woman, not in that way. But she was solid and had a huge mind, gracious hands when they touched a shoulder, and she understood all those looks that passed between Will and me, knew how much the connection meant to the both of us, and because of this she was part of us, always inside of us no matter how far we traveled from the warmth of her ranch house.

"Rain, you've been away awhile," she looked at me, "and you look tired. You stay here awhile and get your thunder back."

I wouldn't argue with her, though I had plans and missed my family horribly. She saw into me, and I know when she put those eggs on the plate she blessed them silently, asking in her way that they give me the strength she saw I needed. She was this way with Will too, always taking care. With a huge smile she'd sit him down when he was exhausted, and with a torn and relieved face she'd welcome him home from a long trip and then talk calmly with him until dawn, if he had to spill it all out from his insides, all the complications of the world laid out on their big table. And she took it all, gave the right advice, and loved him.

She was to him as my Sweet Hunter was to me, kind and understanding, complex and far-reaching, brilliant in acceptance of all that the world brought down upon our shoulders. She was tough and beautiful and profound, a force larger than most people around her could ever imagine. She was Will's foundation and his inspiration, and in this way she was my sister at the center of the world.

"When you finish eating and catching up, you go into the corner room and get some sleep, as long as you need it. We need you fresh and healthy." It was an offer and an order, and I obeyed.

I walked slowly, savoring the smells of the house and its colors, the morning light streaming through the windows, the soft voices of Will and Betty still at the dining room table. I undressed and showered under a hot waterfall of beautiful clean well water, letting it pour into my open mouth, letting it pour across my eyes and down my shoulders and belly and legs, and I stood there listening to the water and the myriad of differences between this world and my own. I smelled the depths of the earth the water rose up through, inhaling its scent deeply, then I dried myself with a huge fluffy towel and fell into bed as the room filled with light. And I dreamed.

Will and I were talking, and I was telling him this story:

"A young Polish woman asked an elder Miwok woman sitting at a classroom table in California, 'How do you deal with the hatred?' She prefaced her question by telling the elder that her family didn't talk about Auschwitz or any of what happened during their time there and after, but they taught her a language filled with hatred of Germans and Russians. She said it festered in the language and in her family even today, two generations later, an unresolved and deep poison she could see and feel. The elder nodded and looked at her steadily.

"'It's a good question.' She talked very slowly, finding the right words, careful words about forgiveness, not forgetting, because 'you can't forget,' but about approaching forgiveness however you can. She said forgiveness has its time and its own way; it can't be pushed, forced, or found artificially, that life has to bring you there. 'It's a complex thing,' she said, 'and important.' 'It's about yourself.' She looked at the young girl. 'And it's about others too.' Silence filled the room. The elder's hands were folded in front of her, and she nodded as she finished. 'Yes,' she said.

"When I heard the word 'hatred' from the young Polish girl, I thought of my Hunkpapa friend on her back porch smoking and saying, 'They hate us, don't they?' She had been asked to do a blessing for an organization of predominantly white people, with certainly no other Indigenous present, a blessing for descendents of the settlers who knew precious few details or the scope of their ancestors' actions against her people. She did it although she had misgivings, because she knew the relationship between privacy and survival, but she did it anyway, and in the doing of it she found the right way, the way in which all were included in the magic and beauty. She could not forget the century of the great storm of settlers that swept most of her people away, but she did the blessing for everyone. Afterward, a woman walked up to her and said bluntly, 'It would have helped to know what all of the words meant,' for parts of the blessing were in the Hunkpapa language. 'I can't translate them,' my friend said, and the white woman was immediately offended. She turned on her heel and left quickly without a word. As she walked away, my friend added quietly to her back, 'They can't be translated, and they take years to understand anyway, even for us.' She told me the story of this blessing and snub, finishing with a laugh and a drag on her cigarette, 'They hate us,' she said. I knew what she meant; it was the quickness of disdain, and the right to inhabit it face to face. People like that woman want to own those Indigenous who are left, even after everything else, even then and now, and the owning is really about trying to satisfy the hunger that came along with the destruction, a natural consequence. My friend's cigarette smoke rose into the redwood trees in an ironic curl.

"The imagination of my dreaming brings the large and the small, and it fits them neatly into each other like Russian wooden dolls within wooden dolls within wooden dolls. I remembered an Apache woman telling me of a jet ride on the way to France, when she was talking with the woman seated next to her, who told of her spiritual pursuits in life, her desire to find some kind of enlightenment in all the confusion and chaos. They bonded around the need to find some kind of personal peace despite it all, the wars in Iraq and

Afghanistan, the terrorism, the class wars worldwide, the nuclear warheads in frightened silos all over the planet waiting to usher in the neo-cons' fiery Armageddon; all of it. There had been personal loss in both their lives, and as the jet winds roared, they became closer in that shared loss. Then the traveler asked the Apache how to say 'We Are One' in Apache. Her eyes were bright, as though knowing this would bring her closer to her goal. It would give her something to share, to bring from America, something genuine from the ancient ones. It would give her credit in her own bank of enlightenment, and certainly with others who banked at the same fountain. Startled at the grasping nature that had so quickly arisen in her new friend, the Apache woman said, 'I can't tell you that.' She spoke not in an offending way, but simply, and as a fact. 'Why not,' the traveler asked. The Apache looked into her waiting eyes softly, with caution. 'Because we don't say that,' she explained, then added slowly, 'and because it's not your language, so anything you might say about that would be your thought, not ours, so it would not be Apache.' The traveler pulled away slightly, though the arm rests would not allow enough distance. She was insulted and frightened that she could not penetrate the Indigenous world. The Apache woman paused, weighed her next words, and continued, 'It would be a misrepresentation.' The seeker looked appalled, or so it sounded by the shrill of her voice. 'Why, you can't own a language. No one owns language. It's for everyone.' The Apache woman said nothing. She just looked down at her hands, then back at the traveler, who had turned away. After this, the traveler did not talk to the Apache woman, who was glad, for she would not be owned either. She was, after all, Apache.

"The dolls continued to open, like they can, when anything can come. I also thought about the young White Mountain boy, Thomas, who always got beat up or thrown in jail on the streets of Santa Cruz, a liberal California town, a seaside watering hole during the century following the destruction of the people they call Ohlone. It had been the home of numerous Indigenous for thousands of years, a town where those Indigenous who were still here had to fight, march in the streets and protest and discuss with politicians, to keep condominiums from being built on the graves of their ancestors, and most of the time they lost those struggles, getting to keep only a few bones the tractors pulled into the light and open air in a burst of diesel smoke and roar, bones that were only tokens to the politicians, truth be told. I wondered which way the hatred flowed, towards the Indigenous or from the Indigenous toward their occupiers, or most reasonably, in a strange stretch of what reason should mean, it goes both ways. Thomas came from the reservation, 'escaped,' as he put it, and it was plain to see he was a strong runner in many ways. He would have been a handsome young man with long flowing black hair and a fine slender body, if his face wasn't peppered with scabs from fighting, his knuckles bruised and swollen, his body bent from cracked ribs gotten in the streets of this university town. He was on fire with his

hatred, and with being hated. We once saw him striding, in between wounds and jail, proud and free on
the damp shoulder of a long road going through arti-
choke fields straight to the sea. We offered him a ride,
and though he knew us, he waved us away. At that
moment he did not want the confinement of a truck or
the company of anyone but the blowing sea-fog and
his unknown destiny for the day. He did not want to
sit captive even with others of his kind, so burning he
was, and we took his awareness of his mental state
gratefully. He didn't want us to be touched by his fire.
In his eyes, he was taking care of us by striding alone
through his crucible, a crucible in the shape of a huge
alluvial plain to the sea, a plain once full with pelicans
and all manner of wildlife and thriving people. Now
neat rows of vegetables lined the land, vegetable seeds
brought from somewhere else, fruits bound for somewhere else, all on the command of what he called the
'green frog skins,' money. The defiant White Mountain
boy Thomas reached his moccasin-covered feet boldly
through this new time on the way to his next beating.
I knew he wouldn't see his twentieth year, and that he
is a mirror of thousands of reservation and inner city
boys, Indigenous boys living and dying in twenty-first
century America. Where is the hatred, and what do we
do with it?"

I told this series of episodes to Will in one of my
dreams on that long-sleeping day, where Will lives
inside my life-force and my drive, and these stories
are modern tips of a buried mountain of images,
postcards scattered across the floor of my memory,

snapshots of Black Kettle staring unbelieving at the charging cavalry, the American flag chattering help-lessly behind him on his lodge like an old madman's tongue. The images fly like blood across the plains, hat bands made of women's skin, hot and steaming in early morning. Children are carried screaming to the waiting cars of government workers, children who will never see their parents again. It starts with wagons carrying the children, then buckboards and rattle-trap cattle trucks; now it's SUVs. These are Indigenous images, whole tribes of South American people going into extinction on a monthly basis as the century continues through the jungles of the Ama-zon in 2012, chain saws blazing, oil rigs going up and down, up and down. These rigs are lonely old men masturbating metallically under an uncaring sky, for there are non-Indigenous images as well, like porno-graphic baseball cards isolated in sepia tones and in high glossed color. The old men are trying desper-ately to remember their love as they pump up and down, but they can't quite get there, can't recall the face of her kindness or the touch of her hand. They can't quite bring it back, but they keep trying, and don't know they're visualizing the very fantasies that made her leave them in the first place, straining for the body empty of spirit, the flesh without the living soul, the image rather than the substance. They want her back so bad they almost cry out, but she moves further and further away the more desperately they pump into her body in their frightened silence. And she is Earth. She is Earth, and they don't even know it.

Trying to escape, my bones aching and my muscles tired with the hatred of the beast in the Vatican, alongside everything else connected to it so intimately, I had tried to find my way, my line of seeing to Grandmother but could not. I had sought dreams all day long in the big soft bed like Grandpa Tree says to do, but even these were replete with the seeds of the question the young Polish girl asked, the question of what to do with the hatred, that in itself an inescapable echo of my own people over time, a question that's a vicious mosquito, a whole swarm of them in the round house in the middle of the night. My head spun, so as the sun set over the churning Pacific, I rose and walked toward the trailhead that climbed the hills toward the rising moon. Surely Moon could help me, for she was used to being in the shadow, and the thought of her made me smile. I smiled even more broadly when I heard Will's quick steps and voice behind me.

"Wait up now, would you? I gotta get a piece of that moon myself."

"How do you deal with it all, Will?" The words burst from me completely out of control, frenzied and in his face. I did not break my stride, nor did he as we climbed the trail, but I did not recognize the voice that flew out of my throat like a young screech owl's. I had to laugh, but in desperation. I was losing myself.

I followed Will up the darkening trail through overhanging oaks and ruby-barked Manzanita to the hilltop, a small flat lookout where we could see to the north, south, and west, a higher tree-covered mountain rising to the east. The moon was up, almost full, lighting the treetops silver, the ocean bright grey and silent. Will was agitated, unlike his cool public self, turning toward me then standing still, waiting anxiously.

"I looked in the mirror when I got out of bed this evening," I said, "the big one with the frame Betty painted grape vines on, and I didn't know myself. The face that stared back at me was someone else's. The purple grapes and green vines made me Greek or Italian in some ancient tragic play somewhere else, and I couldn't see me. Oh, I knew it was me, but the lines around my eyes and mouth turned me into someone else, not older, but different. It wasn't the age, but something else, something worrisome. It just wasn't me I saw but something on top of me or inside me, something not me." I rattled on until Will interrupted.

"It's the forgetting, is what it is," he said, then repeated it. "That's what it is, the forgetting." He took off his hat and put a finger to his lips. "That's what you got, the desire to forget, but you've got to reverse that. Now think about it, and remember what happened on this trip."

Ah, there it was. I was suddenly back in the Vatican, when the witch revealed himself, claws on the tabletop. There was a moment, an expanding moment when he was gone, lost, when he himself didn't know who he was, and he was floundering around like a fish on a dock trying to flip his way back into the water. Yes, he carried the fury of being opposed in his power; it lit his face, magnified by the fear of exposure too, but there was another thing there too, a growing thing with frantic eyes searching everywhere at once with flailing hands like a drowning swimmer. It was only an instant, but it was a huge thing, and it was showing me the way that desecration works, and I'd missed it, so caught in the possibility of violence and feeling the blade handle in my suit pocket. The witch really didn't know where he was or who he was. He too had been lost, and if he'd looked in the mirror he'd have asked himself the same questions I did this evening; that is, if he was still capable of reflection.

"That's how powerful it's gotten to be," Will said, seeing my revelation, and I turned a circle in the moonlight like a dancer, hands spread out in the night. "You can't forget," he said with force his voice was unaccustomed to, then he calmed down. "Now, you ask me how I deal with it all, and I'll tell you. At least I'll try." He grasped my shoulders and held me strong, staring quick and hard to calm me enough to listen.

An old oak round lay on its side next to another round, set upright like stools on the edge of the clearing, and he stopped talking long enough to roll them both to the center, one at a time. They shone in the light, and with a sweep of his arm, he invited me to sit. The wood was soft and warm against me, the night cool.

"You see, the Trail of Tears wasn't even a century ago, and our people are still scattering all over this land, you know that, still scattering today in 1920 because the Indian Territory is a tough place to call home. And it's not our home. Out in California, they just put 'the last Yahi,' a fellow named Ishi, to rest after he showed those folks out there what his life was like for forty years of hiding from them very same folks. Had him in a museum in Berkeley, they did. That was only yesterday, about the time my young son was born. I can't forget that, my son being born. You don't forget something like that. And things are attached to that kind of being born, things we see in the papers and things people talk about. They're stuck to them, and there's no getting away from it."

He gathered more words in quiet, looking up at the moonlight on the oaks. A white owl cut an arc across the north end of our clearing, in the place of wisdom, and swept out over the hills to hunt in silence.

"The way I see it is that if I forget, I limit my mind, you know, I shrink it down into what I might think for a moment would get me by, but it turns out it's not enough then. I got to remember. I just got to because it's there. It's all there for the remembering. Now most folks around here don't want to, and that's to their loss, if you know what I mean. That's a limit to their minds. And when you limit your mind, you shrink your heart, and I'd never want to tie my heart down, or to shrink it in any way. There's too much going on, too much out in the world to get touched by and to touch. It's all just too big, you know? And if you shrink your heart, why, you shrink everything there is in this world."

I could breathe now, and as Will talked he listened to my breath and his words dropped down into me differently too. We found the ground, and I realized he'd been frightened for me, frightened because he saw how I'd gotten lost, even though everything sounded right on the surface of things, the talk in the tack room and at breakfast. But he could see what my dreams had done to my spirit even more than I could, and what those dreams attached to, and it troubled him.

"We need you, Rain," he said. "You've got a big thought and a big seeing, and an even bigger heart. I look at you feeding the horses, and I know you have something inside of you I can't even imagine what, some kind of seeing that's just all yours. And this is why we need you with us when we go talk to some of these folks tearing up the world. I can't put my finger on it, but I know it's right."

I stood straight up, raised my hands to the night sky, took a huge breath, let it out with a sigh, then sat back down again and listened to him.

"You asked me how I deal with it all, and my answer is 'the best I can,' and that may seem simple, but it's not. I got to gather people around me to help me, people who like life, you know, who just like living no matter what, drinking a cup of coffee and going for a ride on a good horse. Or going to a good movie. Those are all little things, but those little things prop me up. They're sticks and branches stuck here and there against a big hot air balloon that's me, holding me in place so I can float up there and say what little I can see." He chuckled at himself, at the direction his words took him, because it was the public man speaking now, the famous humorist and orator, the

Cherokee Kid roping his way into people's thinking all across the world. But he came back to the clearing, back to me.

"Truth is, I don't deal with it all. I only deal with what I can, and when I can't do it anymore, why, I stop and rest, and I fall into my Betty's arms. There isn't any secret, none at all. I'm grateful the world listens to me, though I don't understand why they do, but I begin to sometimes, and it seems it's just about telling the plain truth in a world spun on lies, spun on lies for some reason I don't get." He stopped, looked at me a hard moment, then went on. "Maybe you get it more than I do. I think so sometimes when you're looking at one of those people in the meetings, your eyes like they're five thousand years long. And that's why I need you around."

The owl returned, this time coming down from upslope and crossing over the southern arc of our clearing, the life path, white wings spread wide in the moonlight, a quiet breath of bird moving through us.

"Don't forget that," Will said, and he meant all that he'd been talking about, and the owl too, and he nodded toward it as it vanished toward the sea. "Don't forget anything, and hold it gently inside of you because it's all still moving. It's all still moving, and when you remember everything, you get a say in where it goes."

GOING TO WATER

24

On my way back from some precious time at home, where all those I love took me into their arms and lives as though I'd never been gone, and where I rested and saw what was truly real and open again, I lifted into the high space above the clouds. I floated there and looked down upon the world and saw it was a perfectly round gourd, a perfect summer squash of brilliant color, of bright blue oceans and green land and pale patterns of swirling and lilting clouds between my high perch and the surface. I saw a glistening woven network of white-gold light hovering and fully connected over the whole earth like a transparent shawl, and it was encompassing time in a whole moment, yet separated into epochs too, and it breathed, pulsated in tremendous, calm beauty, feeding all that lives on the surface of Earth and in her skies and her oceans. All across Turtle Island, long before the invasion, the shawl floated and shimmered, and to the east and west, clear to the European and African continents and beyond, over the Eastern lands it floated and sang its way across the seas, free and necessary, holding all in its nurturing light. But here and there I began to see it constricted, pulling down tightly into itself, in this epoch or that, like a fist had reached up from the land below and grabbed a handful of the shawl, trying to pull it down into a hole, like a frantic gopher cutting the roots of a young corn plant and tugging it underground into its sunless lair. I saw spots of this constriction scattered across time, across the globe, where the tightness strained at the entire weave, pulling at the vast strands. In Mesopotamia, and places in China, pockets of constriction dotted the land, and in Central America, Mexico, South America, and the islands around the North Sea. I could not see the origins or causes, but they looked the same from high above, from the place just between the atmosphere and the beginnings of starlight. In the Americas, I looked closely, squeezing my eyes down into far vision, and I saw stone temples of cities rising up through the clouds, pyramids and armies gathering around their bases then marching out through long valleys, and where they landed they reached up like the gopher and pulled the fabric of life into their ceremonies, and blood ran red into the golden lines of the shawl, and the shawl quivered and resisted as they sought to pull it all in, all of it.

To the north in that epoch, on Turtle Island, I saw no temples, but huge numbers of people were there, pushing sharp polished digging sticks into the soil, moving bulbs from one place to a better growing-place and waiting patiently for the next season to feed them. They hunted, and they farmed, and they walked far and wide to trade their skills and goods, and they thought deeply about the tremendous complexity of the life they were given. Their fires dotted the continent and their dances softened Earth, and when I looked to Europe and beyond I saw that the people were more spread out, and there were many people, not so many as in the Americas, but many all the same, and the fires in their cities were hidden under roofs, but I could see the smoke drifting out over the snows of the countryside. I saw very old villages where people thought about the complexity of things too, and I saw changes in the thinking begin to emerge, something new coming north and west like a slow cloud. I saw the fires in Africa and all across Asia, people everywhere, nowhere empty, and I knew this was a time long before the great migrations they call discovery, before it changed, tumbled over, and after this tremendous shift the thinking became much simpler, more basic with the need for acquisition, position, kings and deified people, stratified life. This change built oaken ships that carried adventurers looking for new places to conquer, to bring the gold back home to build bigger armies. Yes, there were those who sailed and rowed and drifted with the blue currents simply for the thrill of finding new people whose stories they could glean, new faces and places to marvel at and learn from, as through all of time, but they were like single ants trekking across a huge flat surface in search of sweetness, and they were scattered across time and did no harm. The flotillas were different. They moved in lines with a singular purpose, armed with avarice and greed and eyes steeled like the shine on their armor.

I saw all this, and I saw that the constriction was not all-encompassing or uniform but was sporadic and in the nature of aberration, a limitation of the mind grasping for more, feeble and angry hands pulling at what they themselves had pushed away with their armies and swords and effigies of themselves. They pulled and tugged at the shawl they had rendered, and the fabric would only heal, would only reconnect itself by itself, when the temples crumbled and it could relax again into its own infinite nature. I saw this rise and fall, again and again over time, and the shawl did not weaken but kept growing and repairing itself where needed, but it sighed and tired sometimes, like an old woman watching the kids make the same mistakes over and over again, shaking her head and going back to her work alone, alone and more than a little sad.

I breathed in, waited and watched, perusing millennia of human experience, and then I suddenly saw it. The centuries from which my two dreams had emerged, the very dreams that began all this traveling and this huge portion of my life's purpose, churned a growing bulge in the shawl, and then the fibers stretched and fell downward from the east coast of Turtle Island, now called the United States, to the ocean in the west. They stretched as if being pulled down into a whirlpool or whirlwind, but they resisted, and all across the whole globe as far as I could see, the net of interlaced light was pulled in the direction of North America, my home, a rising tone and ring of brass and steel and cries extending all the way out to where I sat on the edge of space. Then the churning subsided, but the coloring had changed, dark and light, for the struggle still held, the grip pulling the fibers of the shawl down, the shawl resisting, resisting, chiding and strong, but held strangely static in the struggle too. And then a bubble appeared across the ocean, another bulge like the first huge one, and it was concentrated over Europe, connected to the Americas by the stretching and straining fibers of light, to my home and my people. It twisted and turned, a splash of red spurting across its surface like a bursting artery, and it sucked all the minds of the people into itself with a huge inhale, and I knew where I had to go next, for this vortex captured the centuries' imaginations, but the people could not see the sources. They could not see that the brilliant black and twisted arms of the swastika were the appendages of a crippled old octopus crawling across continents and spanning seas, connecting everyone in its love of death and power and perfection, connecting everyone in its particular and insatiable hunger for more, more of everything it laid its shining eyes on. The people were isolated in their own tragedies and could not see the larger pattern. They were blind in their own pain and horror and their strange patriotisms. They could not see the pyramids and stone jaguars alive again in new shapes because they'd torn the structures down and rebuilt their temples only in their minds and ideas, invisible to the naked eye and therefore even more powerful than ever.

GOING TO WATER

25

I planted myself beside the trail in full deerskin because I knew their fascination with American Indians. I was laying a trap of a sort, and I thought any guards that happened along the way would think me part of Eva's retinue, but as it turned out no one came along until Eva Braun herself wandered my way, camera in one hand and a book in the other, eyes lowered, scanning the grasses, wildflowers, and butterflies crisscrossing the mountain path. It seemed surreal that the lover of such a powerful man would have no guards, since he was hated as equally as he was loved by so many people. As Eva walked closer, danced really, in an athlete's long stride full of rhythm and connection to Earth, she looked up and saw me and suddenly stopped five or six strides away. Her pale yellow dress wrapped around her from behind, like waves surrounding a boat that suddenly cuts its motor on a blue lake, the sky shining bright blue behind her. She stared and her eyes widened, then she burst into a broad smile, as though I'd given her an unexpected present, some kind of gift she had no idea was coming her way.

This was true; I was a gift to her, and I hoped she'd find me that, but I doubted it, though I never really know how people might finally take me. As she smiled, she quickly stepped up to me, covering the short distance with confidence yet with a peculiar shyness too.

"Who are you?" She looked down at the book in her hand briefly, then back to me.

"My name is Agana, Rain." I smiled, for she had a quality that brought my enjoyment of the sheer beauty of this place, this mountainside, to bear between us. It was her vision lifting over into mine, meshing softly, and I let it happen. I wanted to understand her.

She held the book out in front of her, holding the cover for me to see, and it was the novel *Winnetou*, by Karl May, a book countless Germans were reading at the time, and had for decades, with a painting of a handsome Indian Brave adorned in the beadwork of the plains people, a man with European features and deep bronze skin. It reminded me of the paintings of Mayan people on the walls of the Mormon tabernacle in Utah, with a white Christ ministering to people who looked just like him but smaller, with golden-brown skin and no beards. These are paintings of the fabled "Second Coming" they believe has already happened.

"And did you spring from the pages of this book for me today?" she asked. There was a tease in her eyes, again with the mixture of shyness and strength. She talked like a movie of her time.

"In a way, I suppose I have," I said, "although we are little like the people in those pages."

"What do you mean? Are you an imposter, someone dressed like an Indian who is not an Indian?"

"No, I am real. It's just that the characters in your book are not. They are inventions, reflections of the writer's mind and wishes, and they think like him, not like us. They see like he sees. They're brown Germans and brown Christians."

We were getting to it quickly, more quickly than I had imagined we could, even though it was simple, but this was only the surface of the meeting, a water spider skimming over the glassy surface of what we must talk about. She was fast on the inside, inviting, and though she was surprised at my presence on her mountain, she knew she was safe, so she held control of our meeting.

"Yes, well, that is very abstract, too much so. And it's a beautiful day at the Berghof, so let's walk and enjoy ourselves. You must appreciate the beauty of the landscape, I'm sure, since you are an Indian, so let's enjoy it together and leave the world of ideas behind us for now. Let's live in the moment."

I rose and looked up the mountain. She dropped the book into a big square pocket on her dress, circled her arm into mine as though I were her sister, and we headed up the trail at a brisk pace, then when the trail narrowed as we got higher, she let go of my arm and took the lead, sweeping her hand across the blue sky as though opening a broad curtain to a magnificent view.

"Have you ever seen a more beautiful place? In one direction are the Alps of Austria, and in another direction the Alps of Bavaria, both rising straight up to Heaven. In the valley is the Koenigsee, such a magnificent lake, and below us lies a village of people who have lived their own ways for many hundreds of years and more. Are we not the luckiest people in the world? And is this not God's own country?" Here was the film again.

She stopped suddenly and stared into my eyes with both surety and longing, as though her words themselves were a prayer. She was raw then, exposed on her green mountain slope in a cool spring breeze, surrounded by blue and crimson and bright yellow wildflowers, in her billowing pale yellow dress and silken hair. Her soft brown eyes flashed with hope for the dream to be true for both of us, as though if I believed, then she could too, and it would be true forever, for all time. But there was a chasm present in her eyes too, like the shadows beneath the mountain crags, the darkness just below the glistening white snow line of sharp peaks. We stood looking into each other while the smells of the wildflowers swirled around us, and the sound of a very distant cowbell rose gently into the sky from far below.

I saw her life then, how deeply and desperately she loved this man she called Adi, a man with a direction that would eventually destroy him, and her, along with millions of others. I saw her two attempts to take her life in the years before now, a faint scar on her pale but sleek and muscled neck, visible when the wind lifted her fine hair away into itself for a moment. I saw how this scar might draw him to her, this fragility and what he would see as her commitment to him as well as to her life in death. The sun shone on the soft hairs of her forearms, and her toned muscles and strong but delicate hands belied her desperation. She was both strength and frailty, beauty in light and dark, and she needed something very deep from life. Something had been taken from her a long time ago, something in her family or in her parents' families before, or in a time even before that, something taken from all of them even while they sought to embrace it. It was something her long walks on the mountainside, her swims in the cool lakes, all sought to regain, rebuild, strengthen, and in this she was like so many young women from Munich or Berlin or any of the country-sides full of small villages tucked into hillsides, try-ing to find their faith and confidence. They cried in the spring rains when the heavy grey skies of winter finally lifted away and the wildflowers sprang into view. They ran in the fields and laughed, swept their bare arms through the rising grasses in the wheat fields, and flashed their eyes at their dreams of young men coming to their rescue. The princes of their stories would come to rescue them from their castles of loneli-ness in these springtime dreams, if only they believed strongly enough.

The hillside dropped away steeply where we stood staring at each other. Though Eva knew I was look-ing deeply into her life, she was unafraid, and was welcoming it, in fact. To her, we were two women understanding each other on a rich and fecund moun-tainside, nothing more, and that was all that was needed. She was living in her moment. She saw me looking into her fear and loss, and in this she was comforted, though she could not see the endless depth and richness of my love with my own family, with my man and child and Grandfather Tree and Grandmother. She could not see any of that, and in this blindness to what living could or should be, her loss and her search was gargantuan, a monstrous thing inside of her that she could not see. But she had grown up surrounded by people denying that this loss even existed, that it . had any shape or history at all, so she took on their method of dying called living, and found her ability to survive in her search for magic and delight through her art, her camera, the capturing of images like trying to capture a forgotten life only her cells alone could remember. And because of this memory she found it too in her love of her body, her physical strength. She saw and enjoyed her beauty, which she nurtured carefully but not obsessively, because she liked the frailty of it at the same time that she built its quiet power and grace. She had struggled her way through all her inherited sorrows and found a way to live, and this man she now had in her heart and mind was the key, and this was all that mattered, so when she saw me looking deeply into her, and she turned away, it was not from fear but from a certain kind of tiredness, a weariness with sadness and a stark desire for happiness. The centuries had built her a cage, but at least for the moment it was a golden cage, with sparkling wines and laughing friends with plans, not the drab grey of a Munich sidewalk or a cold stone church whose walls took the fevered and frustrated scratching of her childhood's fingernails without care. This man Adolf Hitler did care for her because he needed her to keep him here in the ordinary world; he really did, for he lived in the same dream as her. I could see it inside of her, that she knew this and had orchestrated it out of her very history, so when she turned away from our knowing too much together, it was with the surety of what her life with him, and death with him, must be.

"But there will be others waiting at the house, and we must watch the sunset from the terrace and play with the dogs," she assured me. "And everyone will like you as much as I do, though you certainly are a redskin, I'm sure." She paused. "Perhaps they will be afraid of you," she laughed, and I shook my head with a smile. "Come. We'll climb a little higher and catch the loop back down to the house. You'll love the view." I followed her, watching the muscles of her calves before me, flexing and relaxing as she climbed steadily. At the trail crossing, she spun in a gymnastic turn and pointed across the whole valley again, but she did not laugh, and her eyes were sober, even garnished with the edges of tears, and she was right. It was a place of great beauty and grandeur, surrounded by mountain peaks that still held bright fires to celebrate the solstices and equinoxes, celebrations my own people have, with ceremonies we have done longer than anyone remembers, the patterns of the stars written in the flames. But here there was something deep and powerful now gone, though some of the form remained. What has been forgotten here in this land?

Even in their beauty, the very mountains seemed sad, and the peaks waited and waited for something they had mislaid to suddenly appear.

We walked the trail as I thought and listened for answers, and suddenly Eva broke into a sprinter's run as the trail flattened and then tilted gently downhill, and I chased behind her in the cool breeze, my hair flying out behind me, the deerskin warm against my muscles. My breath came deep into my lungs and I exhaled with relief, even here, even in this place where horror was spawned, and where that horror took a break from even itself. It was good to run, to really run hard. The house appeared as we ran out of a stand of sweet-smelling pines, and a group of men and women on a broad stone balcony turned as one to watch us as we raced toward them, Eva's laughter running before us like a messenger, and I could see quizzical smiles gradually breaking across their faces as we neared, running straight towards them out of the pages of *Winnetou*, and they laughed, raising their crystal wine glasses toward us, high into the cool mountain air.

A handsome young guard in uniform opened the heavy wooden door for us with a polite smile of deference to Eva, his eyes looking me up and down discretely, showing his perusal as a matter of duty only, and we walked through a green carpeted room with plush chairs in floral prints. A needlepoint design of rich orange flowers in a red vase, framed in gold, adorned the wall behind a round table covered partially by a square of intricate white lace, making me think of the blouses of some of the Mayan villages, whose women of the late nineteenth century admired the German craft and put its patterns on their shoulders and breasts. Tourists from North America would later call the designs "traditional" Indigenous art without knowing that the roots lay in a country those same Americans would later be brought to hate for generations. On the white lace, two of the *Winnetou* books lay neatly placed, obviously and recently read. It was strange to see brown faces staring up with courage and pride into that broad-beamed ceiling in Bavaria. I knew I was in for something momentous as we walked through the house to the doors opening onto the deck, with perhaps twenty people talking there, some in uniform, most of the men in lederhosen and thick woven jackets of green and brown, the country festival dress, the women in loose-fitting flowing dresses, skirts and blouses, comfortable and feminine. The guests were laughing as we opened the doors and walked across the grey stones, laughing even as they turned to stare, unfazed by my appearance. I must have been so securely placed in their imaginations by the books and their hosts' fondness of the stories, and by Eva's smiles, that they did not question my sudden and very real appearance in their midst. It was a demonstration of imagination and reality melting without making any sense at all, of how fantasy and what is in front of the eyes can suddenly dovetail and be accepted without question.

"Adi," Eva called, "Come meet my friend Rain. She's a very strong runner, and she's a real Indian." She looked at me with the corners of her mouth in a wry smile, emphasizing the word "real."

A small man over in the corner, with sharp dark eyes and a slender nose, studied me carefully as I followed Eva's lead toward her Adi, who stood at the center, but nearer the terrace railing. The watcher held a tall crystal wine glass and stood next to a tall and imposing woman with careful blond hair that framed her beauty artfully as she glanced my way. Her hair fell like water rippling down over stones in a descending stream, and the woman quickly looked away and resumed her talk with a man in lederhosen, but she took my image with her. The watcher wore dark pleated slacks and a fine cotton shirt of high quality, obviously proud of his style, and his eyes stayed on me without wavering. I felt no physical threat, but something else sharpened in the air, and I knew we would soon meet.

Eva's Adi did not extend his hand, and I did not extend mine. Perhaps it was a health issue, I could not tell, or his sexual reserve amidst all these men and women who I quickly saw did not share that reserve. And yet he was their king, the chaste king to the lusty court. How strange the world is sometimes, at least in these lost centuries, where contradiction piles on top of contradiction, and people amuse themselves trying to discern and chase down what is true and real, when it should simply be apparent. But these were times of great illusion and preposterous dreams, and I was in the nest of those who would change the world for what they thought of as all time. Perhaps they were right; perhaps they did change it permanently, but this was why I was here, to find out who they were and how their final dreams might be changed when it came time.

"You are American Indian?" my powerful host inquired, holding a plain glass of water in his right hand.

"I am," I replied.

"And what are you doing here?"

"I've come to meet you and talk. I am a friend of Will Rogers, and his untimely death prevented him from coming. He wanted to meet you and get to know you." I paused. "As his companion in trust, I wanted to fulfill his wish."

He nodded, placing his left hand into the pocket of a long black leather coat that reached to his knees, and he seemed chilled by even this light breeze. His hair lifted and dropped slightly with the breeze, but stayed in place, and he seemed very attuned to his appearance, very conscious of how he appeared to me, yet he was not the least bit nervous.

"That is an honorable sentiment," he nodded plainly, turning his head slightly to the side in appraisal of my reaction.

"It is what Will would have wanted." I held his eyes without emotion, but he was able to discern what it meant for me to be here as Will's emissary, though no one would ever know about it in history, so different than Will's visit would have been. It did not seem to matter to the Fuhrer that I was not Will in my capability to talk to the world about this meeting, and

I thought it curious and revealing of his insight that he appeared to be aware of these thoughts of mine.

"Yes, I remember the meeting being talked about," he said, "not many years ago, and I remember the airplane crash." He paused, looking into me. He inclined his head ever so slightly toward me in genuine sympathy. "And, I'm sorry for your loss."

"Thank you. It has been a loss for the whole world."

He straightened, nodded, looked around him as though suddenly distracted, then motioned me to the railing overlooking the valley. I followed, and Eva walked with me, pleased to be part of the discussion. As he reached the edge of the large balcony, he placed the water glass on the rail and looked down toward the village below, smoke rising from several chimneys as late afternoon shade angled down off the Alps.

"Your Will Rogers was an American Indian as well," he questioned, "if I understand correctly?"

"Yes, he was Tsalagi, or what most people know as Cherokee, and I am of the same nation," I offered.

"But he was of mixed blood, was he not?" His eyebrows rose momentarily, then resumed their noncommittal politeness above his dark eyes. He cleared his throat and waited for me to speak.

"People speak of him as 'part Cherokee,' but for many of us, this does not exist. It is not possible to be 'part' anything."

"What do you mean?" He was genuinely surprised, and turned his body from an angle to directly face me, his leather coat crackling softly.

"You are who you are. This is how we see it. His mother was Tsalagi, and his father was Tsalagi, and though their parents married Europeans, they were still Tsalagi, since they served the community. That's how they saw the world and themselves. And it depends upon what you believe. He called himself 'The Cherokee Kid' for a reason, and he was proud of his heritage. It is measured in how you serve people, and he served well with his life."

The Fuhrer nodded. "I see," he said quietly, and put both hands in his pockets. He looked around him at his companions, blonde and blue-eyed, dark-haired and brown-eyed, all in service to his party and to him. "I understand this," gesturing toward the others with his chin, "but there is also the matter of the blood."

"I am what you would call 'pure blood,'" I said, "but this makes me no more Tsalagi than Will. In fact, he has done more than I have for all people, Indian and non-Indian, and I can only hope to serve his memory with dignity and courage." I faltered in my quickly rising emotion, then added, "All of this is for the people, everything we do."

"I see." He studied me, pausing for a long while before speaking again. "It is about your honor, isn't it, and this is what I respect in your people. This is what I know about you. I have read books about you, and I know you work tirelessly for your people, just as I do for Germany." He looked into me and measured his next statements carefully. "I too live only to serve my people. Like you might say, without them, I have no life." His baritone voice was calm, but his eyes flamed with these words. "We understand each other well, don't we?" He did not wait for my reply. "And you are welcome in my home."

The intensity of his words silenced me momentarily, for I'd been to Dachau at this point, heard the stories of the camps in the east, and listened to voices echoing through history for generations, his speeches to his troops storming the Russian front, exhorting them to "drive the Russians out like they are redskins," a bizarre contradiction to his admiration of *Winnetou*, but then this too fit in a world where the maze of contradiction held sway. There would be space for the Germans to live as God intended, like the untrammeled Wild West for the European settlers to expand into, or the continent for the Romans to live in, always enough space for "me" to have dominion over "you," all spoken softly in logic, reason, and in passion too with grand gestures of raised fists, open arms to the Western sky, incense floating to the gods, all in the name of myself, whoever I might be in this strange brand of exaltation and extermination.

"And now, if you'll excuse me," he apologized, "we'll talk again later." He quickly walked through the party and headed inside, Eva on his heels. He stopped only to bend down and jostle the face of a golden brown shepherd that ran across the terrace to greet him enthusiastically and lick his hands. Suddenly alone, I watched them go, and I realized his exit was simply to use the toilet, and for the couple to check in with each other like lovers do, like companions do. Things had not been going as well as he'd have liked at this point of the war. Stalingrad had not fallen to his onslaught, the "redskins" had eventually resisted successfully, and it looked as though there would be no cavalry to ride in with bugles blaring to rescue the stranded German soldiers, no next wagon trains of settlers to flood the Russian plains. The enormous mass of Russia had become a wall, and would soon enough lower an iron curtain of the Nazis' worst fear, a different complexion of abject power, a complexion that would also take millions of common lives in its turn. The grand plan had ground to a halt in the direction of the rising sun, and nervousness filled the air this day, and for some there was even a vague sense of dread and impending doom. In reaction to this sense, the eastern killing fields were both harried and hurried, for even if the "living room" would have to succumb to a more modest architecture, the mission of ridding Europe of Jewry would still have to be accomplished, and there was nowhere to send them now but into eternity. Regardless of the plan, the mission must prevail, and the leader of it all, the spokesman, needed his woman's consolation today, in the face of what his internal and very personal God, and his plan, intended him to do. It was all very mundane, this insanity, even banal in its neediness.

In the midst of my observations, the small man I'd noticed earlier, with the sharp nose and penetrating eyes, limped to my side, wine glass in hand, the silver glint of a leg brace shining on the side of his polished black shoe. Here was the true architect of manipulating a weary population into enough frenzy of fear and ego to get the job done, Mr. Goebbels, and he was smiling at me.

"Ah, such a beautifully dusky creature you are," he exclaimed quietly. The tall woman I assumed was his wife had her back turned, and was now facing a square-shouldered general in uniform who draped his arm over her shoulder in friendship, her free arm gesturing, her shoulders shaking under the big man's arm with laughter I could not hear. With the leader gone, a shift in the revelry came quickly, the sexual tension rising measurably alongside a forced subtlety because of the place, the Berghof, and the presence of the Fuhrer. These people were not stiff like him, not reserved and held, but wild in their hearts, excited at the chase and the conquering, men and women alike. They were the ones whose eyes glowed with tears when the leader spoke to sixty-five thousand people cheering and raising salutes to victory in unison, tears of gladness and relief from their sadness and confusion. "You are a truly magnificent creature," the architect repeated.

"Am I a creature?" I chafed at his intentions immediately.

"Well, you are from a wild place and a wild people, and you are quite exquisite, very strong. So yes, you are a creature, and a delightful one at that." He looked up at me because I was slightly taller than him, and as I took a breath, I was tempted to spill my power over into him through his eyes, but I refrained. My anger has been my undoing at times, and Grandmother warned me about using it wisely, not wasting it where it would not accomplish what I wanted to happen. But his condescension was so overbearing that it almost made me violent. Why not just slit his throat and get it over with, save a lot of lives and be rid of this preposterous man? I checked myself and realized that the tension of being civil, normal, contained, in such an atmosphere of inhumanity was churning me into someone else, someone less than who I must be, at least at this moment.

"We are not wild people," I said, "but free." The words came slowly and with surety, measured for impact and depth, and the meaning was not lost on the architect.

"Yes, I have read reports by the earliest colonists to your land, reports with lofty sentences. He closed his eyes to remember, then spoke from rote, "Of all the men on earth, no one is more free than the Red Man, for he has no king to tell him what to do, and he goes here and there according to his will with confidence that none will thwart his freedom." He chuckled. "Is this true? I would suppose it is, since it is written by a European witness, so it is therefore a picture of a wild man, one with no control by society or obligations to it."

"Or it is a picture of a civilized world," I retorted, "and therefore a free man within it."

The architect was pleased. He had a chess game going with a "dusky creature" he wanted to bed, all in the manner of a brand of sophistication he loved, the world of philosophy and drama, for he was a truly frustrated play-write whose plays no one would perform, despite years of entreaties through all the

German-speaking countries. But now he was successful. Now he had a whole nation as his cast, a whole world living out his vision of what the human story is. And in the midst of this great drama, here was another grand story; if he could convince the "creature" before him of his correctness or accuracy of vision, then perhaps he could bed her, and the best of all worlds would be his to enjoy. And as a complex dramatist, he must have thought that if her submission didn't work, he might play upon her sympathies by references to his limp, his war wound, he called it, which was in fact not a war wound. Then if sympathy didn't work, he had the option of pretending to be convinced by her that her way of seeing life could change him, that his cynicism could be molded into something grand and marvelous by her love, the promise of conversion that would make her the holy mother. But what he did not reckon with was that I am an Indigenous woman, and I know in the depth of my heart he could never understand me, just like the Apache shot out in the theater parking lot one day, "They will never understand us, Agana, not in a million years." Of course he is right, but then that is not my aim or expectation here today. I ask only that the people I visit begin to look into themselves, and truth be told, I have no idea what they might see, or if they are even willing. I simply know that in the process and power of looking, something different becomes possible, that simply looking causes a motion that is new and free, at least in its potential. That was why I was on this cold stone terrace, to see, to listen and to see.

The architect looked at my eyes steadily, but not into them, for I would not allow that violation, would not allow his violence to come into me. I held him out carefully, firmly and gently, as the afternoon shadows began to fall and envelope the valley in angles of darkness. Here was the true dusk, not in the color of my skin. The breeze that had gently cooled the party earlier took on a harsh bite, and many moved inside, quieting in the chill, but the two of us remained outside. My deerskin reflected my body's warmth and protected me, huddled closer to me on its own, and he wrapped his long black leather jacket over his thin chest. He leaned against the railing and I stood squarely in front of him. I could see a stand of pines on the slope behind him over his left shoulder and the darkening valley over his right shoulder. Bright light still spilled over the white peaks of the Alps, and I saw the motion of the wind in the stand of pines, and then another presence as well, something quietly watching. I listened to the man, and to the pines. My eyes softened in listening, but remained wary.

"If your 'free' man meets a bear or a lion, then he will likely be free no longer," he said with a smile of self-satisfaction, still attempting to convince me. "He will be subject to the order of Nature, in which he as a man in the wild is not the top of the food chain. This is the natural order of things, quite simply."

"You know nothing," I replied, matching his arrogant tone, "while claiming to know everything." My world was fuller and richer than he could imagine. "The man would not be hunted by the lion or bear because it is not in their nature to hunt him. He would only be in danger if he violated their place, their home or hunt, or blundered into them without paying attention and frightened them, which sometimes happens. Even then, he knows how to apologize to them if he is truly free, how to back away, or how to deal with an animal who has somehow lost his nature through disease or magic, and he knows his obligations to them, and the power he can gain from right relationship with them. Yes, he must take care, but he knows they were there long before him, so they must be respected. They are very strong, so one must have respect and take care."

He laughed. "You sound like a dime novel of the Old West, with your idealization of Nature, but I understand you and your need to do so," and then after a pause, he added, "and I see that you idealize humankind as well, as Nature and humanity mirror each other for you."

"I only observe, and tell you of a world you'll never see," I shot back quickly.

"Well, I have never been to America, so I don't really know," he said deferentially, again not losing the possibility in his strange mind that the vast difference between us might somehow bring him between my strong legs, if he could only find the right avenue. He was very practiced in his art of seduction, and blind in his singularity of purpose at the same time. He wanted what he imagined I had, and at the same time he wanted what I actually had and actually am, like he was digging for an old memory that is crucial to where one goes from here, but the memory eludes, goes further and deeper into the imagination like a lost boat on a storm-darkened sea. He wanted to fold into this elemental strength, and he wanted to possess it too, so deep was his hunger and love of power.

"What I do know," he went on, "is that all people are creatures of Nature, and that because of this fact, they live in a natural hierarchy. If we are to survive as humans, we must have dominion over nature, over our base selves, and over those who would debase us. We must cultivate our better selves, our most potent higher selves. This is an intellectual pursuit as well as a spiritual pursuit, if you will, and in our case now it is a national pursuit as well. Someone must dominate and lead as a reflection of the natural order of life. This is a matter of will, of the creation and imposition of ones will over those who do not have that same degree of will. And, in this act of the will, the ultimate force is love."

There it was, his vision, an old and simple story and argument repeated in parlors and over chess games, in bedrooms and churches and schoolhouses so often that it makes the head swim. But now, against the fear of communism and capitalism, two seeming poles of thought, and in a large national impotence found in pervasive poverty, his vision took root in the people's imaginations, and he supplied them the ultimate father, a man betrothed to all of them, married only to all the country's women and none other, brother to the men and father to the boys. This architect supplied the people a visionary man whose promise was simple, direct and profound; prosperity and happiness through expansion and 'purification' on a biblical scale.

"Love?" I asked. "You said the force is love?"

"Yes, the love of a father for his children, of a leader for his people. Do you know that people travel from far and wide to collect the sand the Fuhrer walks on when he changes from one car to another, here in the village below us, when he stops to greet the folk? They put this sand in vials on their altars, and they believe it gives power to their prayers. You see, this is love, love and adoration."

We were alone on the terrace now, and the wind swirled the tips of the pines. If I'd been on the mountaintop that was visible behind him, the snow would have been whipping through the air, but from down here I could only imagine it and smell its sharp taste in my nostrils as I took it in behind the black leather of his shoulder. The cold didn't faze me, nor did it seem to affect him, so caught in his pursuit he was, and me in my controlled rage. But it was all so grotesquely civilized that I could not be silent about the larger scheme of his drama, his personal play, any longer. Alone with him, I thrust my hands deep into the carrying pockets of my deerskin, my right hand closing around the handle of my knife, my left hand around the small medicine vial I always carried deep in the folds of skins. As my fingers touched it, I remembered the deer that gave her life so I could be warm on this mountainside so far from my home. I remembered her soft brown eyes as she died, and I said a silent prayer to her.

"I have been to Dachau," I said, and the architect's eyebrows rose, "and I have been to your camps building in the east and watched your trains and seen what you are doing and planning on an even bigger scale." I waited for his response.

"And?" He showed no emotion except for surprise, for perhaps he was wondering how I might know these things, but there was no sense of having been exposed in him, no sense of shame. It wasn't that I expected it, but his coolness surprised me.

"And who is the loving father in all this killing?" I asked sharply. It was still a discussion, but it should have been a murder, a revenge exacted by me on what I knew would happen in the next few years, but I knew I could not do that. It doesn't work that way, for many reasons. It was larger than this man in front of me in the black coat and sure eyes, who still insisted on seeing my body through his twisted philosophy, still wanted my vagina to satisfy his thirst for the primitive in himself, all in the middle of his horrible and gory journey to find his distant God by showing up flaming and smoking on His back door.

I went on. "And what is the love you talk about?"

"The people must be loved from above in order to love themselves, loved by the father," he said plainly, as though describing a recipe. "Dachau is for those among us who defer, who mire the love down with their doubts and unfocused fears, and with their own desires for personal power. If they work and mend their ways, and join us, they will be freed in more ways than one."

"And the trains, and the eastern camps?"

"Yes." He feigned sadness, but only for my benefit. "This is unfortunate, and it is not what we originally wanted. We opened the door for those who were destroying our society with their greed and obsession with material wealth to leave, but no other country would take them, and although some did leave, it was not in appreciable numbers. But now it must finally happen, this purification. It is a sacrifice, if you will, which you surely must know in your world of hunting to live, and it is for the ultimate bettering of society, and eventually the world as we know it. You will see."

He spouted the doctrine the world would come to know and never to understand, but to condemn, as it should, yet when I looked at and inhaled all of history, what they call all of time spread out in a thin sharp line, the condemnation of only this one nation that fleshed up and burst out in manifestation of this doctrine bothered me, made me nervous over all the vast number of epochs my mission would take me to see. Surely people must see the true size of this thing, this aberration, and truly they must be able to get to the roots of it.

"Look at it this way," he went on. "Your people were noble and free, as you say, and even as the famous statue of the Indian on his 'spent pony' at the San Francisco Expo recently said, it is 'the end of the trail for a race of once-mighty people.' Look at the bent and sad posture of the Indian on his pony, and at the statue of the white pioneer erect in his saddle in the very same expo, and you see how the art expresses the truth, that it is a matter of survival of the fittest. And, most importantly, you must always remember your race was conquered for the good of the whole country, of the whole nation, as a result of simple evolutionary law. Your kind of freedom was an anachronism. Surely you must see this. You were obsolete. Your type of freedom could not live in a larger society based on the greatest good for the greatest numbers. Your people were put into camps where many died, and where they are still contained and restrained from living how they see fit, and we saw this, how these camps help to solve the problems your freedom caused for all those pioneers simply seeking to expand their lives, and to bring civilization to your wilderness, your continent. Some of you stood in their way, so all of you had to pay the price. It's sad, because many of you had such noble potential, but we are now back to the laws of nature, you see, and the love I speak of is for the ultimate good of all, not for only the few insisting on their own sense of what it means to be free in the modern world."

I did not pause in my reply. "Then your love is nothing but terror, fear in its ultimate form." I relaxed my grip on the knife, took a breath, and saw where all this must implode with time into its own unnatural momentum.

"Well, yes, of course this is true toward a purpose, and this fear is not a bad thing. It's like the fear of God. When the will of the people relaxes or becomes lazy, fear must be used to coax them back into the larger vision. They must realize that their laziness will make their children's world unacceptable, bound to beliefs and ways of life that enslave them. To be free, and to build freedom for their children, they must remain strong. With their clarity of will, and their 'terror,' as you put it, which is nothing more than fear of living what is quite simply the wrong way to live, this Reich will last a thousand years. This is our dream. And it's a worthy and beautiful dream."

He smiled, and I was shocked to see that he still desired me, caught in his own rhetoric, so enamored of his grand scheme that it physically excited him to tell me all of this so clearly, his eyes glowing. Amazingly, he could not see my hatred boiling. Or maybe he could, and he still wanted me in his outrageous sexual drama, but if so, the game of winning me through cool reason was now gone, and the technique of sympathy was dead too, and the calling forth of the great mother I might have become in his pantheon of what women should be was completely erased, so all that was left was his hope that I would somehow be vulnerable to his statements of abject power and the Reich's ultimate success. Maybe success and its attending powers would bring my surrender. Maybe he thought I would sleep with the devil in order to ultimately do good in the world, and he himself was that very willing devil, and he hoped for a concoction of trades he thought I might make, so he could have me. Certainly he was surrounded by such trades, so why shouldn't I make it as well?

Since he could not sense the depth of my resistance, and he would not be stopped by reality, he forged on. "There were many of your people who surrendered their souls to the conquering civilization, and many came out ahead for doing so." He could not understand the steep price those same people sadly paid, nor could he fathom how our natural impulse to include others, strangers with different stories and different ways, was at the heart of many of our people's initial acceptance and embrace of the newcomers. This was before we began to know better, before we learned from experience of their meanness and blindness and sickness. But by then, the floodgates had been opened, and everything had changed. And it changed for a very long time, for generations, and our will was stretched and tested and torn apart, but it never gave in, never gave up, and even by the twenty-first century, after hundreds of years of obfuscation and being surrounded, our way to see still survived and grew, albeit invisibly at times, and all of this tried our patience to our very bones. And why did we never give up? Because we cannot. It's not possible, because our very thinking is part of Earth herself, something grown out of our simply being. When we walk away from that, we walk away from everything.

"No," I said. "You're wrong. There has been no winning in capitulation. We win only through maintaining who we are, and through a long seeing, and through resisting everything that you are, resisting who you were back then in the colonies, and long before that, and who you are here where we are at this moment on this stone terrace, and forever into the future. You are nothing more than a cannibalistic blight to us, a bad choice in the midst of all this beauty," I nodded toward the mountain and valley, "and the deeper beauty will shrug you away because you are nothing in the face of it, nothing but a huge mistake in different shapes and forms." Scorn picked my words and carried them coldly through his brain, and then like a glint of light off a distant lake or pond, like something high in the mountains seen from afar for only a millisecond but that changes the entire appearance of that mountain, his excitement and desire and heat for me suddenly and instantly flipped itself over into icy hatred, for hatred was finally the base of his sexual nature. It was at the core of his being born, of his god, of his life itself, though he might call it love and desire. The most peace he could ever imagine would be in his death, but not in Shakespeare's sense of orgasm with this Indigenous woman, and now his depth of knowing that he could not have me in any way infuriated him beyond control. I was his Stalingrad. He shook with anger as I leaned forward to speak into his ear with words that were knives.

"Your world will soon end, and you will kill yourself, your wife, your children, and all your dreams of grandeur will turn to shit. Your precious leader will become a shadow of evil in the wind for as long as people remember." I broke my own rules, but I could not help it. "Your own children," I repeated with dismay and anger into his startled dark eyes.

He stared as I pulled away, knowing the truth of my words, as though a mystical part of himself had been waiting for this voice of his deepest knowing and most horrible suspicion, yet still he would not be outdone, for this was all his play. He wrote it, and was writing it in every waking moment. "If this is so," he said, "then it is better to pass into the next world, rather than to suffer in this one without our dream, and without the perfection the dream brings." He threw the defiant face of nobility in death, his alternate and noble ending, straight at me shamelessly and triumphantly, both hands firmly on the railing behind him, jutting his sharp chin out in violent petulance and tremendous power. He wanted to kill me, I could see it, but he could see it was not possible, not by his own cowardly hands or even by the hands of others nearby at his beckoning, and he was riveted to the stone railing by frustration and martyrdom, by confrontation with his own destiny, and I turned my back to him and strode toward the big wood and glass doors that would lead me out of this place, out onto the hillside, out toward somewhere quiet and sane and possible.

I moved through the house so quickly that no one really noticed me, like a shadow against the deepening evening that glowed through the windows facing the hillside. The guard opened the doors for me just as I pushed against them, and I did not look at his eyes, but headed back up the trail past the pines. Soon the building was below and behind me, a rectangular chimera as the sun vanished behind the mountaintops and cold darkness began its quick descent. My breath steamed the air as I rounded a corner in the trail, a stand of pines hiding the house from view. There was only the mountain, the trail gently climbing, the cold sky, the black pines, and now, a laughter coming from within the sharp needles and pungent cones and branches. It was the presence that had been watching me on the terrace. I stopped, listened, and the waves of sound pointed directly at me, calling me. I felt no immediate danger other than from the direction of life that was the totality of this place, and I did not have enough medicine to counter that force, nor a method to deliver it if I would have had it. I was talking and listening in a void of normalcy where no one saw their inevitability on the surface but where everyone knew and lived it on the inside. I walked carefully toward the laughter, step by step, looking directly into the spot it came from. Then as I stepped beneath a tall overhanging branch, I saw him.

He perched on a thick branch twenty feet above and in front of me like a grinning Cheshire Cat, half-way up a sturdy pole-like tree with few side branches. His gnarled bird's feet clutched the branch, claws dipping into the soft white wood, golden sap dripping down from the open gashes. The blue silk stretched around his legs and arms, and his face was the man's face, the handsome gentleman, his black hair jutting up like a jay's top knot, long fingers playing the air in front of him. Neither of us showed any fear, for there was none. He was fully confident in this place, and I relaxed the grip on my knife, realizing I could not reach him, and even if I could, it would do no good. It would not change anything now. He wanted only to talk, to parley, as he put it in his smooth voice, a voice that began as smoothly as the blue silk then finished with the harsh scrape of a crow's call of annoyance when he does not get his way. But here the witch was getting his way, so the sound was simply habit, his nature of irritation.

"You see how it is now, don't you?" he said, tilting his head slightly back in laughter. "I have nothing to do here, nothing at all." His eyes stayed on mine, as he could feel my resolve and sense the knife and my power, but there was no trepidation as he went on. "There is no convincing to be done, no arguments or promises to people. They are doing it all themselves now." He laughed again, waiting for my reply, his sharp eyes a bright black and red invitation in the growing darkness, a dull and pale white light surrounding his constantly moving form. His arms fluttered in their readiness to become wings again at any moment, anxious to fly quickly through the trees into the open night sky.

I nodded. "You are right," I said. "But it won't always be this way."

"Ah, but it will, beautiful beloved woman. It will, and there is nothing you can do about it. Your beauty, your power, and your desire to change the mind are all nothing here. This is the trajectory now, and the way it will continue to be." He smiled and invited my response with a glint in his eye.

"It will end. I promise you that." I said the words, but I was already done with the conversation. It could only descend into two opponents in muscle tee shirts shouting at each other in the parking lot, the same curse over and over, like a comic skit done on the edge of doom, strangely humorous in a perverse way. But there was indeed more to say. I was simply done talking.

"Yes, it will end," he said, emphasizing the word 'it,' "but not this, not what we see today. And do you know why? You spoke with Goebbels last, didn't you, he who is my work of art? You see it, don't you, how his vision of life is what most of the people believe now, and they believe it about themselves. They believe that from the beginning of their lives, their births, they are fallen from the grace of their pathetic little God, and in this fallen state, they give it all away. They teach this to their children, and they call it Nature. They give him, my Goebbels, power over their lives. And they give me power over their lives though they do not even know I exist in their trees and skies. These are my centuries, 'beloved' woman, my centuries." He laughed, his big shoulders bubbling up and down in delight and surety.

"You have come a long way," I said, "from your rabbits in the woods, and your crazed dancing. But this only means your end will be that much more profound."

"You remember our last conversation, don't you, at the big oak table," he said, "and that was sixty years from now into the future, so ask yourself what will have changed even in this short time. You know that in the future they will believe it even more than now, that it will cement itself into their minds and they will call it evolution or some such thing, or that delightful little phrase 'the way of all flesh.'" He raised a sharp finger to smooth his eyebrow slowly and carefully, still smiling down at me.

There was nothing more to say, and nothing more to listen to, so I turned my back on him and began walking slowly out from under the pines. Enraged, he shouted after me, spitting the words.

"They will call it 'human nature.' You know they will. They will say 'It is what it is,' and they will live it out, and I will have to do nothing, nothing at all."

His voice grew fainter as I climbed the trail up the slope.

"I will only have to watch," he cried out, "just watch them all, so why don't you just give up and quit trying? Accept what is real, 'beloved' woman, and join me now. It's time for you to switch. It's all done now, so join me. This is what I wanted to say. Join me. Think of what we can accomplish together, you and I, with my power and your sweetness. Don't fight me, because it's all over now for these people."

But I kept walking as he went on and on, and I listened for all the voices that were not there right now but that had to come. I walked and I talked to Grandfather Tree and Grandmother in the wind, and to the Apache and his warrior ancestors, and to the grandmothers of his clan, and to the people at home who missed me and gently talked to me in the forest at night, asking me to come home. I climbed the mountain until the witch's calls were gone, and then he burst out of the trees with a flurry and circled me in the dark sky once, then vanished, his voice a crackling hoarse cry, for now the protection songs were surrounding me from antiquity and there was even less that he could do to me. I called all the spirits, all the walk up to the icy tip of the Alps above me, and from that snowy cold perch I turned to look below me, but the valleys were only long thick black lines in a black night written over with bright silver stars. I looked down and saw the future, again with the most potent army the world has ever known gathered on the once-lush hillsides and in the beautiful valleys of my own Turtle Island, then I sat in the snow and sobbed, until the tears became ice and cut into my skin like cold sharp knives that woke me to the voice of my love. I stood then, looked into the Pleiades, and with a rush of song, I flew on home to where I belonged.

GOING TO WATER

26

I was polluted, coming from a time where death had become escape, a hunger for the divine in a profane world, so I went straight into ceremony. I went into the dark womb, and when the thick hide door dropped down and darkness encompassed, and the water hissed on the deep red stones and misty fire circled around my back, penetrating my kidneys and spine and shoulders, I surrendered to it, and a bright blue and black turtle suddenly shone above, between twin eagle feathers that hung from the roof, invisible. His head was luminous and his neck black, his legs bright with black tipped claws, his shell a pattern of bright and dark in the shapes of the directions, quadrants of sustenance. He pulsed against the roof of the womb and comforted me, and the songs carried through me, the drum filling me, filling the cavity of my womb and of the womb in which I prayed and listened.

I gave thanks along with the others, the water hissed and the stones sang, and then another round came and we fell into silence, the prayers going personal, and faces ran through my mind. My son Unole, Little Rain, Sweet Hunter, Will, the Apache, Johnny, all took turns staring into my eyes. More water hissed on the stones and curled around me, lifting my body and placing it gently onto the earth, where the grit and smell filled my prayer, came into me as straight strength, and with the strength I floated up into the prayer, a flying and touching and listening and watching. Little Rain, with her pale heart-shaped face framed in long black hair watched from a distance, by her woods, and news photos of frightened children running out of a school building flared up. Oh, no! Not here! I touched them with my eyes, and behind them stood a young man with an automatic rifle, eyes like saucers. Darkness flashed, and like in a slide show, another small boy emerged, taller and bigger than the child he spoke down to in derision, and he said, "I will kill your mother," and the smaller boy shrugged and walked away, but he had been penetrated and his lips quivered when he described it later. I touched this conversation with my eyes and struggled in the prayer, shaking my head in the darkness, rubbing my cheek into the earth, and tears fell into the sweat pouring off my body, tears for all of them, for all of us. I saw a century of such scenes in increasing frequency, like a film speeding up faster and faster, frames flying by until the celluloid spins off the reel and slaps against the projector over and over in the silent theater.

I had come to give thanks and to cleanse, and so I did, but even here in the womb there was this future, even back here a thousand years before the invasion it came and circled in the fire and steam and had to be dealt with. "Uneque, wado," I heard in the darkness. "Nawatte," I heard, Grandmother and Grandfather speaking, asking, thanking steadily, as though they could see what I could see, from wherever they were at that moment. It circled through all of us in the heat, and I fought for something else but knew I could not win that battle to inhabit my own mind and heart privately, not privately, and especially not here. I took a breath that burned all the way down, that stayed burning in my lungs, and I felt a long river of sweat pour down my face. A beetle dropped out of the hide behind and above me, landing on my bare wet calf, then scampered across my slippery skin to hide in the soil around one of the womb's wooden ribs. His panicked flight made me smile, brought me back, and I could feel him nose down into the rich damp earth, motionless and hiding. I wanted to be him, forever, or if I couldn't do that, then I wanted to burrow together with him nose to nose, commiserating and bitching together about all of it, every last stitch of it, me and the beetle.

This was the cleansing. It was not a pouring out as I had known many times before and hoped for, expected even, though I should know better than to expect anything from a ceremony, for each one carries its own life, and what is found and given is made by more than I know, each time. No, it was not a pouring out but a filling in, an inundation like filling in every single tiny space of whiteness in a coloring book, leaving nothing behind. Nothing went away, and the songs and prayers and visions were like an engine on a pump, grinding away through the night to empty a sump that can never be emptied. The engine is an old sound, a simple mechanical banging away, the cylinder slamming up into the head without sophistication, no gear-driven valves and smooth exhaust notes, but a working song of simple pushrods and rocker arms moving like oil wells up and down, the exhaust a steady labored chuffing of white smoke pushing into a cold night. It's simple, and it goes on and on as though it could never falter. It can't falter because if it does, the sump fills to overflowing and you've got a huge mess no one knows how to address. This is the ceremony.

When the last round came and I saw the afternoon light stream through the opened door, I simply lay there and watched the steam float out the door up into the walnut tree. It was good. Though my mind was still full, my heart was too, and while the pollution was not gone, there was enough grit to hold it in place, to realize it, feel it, taste its bitterness without consuming it or being consumed by it either one. It was matter-of-fact, like when you're in the back seat of a car and the driver starts to make a wrong turn, and you know the way, you've got to speak up, that's all. You just hope he's listening, or if he makes the wrong turn because his iPod is too loud to hear you, you can eventually get him to turn around and go the right way. This is what it's always been, always the practical side of things in dealing with monsters, and this is what it still is. The steam rises into the green leaves, and I crawl out the door to unfold my glistening body into the sun, while the fresh smell of cooking meat, juicy and spitting onto the hot coals, calls me to the cooking fire. That's the way it is.

27

She was numb, caught in stasis, lying on her back staring into yellow sky, eyes in slits. I brought the ceremony with me and poured it onto her from my hands, spilled it down on her in a smile, for by now I had the confidence I could reach her, even if I couldn't cure her. If I could reach her, then maybe I could heal her, for there is a difference between a cure and a healing, the difference between the body and the spirit, and her healing would unquestioningly be a matter of spirit. In this, she had become my teacher now, for I had to follow her direction, though we did not know where this might go, whether her death was imminent and might pull me down into her like a whirlpool on the town's stream, or whether we would triumph in some way we could not yet see. It could go either way, or in unimagined directions. We knew only that we were connected, and that this direction, this going back and forth, had meaning. I straddled her, my deerskin dress touching her stomach, and I poured the ceremony over her like it was warm water. Faces crossed my imagination, and I listened to hear whether they might be coming from my memory or hers. I knew this now with her, that if I listened deeply enough to my own experience, I could tell where the images were coming from as they walked into the center of my mind, from her or from me, while present in me. And there were faces we knew together too, where my people had come to visit her, making the long trek through the woods to her town, or traveling through their imaginations to her sleeping form, or to her spot of quiet sitting by the woods.

The ceremony eventually worked, and I smiled down to her as she opened her eyes a fraction wider and the faces went away, replaced by her being here now, here with me under the yellow sky. She rolled over, got to her feet, took my hand, and we went into the woods to the edge of the pond, to the side where there was flat dry sand spread out in the shape of a fan. She sat, leaned forward and drew, focused onto her fingers where they gently pushed the sand aside, and at first I watched, but she glanced up at me as though to say it might take time, and I should not watch, so I turned into the small meadow and walked slowly around, looking at beetles scurrying under leaves, spiders waiting patiently at the edges of their webs. A hawk called his screeching call above me, and I turned to wave at him. He circled one more time, dipping his wing to me, lower, then went on about his hunt. I lay down under a silver-barked ash tree and slept through the day. After a very long while, I went back to Little Rain, and she was sitting very still looking down at her sand drawing. She looked up at me, then back down to the drawing.

It was like the sand paintings of the southwestern peoples, beautiful in its symmetry, with raised portions here and there, but there was no color save the gold and brown of the sand, and it was not an isolated perfect circle or square. It arched down from the imperfect curve of the pond's edge and spread out into a perfect circle below, as it got further *from the pond, so the top was open to the water's shaping of the land, and the rest grew into the fine shape of a globe. All around the edges of the circle were terraced fields, surrounding the drawing as a neat border, and at the top were volcanic mountain tops leading to one slope that peaked them all. The slopes of the mountains carried careful orchards, neat rows of trees reflecting the ordered fields below. Moving inward from the border, in geometric precision, were houses forming villages or towns, with meandering streams weaving through them, snaking down from the mountains above. Small dots of tiny pebbles floated around the streams in random places like things flying, like birds. The villages were still in the outer layer of the drawing, separated by small forests, joined by streams and paths, and as they moved further inward the houses grew closer together, eventually forming a huge tight complex. It was a city in a big circle surrounded by villages expanding out to the defining border of manicured fields, and tiny stick figures of people all stared to the center of the city under the mountain. At the center of the city, the stem of an overarching shape began, a shape that was the center of the drawing, and it rose up through the center as a column, expanding ever wider as it grew in height, reaching up toward the mountain through the villages and fields and orchards on the mountain slopes, expanding wider and wider until it exploded out the top as the head of a huge mushroom cloud.*

Little Rain let me watch the drawing alone in myself, then she looked up toward me. I knew she was both knowing and asking. Pain constricted the muscles of my eyes into resolve before I met her gaze, and when we met it was as sisters knowing another layer of our connection and mysterious purpose. I nodded to her gravely, that what she drew was true, and she held onto my eyes, with no expression, for a long time before looking back down. I stared at her frail shoulders, then rested my right hand on her as evening tilted toward darkness, and we waited.

There was an old Mayan man, Jose Maria Perez Cux, who told me once that a young man from California had told him the people in North America created a bomb that could destroy the world. He had waited a long time to ask me his question, and to tell me of this, and one night he came to my hut. He said he'd been thinking about it for some time, and had been watching me to know whether I would tell him the truth, and now he trusted me.

"Is it true? Have they made a bomb that can destroy the world?"

I looked at him steadily before answering, and in that time, Little Rain's sand painting swept through me. Jose trusted the world, and he trusted life, though he'd spent time in prison for teaching the old ways to the people of his village, for prisons and banks and politicians were another matter than the largeness of his life, so I had to tell him what I thought. He saw my deliberation, and in this he knew of the bomb's existence, and anger crossed his brow, impatience and frustration, but he came back to the essence of his question quickly.

I spoke slowly, in evening light above a vast lake, under the shadow of a living volcano, a volcano his people had lived on for two thousand years. Thick stone blocks formed steps up the steep slopes into ancient onion fields, and they were worn halfway through by generations of bare feet and simple leather sandals.

"No, it's not true. Only the Creator can destroy the world the Creator has made for us," I eventually said.

Jose nodded and smiled, his eyes sparkling with age. "I knew it was a lie," he said.

We drank cold beer together, sitting on a stone wall facing the lake, before he shook my hand and headed upslope toward his home, evening smoke curling around the barely visible thick brown thatch roof. He knew it was a lie, but he understood me too, and he would not see the world the same way again.

GOING TO WATER

28

Easter had come and gone, but there was no celebration in Germany, and resurrection was present only in a twisted kind of way. Everything was falling down, all the houses were falling down. The Fuhrer and Eva were in Berlin, underground in a concrete bunker shaken repeatedly by Russian mortars. Goebbels' six children were silent, somber, and when mortars would shake the walls, the older ones would cover the younger with their bodies out of duty and love. The resolve of insanity inundated their dreams, and they waited in the shadows of their parents' vision, all but one 12 year old girl, who would struggle against a fate too big to fight. It would come around as the sharp-dressing man with the leg brace foresaw, the whole family gathered together huddling on God's back door, and I wondered if even their God would let them in, despite all the talk of his forgiveness and the storm raging about their souls.

It was afternoon when I walked unmolested into the private quarters. Adi and Eva were not surprised to see me, and they motioned for me to sit, then stared into each other's eyes to finish a deep but sparse conversation. I had interrupted, and it didn't matter to them or to me. A pistol lay on the table, next to white capsules and papers. I waited, taking out the medicine vial slowly and unwrapping its hide cover carefully. A single small turquoise stone sewn into the deerskin shone in the dull electric light of the bunker. I stared into it as I waited, then when it was silent, I spoke.

"I have this for you," I said, holding the vial before me, "and it will help everyone after you, and before you."

Eva's eyes were full of love and fear, adoration even at the end of her road, and she was asking Heaven questions, but Heaven was not answering. Adi was there with her, and she fingered the scar on her neck as she looked at me steadily.

"Will it help us die?" she asked. "Will it ease the pain?"

The Fuhrer was numb, his face swollen in grief and spent rage, yet his eyes glowed with a strange fire, like one seen from a far distance where a fire shouldn't be, not on that mountain, a mystery to behold. He wanted to speak, but the words troubled him. He had spent his words telling Eva things I could not hear, things the world would never know.

"It will help you see all you need to see," I said, and for reasons I can never find in myself, they both trusted me and listened to me. In reflection over all my time, I think it must have been the depth of the novels living within them, a sure testimony to the power of stories to make people become the stories, for surely I must have been the Indian shaman on a Western plain, a strangely holy and ancient being who would deliver them to their world beyond, their next step, in the manner they perceived it should be. I was Earth's magic in their own deep memory, from long before the Roman Church. Why else would they have welcomed me and my medicine in these final moments of their lives?

"Then give it to us," the Fuhrer said weakly but decisively. "Give it to us now."

"I can only give it to you in the moments of your passing over," I said, and Eva pulled back startled, as though she'd been expecting something to make the death of her beautiful body painless, even pleasurable, as though she would not really die from the white capsules on the brown table, but she would be lifted into another Berghof with Adi next to her for eternity, never gone to meetings with foreign dignitaries or speeches to the multitudes in northern cities, never gone to pore over the war maps spread out in gray rooms with hanging metal lights and men in uniform. It would be only the two of them, with the dogs, beside a pristine lake, their returning to their own strange water.

"Will it hurt?" she asked.

"You will only see, nothing more than seeing, and the medicine will not make physical pain. You will see all of your life, and in this you will have a chance…" I could not go on and tell them. I looked at the Fuhrer and spoke calmly.

"You told me it was about the people, and this is about the people. It will help the people if you see what the medicine can show you."

He nodded slowly, trusting his vision of me, and I saw with a pang of quick remorse that I was somehow lying to him because I could see in that moment that he was not considering that it could really be about all people, not just his people, and I did nothing to change his perception. Was this a lie? I believed for all our sake that he needed to take the medicine, so I remained silent about the truth and let him believe what he would.

"Then give it to us when it is time," he said, and turned to Eva. He reached out to hold her hand, and their knees touched where they sat together on the green sofa. I turned away, stood slowly and walked to where they could not see me in the small room, waiting with my back turned to them.

After some moments of silence, Eva coughed, and when I turned to look, she was holding the capsule to her mouth, looking into his eyes, into her Adi's eyes, and he held her free hand. Another capsule pointed out from between his thumb and forefinger, poised in front of his lips, and as she quickly put the small cylinder into her mouth and bit down, he did the same, and their eyes started open in astonishment together. I jumped to them quickly, pulling the stopper to the gourd vial and pouring the green liquid through the smell of burnt almonds that rose from their open mouths. The pain of the cyanide burned in their expressions, then the passing began as the acid did its work on the body quickly, and as this happened, the medicine took hold. At first, peace fluttered through them a brief wind, leaving silence behind it, and Eva looked up at me for a split second of gratitude.

Hitler dropped Eva's hand and grasped his knee with one hand, his heart with another, and it happened as fast as a swallow moves across the vision, as fast as he turns in the sky to catch a dragonfly.

Eva's eyes widened, staring at Adi, then her body stiffened and she riveted her gaze on the grey cement ceiling. I was in her peripheral vision, though her eyes were pinned on one point, a water stain in the shape of a moth's wings, dark grey fading into black on the concrete. She could see me, and I stepped closer to look down into her, through the doorway into her mind as it both expanded and flew away at the same time. She saw eyes wide like her own, peering from behind metal barred windows at Dachau, grey and black stripes of prison clothing on gaunt bodies no more than skeletons; Germans, Gypsies, Jews, dissidents and children, people of all kinds thrown into a grey hell, and they stared their hunger into her. She saw champagne glasses and carefully sliced pieces of Black Forest cake, heard the tinkling of glass on glass, toasts to freedom, liberation, victory, expansion, God and family. She tasted the chilled liquid going down her throat and felt the scar, tried to reach for it, but her body was already gone from her will, and the smell of burnt almonds became an almond cake, a tart that was done perfectly by the adoring hands of the old baker in the village below the mountain, and a skeleton hand reached out, picked it up and put it tenderly between a child's dry lips. Eva

saw me, and saw all she had turned away from, justified somehow in her turning away, as though if she did
not see it, it would not happen, as though thinking it
would make it happen even more horrifically, but she
did know about it all, and so she said to herself then,
"It has to happen, but…," and her thoughts spun away
in a night dance on the cold balcony, hands open to
the stars. She looked into me and the medicine pulled
at her, and I nodded, and she let it take her. All those
years tumbled through her then, and she saw the hunger in her own childhood, the fear, the dreams, and the
tanks rumbling out of her homeland across everyone's
fields, the horsemen in their tunics crying out for victory, charging metal rolling steadily in efficient pride.
She heard the architects planning in her dreams as she
lay under rich covers, and remembered the tears and
saw the truth, and in this she began her own reconciliation, and I nodded down into her eyes as her world
exploded and she fell across the couch, away from her
love. The grey moth stared down at her from his frozen
perch, and Eva was very still.

Adi saw his own truth in these seconds, and I
turned to him then, one hand steadied on the couch
behind his shoulders. The almond smell rose in a wisp
from his nostrils, the green medicine dripped in a tiny
rivulet down from the corner of his mouth, and he
stared upward into a high corner of the room. I poured
another few drops between his open lips while his eyes
widened a fraction more in resistance, but he could not
pull away. Everything ran before him too, I could see,
but he fought it. He refused it all, turning back the faces

peering into him from Treblinka's barracks and burial pits with deep resolve and righteousness. I poured another stream into his quivering mouth, and inexplicably, he turned his face up to me, fixing my eyes with his. He could not speak, but betrayal filled his mind and he spilled it upward toward me, projectile betrayal from his powerful will, from the depth of his perfect dream as he took truth after truth and tossed them from his mind, from his realization, and from the possibility of his revelation, and they scattered in the air between us like ashes from burning newspapers. In his own personal and intimate revelation, which was more like the biblical fires of Revelations he brought to those under his dream-gun, there was no need for reconciliation. His will conquered everything as his body shook in spasms, and he stared at me in defiance. And then, I could swear a smile crossed his face, though it could not have been physically so, as with superhuman effort he reached to the table, grabbed the black pistol with a wild but sure hand, and raised it to his temple, all while staring into my eyes. His pupils contracted into his power, into his consummate refusal of even his most ancient knowledge, and he held his superiority over me in this split second before death, as though to say, "You don't understand. But this act you will understand, and in this you may remember me. I turn away from your truth and live my own truth forever," and with this he pulled the trigger, and the glistening bullet drove through his dream instantly, and he pitched forward even as the blood spray fell through the air.

29

Goebbels was my undoing, and I should have known better. It was the morning of the next day, and a man who would be taken for a doctor walked into the children's room on the heels of their mother, who had been crying for a long time, but what she cried for could only be guessed at. Certainly it would be for the death of her children at her own hands, but it might have been more for the demise of the Reich, since she had made her decision based on imagining her precious children in a world not of her making, not under her control, not on her terms or the terms of the men and ideas she served. But I wondered, did those men and ideas serve her too? Did the men and women serve each other equally? This is a question echoing through three hundred and fifty years of African slavery on Turtle Island, on top of the ongoing destruction of our Indigenous world, a question of who is served to the point of turning away from the most elemental bond of mother to child, child to mother. This is not the question of the slave mother who kills her new daughter to save her from a life of torture. It is not the question of the Taino mothers who drown their babies to save them from Columbus's hounds. In this killing today, does the woman who is master of death serve the man's ideals, or is there something else? What switch is turned in this mother's heart to accomplish murder for a set of ideas?

The morphine given was explained as inoculation, and the obedient children acquiesced. Only the twelve year old daughter questioned and protested, resisting with an angry look. Goebbels was outside, smoking a cigarette furiously. The mother came out and joined him briefly, waiting for the sedative to expand, then she quickly returned to go about her horrific task as though she were bustling around getting the kids ready for bed. I stood between her and the children and raised my hands, holding her for a moment.

"Are you certain?" I asked, though I already knew the answer, and I could not change what I knew what would be done, but I could not be silent, could not hold my tongue. But it didn't matter. I was a ghost to her, and my words were smoke, nothing more, a disappearing breath on a cold morning. She saw me, heard me, but I did not really exist. How could I? As far as she and history were concerned, I was a hallucination left over from Eva and Adi's novelistic fantasy world, floating through the room where a real job was to be done.

One after another she dispatched the children, an efficient woman fulfilling her destiny and manufacturing her children's passing. Their eyes wavered up into the ceiling in narcotic delirium until the poison hit, then they were shocked into sudden wonder as they faced their hurried deaths. The little one looked at her sister next to her and reached out as though to hold her hand, but the nerves in her body would not work and she fell back away.

Then I was drawn into it too and without thinking, I quickly opened the medicine vial and rubbed a drop into the little girl's mouth. She stared and died as fast as a flash of lightning on a dark sky, and in that moment I saw peace, and I saw another use of this deep green fluid laboriously and lovingly made by Grandmother, a different use, but one that had to come to fruit now in this moment. Following the mother like a nurse on a hospital assembly line, I dispensed the medicine as the children left the world, and they all found something in that moment of leaving. Maybe they were relieved. I could not tell, could not see into them, for the doors were closed so fast, like infants' hearts beat so much more quickly than ours do, exhilarant in the promise and passion of life. Their deaths were like this, urgent and fast as a child's sudden turn while running on a green hillside, chasing yellow butterflies.

The mother had her back turned to me, hovering over the oldest girl, who I could not see, and she was speaking sharply, harshly comforting, exhorting to the child, as I put tobacco and pollen across the other children's eyes, closing them gently. This prayer was fast too, and I came to the mother and daughter quickly as the mother grasped the struggling girl's cheeks in one hand and worked at forcing the capsule between her lips with the other. Morphine clouded the girl's eyes, but she had seen enough through her opium dream. She had seen her brothers and sisters die silently, and she fought for her life, fought her mother's strength with all she had left, her small arms nearly useless, like she was trying to run away in a nightmare, but the limbs just wouldn't work, no matter how hard the mind screamed "Run, Run," and the legs moved in thick dark water, and the body went nowhere.

I grabbed the mother's arm to pull it away just as she forced the capsule in and it broke between the teeth, and in that moment the mother stared at me, tore her arm from my grip, and stared one last look at the struggling child. The girl now began to fall into the cyanide, and her mother ran out the door. The girl looked straight upward, and I poured the liquid into her mouth. Burnt almonds again, the scent of centuries.

The girl saw it all, I am sure, and for her there was no need of reconciliation, but only recognition, for she was the one who did not trust, ever, the one who had the unsure gaze as she watched the parties and sat against her will and comfort on Hitler's lap. She was the one who stared at Eva's camera with distrust, her face turned away, eyes dark and questioning. Now her questions were answered, and certainly she faltered in the enormity of it. What suspicions can be confirmed in a twelve year old girl's mind? What could she see, or what would she see? I could not know, it was all so fast, so frenzied and unnatural. I could only kneel down and stroke her face once, slowly, looking into her eyes gently, then fold her to my breast as she died.

I felt her breath against my hand where I held her against me, her weak grip on my arm, squeezing gently then relaxing, and she was gone.

I burst out of the room furious, flaming, and I did not know myself. I was uncontained, frenetic and intensely focused at once, and I wanted revenge. My mouth was open, teeth bared like a big cat, and I stalked the air bent over and ready. Cigarette smoke curled thickly through the air on the garden slope, and a pistol shot rang out. The mother fell onto her side, onto her smoking pistol, and I ran upslope past Goebbels to her, kneeling in the dirt and grass. I pushed on her shoulder with one hand, pressed her hips over with my knee, and her body fell face open to the sky, heavy and pliant. I poured the medicine quickly, registering how little was left in the light gourd vial, only glancing at the mother's face and eyes. I did not have time for her, and I spun toward where Goebbels stood.

He held a blued Walther in his right hand, only feet from me, and for a second I thought he would shoot me as he raised the tapered snout up off the ground into the air between us. The thought crossed his mind, I could see, but something much bigger was in him, and his eyes shone. His face was blotched with anger and fear, and hours of amazed dismay stretched his skin into sallow colors and shapes, and there was nothing left of the precise beauty he thought of himself as presenting. But his eyes blazed. He was chaos and escape, a once-powerful man realizing his doom, and after looking around this world frantically and finding nothing, he sought and found triumph in the same place he'd always found it, in his imagination. He glared at me, his lips twisted in scorn, twisted in a cold metallic smile that was also somehow warm in its unwavering condescension.

"You can have this world," he said, "and I will have my dignity, my honor, and my glory."

He fired and fell sideways onto the grass, head turned toward me, and I knelt quickly, vial in hand, then the ill wind caught me and I came undone. A quick spring breeze crossed my neck, just a whisper, and I felt the child in my arms, saw the others laid out in a ghastly row, and they joined all the others over the last fifteen years of the Reich, and those faces and thin hands joined all the dreams over the next generations, and those generations echoed back in time across Turtle Island and through all the Americas, all through the world. It tumbled, like it does sometimes, and there is no real escape, no ordering of things, just a mass surrounding me that makes no sense, and it formed itself in the shape of this one thin, bleeding, sneering man at my side, and I lost myself and turned away. I clenched my fists, looked into his eyes and spit on the ground. I said nothing, but I thought it. I thought, "You will get no chance to see. You deserve nothing," and I stood and walked quickly away toward the garden gate between two broken stone buildings, charred bricks dangling around twisted metal re-bar in the faint smell of exploded mortar rounds. My fury burned itself into disdain, and I stomped over Earth cursing under my breath.

Then as I rounded a tall broken wall, I woke up. A captured pocket of mortar smell at the corner lifted out and drove more pungently into my nostrils, like smelling salts waiting in a quiet hidden cloud between the buildings, and it shook me awake, and I spun on my heels and ran back to where the man and wife lay on the ground. Her spirit was gone, I could see it in an instant, and I prayed for him to have even only a moment left, but as I threw myself down next to him, I realized he was gone too, and I was too late. I had pulled the vial and readied it in my headlong run back to him, but it was over, and I had succumbed. Now, as I looked down upon his body, I could see how small he was in death, diminutive even, but I had let it be personal. I had let him penetrate me after all, if even for a moment, but it was a crucial moment, and now it was on me, and he was still inside because I had let myself become him. I reached down and put a smudge of green between his lips, then brushed tobacco and pollen across his eyes as I closed them. I prayed, and my prayer was real, but I knew there was something else awaiting me now, something I could not see, and I hung my head in sorrow.

GOING TO WATER

30

I threw myself over the high cliff with a piercing scream, naked and falling through the icy mist and long reaching fingers of the waterfall, an open mouth of water waiting to suck me into its depths below. But I never wanted to land, not like this. I only wanted to fly and have the home mountain air slice through my skin into my heart. I wanted the mist and water to become Grandfather Tree's strong hands throwing me into the sky, but he had only looked at me and turned away quietly, knowing what had to be done. No one told me. Not Grandmother, who did not smile but only fed me in silence on my return, then walked into the evening forest. The water splashed against my back, my neck, the backs of my legs as I plummeted, and I looked across the tops of tall trees far below and begged for release. Even a flight in the air, even that, could not release me, but I knew the avenues, though I'd never been here before. I knew what I had let happen to me in hatred, and I had to go under the waves of the gauntlet I must shape for myself, for this was no one else's doing and no one else's job to change. I prayed in my fall that gravity would suspend itself on my behalf and give me enough time in the cutting wind to let my shame be carved out from me.

I thought of one of the western Indigenous people, and stories of how when they fell away from themselves, they came back to the people and asked to be lashed publicly, and their own asking was enough to help them carry what they'd done, and in the asking and receiving the sharp bites of hide on their flesh, they could feel the others helping them hold the pain, the mistake, the misdirection that might have been a flight of the moment, but that would change everything for all of them. But my people have no such lash, no whip. We have only the water and our memories. I had forgotten, and now I must remind, remember, put back together what I'd let be torn apart, which was my purpose. I had to remember my purpose, and the frustration was that I knew it all along. I had only let it go for a moment, but that moment exploded like a gunshot, and I had to do something other than to reverse time and change what happened because I know it does not work that way. It cannot be done.

Falling through the Tsalagi air, I thought of African villages and tribesmen with machetes running through villages wreaking havoc, and not so many years later, those same tall dark men standing before the survivors of those raids saying what they did, and what was in their hearts when they did it. They looked at teenagers with severed limbs as they spoke, limbs taken in childhood, and said they were sorry, asked for forgiveness, and in their speaking out what happened, in their voicing the truth in shame, reconciliation could begin for all in the village. No one would forget, but they would know how to carry what was done through the spoken truth. Without truth, there can be no reconciliation. Without truth, there is no revelation, and without that, well, nothing furthers. It's a simple thing.

I thought too of the weathered old Arapaho woman sitting on the steps of the White House on an evening, saying to the newsmen who questioned her presence, along with the presence of her compatriots, all old and concerned, "America will never be free until it comes to terms with us," the enormity of her meaning lost on the men and women with cameras and ignorance in their lenses. "What does she mean? What do they want, those Indians? They have their reservations and their casinos, so what do they want?" She said to them, "You must deal with us for your own good, which is for the good of us all," and that part of her truth disappeared like a misunderstood Zen koan in a stack of papers on an editor's messy desk, like the message of so many Indigenous writers, artists, singers, poets, teachers and healers all across the land, unheard in the land of them and us, us and them. The cold air cut through my eyes as I flew downward. There was a ceremony at Dachau on a rainy summer day, umbrellas of orange, green, brown, black, red, yellow, all pattering steady rain sounds to the strains of a symphony orchestra half-sheltered on an open stage, sheltered only by a slanted tin roof high above, a roof that also sang the rain. Mist circled above the umbrellas, and sometimes the rain stopped, and the sun poured into the large square and made steam rise up from the wet grey ground. Thousands had died here, and now at the turn of the twenty-first century this music played, soaring music composed by a fifteen year old girl who had died here, and the conductor was an old Sufi man who was her uncle. He was old, and sometimes forgot where he was in the music, so the orchestra faded gently, in unison, or held a note until someone could turn the page for him. Nuns prayed in a small cloister on the camp, keeping candles lit, and people from every world faith stood in the rain together, while the barracks and displays taught German school children in smart fresh clothes what had happened. The children saw the pictures, examined the plan as it was written, traced the large map of train tracks leading to the other camps, the map that stretched across the whole wall like it stretched across their known world. Truth, reconciliation. Revelation to the German children.

I kept falling, and I saw fourth graders at Mission San Juan Bautista in California in 2010, all standing in trust before a uniformed ranger who told them the mission was built in the shape of a fort because the padres were afraid of the "Native Americans," a politically correct identity used to mask the cool driven lie she then told them, an incorrect story that the Indigenous people who built the mission did so voluntarily, that they came of their own accord and worked for the padres freely. She went on with stories and analogies to portray a simple, primitive people bought off by baubles and awed by civilization, by "la gente de razon," "the people of reason." Several of the listening children were descendants of those same California Indigenous, and they fell deeply silent into themselves as they listened to the woman with a badge, disappearing from their own existence. This was a cruel fabrication, without the numbers of dead, without the truth of forced labor, forced conversion, whippings, stocks, horsemen gathering whole hamlets under the sword and gun, lashing them together by their thumbs in long lines and marching them to their deaths in pestilent mission barracks not unlike Dachau, barracks with only the reasoning being different. But no, even that was the same, or similar enough when measured in numbers, in percentages of a people dead, and where now was the truth? I saw this as I fell and the water roared around me, and it took so long, and I was grateful for the sound of rain on umbrellas and the flickering of nun's candles on their altar, and the African tribesmen standing in open shame like open sunlight, like water running through the center of the men a great river of understanding and courage.

I plunged into the water and fell down into it until my feet touched the rocky, slippery bottom, and I curled into a ball down there, held my knees in my hands, my head between my thighs, and looked into the darkness with gratitude. I waited and listened to the falls crashing into the surface above and behind me, and the freezing was a good and cold hand holding me there, a hand of mercy, for that was what I needed and asked for, over and over.

GOING TO WATER

31

My hair was still damp, the shining black tips brushing the small of my naked back. I found my Sweet Hunter in his favorite hunting spot, the place he went to provide quiet for himself and food for us. He knew I was coming up on him, though his back was turned. His shoulders raised and lowered, breathed recognition, and I could feel the smile on his face. This was his place, his sanctuary, the center of the world from which his prayers expanded, where his worries for me in my travels concentrated themselves more and more densely until he held them like the knife he held when a lion stalked through the woods near him and he spoke to it. "I am in peace with you, and I am the most ferocious thing you will ever see." Predator speaks to predator in respect, knowing who is food for whom, and who is not. He did this with his fears for me, here in this quiet glen, this hidden gem in the forest. And now I came up behind him and threw my dress onto the ground before him, arching it through the air over his shoulder to where it spread gracefully over the soft cool grass. I wrapped my arms around him and pressed my bare breasts to his back, burying my face in his hair and strong neck.

"Aahh," he sighed and reached up to hold my arms close against his chest and heart, and I felt his tears spring across my bare skin. I held him as though my life depended upon it, and it did. I inhaled and squeezed him into my hungry lungs and pushed his being into the cavity of my chest, stuffing him into me like pushing something precious into a sacred gourd, some herb that must be encased quickly, before its essence dissipates into the air. It's like collecting a certain flower with the wind coming toward it, not from behind, where the human scent would come upon the blossom and change it. Approached rightly, the flower's delicate strength is pure and the medicine will do the most it can. The wind was scant in the forest, but it came toward me, and my Sweet Hunter's essence came to me, and my damp hair fell across him as we clutched each other in desperation and gratitude.

Then, as the forest birds gradually came back into chattering from their watching silence, we became man and woman, and my teeth bit into his neck and I growled our growl, and he pulled me around to face him, looking into my eyes. I grasped his face in my hands, and my pupils constricted just enough so he could see something was in there, inside me, but he stood and picked me up just the same. He did not hesitate, but he saw, and I loved him even more for his lack of hesitation and his not asking anything as he bent forward and laid me down gently on the brown deerskin and green grass. He stood and looked down on my naked body and smiled, then pulled his shirt off and slipped his pants away quickly but without hurry, looking at me the whole time, and I shivered under his beautiful gaze. I reached up to him, stretched my body in memory of what it meant to be with him, a memory of cells all my recent traveling had buried somewhere too deep inside me, and I wondered what I had been doing, wondered in my skin, the skin that was telling me that yes, here is my life, here is my joy, and here is my place. Where else could there be so much? I wandered in recognition of where I'd come back to and where I'd been, and then he was there again, smiling and watching. I arched my back and grinned into the trees and sky, stretching all the other time away, expanding my muscles, and he bent down to me, knees between my thighs, and stroked me with his hands, from shoulders to breast and stomach and hips and legs, one long slow stroke with his powerful, caring hands, and I softened and let the grass smells surround me, as he covered me with his eyes.

I could do nothing but accept him as he looked down onto me, at my feet and calves, thighs and stomach, breast, neck and hair. And when his eyes touched mine again, he saw it again, for I could hide nothing from him even though I knew of no way to tell him, but he did not need to know the people and their stories. Instead, he spread his hands on either side of me, on his hands and knees, and let his soft thick hair brush across my breasts. He smelled between my breasts, down my sides, then up to my neck and each ear, and everywhere he went I could feel his tears warming my skin. Up and down my body he went again and again, following his desire and love and care, touching me everywhere with black hair and silver tears, and my mind remembered, it remembered while my body fell and fell back into itself. And then his lips touched my breast tips, and the memory of where I'd been shot back away, racing into a corner I could not see but only feel as light pulled at me through my nipples and warm water seeped between my legs and the grass smell rose green. He kissed my sex, and my legs fell open, muscles pulsing and relaxing at the same time, and the lurking memory called out dull from behind me, and then he came inside me. He settled on his knees, holding himself just above me with his elbows in the grass, so all of him touched me but his full weight hovered, a hawk motionless in the wind, and his spine was the tail, moving imperceptibly inside, dipping into the breeze, and I was the sky and the day. But the memories called me, of dying children, hatred in the future, a violent dark purple blood stain on a couch, on a grey and black striped shirt, and my hands clenched, my face turning to the side.

Then he was still. I had to speak to him, tell him, but when I turned my face up and my mouth opened he kissed my lips lightly, eyes wide and staring, intent and kind. He stalked the memory that stalked me like it was a broken bear, a renegade in our forest, a man sickened by war who could not be healed in the ceremonies, who wandered the forests alone and haunted, a wounded animal who could no longer fend for itself so was a danger to all. Sweet Hunter looked at me unflinchingly, scanning and ready, and when the memory dashed through my mind he held me closer and came deeper into me, pressing into me. He moved his hands to my face, to where I could not turn away, and he smiled a burning smile I'd never seen, the hunter's smile, and I knew I'd never seen this face because it had never been needed between us before now, but now it was.

The memories were strong, but I dared not think the names, dared not go there. I accepted my protector now as I was protector to him, and we traded then and there, in my surrendering and his seeing, in my surrendering to his knowing even though I could not imagine how he did know. I went out into the world, and he stayed at home, but now he went out into the world through me and brought me back into the home of my body, into the womb from which our magnificent son was born. He searched out intruders invisible to him and vanquished them with his love, and I gave myself suddenly as I realized what he was doing, what he knew.

I called into the sky as he took me and burst into laughter so deep and strong and joyous that my eyes widened in disbelief. I laughed too, and he drove into me then, cupping my shoulders in his hands and flying more deeply into me than ever before. He came to the end of me, the very end of me, and still we found an opening, and what I'd thought was as deep as I could be opened into another layer of expansion, flesh giving way in the center of me, flesh turning into light, and I was even more than that, and he was more than that. We were together, soft, powerful, exploding, muscular, yet in all of it I was giving myself to his purpose, watching his joy, and watching my own ecstasy watching his. I was unmoving and undulant at the same time, still and squirming, the woman he wanted and loved and laughed in sheer pleasure for. We were animals from forever, all humans, and this manner of love gave birth to us as surely as it would make the sun rise whole and burning. In the face of this love, the memories stepped back from us, afraid, away in the darker reaches of my mind, as though they feared so much light, so much fire, so much power, and so much courage, for this is what it's all about, the courage to love, and more, to let ourselves be loved, no matter what.

Then my Sweet Hunter held me, folded me into himself, and I nestled inside his strong arms. I held him too, the very same way, for I knew he needed me as much as I did him, even on this day, and we fed each other time, all the time we needed before taking the next steps toward home. I would have to face myself alone there still, but now his life was alongside mine, separate and joined, and it would not be so hard because of him.

GOING TO WATER

32

She was at the pond's edge, kneeling in the light brown sand, focused on the hand-smoothed earth before her. She turned toward me when I entered the clearing, and I saw what I already knew, though I'd hoped it would not be true. But she held together with me in her concern, for she trusted me now, or at least I thought she had until this point. Yes, of course she did. It was only my distrust of myself that made me think she might lose faith in what we were ultimately doing together. But while all this was true, and while the love was certainly there, her eyes gave away her struggle, the eyes that were her main tools of expression, one open wide in trust, the other squinted down in wondering and trepidation. In her mind, if I would fall, then where would it all go? This is a hard thing for many to understand, how so many rely on even one person, yet it's true. People ask how we can feel freedom with so many counting on us doing the right thing. But the truth is that the freedom is found in the obligation, in the power of the connection across time and individual experience.

It was in her face, and she reminded me of an old Filipino friend, a sparkling old woman whose face changed daily, one eye from the Chinese side of her, and the other

*from what she called her "jungle" side, Aeta. She would
laugh, but it was a way to disperse the pain of her people's
struggle to remain free, or to remain at all, and sometimes
she told me of the dances before fishing, like we do, and of
the herbal healing abilities of her people. She said we were
the same people once, and she was an excellent doctor with
a sharp but kind tongue, and a quick and steady knife with
the herbs. But through much of her early life, she struggled
with the two races in her, despite her growing wisdom, then
finally over time she learned to use the two different eyes
as signs of what was in the air. If she found herself peering
from the Chinese side, she'd look at the world through that
lens to make a decision, and the people who usually came
to her on those days weighed on the Chinese or the Spanish
side, embracing what they called reason and philosophies.
On the Aeta days, when that eye scanned the world full of
so much change, for her Aeta people were now few and not
seen, and they stayed hidden in the mountains all during
the twentieth century and beyond, on those days the people
who came were full of magic and another kind of wanting,
listening, and knowing. They saw things before them, and
asked my friend for her help when they didn't know what to
do, or when they were ill. While I thought of my good friend,
Little Rain looked at me with one eye open and trusting and
seeing, and the other waiting, evaluating, and tense.*

*She turned to her blank slate of sand and began draw-
ing. I walked to her side and watched, bent to where I could
see, but still standing. Faces formed in the sand, skeletal
faces with reaching hands beneath bony chins, but they were
half-formed and diffuse in the sand, and she was hesitant,
not capturing her usual steady and uninterrupted motion.*

She looked up at me then back down. The closed eye reigned for a moment and an outline of a barracks appeared. Then she looked up again, and the Aeta eye took over and when she turned back there was a lone tree behind some lines that turned into outlines of barbed wire, a fence beginning its skinny horizontal stretch of holding people in. She looked up again and both eyes strained, and one was from the dying of the Nazi mother Magda, the wife, the murderer and what she saw as she died. This was the soft eye, a dark brown pupil of compassion and harsh reality, unforgiving but understanding, like the Aeta eye comprehending the forest's labyrinths of experience for all who lived and died there. But the little girl went back and forth, and the other eye went crazy in seeing Goebbel's refusal, a husband's refusal, a father's refusal, and more, she went crazy in seeing my fury and failure, and when she turned and looked up at me, I smelled the pungent mortar that drove me back to myself. Little Rain drew a pistol in the sand, a rough sketch that burned her fingers as they moved through the grains, smoke curling up from the barrel across the faces in the barracks. Back and forth, she looked up at me then down, like a frantic machine, and finally, after a hard stare at what had appeared before her knees, she swept her hands through it all and fell face forward into the sand. She lay motionless, then turned her face to the side, and it was covered with fine brown grains, across her lips and into the damp corners of her mouth, up across her cheek and crusting over her eye. Her hair splayed out above her in a fan, reaching toward the water, her slender neck exposed to me, a fragile and beautiful girl lying before me, her hands clenched in tight fists.

I put my hand on her back, on her cool spine between the tender shoulder blades, as I settled into sitting next to her on my knees. After a moment, she lifted her face up onto my knees and wrapped her thin arms around my legs. She did not look up at me, and for that I was grateful. There was nothing to say to her, and I leaned forward, closer to her, and breathed deeply. She sighed too, and the sound of our breathing was the only sound in the clearing. No birds sang.

GOING TO WATER

33

This is about the despair and how far it's come, how far it penetrates, and what we do about it. It's about the despair I had because my own hatred of Goebbels threw me tumbling away from my own vision, my own task, what I knew in the deepest part of myself was right, what must be done. It's about what I saw in the girl's eyes when I went home and knew I'd failed, and what I felt, alone and for all of us. The Apache, who lives with the despair of the blood war three hundred and fifty years long in his family, who lives with the despair of the killing and dying in the Vietnam war, and with countless deaths and dispersions of the possibility of goodness throughout those times and since those times, sat in a silver Chevy pick-up and said, "We have our sorrow. We all have it. If they all got in their boats and sailed off this continent, I'd be a happy guy, but it's just not gonna happen. We're here together now, and we have to figure out how to do it right."

A group of five young people, kids really, came to the tree house to get me, through the snow and cold. Sunset was near, a grey and somber thing that time of year in the foothills above Fresno, California, in the latter part of the twentieth century. I was staying in a shelter built by a twelve year old boy twenty feet up an old oak overhanging an icy stream. Their friend George had been motionless in fear for hours, they told me, talking of demons out to get him. He was from the nearby reservation, an artist and mixedblood boy of sixteen years, long brown hair straggling down his face, a nice kid teetering between two worlds like so many, too young to have figured out that the two different worlds didn't matter, not finally, that the heart is what we finally see, not the blood or the skin. The evening bite was on the air, and the kids shivered.

"He's been sitting there for three hours," a hard-faced thirteen year old girl told me. These kids were sent from probation departments all over the country, white kids, Indigenous kids, all mixed into craziness together with Jimson weed, Colt 45, LSD, mushrooms, and everything else they could get their hands on. This girl had been around the block at thirteen, thirteen going on seventy, her spirit harsh and condemning yet inexplicably tender and hopeful. The kids all lived together in the mountains in homemade shelters and a few ramshackle farmhouses and barns, with course brown grass, cow trails winding up through the oaks, and crystal green water grottoes hidden beneath innocuous-looking gullies packed over by huge granite boulders. These hidden grottoes held old grinding stones fifty feet under the surface, in broad caverns with high boulder walls, a sharp shaft of sunlight striking down on a flat rock in the middle of an underground stream. Here is where the people had come in the blistering California summers to gossip and grind acorns, and to sing. Now their descendants came with descendants of the settlers to do drugs and try to remember, to think of their parents' sorrow and longing for what had been destroyed with ruthless concentration and purpose, an intention no one at this point in time wanted to think much about. "Let's move on," the teachers said. "Time is a straight line," the pop scientists said. "That was then; this is now," the businessmen said. "There's nothing we can do. It's inevitable," everyone seemed to say. So the kids took LSD in tiny orange barrels and transparent squares the size of a fingernail, drank whiskey and beer, ate Jimson weed, all at once, and attempted to fly from silver granite boulder tops when they got really crazy, and in the hospital later they were silent, all of them captured by the world and by themselves, and no one understood their grief, for it was too long in coming, and they themselves didn't understand it, so there were no words. How could anyone know?

George was glued to a huge oak trunk on a dry patch across a small meadow from tangled brown winter brush, no leaves and plenty of sticks, like a briar patch out of children's books of the times. But it was not a friendly place, no escape. He was stuck to the tree by his terror, which seeped out of every pore in his body, shaking and angry, but more terror than anything else. It all came together in him, what they call history, a preposterous and inadequate word living in this child, and people turned away and acted busy.

"What's going on?" I asked, more just to make the sound than to have any meaning, like reaching out to touch his shoulder warmly. That's all it was, nothing more, just a human sound among the monstrous sounds he heard surrounding his mind.

He pointed with his face toward the underbrush across the way, and clenched the heavy black bark of the oak in his strong hands. A fire had come through decades ago and scorched the tree, but the tree survived, like George's family had, burnt but alive, and now he searched for them, for his gone father, his desperate mother, brother and sister swallowed by Los Angeles, the city of lost angels, having run from the reservation sadness, Indian Territory sadness, long before he himself reached out to this world he made no sense of and got into trouble, trouble that to him was simply firing back into the darkness, into the general area from where the assault had come, the anonymous gunfire aimed at him, and the blanket of invisibility stuffed onto him on his own land. He was just fighting back. But his parents had tried to put it together, white woman and Indian man, and they had loved across the divide, but ultimately it meant nothing to George, so he shot blindly at everyone and anything, and it landed him in Juvenile Hall, next door to doing hard time, and now here he was against the burnt tree in the cold mountains.

I sat down next to him and pushed my body up against him, and he didn't move, but he didn't resist, which was a good response, the best I could ask for. I looked where he was peering and waited, my shoulder and thigh close up against him, and he was pliant and soft but fragile, ready to fly. The other kids walked to the edge of the small meadow and sat, after saying, "We're here, George," and they waited a long time. He didn't acknowledge them, not with a word or glance, but it meant something to him and they knew it, and they didn't leave until they felt it was okay, that he was safe. They were bound to one another despite their collective insanity, one body of six kids, six different ages. They'd brought me because they knew he trusted me in his wild grief, because they felt my grief, then they waited, and they left when it was clear it would take time. It was getting cold. I threw a beat-up wool Pendleton blanket I'd brought over both of us, and we huddled together and watched the night come onto the branches.

The moon rose strong behind us and lit the tangle, and we stared. He looped his arm over my knee under the thick blanket and was motionless for hours. His eyes dropped and mine followed, and we drifted in between the worlds together. My eyes rested, but my experience echoed, looping, with his brothers and sisters in arms here on this mountainside, kids like Lee, the psychopath wielding his Japanese oak staff with deadly skill and accuracy, terrorizing everyone, and everyone giving him space. There were binges hidden away in makeshift shelters, howling at the moon, cold sex on the ground trying to find it at twelve, thirteen, fourteen years old. What could they find? A way to speed up the years, pack in disappointment like nobody's business, and catapult themselves into a semblance of adulthood, all while completely and utterly rejecting the adult world they hated. Indian kids, white kids, mixedblood kids, all living on the reservation called America.

George moved, thrust his hand out of the blanket and pointed. There it was. Something flashed through the thicket, stopped, turned and stared. The outlines of the face melted into the shapes of intertwining bushes, then came back.

"There, you see," he whispered frantically, the whisper almost a voice but subdued by fear that the sound of his full voice would bring the demon down upon him, leaping across the clearing to pounce on him. It was something like an angry animal, or something even worse, something so bad that it would simply dissipate softly, then return to the landscape to quietly stalk him. It would remain only a presence in his mind and heart, something he could expect to return right at the moment of love, or of seeing something good, laughing really, laughing down in his belly. Then it would come, and he would be back into the reality of the quiet, steady, reliable demon.

But the demon had come back again right now and I saw it too this time, shifting behind a tangle, watching us with big oval eyes. It streaked to the left, almost disappearing where the moon couldn't find it, no matter how frantically it reached its blue-white fingers into darkness, then it raced back to the far right equally as quickly, then it drifted back to center steadily, confidently, and peered at us. It had a big round face like the moon, a circular toothless mouth and a mean intention that lay in a straight line across the moonlit clearing to the big oak where we huddled together.

"See it?!" George yelled in a whisper.

"Yes," I said quietly, whispering back, "I see it."

"What are we going to do?" He was in a panic, clutching my knee. The demon was motionless on the other end of a line of hatred, motionless but vivid and real, and the line stretching between us was like the light of an old projector in a theater with people smoking, and smoke lifted up through the light-stream to reveal the source of the images on the screen. A cold mist rose slowly off the grass. Where did the demon begin? In George's mind or in the world he inhabited? It went both ways in equal proportions, as his living thought, because his existence was a shape of its cruel intention. Was it thoughtless? No, it was a logical progression of lies and omission, silent and real in the bush, a stalking kind of thing.

"We have to talk to it," I said, not taking my eyes off it.

"Okay," George said quickly, and I began, and as he heard my words he joined me, entered my voice with his own. We started to talk in hoarse whispers.

"Get away from us," we said again and again, and it moved as though struck by a gust of wind, shifting its weight but staying, dogged in its purpose and long-standing confidence. George was only one among many, and the demon knew this well. It threw kids down long prison wells, tossed them fighting each other into the streets, watching the show like the slave masters pit slaves against each other for sport.

"Go away from us," we repeated in its face, our voices gradually but firmly coming into their own strength, expanding into the moonlit blue clearing.

"Go away from us," we said over and over, and the face and diaphanous body moved back a notch into the brush.

"We are stronger than you." Simple words, over and over. "We are stronger than you."

This was our night chant, thousands of years old in this land, new in this language, and our fathers and mothers knew each other for this time, his and mine, because that's the way the desire works when it realizes it has to make a choice to live, no matter what, no matter when, no matter where.

Not long after this cold evening, in only a matter of a couple of decades, I watched a conversation with a young Indigenous story-teller, who referred to the pollen and tobacco of Indigenous as "shit," and he was speaking to the audience of the whole world. He was said to be the new voice of Indigenous America at this time, and while he seemed in disbelief of it himself, he rode the adulation in a white shirt and blue tie, with a sharp sport coat and a quick tongue, for he'd been given the gift of language. His stories had begun to traverse the globe, stories of reservation life and hopelessness, alcohol and violence, telling "the real story" with a tone people called satire. Things hadn't changed much for many of the kids, it's true, but at the same time, I thought about how the ceremonies could now be done in public, and how people stood proudly and prayed to the directions, used that tobacco and pollen from their hearts, formed Indigenous language pre-schools to bring back their old ways, their values, and they rode and walked the old trails where the killings in America had happened not so long ago, trying to help people see, trying to help themselves heal, not so much to be cured from their ailments, but healed in the mind and heart and memory. They were collecting things important to them and shaping them in ways they could use now, and this story-teller spoke out into the world that had conquered his people, that had forced all of the pain onto the people. He said in his sentences the Indigenous were a "broken people," and it troubled me to hear this said so many times in so many ways, even where it is true. Is there nothing else? Many elderly people turned away from him sadly, and some other story-tellers spoke out and said, "You're telling the white man what he wants to hear, that we are vanishing, obsolete," and he nodded in his writings and said, "Well, this is my life, my truth." They agreed, and they told him he had a responsibility to say more, alongside of his own experience and his right and need to tell it, not instead of it, but to also tell of the children learning their values, spurning alcohol and drugs and self-destruction. "You're the voice now," some people said to him, "whether you like it or not, or agree with it or not, because this is how they see us, as one body of people. We are only one thing to them, the body they have displaced, the 'once-noble' people whose land they now build strip malls and factories on. We are one thing to them, invisible, and you are popular now, and they pay you to tell them it's all okay, that we're sad relics and that nothing can be done. You're the man now, the Indian, so do the right thing." They begged and cajoled and criticized. "Hmm," he said to the story-tellers. "Maybe I'll think about that," and then he made a joke and continued, "and maybe not." Ah. Another story-teller said this young man was a trickster and a heyoka, a contrary and a clown, embodying ancient traditions, and that he was therefore as traditional as the men and women of the directions, tobacco and pollen, but in a modern form, a new form the Indigenous needed, a form the world needed. I thought of the contraries I have known and still know, as I watched and listened to this debate, and I could not imagine them saying the pollen and tobacco and the prayers to the directions were shit, especially not to the whole world through the media. They might tweak a person's sensibilities hugely when needed, turn the world upside down to wake a person up, or bring a laugh when the world was too serious to be manageable on any level, but they would never dismiss the pollen, never talk like this. Was this the trickster, the being acting out in greed and cunning to show us how not to be? Or was this a new Coyote wanting to make a world better than Silver-Grey Fox did? Was this him, wanting all the women to himself, a constant reminder of who we should not be? A heyoka knows his actions must be for the benefit of the people; he sacrifices for it, and I could not understand this young man's laughter in what felt like loneliness, though some young Indigenous men often said he gave them a place for the pain, a place to put it in a moment of relief, a sarcastic chuckle stepping away from all the overwhelming reminders of erasure. Okay. Is this where "Even the drunken Indian has his place," as the poet said? In this, I stand back and listen, since I do not know the pain of their age, though I know George and his demon well, and many others like him. I do not live like him, have not lived his sorrow. Though I see the demon in the thick tangle in the moonlight, I come from another age than this story-teller, so I have to step back from his fire and watch, and listen.

It's the ownership again. That's what it is. That's what I hear. The settlers want to own the Indians in their stories, like they own the mountains and lakes. Can it be this simple? In a large meeting, a mixed-blood college professor complains to the historian at his school that precious few of the students coming into his class know of the boarding schools spanning generations, whose sole purpose was to obliterate the cultures. They don't know of the forced sterilizations in the twentieth century, the violations of 'rule of law' in all the broken treaties, the statistics of his day in the twenty-first century, the ones that show one third of Indigenous women will be raped in their lifetimes, and eighty five percent of the rapists will be non-Indigenous men, most of whom will not be prosecuted because of confused jurisdictions in a divided land, divided by the illusion of unity and the overbearing silence. Because they don't know the history, they will not understand the young storyteller, and if the Apache was right that day of anger, they will not care enough to find the history. The storyteller says the same thing, that America will never look at its genocide, yet these two men are far apart in how they live, one by his quick wit and cleverness and books, the other by the tobacco and pollen and ceremony handed down for generations in his family. Both know pain very well, and into this deep struggle within these Indigenous men, the history teacher announces that he feels defensive listening to the list of Indigenous issues the students do not know about. He does not speak of the mixedblood professor's pain in this, how he might feel defensive too, attacked by the absence of historical fact or even discussion of it in his life in a modern college, attacked by the abyss in a place of learning and understanding how we must do better. Trapped in his own legacy, as deeply as the Indigenous are trapped, and while being a very good man, the historian still does not think of how the Indigenous man must feel about his very survival in this strange world, where somehow it's all called real, this absence and erasure, and Indigenous people are silently asked to swallow it and be still, and be silent themselves. The mixedblood professor tries to answer the historian's feelings quietly, kindly, as he was taught, and all those who taught him stride through his mind. He thinks of his grandfather, born in 1894 in Indian Territory, chased out of the land the Tsalagi were forced onto by the Trail of Tears only decades before, scattered by the move West and the white man's thirst for oil on land promised "for as long as the grass shall grow and the wind shall blow," and this is the man who brought him up, taught him steadily into Tsalagi thinking from 1949 until now, and it continues long after his death, never going away. The professor thinks of his mother's words to her father when he was five, when he finally retreated from the world out of frustration. "Our way of life is dying. You raise this boy, and teach him." He thinks of his grandfather's mother, staring strong and resolute out of a picture in an old cane rocker on his desk at home beside a stack of papers to correct, a woman who saw all the ravages of Manifest Destiny, a teenage girl during the Civil War, a child who endured it all, who saw them all on horseback and in wagons ripping through her life so hard she could only hunker down and watch them all, all of them frantically killing in their search for a better life for themselves, not for Indians. She watched the ragtag veterans, the Buffalo Soldiers, all the entrepreneurs of Indigenous destruction, and her eyes grew hard, but she held onto her love, and when she became a woman she loved a courageous English farmer who came through with kind eyes and a song and his own story, and they became share-croppers of corn, the ancient seed of her people. She lived through everyone tearing through her tenderness, and still she taught her sons what it meant to stand on the earth rightly, in respect, honestly and with care for all good people. This is our history. This is the mixedblood professor's story, but the silence around it is okay, needed even, to keep the central machine oiled and smoothly running, the perfect dream with only jocular rough edges to talk about. Even in the twenty-first century the position of power is not transparent, not seen in the room, not when it comes to the person, in the face, to me, to mine, to what I do to you, what you do to me. Who thinks the Indigenous man might feel slighted or personally insulted by the burden of the status quo? Very few. Ah, it's all gone away, I think when I watch this program, and I think maybe the young story-teller is right. Maybe he's right after all. It's all shit, all lost, and you just have to watch out for Number One. And then I wonder what I'm doing here.

But I look onto a shelf when I get back to where I'm sleeping, back from observing that curious school meeting, and I take down a stone George gave me, a dark blue stone he sent me a year after that night against the cold winter oak. I pick it up and feel its smooth round body and think of the young boy's hands. He'd left the ranch shortly after our night at the tree, left the mountain where we met and talked, and gone on long walks into the wilderness. He left and went to an art school in San Francisco, and one year later he sent me a single message in the shape of a stone. He had one of the kids search me out where I'd gone down to the coast, deep in the towering red-wood trees. On one side of the stone is the face of the demon, glaring and hard, and I stare at it, feeling the strength of the fingers that shaped the image in rock. I turn it over and look at the flip side, and it's the same face, but no longer a demon. The eyes are softened into slits, and the mouth is shaped into a gentle smile. I turn it over and over, this side and that, and as I turn it, I see a streak of gold in the dark stone, a clear and strong brush of pollen George put there when he finished the carving and sent it my way, pollen from San Francisco, a bright city pollen that penetrated the carving and never left it. You see, the boy had found his way home amongst tall buildings and grey sidewalks, amongst shadowy homeless wanderers, and in this I know what is most deeply true. The medicine is everywhere, not to be denied for long, no matter what the pundits or coyotes might say on their way to the Bank of America, in this strange epoch, this culmination.

GOING TO WATER

34

A broad alluvial fan spread before me toward a wide, powerfully flowing dark green river. The mountains were behind me, and I was exposed to the sun and flat plains beyond the river, endless flat plains, as though I'd come on a long journey to another world, but it was this one, my Earth. Grandfather had put me on my own, and Grandmother too, with a touch on the shoulder and a kind look. They weren't rejecting me, but they recognized that I was not with them in the way I needed to be, that I was still undone. It wasn't about finding myself alone, for I could never be alone, but there was something more I needed to see in the whole collection of my life, not isolate, but together in its enormity, in order to bring back my power. Leaving one's own values is nothing to shake off and walk the other way from. My family understood this too, watching me tend the fire with deep concentration on the tip of the burning red poker, the red glow holding a million thoughts from somewhere else, and I had to hear Unole's questions twice before I could answer them, so he looked at me with a quizzical smile. Despite Sweet Hunter's powerful love, his dragging

243

me into myself laughing, and the town's welcoming me gladly in feast, and despite the ceremony and the leap through the water, I still tilted back over into astonishing fear. It was my own doing, the place again where fear and hatred came together, and disdain too, the pesky cousin that likes to remove herself from the immediate fury and sit in complacence, surveying the kingdom of her own misery with a knowing smirk. I disdained Goebbels, and I disdained the evolution of the decades following him, for I thought far too little had been done to unveil the depth of the problem, the source of the horrible disease. I gazed out toward the river and searched inside myself.

An old man crouched at the rapidly-flowing river's edge, dangling a long stick into the eddy along the muddy sides. Hot yellow sun poured down, and a broad rain squall moved steadily over the plains beyond us in the distance, vertical columns of rain pouring grey lines down from tall thick clouds, black on the bottom and brilliant white on the top. A distant broken rainbow straggled along behind it like an old, once magnificent dog.

I squatted for a long while and watched him from a distance. We were the only forms sticking up from the brown flat soil, lines of water snaking through the sand toward the river, and we two were the only things upright but for an occasional lost and bare tree branch. Sweat beaded on my face and arms, and my feet ached from days of traveling, and I tucked my bundle onto my lap, watching the man. He had power, I saw this, but it was not good, so I watched and waited. Then he turned and beckoned me with his stick, and in that moment I knew he was part of why I'd come here, part of why I'd left the comfort and safety of home. It was clear, like an appointment, but an unknown or forgotten one I suddenly remembered with a start. I watched for some minutes more, and he did not raise his black stick again, but the invitation hung in the steamy air, so I rose and stepped carefully toward him.

When I reached him, he did not turn around, but continued his dangling of the stick in the water. It was not an aimless movement. I could see this as I squatted next to the river's edge a few feet from him. The long curved stick dipped its sharp point into the whirlpools in the eddy before us, one after another, the green water sucking around the stick noisily for a second before the whirlpool disappeared. It was as though he was taking the swirling power into his stick, but I saw he was breaking the circles apart, and then I realized he was doing both things. I am not a magician or healer, only a traveler and dispenser of medicine, but I knew the acquisition of power when I saw it. I waited, strangely unafraid, just as I had been on the slope above the Berghof. But this was not the witch. It couldn't be, because the witch was still developing in our time, a relative fledgling. He had not progressed into the full-blown monster yet. This was another person entirely.

"I'm glad you could make this meeting," he joked, turning suddenly toward me, and I saw a broad smile on a face that was both young and old at once. "I've been wanting to talk to you." He knew me, yet I didn't know him, despite a certain familiarity that unnerved me. There was no point in asking him who he was because that would be revealed or not, and perhaps his identity was not what this meeting was about. That much I wondered about, though I could not say why.

"What do you want?" I asked, just to open the door, and he smiled and chuckled.

"Oh, it's not what I want that's important, but what 'they' want, isn't it?" He would talk in riddles, but the words were quickly not riddles. He spoke into my pre-occupation.

"They are caught in their time, and acquisition is what their time is about, among all the other things that come with acquisition, which are many, and that's nothing simple or cliché." He turned his sparkling blue eyes away from me, back toward the river, blue eyes, dark brown skin, black hair and a woven brown robe tied with an embroidered belt, flowers in needle-point designs blended with ancient shapes from rock walls. Who was this man?

"You don't recognize me?" he asked. "No, I suppose you would not, being so new and young. And it's true I've never come this way before. I've never had to, but now because of you, we have this meeting. And there is much to discuss. That is, unless you simply want to listen and defer, which is what I advise, of course."

"Who are you talking about? Who are 'they?'" I asked, goading him, though I knew, and he laughed at my clumsiness. I felt out of my league with this man, and I searched my memory to find those eyes and the confident smile that were before me now, but there was nothing there, nothing jumping out in revelation.

"I repeat to you that they're caught in their time, centered around it as though it is the only thing that matters. They imagine themselves the head of the flying arrow, and the wind blows by their forward-facing cheeks intoxicatingly." He laughed, still facing the river. He pointed in the direction of the river-flow with his stick, "That way. It all goes that way." The river went to the sea, but that is not what he meant. His meaning stopped in the direction we could see, as though there were nothing more. One direction only.

"Once people were smarter," he said, "when they had to use their wits to survive, when each individual would only survive if he could sense the world around him. The individuals who could sense the world could feed the children and could stay alive. The foolish and stupid ones wandered without thought into the path of the saber-tooth and were eaten, so the smart ones survived. You know this. You see the difference, don't you? Today the stupid are protected from harm, and so the stupidity goes on."

I knew this story. I'd read it in a magazine from up there, but this man hadn't read it. He knew it like I knew it without reading it as a sardonic theory about human evolution.

"They think it's all gotten better. And that they are more advanced." At this he laughed and turned to me again, his mirth deep and genuine, from the belly. He had to contain himself, it seemed, putting his free hand to his stomach to calm himself. He squatted still, his robe covering his feet, and he was strong on the ground.

"You are here today because you know better, that they're not advancing. And you know this because you yourself fell to what they've done with themselves. You got too close. You fell to it, ran back away from it, tried to fix it too late, and now you go in and out of it, and you're tired. You're very tired, like they are, because going in and out of it makes you weary, and you want to give up the struggle but you can't. You know you can't, but you don't know what to do. You're tired, but you can't sleep your way clear. Your sleep turns on itself." He did not laugh then, but turned on his feet in the slippery wet soil and pointed the stick in my direction. Murky water dripped from the tip. He circled it slowly, like he did with the whirlpools just before they vanished.

Though I'd already known it, I admitted to myself that although I did not know him, I knew his sources, that he moved freely too, or at will, but what his will was, was not clear to me, and as the stick turned, my stomach followed it toward nausea. I opened my palm toward him softly, warding him off, discreetly from between my legs, behind the folds of my gown, and he smiled and turned back to the river with his stick and his eyes.

"I know what you think," he said, "and what you feel, so you should just talk to me."

"I don't know who you are," I said, "or what you want."

"Just tell me what's in your heart," he repeated. "I run parallel to you, so you can tell me. It's all right."

What did he mean by that? Of course I knew. The warm mud of the riverbank oozed up around my moccasins, and the water began to seep through to my skin, starting as moisture, then it became water, warm between my toes. My muscles ached from squatting so long, so I shifted my weight from foot to foot. The man glanced at me, smiled again, and turned away.

"I am not the enemy," he said. "I know you very well. I know it's the despair that's eating at you. It's the scalps in the president's parlor, behind polished glass on neat mahogany shelves, isn't it? And his bridle made of human skin?" He turned back again. This was his method, looking away, speaking softly but powerfully, shooting back with his blue eyes, black hair hot in the glaring sun, his lips young and old, old and young, a shifting kind of man.

"Yes," I said, "that's it. That, and the hopelessness, and it's different in the two worlds, Indigenous and white, a different kind of hopelessness, and yet they blend into each other and rise out of each other."

"Exactly." He had me now, so he turned entirely toward me and thrust his stick into the mud beside him, leaning on it slightly to talk. He shifted his weight too, like I had, his back toward the blazing sun now, and he pulled his robe open at the top of his chest, open enough to let the still moist air against his skin. He had a strong neck, and like his face, it was both old and young, experienced, smooth and resilient-looking. He went on.

"It's the two worlds, and how the despair weaves between them. The world you come from feels the pain of the difference, remembering what was, remembering in the blood, and it screams out in pain until it cannot scream any more, then it falls into the despair. You see the children jumping off cliffs in themselves and in the mountains, trying to find the world their hearts know is there, but they can't find it." He paused, a strange smile lighting his face, not at what he was describing, but at something I could not find, like a pleasure in his fatal vision, like the realization of an end-game in chess. It was a comfort that there would be an ending, just that, an ending. He smiled.

"The world you don't come from, the world that came to you from across the ocean feels the despair too. It feels what it did when it hit your shores, a reflection of what it had done to itself long ago, and what had been done to it too, and it feels what it continued doing when it spread across your lands, and it knows the loss in its blood too. It knows your loss and its own, and it knows how they are intermingled, impossible to separate. Those children are reaching for it too, trying to find the world they know is there, but they can't find it either. And it keeps on going, like something trying to re-create itself, perpetuate itself, despite its ever-deepening sorrow. It keeps on running headlong into doing the same thing over and over because it can't help itself, like an old dog chasing its tail." He smiled again, the same smile of pleasure with finality.

"In both worlds," he added, "it will be finished, and when it's finished, Agana, why, then you can rest." He nodded, almost grinning, his smile friendly and reaching toward the comforting smile of an elder, one who has seen so much that it stills the frightened and anxious younger heart. Everything comes into perspective in that old smile, the whole world becoming much larger than my own small problems. But behind the smile something else was lurking, and I would not be easily fooled, not again, not so soon after I had fooled myself so catastrophically.

I realized he was following me, dipping into the thoughts about everything I'd seen, things about the movies I'd seen in the other times, even things tucked away in the minutia of particular times and events, like how the white critics said a movie about a young Indigenous man's suicidal despair was unrealistic. "A Native American would not feel such a level of despair," they intoned authoritatively. What could those critics know of Indigenous despair, or more, what right or ability did they have to define it? This movie, the medium of most influence in the world, was made by two of the most famous actors of the time, almost as famous as Will was in his time, though for very different reasons. But even with their collective fame and money, talent and vision, they could not show Indigenous reality and have it be seen, could not reach down the throat of modern twentieth century Turtle Island and pull the heart up and out into plain vision. They could not expose the momentum of the beast and the despair he caused, the despair that kept us all apart.

The man squatting next to me in the mud had followed me at the mission in California too, listening to the ranger lie to the fourth-grade children, watching their confusion and submission. "They built the mission as a fort because they were afraid of the Native Americans," she said. Then, "the Native Americans volunteered to build the missions." Where did the idea about the fear go then? Where is the thinking, the follow-up, the logic? Eight year old children must simply accept, no matter how little sense it makes even to them, for they are simply children living at the bottom of the ladder, with no smile.

And where were the numbers of people who died and continued dying? Where were the connections between Goebbels and the men who killed a hundred thousand Mayan peasants right under the chin of the twenty-first century, and where were the teachers and world courts and nations and those who could shift this huge boat in another direction? These were little things, daily things, Indians as mascots and butter containers and people of ancient worlds living today on top of oil reserves in the jungles, people as things, people in the way, a collection of unnamable tortures refined down into toilet paper labels and oil smoke snaking through green tropical leaves, all connected, connected in my mind, in my bursting imagination.

"You're right," the man said, "it is an important time, and all your thoughts are little more than minuscule thoughts on the surface of a gigantic underground lake so big you could never conceive it. You're right about it all, so now you should listen to me well and find comfort in what I'm telling you. Listen carefully."

He became grave then, still leaning on the black stick, tilting ever so slightly in my direction. He spoke slowly, enunciating each word carefully, giving each word its own power. "Go home and tend your fire and forget it. Forget them all. Live your own life, and find your love where you know it's real. It's a choice they've all made and continue to make, so let them live and die in it."

The rain squall had disappeared, and the clouds retreated to the very edge of the horizon, where occasional flashes of lightning played with the light sky. Green grass turning brown in the irrepressible heat spread from the other bank of the river as far as I could see, without end, so flat it showed the nearly imperceptible curve of the Earth curling down at the edges like a rueful smile.

I closed my eyes against the sun, now descending from its apex, creeping down the sky to the west. I saw Will's face, and the Apache, Unole, Grandmother and Grandfather, and Little Rain, and Betty's chiding smile and finger pointing at me, telling me to sleep well in their house above the sea, piled into plush down comforters. I saw George's face and hands, and then a dignified man in a boat wearing a robe and ceremonial hat, followed in his course across a bay by other boats like his, carved from trees and adorned with animal faces, fish faces, and behind him there were speedboats and fishing boats with high cabins and trawling poles reaching high into a grey sky, fishermen watching the Indigenous reclaiming their sea. I saw allies, white people and black people, and brown people with resolute eyes, and paler mixedblood counterparts too, holding unerring bows and rifles in simple defense of what is right, and I took a deep breath on the hot riverbank.

"There are no allies," the man said, reading my mind, and he pulled his stick out of the mud with a sucking noise and made small circles in my direction. He focused his blue eyes on mine. "No allies." The stick circled and his eyes smiled sadly, knowingly, secure in their reality. "Believe only what you see in front of you," he said softly, "and we both know what that is." He smiled sadly. "You are alone, and that's as it should be. In fact, as you well know, being alone is actually quite beautiful. It is absolute, vast and beautiful. It is the magnificent face of creation itself. You know this."

He shifted his weight and reached his hand out to touch me, a familiar and soft hand, but I pulled away, for when he moved, his robe opened away from his feet and I saw his soaked moccasins, and his breasts budding out where the robe had opened too far. He quickly pulled the robe shut, but it was too late, and in the sudden movement he lost his secure footing and thrust one foot out to steady himself. I saw the small quill design on the upper part of his foot, my own yellow and black pattern against the wet deerskin I knew so well, and when I looked into those sharp blue eyes then, he knew I saw him, saw who he was. With that sudden clarity, we both stood erect at once, facing each other, my dark eyes, his bright blue, staring into the mind we shared, and I quickly put my hands on his shoulders without any resistance from him, grasping him firmly. I shook him, his hair tossing back and forth with the motion, and his face was expressionless but very present, waiting in the mirror. I smiled, not a smile of pleasure, but simply of recognition. There would be no end game today. Not today.

GOING TO WATER

35

She's a small woman in stature, this young Anishi-naabe fighter, but huge in spirit. She stands one day at the edge of her people's lake, a blue lake that owns the people rather than the other way around, watching with a smile that rises from the bottom of her belly as the rice harvesters paddle out in their canoes into the tall full rice plants. On another day she stands erect and intense, yet relaxed in her firm conviction, before a polished old courtroom, before a judge who does not understand how a lake can own a people. It may be that, as a wrinkled and tired old man, he might come to it at this point in his life, where he has seen so much senseless but logical loss, but the tradition of law he obeys does not see it, and he must return to that legacy to call up his decision and his position, the rigid position of his culture. It's strange that his culture does not even define itself as a culture except for in its music, popular music and blues and jazz. These are the famous signatures, but law and property, decid-edly cultural positions, are defined only as what's right, ontological even, given, evolved and evolving from a moral base that is assumed and never defined

256

but for in position after position, the posture that too often gives those who wield the gavel what they want. Again, I am struck by the strangeness of it, but no longer surprised, and this small, beautiful woman standing square-shouldered in front of it all, in front of the centuries of it all, fills me with pride and gratitude.

When the harvesters return, the smell of the rice fills the air, and there are tired smiles and celebrations. They are not rich, but they have survived, and they continue to survive, for through their very strength of spirit they have convinced the law the rice is theirs, for almost two hundred years, in trade for almost all of their land. They have found enough like-minded old white men to form a trail of precedent that holds precarious sway from 1837 to the first decades of the twenty-first century. They climb into old Ford pickups and make their way home, a man driving with one hand and caressing his wife's knee with the other, glancing to her as they remember all the years of poling through the shallows, carefully threshing the grains from the plants overhanging the canoe bottom. They recall not only their own years, but the years of all those before them. Reflections of long walks home carrying hand-made baskets shine off the truck's dusty windshield, and they smile the same smile the young woman does, from deep within where their lives begin.

In the courtroom, young finely dressed lawyers who are not owned by a lake, but by pages in a book and their own deep desires, tell how their clients can grow wild rice in paddies in California and market it as "wild" rice even though no Indigenous people grow or harvest it. "It's a term," they argue to the old judge, "owned by no one in particular." "Wild." Their clients took precious kernels and put them in their test tubes, Petrie dishes and centrifuges and planted their grim-faced engineers in the genetic stream of forever, and the engineers spun round and round like kids in a tilt-a-whirl at a cheap carnival, and came out smiling, with "wild" rice in their hands. And then they named it, and sold it in plastic bags with pictures of Indian canoes, two people to a canoe, paddling softly into the lakes. The Anishinaabe woman, and many alongside her and before her said "No," and the smiles fled the engineers' and accountants' and artists' faces, and everybody went to the big stone courthouse to decide between right and wrong, simply because there is no shame in those who think they own the land and the lake and the sky.

I stood beside her one evening as the boats came back, as she watched her teen-age son empty their own canoe of the rich, nutty brown and tan harvest. I had been looking for her because I had to feel her strength, woman to woman. I hoped it would not be a one-way thing between us, me taking from her out of my own need during a hard time.

"This is good," I said, "that you are fighting." For me, two hundred years was both very long and very short, the time it takes to take a breath, to glance from here to there.

She looked up at me in silence before she spoke, a calm expression on her face. She nodded toward her son, who worked silently without his cell phone or iPod, listening to the others working and laughing, and to the sound of grain on old wood swishing into evening. Tiny flying insects of many kinds rode paling light. She nodded.

"We've been fighting this fight for a very long time," she said. "Centuries."

Later, as we sat at the lake's edge, looking across it and back to each other, she told me that most of the world's diverse life forms, plants and animals, live on land inhabited by Indigenous peoples, some ninety percent. She told me in her fact-filled, strong and gentle voice, while the sun dropped lower, that food corporations and medicine corporations were going into these lands with lawyers and scientists to buy patents, the rights to own knowledge exclusively, knowledge Indigenous people have held and shared for thousands of years. She said Indigenous people were banding together now, and that they must continue to band together to fight this intrusion, because as the scientists twist the inheritance, the lifeblood of the plants, they play with things impossible to know, simple things like where an adventuresome blue-necked duck might fly with a sterile pollen, a completely twisted concept of contradiction, for how and why might pollen be sterile and have no power? They toy with more complex things too, like where wind might carry something they've made that is mechanical and deeply internal and mysterious, a tiny grinding steel thing like the tilt-a-whirl, a shiny steel face of one grinning particle of pollen, one "crazy" particle tossed into a world that has been stabilized forever by simple respect and admiration and sunlight and rain. What might happen in this meeting?

She told me all of this and more, for hours, as though spilling so much of what she knew of time and science was casting it out into the world for all people to hear and know, out through a horn of plenty. I was a vehicle to her, though she did not know me, and as she talked and night came on gently, with the lake lapping at the shore only feet from where we sat, I thought of where knowledge comes from, how it takes form, finds a voice, then flies like pollen from plant to plant, mind to mind, imagination to action, and I felt good, even redeemed by so much of what she brought to the world out of her own simple desire to live the way she had to. I thought that all of her knowledge and caring could only return to both of us. It could never have been one way between us, not with this woman, and when she finally went on her way with a departing nod and warm smile, I knew how deeply she was an ally, not only of mine, but of everyone. In this, there is great comfort and more. There is possibility.

GOING TO WATER

36

It was a conference call of sorts that brought me back to Will, Johnny, and the Apache, a racing through time to get the strength I needed, and I told them everything for the first time, about how I fell from myself, from what I knew was right.

The Apache listened and growled because he sees all sides of what's happening, the forward and the backward motions of the time he's trapped in, and his heart chafes at it, chafes away as he tends the place of wonders and miracles, the lodge, blesses the stones on the wooden pallets, straightens a length of wood waiting to make a cradle for the stones from Akoo-Yet, Mt. Shasta, pulls black plastic tarps over the firewood before cold winter rains. He sings under his breath and dusts it all with pollen, and then he goes to work in an old Dodge truck, a slant six that'll last forever, or at least as long as he needs it, which is his lifetime. He sings songs thousands of years old, even older than the rusty Dodge, but he still smiles when the spark plugs ignite and the engine fires to life. "You believe in people," he said to me, touching my arm. "And that's a good thing." He smiles. Rock and Roll bounces off

261

the bare metal insides of the truck, and he is caught by its exuberance and love of living. He remembers sitting on a rock in Apache country looking in all directions, knowing that someone of his kind, his family, has sat on that very spot for thousands of years, and he drives to work, to the job he must hold now, as one of those same people.

Johnny listened and smiled because that is what he does in life and in death. He nodded as I talked, offered me a glass of fine-tasting sake, looking out the window of his room onto the garden below. He said little, only putting comments in where needed, "You missed it," he said, raising his eyebrows. "That's okay. We do that sometimes," he said, then listened some more. Because of his style of talking, I too said little, but just enough, and I came to him not because of what his words might be but because of his stillness, and because next to the stillness was a bubbling laughter, a giggling at so much of what was happening in his time, which was now my preoccupation, for it was into this time that I'd lost my resolve despite where I could see it going. I didn't need consolation, an impossible thing anyway, but another ear, like the Anishinaabe woman's voice stating facts and directions, admonitions, and by talking with Johnny, my feelings found form and direction. "We do that, and it's okay," he said, knowing I knew it wasn't okay, and he also knew that it wasn't okay, but it had happened. "Yeah, you can't stay there," he said. "There's too much at stake." He nodded at the sake glass. "You want more? You okay?" "Yes, I'm fine," I replied, looking into the half-full blue cup, a standing white crane painted on its side. Alongside his giggle at it all was a clear shining tear, and the powerful resolve of a solid, stocky man who had played offensive line on a football field full of tough brown boys full of rage, confusion, hope, and promise all mixed together in a potent brew, the pigskin the place where they resolved it all, crashing into each other with loud grunts and snarls and helmets clashing, surrounded by agricultural fields that feed America, fields they and their parents worked. This was there next to the quiet poet, the man who gave meaning to the term "gentleman." I sipped my sake, a refined taste of rice from across the sea, and I listened, domestic rice refined by the right thing to do this day, echoes of wild rice reaching into a lakeside night, rock and roll and Apache songs, and Tsalagi songs all dancing with each other.

Will listened to my story carefully, hands folded on the big oak dining table, then he motioned me outside. I had stretched all my rules and told him everything, how and why I moved in time, and I showed him the medicine vial, a huge thing I thought I'd never do, but he just leaned forward and smelled it, sniffing carefully at first, then inhaling deeply.

"You've got a beautiful mind," he said, but his face was troubled. How could he know what I was really saying or doing? We sat at a picnic table in bright filtered sunlight under soaring green pepper trees, and his strong fingers folded together again, turning around each other slowly. He sat for a long while before speaking again.

"You know, the world's doing strange things these days, murders for oil in Osage country, putting so many kids away in what they call schools but that ain't schools at all, burying the languages and ways people pray. It's just never stopped, is all."

I waited and watched his thoughts build under the overhanging long-fingered leaves that reached down and pointed at us, drifting back and forth in the occasional breath of wind.

"You say you travel in time, and I'd guess I know what you mean, though you got something different in your eyes when you say it, that's certain. It's something mysterious you got. But you make me think about what I do out there in the world, about the blessing I've been given, and how I think about that very thing, about time, and about where we live."

He pursed his lips, then smiled at me. "When I go to Indian country, not that all of this ain't Indian country, but when I go to where the people live in the hills the way they used to, I see it and feel it, and I know that what I do and what they do is connected real close. Sometimes when I'm flying, way high up there where I can see the whole world laid out beautiful before me, I look down and I swear I can hear some old woman or old man singing somewhere where they can't be heard, somewhere safe. It's in my mind, and that makes me feel good. It stretches me, like being up there in the plane does, into a bigger way of seeing."

He looked at me with a big question in his expression, one needing no answer from me because I couldn't answer for him anyway, and it was his own question. But he was still wanting something from me, like I was from him, and we circled around it.

"I'm proud of being Cherokee," he said, coming to it, "and I'm proud of my people for having survived, but I know there's folks out there I've never seen who got a better handle on all of this than I ever will. I think of them when I get up on that stage in Hollywood or New York or London, and I give 'em a silent nod because if it wasn't for them, I wouldn't be here."

"You get me thinking, Rain, and it comes down to this. I see Indian people in many places in the world, and they ain't called Indians but for here in America, and there's something the same in their eyes, and it gets me thinking, like you do. And here's what it comes to. They've all been on that piece of land for longer than modern man can think of with his calendars and all, and because they've been on that very same chunk of land, more or less, well, that does something to 'em. They get to know that land, and they form a friendship with it. They ain't enemies of that land, but friends, because over that much time, they got to be friends or they just wouldn't make it. They ain't just passing through. They may tussle with their neighbors time and again, but with the land, it's different. They go way back together, and because of that, the people see time different, different than someone who moves from place to place. Words like 'always,' and 'forever' got a meaning to them, something like how fifty different words for snow are said by people who live in snow all the time."

He looked at me with that question again, and I grinned at him. "That's it, Will. You're right. It's a different way. Very different."

"It's in their eyes, Rain, I tell you. And it's in how they value each other. They use words like 'we' a lot, referring to each one of themselves, and I get back in the airplane after visiting some of them somewhere in the world and think about some of the Cherokee I know who talk like that too. Now, I ponder on it, and looking out the window at the clouds, I figure that if you see time as forever and your place as forever, why, then you got to treat each other different somehow, because there ain't no place else to go, and all those people and their kin is going to be around you and your kin forever, so you think on things different, maybe being more careful."

I leaned across the table and put my hands on his, holding them firmly. What would I do without this man? He went on.

"This is what I see on our home country with them Dakota fighting for their hills in the court the last sixty years and more, them folks up in the lakes fighting for their right to live off that rice, fighting in the courts for a hundred years, and it seems they each all think about how their fight fits into the other's fight, coast to coast, and they talk about that. So I go out into the world in a different way, into the craziness of what's happening in Europe now, and in China. Now I can't believe what I see happening in China with that invasion by Japan, and it scares me deep, real deep because of what I see in the soldiers' eyes, or more what I don't see in them, and I told the president that, and I'll tell you, Rain, he's worried too. The whole world's worried about what's going on."

His hands came apart and formed fists on the rough table, and he pounded a slow rhythm gently before he brought them together again.

"It's a perplexing thing," he said, looking up into the sunlight streaking through the trees above us, then straight back at me. "The Indian people got to fight for their own rights here on their own land, where they been forever, with the country that says it's here for their own good but keeps proving it ain't. It don't make sense. And at the same time, I'm telling the politicians this country's got to build a bigger navy to protect itself against the craziness I see happening out there in the world, and I say it because I live here, and my people live here, and I'm an Indian, on top of it all. What kind of sense does any of it make?"

He shook his head and bowed it down to where his forehead lay on his folded hands, and the smile was gone even before his head dropped, far away, and I missed it, missed that sparkle in his eye. It frightened me to see a man this big of heart and mind disappear into himself so suddenly, and I looked at myself to see whether I'd made it happen, but it was clear this was him, his reflections, his vision from up there in the sky he loved to see things from, his hideout and his vantage point. I stood quickly and moved around behind him to wrap my arms around his shoulders and lay my head next to his. He took a deep breath and sighed big, then his hands reached up to hold my arms, his elbows on the table, head still bowed, but his voice was strong.

"I thank you, Rain. You keep on it, keep doing it," he said, "and I'll do my part too, the best I can. We're in it together, and we sure do need each other. All over the world now."

A wind swirled in the overhanging tree, and errant pepper pods bounced down off the table top with a quiet chatter. The smell was pungent and bright, like the southern California sunlight shining down on us so far from our original homeland. I thought for a moment that we were home just the same, but it was only a strange kind of traveler's longing, like a brief kneeling on the ground to remember where we were coming from, and the place we hoped to return to, one way or another.

GOING TO WATER

〜〜〜〜〜〜〜〜〜〜〜〜〜〜〜〜〜

37

I found her at the pond's edge, predictably, where her family said she'd been constantly these days, working on a large painting in the sand. The sun was straight overhead, yellow light falling down through broad-leaved ash trees onto her workplace. She was deep in a painting, and her body glowed in the dappled light, even where dark shadows danced across her shoulders, her bent-over back and loose hair in a barely audible breeze, a whispering breeze. She knew I was there, and I thought I saw the corners of a smile, but it could have been shadows because when I got to her, her face was like always, not expressionless but impossible to define, impossible to discern what was behind her look and the firm set of her mouth. She looked up, nodded, and kept on with her work. I settled in next to her and studied the delicate images before her knees.

Instead of forming out of the pond's edge this time, the painting was a circle unto itself, a full footstep away from the water. There was a broad lake in the top center, moving out toward the dark borders defining the circle. Two canoes, with small stick figures in them, paddled into tall thin plants reaching out from the lakeshore toward the center. As I realized what she was drawing, sifting fine

269

sand through her hand onto the surface with smooth sure motions, she stopped and looked up at me again. It would take time, she seemed to say, so I sat back and looked across the dark pond to think about this change between us. A fish nibbled around the edges of a tree blossom that had fallen in, searching quickly for insects hidden in the soft white folds. I exhaled, and asked myself if this new shape of our life together could even be possible, that something this astounding could happen. I looked over at her profile and saw an older child, a stronger child still frail in her body and mind, but with a filling kind of imagination that she seemed to understand and welcome. It was huge and frightening, but it was a tool for her, something she really knew was hers. I ran my fingers through my hair and waited, and a scarlet bird darted from bush to tree branch and back, coming closer and closer with each leap. Finally, he hovered in front of Little Rain for a moment, looking at her working hands and steady face, as though trying to get her attention, or maybe staring out of curiosity, then he perched on a bare branch and began to preen himself. I was afraid to look at the painting for fear I would stop it, or change it somehow, my expectation was so strong. I knew it, yet I feared its power because this change shifted everything. To be sure, it was in our direction, something to build in us, yet I was afraid, as though I was afraid of how good something could be, like being afraid of love. I closed my eyes and let the sun warm my shoulders, listening to the leaves, thinking of the recent days and how deeply I needed my allies.

She touched me on the shoulder first, then her sandy fingers stroked my cheek, and she guided me to the painting. It was the lake, as I'd thought, and the rice harvesters, and underneath, both right and left, arching along the bottom border, were stylized but rounded faces, one of a woman with a strong sharp nose, one of a man holding an eagle feather. It was the Apache and the Anishinaabe woman, I was sure, and in the center, right at the bottom, was a simple stick figure airplane, like a bird but with straight wings, fuselage and a simple tail, nose raised in a gentle climb toward the stars. Just above the airplane she had prepared a perfectly round sand pallet yet to be finished. At the top of the painting an Asian face stared quietly out at us, done in round smoothness like the faces below. It was Johnny.

My eyes widened in wonder, even though I'd known what she was doing. Behind my closed eyes, listening to the day, I'd known. She began finishing the painting, focusing on the circular pallet at the bottom center. She moved quickly but carefully, and the face took shape. As it did, the painting seemed to move. The sun shifted and light played at the circle of sand and it seemed to lift up, or the faces moved of themselves, took on expressions as if to speak to us, and the rice plants seemed to shift in the breeze coming down from above us, the air reaching down to ripple the pond's surface and curl around our shoulders. She paid no attention to the breeze and the changes in the painting and the weather, but worked on, taken in completely by her task, and her body gained strength as she moved. The eyes of the central, final face were the last shapes to form, but I already knew them, and as Will's big warm eyes fell into place in quick circles of fine sand, I laughed out loud. The painting jumped out at us, and we watched it unfold.

Allies work over time, I saw it explode right in front of me then, and Little Rain pushed my shoulder with the back of her hand. She put her small hand on my chest as I turned toward her from the shove, then put it on her own chest quickly, back and forth, leaving tan sand prints on both of us. The painting glowed, Little Rain glowed, and the breeze rose to a light swirling wind, the faces staring up at us both static and vibrant at the same time. The wind increased, whipping the pond's surface, and the birds darted into the deep brush far away from thrashing branches, quick flashes of color. A summer squall flew over us, and the painting held strong in a flurry of raindrops flying horizontal in all directions. I looked into the bright sky as a quick lone dark cloud came over us and kept on running to wherever it was going in such a hurry, and then I looked back down at Rain, and she had the slightest turn of a smile on her upturned face. It was the first time, her first smile. I grinned and stared and saw an older child becoming even older as I stared. Then we turned our faces down to the painting once again simultaneously, and it subsided, like it was breathing down or taking a breath, something cooling but still living hot. Then she bent forward without hesitation and scooped her hand into the lake, into the faces, the canoes, the airplane, and steadily cast their heat and life high into the wind, one by one, trailing wisps and tendrils of sand into the wind until there was nothing left on the ground but mounds and cavities by the pond's edge, as though a small child had danced there and left her footprints of joy and abandon. But she was earnest, not gleeful like a child. She was purposeful and resolved in the way she dispersed the sand, as though knowing it had to go back to its source in order to live again another time in another way, as though she knew absolutely everything about what she was doing.

GOING TO WATER

~~~~~~~~~~~~~~~~~~~~~~~~~~~~~~~~~~~~~

38

Grandfather poked at the fire and leaned back on his strong haunches. "They say her family came here from the west, nobody knows how long ago. It's like our stories, how some of us came from the north, and others say we were always here. My family too comes from somewhere else, so long ago even I don't remember, and I know you can't believe that, can you, that I'm so old I can't remember something?" He laughed his old man's laugh, becoming more thoughtful and humorous about his aging these days. "Why, I remember..." he scratched the words out in a mock-ancient voice, then let them trail away, and turned to me with a blank stare. "What was it I was going to remember?" He leaned forward into a standing position, bent over, then hobbled around the fire, laughing.

"The little painter is remembering," he said clearly as he came around to me again. "because it's in her blood, and she's at that age. We listen to our blood when we're very young, and then again when we're very old. In between, well, it's a matter of luck. But if we don't listen at all, on either end of life, then we have problems." He paused, picked up an errant stick near the wood pile, and tossed it with perfect accuracy into the fire, filling the vacant spot expertly with a simple flick of his strong wrist. "It's the same as your Grandmother and me. We're out here in the woods because this is our memory, our blood. It's what we saw and came into as we grew and began to know what it meant to be a bit different from this old clan or that, and that's when we remembered bits and pieces of how our line came from somewhere else, somewhere that was inside us, and we learned how to act on that, to do what came up through us over time." He stood straight up then and smiled down at me where I sat by the fire. "And old Uncle helped us remember. We can't forget that for a moment."

"She's painting pictures in the sand, of things that haven't happened yet," I said.

Grandfather nodded, put his hand to his chin and walked another circle around the fire. "She's working with her dreams," he finally said, repeating "her dreams," and I thought of the Atsugewi elder up in the twenty-first century, who gathered dancers from California nations, Central American nations, and South American nations, to take them across the ocean to dance down the Champ-Elysees in Paris. He said his dream was to take the original purposes of the dance back to the shores of the people who had brought their dreams of destruction to California, and to all of Turtle Island, and to plant the dream of beauty and gratitude there in Europe, instead of destruction, to awaken something even older and more truthful over there. Then the dancers would dance all across Europe and eventually back under the Golden Gate Bridge, where they would dance on the decks of boats as they came into the bay under the huge steel spans, and from there they would go to the Great Wall of China and dance the dance of Ye'Ja to heal Earth there too. They would dance on the ancient stones of the Great Wall. This was a big dream, and it still is, and when the elder told me of it, he said it's all about the dreams we plant in the minds of children, and that this is our obligation, something we can recognize, something not to create artificially, but to recognize that we are capable of, and what Earth wants for us when we see we belong to her, rather than the other way around. It's no symbol, no metaphor, no fantasy, but a living dream we have allowed ourselves to forget during a crucial time, this elder said from his battered old wheelchair, and he's right.

"Not long ago, when I was still very young," Grandfather chuckled and then said soberly, "a traveler from the little girl's country passed through here trading beautiful things her people had made, and she told us about the paintings in the sand, how they held the world together. She said they were living things, like dreams are, and that as they were completed they came fully alive, and they reached out to gather the corners of the world together like the edges of a blanket holding something inside it, something very important."

Grandfather mused again. "There was something I was not supposed to forget," he pondered, hand on his chin again, turning slow circles in the orange firelight.

Owls talked to each other in the distance, as usual. "Oh yes. I remember. It's been a long time since I've thought of these things." His laughter turned away, and he became quieter and stronger, like Little Rain had been as she dispersed the sand. "Some paintings remain whole, hidden in caves, and the painters go into them to maintain them, freshen them, adjust them, repair them, and they are like gateways to the minds of the people who live under their pictures of unity, their pictures of what makes sense for those people on that stretch of land, the land they come out of, the land the paintings are made of. She told me that if the painters cannot work with the paintings, that if they fall into disrepair, things go off kilter in the surrounding world." He spread his hands out wildly, imitating chaos and confusion, shaking his head and tossing his hair. "Things get crazy." He shook his head. "But she told me that other paintings by those very same people, and by others living in the places surrounding that country, can only live for a short time, and then they must be dispersed, given back to the wind they came from. They are not allowed to become static in any way, sedentary, and they live only for the purpose of that moment, or for a particular ceremony, and when the ceremony or moment is over, they must go back into the earth, and back into the wind, or the wrong thing is left working on its own when it needs people right there with it, guiding its purpose. She told me this is what she knew, and she must have been of the same people."

I began to understand Little Rain more deeply, and how her art and ceremony, for that is what her paintings were in the most profound sense, carried a power of understanding and of placement for both of us. They put her impossible dreams into a form she could begin to manage, something she could see that bound us together as the dreams changed with my coming and going, with all the people I met and things I saw, something she could manipulate and work even as it poured out of her, as though the sand in her small hands flowed brightly through the dark veins in her wrist, shone from her wrist directly into her palms, then spilled through the open venturi at the base of her palm onto the flat ground, ground prepared by her deepest need and drive to cope with the world that had come upon her and was even now coming up through her like a river.

The Anishinaabe woman said something once that stuck with me, speaking at a university on a hill overlooking the sea, a beautiful place much like Will's ranch, with a bright blue horizon sparkling outside the grey walls of the small auditorium. As we sat on hard, cool folding metal chairs, she told all of us gathered there the original name of Amherst, Massachusetts. I don't remember it, much to my frustration today, but I can still feel the beauty of the name as she spoke it, even without the syllables clear in my mind today, and how it called up images of waters meeting, how it made us all feel good to hear the sound and attach it to the meaning. I knew this because I looked around the room and saw the smiles, and it still brings that feeling today, so far away in time and place. Just a memory that the sound is there brings joy. She went on to detail Lord Jeffrey Amherst, and how he purposely gave smallpox-infested blankets to the Indigenous he struggled against in the battlefield, and how many thousands of people died as a result of those gifts. All of us in the room recoiled at the ugliness and cowardice of his actions, the brutality and inhumanity, the sheer numbers of dead in the tens of thousands, looking at her face and then up at the high ceilings of the hall to escape from the pain, or down at our feet, and I thought of the cold lack of remorse I saw in Goebbels, imagining the same in Amherst, yet a beautiful name and place lies buried under his memory, under his name. She talked about how names are sacred, alive, and that we must rename the sacred in order to get it back, if not in paper deed, then in how we might feel as we walk the streets of that town, or sit at a sidewalk café and drink a chilly iced coffee on a hot summer day. We must know in our hands, our clenched fists and open palms, how the name can meet the feeling of the earth, of the underground water, where it sends its fingers of gravity up through the asphalt, cement, and souls of our shoes as we sit there. We must be able to grasp it in our hands. That's how we begin to get it back, by that kind of gracious, tenacious knowing.

What are we surrounded by? That's the question. California towns in the twentieth and twenty-first century are the same almost everywhere, two hundred years of renaming, all named after those whose dreams terrorized and smothered Indigenous dreams, and how do the Indigenous of that time recover the origins if not through language and image, alongside all the other ways they may struggle? Through story and song and names? Yes. As Little Rain paints her way out of death, so the singers sing their ways back to health, speak their ways back home to their own way of seeing. And they do this for the non-Indigenous as well, for the settlers' own naming traps them and their offspring in a bloody history, a nightmare, and in that nightmare they cannot find the connections they too so desperately crave.

Grandmother came and led me into the lodge later that night, her personal womb tucked away in the deeper woods. As the heat and bright stones and songs planted us into our most elemental, honest selves on the cool ground, the power of Little Rain's painting rose up and glowed in the canopy. It came alive and then, quickly, the turtle superimposed itself across the painting, joining in the strength and purpose, traversing the images from another century, shimmering purple over the faces and the lake and the stick-figure airplane. I watched, and Grandmother sang another song of protection, and then another, and the tiny lodge squeezed down around us, holding us as though in a spin through an unknown universe, hostile or benevolent we could not know at any given time, and we turned circles as we flew, lifted up and away in our minds into this living dream. The eagle feathers shook, and I thought of all those people ripped away from their traditions, their songs and languages, of how hard it must be for them to find their places in all the chaos, all the isolated caverns of personality and cult and class and race and goods and jobs and schools and churches. The painting and the turtle took turns expanding above us, and Grandmother sang the protection song over and over, and even when she was silent the song kept going on in me, like the woman's name for the town but formed, tangible, carrying, a base and a shield. The world outside the lodge alternated between blaring sounds of centuries-to-come and floating away into invisible quietness, softness. The usual expansion through Earth out into the world tugged away at us but did not come, giving no integration, and my palms pressed into the ground and grew hot and sweating, and I spread the mud onto my face and neck, feeling the soil, and we kept spinning, rushing through the unknown. Something ominous and troubling was there, and we held it off at a distance, but it was insistent even in its not appearing, not inside with us, but out there somewhere, and Grandmother held sway through it all, though I could not see her, as though she'd been here many times and knew just what was happening, yet it was still all brand new, even to her, a world of strange contradictions we shared and rode together like an unpredictable horse with way too much fire in its eyes, and complete loss of even its own intentions toward itself. And it was out there building, out of control.

GOING TO WATER

~~~~~~~~~~~~~~~~~~~~~~~~~~~~~~~~~~~

39

Little Rain was sobbing, and sounds poured from her voice for the first time, and like her first smile had been, the sounds were full with all the absence that came before them, full with the enormous time of building into something from nothing. No, not nothing, but something so confusing and terrifying that it couldn't have a sound attached to it; it wouldn't stop long enough to form into sound, but crashed against itself her whole life long, and even longer, because it churned through the air long before it came into her tiny body, and when her chest finally heaved the emotions up through her throat the sounds that came out silenced everything and everyone around, the people and animals and trees and wind. They were the cries of soft stones long in the making moaning out into the light of a yellow hot muggy day, and her thin arm reached out steadily over the earthen pallet by the glassy pond's black surface as she painted.

Her family had sent the fastest young runner to get me, and I fell behind time and time again, following him through the trail to her, running at the edge of my speed and endurance and beyond it, and when I fell into the clearing before her I was a flurry of motion and sweat, heaving breath, and

I stopped to catch myself, hands on my knees, head tilted up toward her because I could not take my eyes off her. The sand fell from her hand and she cried so strongly, with so much power, that no one watching had room for even a tear or tremor, for her tears were more than anyone could stand. Another sound would tear their world apart. But her hand was calm and sure and moved solely in its purpose, even as she looked to the sky, then back down to the painting as she cried.

Finally, I jumped quickly to her, kneeling next to her. I touched her back, behind her heart, and rested my hand there, and she calmed slightly, but only slightly as she looked up at me quickly, her mouth open as if to speak, but we both knew that would not happen. That was not possible. It was only the shape and motion of the lips before speech, but nothing of words or naming or song or anything; it was only the voice of sobbing.

I saw she was afraid, but I had seen deeper fear in her before now, so it was a strange fright. It was something else now, an intelligent dread that was brand new to her, like when something is new yet expected from someplace inside we've not met, and when the feeling comes, it's known, yet not known, then known again. She poured the sand out of this kind of knowing yet vacillating hand and beckoned me with her whole face to look down, and when I did I saw a complex scene of the town and the round houses and wood smoke and Grandmother's place outside town in the woods, the stream running through, and Grandfather's fire and the trails winding through, and Sweet Man's hunting place, and myself running full speed to where she now sat and poured at the edge of the pond. And above it all, onto a broad spread of lightly wetted sand, she poured, and as she did, her shoulders steadied, subdued themselves as though preparing for a long hard physical fight. She shuddered in new-growing power, and poured the painting she did not want to see yet knew she must see, the painting she wanted me to see but wanted not to happen to me or to anyone she loved, and by now I knew her amazing love, so I knew what was tearing at her insides. She painted her deepest caring, and she lived it as it formed out of Earth, and when the foreboding shapes formed above the town and all of us, looming, her love turned to anger more intense and concentrated than any I'd seen bursting out in combat, not rage that is out of control, but outrage and determination mixed into sadness and grief to form a high-pitched battle cry where there had been only silence a moment before.

The grotesque shape of the beast himself rose up grinning through the sand like a face out of a terrible nightmare, the witch boy growing into a man and flying beast, along with his many shapes over time, kings and emperors and dictators and chairmen, their numbers rising and rising in momentum, increasing, forming out of their own accord now without her hand. Instantly, once she had quickly determined who was before her, she leaned far back from the painting and opened her hands to the sky as if to surround the images she'd just created. Then she inhaled a long and deep breath, her lips peeled back to let all the air in the world in, and she screamed the scream no one in her time had ever before heard.

It was not long or drawn out, but short and pointed, abrupt, and it flew everywhere, filling the people who stood like stones around the edge of the clearing, filling the trees and the water of the pond, shimmering on the surface, and filling me with steeled trepidation, pride, and resolve.

Then she leaned forward quickly, and with both hands she swirled the painting into a huge round mass of sand, from the west to the east, north to south, in a fast circle the opposite of the sun's direction, over and over, as though unscrewing a lid that had tightened itself down on Earth out of its own volition and for its own violent and hungry purposes. She blended the sand in a circle with strong fingers until there were no shapes left, and as she did this, the beast's sandy face was shocked for a split second, in the moment before there was no shape there anymore at all, vanished, as though he was caught in an unexpected cyclone with his minions tossed all around him, and he could not see what was happening to him. Then she threw the sand in every direction until it was done, and when it was over, she leapt straight to her feet and stood, thin legs apart and planted, fists clenched. She took another huge breath, then walked straight into the pond, into the dark water that surrounded her softly and quickly, with no resistance or surface motion, but with gentle acceptance and the density and power that water alone possesses.

The people slipped away into the woods and went home, and I moved quietly to sit and wait at the base of a huge white ash tree just out of the clearing. It was a long wait, and in the time of sitting and listening, all the other sounds of the woods returned from hiding, and soon the clearing was dotted with bird songs. And then the hum of wings from a gathering of bright turquoise dragonflies suddenly filled the air. Their black eyes peered at me and Little Rain from the ends of their needle-thin bodies, as they flew back and forth between us, back and forth on quickly-moving bright paths of horizontal light.

40

I had to go out into the fray again because the beast was gaining power. He'd come back to his origins, or to some place just past them where time can be a straight line, against all reason and reality, which depends on how tenaciously the people cling to the idea of it. It's like race theory, like the idea of white supremacy, or if not outright supremacy, in an effort to hide the obvious, then white centrality, or the centrality of one's own "civilization" no matter the hue, a softer form of the same brutality. That's how time works in the mind too, a collection of how people see something so strongly it finally shapes itself into that vision, and the beast jumped on that train and brought them all back to us, brought himself and all his friends. Maybe the door was opened even wider through the little girl's dreams as she gave them form in the paintings, or maybe it was opened by my coming and going and changing the imaginations of the perpetrators in their final moments, or maybe it had always been open and our time without the evolutions of the witch boy who came into the painting was the aberration. Maybe we'd just been lucky, living in a window or capsule of time and

existence free of that kind of horror, like a whole pantheon of sea life living at a depth no one had known
could sustain life, and one day an unmanned sub with
its bright incandescent tentacle lights opened the door
to all the stunned creatures having lived there for a
million years undisturbed. Maybe we were like that
world, floating through time relatively unmolested and
naïve, until something mysterious opened and we were
exposed, naked before a steely probing eye. Maybe we
are still like that.

I stared into the star-filled sky, the pre-industrial
sky no one in those centuries could imagine. I remembered an early settler of Turtle Island telling me the
story of how a California Indigenous family he met
once described a great lake of beautiful blue water
beyond the mountains, and late that spring he and his
explorers had trekked to a high mesa above what they
were absolutely certain was the right spot, but they
only saw a long and wide valley filled with birds, as
far as the eye could see, and they saw no water. The
brush was so thick on the slopes leading down from
the mesa that they turned around and headed back,
pulling their tired packhorses behind them. When they
returned to the family's home weeks later and told
them what they saw, and that they could not find the
lake, the young mother laughed, "Oh, then you must
go back just before winter comes and the birds have
gone back north. Then you will see the water." She
told her children the story, and they laughed too, but
the settlers could not believe it, not until they went
at the beginning of winter and were thunderstruck

at the vast, crystalline blue lake spreading out below them from the very same campsite on the high mesa. Their imaginations soared like the birds had, up into a night sky with as many stars as their minds held birds, bright white and inestimable in number and beauty alike. They could not have imagined such a thing.

This is the brilliant living sky I stared into, listening to where I must go next, and I saw place after place, person after person. A Mayan king grumbled to his servants that he was dissatisfied with his meal, that the fruit was not peeled right, speaking to them in disgust and making them fear for their lives, while a dictator who was called a chairman ordered his armies to eliminate the Indigenous people of a Southeast-Asian jungle, standing glibly on the formality of his ideology, the correctness of his concept of brotherhood and obligation passed to him by still another of his kind. He picked at his rice and vegetables as he spoke to a broad general with a chest full of medals and a hard face, and on the other side of his tasty but politically plain meal, hundreds of miles away on a green jungle hillside, a young Apache Marine made abandoned sweet love to a beautiful and delicate Indigenous woman. A child was conceived that day, a mixed-blood from across continents, like Little Rain's people had mixed with our people across one large continent a thousand years before, like Grandmother and Grandfather's people had mixed, who knows when and from where, blood memory spreading like shooting stars across the Indigenous sky, the Indigenous land. But the conception, the boy born of young love between two Indigenous who were only beginning to learn each other's languages, would never grow to be a man. He would be cut down by a thin brown soldier in green, snaking through thick jungle with a chairman's idea in the chamber of his rifle, an idea in the shape of a bullet with that child's name on it, and with the name of his mother on still another. The Apache, whose family on Turtle Island had already known far too many centuries of fighting for his own home, now fought to protect the homes and rights of Indigenous people thousands of miles away, far from the land that had been stripped from him by the very people who sent him here to fight, and now he would know still another layer of grief and insanity. And the masters of both these wars would not think of him or his new Asian hillside family, nor would their offspring think of him in their daily treks to the supermarkets and long boring commutes down the freeways back on Turtle Island. And in this Asian land of the newer great killing and social and economic transformation of communism, they would not think of this young mixed-race Indigenous family who died here either, as they built malls where the people would buy American hamburgers tasting like lemongrass, ginger, and Saigon cinnamon.

I heard the names calling down out of the sky like distant single-engine airplane sounds, Chiv-ing-ton, Pol-Pot, Mao Tse-Tung, Ray-Gun, Ho Chih-Min, Sta-lin, Jack-son, and I could not decide, though I knew it was not up to me but to gravity. I could only watch the parade. It seemed overwhelming, a matter of sheer numbers beyond what the mind can hold, like my old Yaqui friend told me of his time manning a machine gun on a South Korean winter plain, dug-in and fortified on a slight rise, firing all night into a sea of soldiers coming at him, firing until the barrel glowed red and began to melt, and then they'd strip that barrel off with thick gloves in an icy wind, burning the whorls of the fingers, and click a fresh barrel into place, tossing the red-hot metal cylinder into the snow with a hiss like a monstrous snake. In the morning, the bodies were too overwhelming to count, just too many, and eventually his little knoll was overrun, and he woke up one cold afternoon with a bullet crease in his steel helmet and the skull underneath, looking at the blurred shins and boots of North Korean soldiers, rifle muzzles inches from his bloody face. He spent the next two years a prisoner of war, enduring the brain-washing pressed into him every day, and when I asked him how he resisted it, he grinned and said, "Can't wash what you don't have," and he laughed loudly before looking away, that Yaqui friend. And I heard Rose-ah-velt and saw even more Yaqui men generations earlier, packed off to the Philippines, where they'd blend with the Indigenous they were sent there to fight in order to liberate them from the other righteous colony, the other one called Spain, in this transfer of the same style empires, a brutal switch. And how many millions died in that liberation, one or two million? Ah, who's counting the digits of madness? What's the difference between one and two? Only one, even if it's a million people on a small complex of islands in a rolling tropical sea. No, it's not people then; it's only numbers and painted faces on a curved tin roller. It's a rolling spinning face like the apples, cherries and white goats in a slot machine's window, the ching-ing sound of bells and guns and engines and shouting in Tagalog, Ilicano, Spanish, English, Yaqui, and the Black English of the Buffalo Soldiers. And a hundred years later a brown German with a Filipino name, son of a vanished American soldier, wakes up one morn-ing to hear a song from under his white pillow, so he drags his tired and confused body to the airport in Frankfurt and goes to what he thinks is his father-land. There he finds his Macabebe clan, and a finger pointing back toward America, so he goes on another long jet ride, and he lands among the descendants of those ancestors who were packed in sardine-can troop ships five generations before, but he cannot find anyone in his family. He cannot find what he needs until an old man at a bus stop points him up north to the Apache country, to his fighting cousins from long ago, Yaqui the sentinels looking south, eyes for the Apache defenders, allies to make sure the south-ern empires stayed put. He rolls north past the slot machines and through their blinking lights, empires of commerce, through Indigenous poverty, searching for what he knows he must find in order to be able to keep on going in Germany, to keep the strength inside him, to keep his spirit alive. In the inevitability of how our time really works, not on those spread sheets and line graphs that run lives ragged, but by something gentler and larger, he ends up singing Apache songs in a small round lodge in Freedom, California, that has been built the same way for millennia, but now it's crafted out of thin fresh-smelling eucalyptus once from Australia, where still other Indigenous sing their own Aboriginal songs. He sings with the very same Apache marine from Vietnam, songs that spring out of times lived long before all the forced displacement of both their peoples was even a dream in the empires' fledgling lusts. He sings Indigenous songs with a man who is cousin to kin he never even knew he had, who allied in defense of both their freedom against the same king who complained about his sliced fruit, or bragged about the divinity of his own savior, or swore to the rationality of his own kind of dollar or freedom or government, and therefore put his stamp upon the land of all our ancestors like it was his to stamp, his to stamp in frenzied righteousness.

I saw all of this and thought, "Where do I begin this time around?" The sky didn't answer, so I went back to my round, low house for a long, much-needed sleep, curling up between my men, my husband and son, and I slept without dreams in a very deep peace. There would be time enough for anxiety. Now was the time to rest.

GOING TO WATER

41

I woke in the morning, walked onto a gentle hillside, and knew I had to speak with John Chivington,
the charging leader of the massacre at Sand Creek,
"onward into battle." He was heavy on many minds,
and had been for a hundred and fifty years, a powerful influence. It was him, the man, and what he represented as well, for like all of us, he did not live and
act alone. He was an arbiter, a voice and a sword of at
least two sides of a nation and a people, at least two,
and what they call his soul knifed out in all directions
to either cut pride or shame into a man or woman's
expression, or confusion, or all three. The beast was
in him and those surrounding him, and at the same
time the beast would form a wall of protection around
his image, either to make him evil incarnate, or to
paint him as a simple product of his time, a result of
his fear and his hatred of Indigenous depredations,
a natural outcome of what they justified as a natural
and inevitable confrontation between two irreconcil-
able worlds, what people then and now would call a
sad yet unavoidable state of affairs. In both cases, they
would resist seeing the depth of dehumanization they

dreamed, and so that dream would continue unabated, once again simply replacing faces over time, one for another and still another.

It was a dark room smelling of impending death by a disease that eats a body away from the inside. The air was thick, and it stunk of the man's history. I could see the blood and killing attached to his bed-clothes by pride and refusal, his never letting go of his right to exterminate all those people camped under the American flag and the white flag of truce. Even when the Cheyenne were fighting, it was to protect their homes, and not one Cheyenne soldier, even among the reputedly fearsome Dog Soldiers, ever proposed taking a detachment of warriors to Washington D.C. to wipe out the leaders having drinks in the White House, arrows and lances and carbines crashing through transparent crystal and delicately-painted china. Brutal as it came to be, it was after all a war of protection of a homeland, but this "colonel" did not see it this way. He had walked into the house of the Cheyenne, Arapaho, and many others, looked around, and called it his own. I could see his obstinacy even now, at the end of his long and tortured seventy-three years.

His eyes were closed when I first entered the room, and when I opened a window to let air and dawn light in, and turned toward him, he trembled in shock to see me. I walked close to his bed, to where pale light streamed through and hit the sides of our faces, and just as I could only see the lit part of his cheek and mouth, and one eye, I knew this is what he saw of me. We could only see each other in halves framed in shadow. Without leaving his stare, I pulled a chair across the wood floor and sat near him.

"I don't know you, Indian," he said, paused, then demanded, "Get out."

"I cannot," I said, reflecting his tone of finality and will. "Not until you're gone."

"Where're my aides?" he asked.

"Asleep."

"Who're you?" he wanted to know.

"I suppose I am your chance at redemption, to use your terms, Reverend," I said, lingering on the title. "I'm your chance to simply see."

As I said this, his hatred rose up through the cancer beneath his skin. Maybe this was his particular form of that disease, I thought, his own form of hatred carried and nursed over a lifetime, boiled up into finalizing eruptions inside his body and mind.

But strangely, he settled into accepting my being there quickly, and I was surprised at how this happened, because it did not seem to fit his obstinacy, but it soon became clear why he accepted me there, a "redskin" woman. He held to his fight, not holding to it out of stubbornness alone, but because he truly relished it. He lived by it.

"Don't expect any regrets from me," he mumbled. "You all got what you deserved, the whole butchering lot of you." He spit the words out, though it was difficult for him to talk with such raw emotional power, but he called it up and it came straight out of his personal brand of spite. "Besides, what do you or your kind know of redemption?"

There was no answering him in that moment, only watching and waiting and wondering at his mind and heart, at the power of his imagination being so turned away from human beings he could not understand, but who were a people he had known in his early lifetime, before his hunger for vitriol and battle had consumed him. I waited until he calmed before I spoke again, breathing shallowly in the sickly air, an occasional draft of outside coolness penetrating the dark, wood-paneled room.

"What is it, finally, that troubles you, Reverend?" I asked softly, once I could see his lids droop down again, down away from seeing me and into his just feeling my presence, as though the image of me as an Indian had tucked itself away somewhere invisible in his mind, somewhere inches away from his disdain, and this allowed him to feel me only as a person, and maybe even as a woman. "What is it?" I asked quietly, almost whispering.

There was a long silence, then hushed but intense words, "They threw me away," he said, "and all I did was what they wanted." He took a deep breath and his chest swelled up under the soiled white gown he wore, and years gathered in his throat to speak. "I heard them talking about redskins in the bars, about what they'd all do given half a chance." His eyes were fully closed now, and he seemed to forget he was talking to me, to someone else at all. "I heard them go on

and on, about the squaws and papooses and bucks,"
he said, "but mostly about the squaws." He waited,
then repeated the words, "the squaws." Now he was
talking to someone again, to me.

The soldiers had ridden into Denver with freshly
stretched pudenda on their hats, and more body parts,
blood and sex all stuffed together like a snuff film of
the late twentieth century, pre-dating those movies
but giving birth to them a hundred years before, still
another birth of violation among far too many, and it
all fit neatly into what he'd done with his mind out
of his own greed and petulance, and out of theirs too,
the masses who spawned him with their theories and
laws built about people and science and ownership
of land and people and time. But he had become too
obvious for them, too much a clear face of what they
could not accept in themselves, too gory a spectacle
even for them.

"We killed so many," he said, "but not enough.
Never enough. And it was good. It was good, thrill-
ing. We were heroes. When we rode into town, people cheered, and they saw our trophies of war and
cheered. They celebrated, bought us drinks, and
the women laid with us, laughing and drinking,"
he paused, exhausted from so many words and the
breath they took, and then he grew dark. "And later
they turned on us," he said. "Cowards." He opened
his eyes and looked straight into mine. "Cowards," he
repeated, somehow knowing I would understand him
as an Indigenous woman, and I nodded in agreement,
because I did understand. I did know, and he saw this.

"Yes," I agreed, and my agreement rearranged something deep in him, perhaps a distant memory of what a soldier should be, not the memory of the soldier he'd become. "You are them, and they forsook you," I added, a biblical term floating off my lips easily.

"You do understand me, don't you?" he declared and asked almost desperately, as though coming out of a loneliness I could not imagine, a long drawn-out loneliness, and here I was, a woman of his deepest enemy, or at least what he thought of as his deepest enemy, and suddenly his whole life's longing burst into the room through his eyes, and it looked as though it would bring him back to life, dispel the cancer, and he would walk to the window, take a breath, and live again, start all over and maybe even do the right thing. But it subsided and remained only as the beginnings of a shifting yet rigidly controlled mind and to him, a soul.

"Of course I understand," I said. "You know that. How could I not?"

A young Indigenous boy from long ago in his life ran across a field toward him, waving, and he knew the boy, knew his family, and he was not afraid of him then. But the push west had come regardless of all the congressional and parlor discussions of how it should be done, and the wars rose up instead of reason, the Civil War and The Indian Wars, and the young boy disappeared in a world of disappointment and death. He'd been a determined abolitionist and a man of God, so you'd think he'd understand we are human too, but his drive for glory and fame and power in an overwhelmingly contradictory world outdistanced earlier memories of the Indigenous boy running toward him, and he listened to the fire and brimstone god instead of Jesus, since fire and brimstone was all he saw around him, and in his growing up all the talk of red devils invaded him because he invited it in. He had to let it in because it was everywhere, a growing way to see everything. He nursed it in pictures of uniforms and brass and smooth pistol grips, and then over time it coupled with his failures, the opportunities that slipped through his fingers because he was too much, one way or another way, just too intense for the church or the generals or the congressmen. And his failures joined all the other failures of the whole movement west, the dried-up farms and impossibilities of growing on lands divided on paper in Washington, having never been seen or walked upon, farms with no water, people with no water. And in this misstep of expansion countless spirits dried up, and dry consciences defied their own gods in suppressed anger, even while standing at the pulpits preaching, and too many people could not understand even their own black book, so tired they were of disappointment. So they fell to drunken exaltation of the dream overtop the reality, and the further from the dream they got, the deeper the drunkenness became, and we Indigenous were the whipping post through it all, the goat they rode to escape themselves, simply because we were there, already on the land of their dream, their dream. We became the faces of their own victimhood when the dream faltered and ran sour, and they could not turn the anger they denied upon themselves. But upon us? Well, it was easy. We were everywhere.

Coming up through this morass of the mind and heart, this man made his choices, and they took him down a bitter road. His son died, his wife died, his life failed his ambitions, he abused women and was accused of it publicly, and he became the shameful man the apologetic newspapers had cast him as, once they saw there had been few warriors in the "battle" of Sand Creek, and that his drunken "soldiers" had killed women and children and old men sworn to peace. He became their open dark side, and they drew him that way then, a caricature of immorality, and even his supporters eventually skulked into the shadows, products of the trend of righteous indignation. "How could a white man do such a thing?"

"It was good," he said to me again, "but they forgot, how good it was." His lips pressed together in anger again momentarily. "They cast me away," he said like a preacher, his left hand moving theatrically but weakly, then falling onto the soft bedcovers, no pulpit to pound.

But he had been taken back in, and even became sheriff of the city that once scorned him, the other face of Colorado coming into light over time again, and his supporters crept back out from the shadows one by one, two by two, and spoke again of his heroism. When he died, hundreds of people stood in the sun and spoke eloquently of his patriotism and courage. "Never was there such a true American," they said, and it would take over a hundred years after his death on this cool morning before his church would issue an apology for him and his actions, an apology to the Indigenous after a hundred years of silence, then a brief moment of sorrow spoken to their ghosts and their descendants, but there was no apology to the children of the settlers, no apology to them because no one could see or hear their grief, not even them. It was only a moment of sorrow surfacing before the silence roared down upon the plains once again and buried compassion for all those left, for all of them, all of us.

"None of it was any good," I said quietly in answer to his honesty, "and now it's your turn to see." I unwrapped the gourd vial, unwinding the rawhide from around its slender brown neck.

"How many of your own died out of Cheyenne revenge?" I asked. It was not a question.

"I mean the killing," he shot back, angry and helpless. "The killing was good." His hands trembled, as if they would like to rise on their own volition and constrict around my throat, independent of his body, as though there was enough hatred in his hands alone, with nothing else to drive or carry them, despite the fact that I understood him.

"I know exactly what you mean," I said, staying calm, remembering Goebbels and my own forgetting. "I know hatred very well." I pulled the stopper from the gourd's mouth, and the rich smells of our forest rose to my nostrils, fragrances ground together in ways I could not imagine by Grandmother's beautiful, strong fingers and songs, songs so strong they had to carry through all the destruction to come and lay truth bare before people she would never know. She called upon everything she'd ever known and all she could imagine, singing through the stories I told her of what would come, through her desire for how it must all come together, singing while gathering herbs and flowers that would be extinct in the times for which they'd be used, carrying her song past her own grief for all of this crazy dying and turning the other way.

The colonel's eyes widened as I grasped his face in one hand and dropped the liquid into his open mouth with the other, light from the window flashing on the green droplets in a quick burst of color and sound as he groaned in his helplessness.

"What're you..." he sputtered, though his strength was leaving quickly. The anger was only his last breathing, his rising out of his body, words like a picture of a soul fighting death, a black and white etching over a thick black bible lying on a hard table, the body arched back, the soul reaching up with a finger on the tip of a raised arm, the mirrored angel of the spirit reaching down, the fingers almost touching, the angel beckoning, the spirit in the body resisting with all its might, one arm pulling up into freedom, the other pulling down into static life. He fought, and words articulated themselves on their own power, coalescing air in the room, words made out of air that he could not make himself anymore, words formed by all those who made him, but he had to let them go.

"It's all right," I soothed him, "so just leave it behind, but...see it. That's all you have to do. Look at it." My words were a soft chant.

A bright green froth shone on his decayed yellow teeth, caught the light from the window and rode it. I thought of the Dog Soldiers in their raging sorrow, riding across the plains in revenge and pain beyond anything they'd ever felt, striking everywhere they could, and of the blue-coated columns of soldiers riding out to meet them in reprisal, and all the blood spent across all those plains, spread like bright red rain into deep green grass, following this one man's lust, one who rode for them.

"See it. See what you've done. It wants to be seen."

He could not talk then, and the sputtering subsided into shallow intermittent breathing, and he looked into my eyes, then away to the smoke-stained ceiling. Where and how he and his soldiers struck the women that day was how he saw the world. It gathered in him, in one man who made himself susceptible, in sexual depravity that is deprivation, deprivation of sustenance from the woman, from Earth, from natural law, from all that holds any of us in place. It grew outward in him, filled the cells of his blood and brain and body, because that is how it works, and it keeps on going until it is seen, for once again I find it laid out before me that the seeing alone gives us a chance to stop it, to make another choice. Only that, another choice, but sometimes that is enough, and it is enormous. But without the chance to see, nothing furthers and it pumps its wings on and on to no avail, stuck to the ground like a clipped raven. In another century, a young man in a courtroom sits in arrogance in a white tee shirt with the word "killer" scrawled in pencil across his chest, drawn in defiant purpose in his cell. In the courtroom, he removes the blue ironed shirt of institutional formality they put on him for the illusion of civility, and he faces the families of the high school classmates he shot down. He sneers to the families, "The hand that pulled the trigger on your children masturbates every day to the memory," and then he gestures obscenely at them, "Fuck you," he says with a pale young hand. This boy rises out of the same blood and mind of the withered old man who lay in front of me on this cold morning, fighting his seeing, fighting it even in the midst of the medicine's working through his mind and memory and imagination. How deep is the anger of the man who destroys the lives of unborn children, Indigenous children lying inside Indigenous women on the plains of Colorado, and white children lying inside mothers to come, all across a nation? Who destroys the womb and all those lying within it?

Then the stuffy air changed, swirled slowly, and the medicine dropped into place. I could see it in the manner of his loosening body and face as he spoke one word, "Soule." He uttered the name of the man he had assassinated for testifying honestly about what happened, then released it again, "Soule." Was it the man, or was he talking about his own soul? In either case, it meant the same thing, and perhaps it was both things for him, for the man Soule was truly his soul, his chance decades earlier to come clean with himself, a chance that had been no chance at all, so steeped in the mind of the beast he'd become, the taste of gunpowder and sweat still on his tongue. But what of this man Soule who lived in him now, and whose name rose up into the room quietly, in these final breaths? I bent over to look into his eyes, but they were no longer mine to see clearly. He began to see only his own landscape now, the glaze of death forming like a faded silver window curtain over his pupils, but the sound came again. "Soule." It rose into the room a delicate bird, and the muscles on his face relaxed, his breath spreading out even shallower, like warm water barely making its way across an alluvial plain.

Then he died, lifting away, the angel's hand clenching his firmly, and I could not see whether he saw what he should have seen or not, but it felt like it because the violence of the room softened into something new and unknown, so I did not look back when I walked out through door of the room, down the stairs, and out the old battered entrance onto the morning street. A thin old man on a rattling buckboard drew up his mule at the sight of me, and he turned to watch as I walked by him with a nod he did not answer. He only stared, and when I turned down a narrow side street toward the open land and mountains beyond, I could feel his eyes on my back, like gun sights on the last "Injun" in Colorado.

A small family of scientists far away from Chivington's moment of passage, leagues away into the world and idea of Future, collected their tests early one morning and told the magazines they'd found the cells of a child in the brain of its mother, decades after birth, clear into death, resting silently in her still body. No one had thought the connection between mother and child worked in that direction, thinking it went only from the mother to the child, like down a pipe through gravity, gracelessly logical and pointed, and only in the womb to boot, but then seven men and women in clean white smocks went further and found cells of the children throughout the organs of the mother, going a direction no one thought of, migrating back up into the mother through the blood and tissue, and penetrating deeply into the brain, perhaps leaving things in the mind the scientists could not measure or even fathom. There was another curious finding too, like a sliver of light under an old rock, something that puzzled and intrigued them, and it was the absence of those same cells in the brains of mothers who'd lost their memories, trailed away in dementia or Alzheimer's. All traces of the children were gone physically and mentally in these mothers. I thought about this, watching this lonely old man die, this bearded face of the beast's victim and hero, a man beloved and hated by both sides of the American coin, a man shriven of his greater memory until dying opened a slender crack of opportunity for him. I thought of it, and wondered what it meant, or which particular memory clenched its legs around the mane of what molecule and rode hard in every direction, remembering again, always remembering in the hum of the tissue and spin of blood, looking for the sense of it all, the connection that mattered. What this science does prove is connection. What people do with it is left to their inheritance of culture. It's left to what they are taught is possible by those who came before them, who listened to the messages of the humming tissues, held them in respect, and passed them on. This is blood memory.

Outside a small country house, after a long ceremony of the changing seasons, I listened to a young Apache's story. I watched him form the story with his hands, his rolling shoulders and tough postures, and I was glad he was my friend that day.

"I was bad," he said. "I was mean," he smiled, but his smile was not really a smile, more of a warning, as if we were going back there together and I should watch out for myself. "I screwed everybody over," he said with a sweep of his thick arm. "I mean, everyone. I figured it like this," he said, changing the position of both feet where he stood, planting himself like a post, immovable in both his memory and on the old wooden deck, then continued. "If you came my way, you deserved to be fucked over. You'd done something so bad you deserved to meet me." He laughed, again not so much a laugh of mirth, but more a release and gathering of the story inside him. "No, you didn't have to do anything to me. Not to me, because it wasn't about me, because I was just what I was, that's all. It was about you, or anyone else at all, and I could do anything I wanted to you just for being around me. If you were around me, it was your karma. I was your payback, ready and willing. It was about you. What you'd done to deserve me." I laughed and asked him if he thought he was the avenging angel, and he chuckled slightly, this time with a hint of ironic humor, but he shook his head at the same time, acknowledging only that possibility, nothing definitive. "I was just bad," he said, landing hard on the word. Bad. It was a single word that contained a whole lot of living, frightening things. He smiled, and it was today's evolved smile, having seen through all that destruction back then, but the other smile was present too, the bad one. "I just didn't give a shit," he pursed his lips in a scowl and shook his head. "About anyone or anything. And I didn't even give a shit about that, about not giving a shit."

Finally he sat down, and while the others smoked cigarettes and looked up into the tall fir trees, he continued. In the silence before he began again, I thought of the Dog Soldiers and blood memory and where grief and anger spill across a person's very being, and how that works in all of us. He was a young Apache, but he could have been a Cheyenne Dog Soldier, for the deprivation and depravity have been vast enough to reach a big hand over all of us, coast to coast and far beyond. The psychiatrist in the prisons that he, like too many Indigenous of his age, had moved through for a decade and more, would not understand the nature of this inheritance, would not even get close, like the civilian psychiatrists of combat soldiers, psychiatrists who'd never served, who wouldn't understand the eventual explosion when they asked the silent and simmering vets to vent their anger. Oh, be careful, doctor. There was no understanding, not in the viscera, not in the gut, not in the mind. "No, that was long ago, history," they'd say to the Apache or Dineh or Cherokee inmate, the past only relevant to how one person understands themselves since birth and nothing before. Is the prisoner assimilated? Swallowed by it all even in whacked-out resistance? What does this mean to a young Apache fighting his way through a hard-packed prison yard, assimilated into the mess of history he knows in his cells, but that may be just out of reach of his knowing how to navigate through it? That's the secret, the navigation, like those ancient boatmen who ended up on the shores of Norway more than a millennium before, only to shock the blue-eyed geneticists over there today out of their own one-way thinking. "Oh my god, they came here before we went there," they said, and went to drink pint after pint of cold German beer to think about it. It's like this, you see, the galloping angry ponies of the Cheyenne course through young Apache blood on their way to vengeance, and it goes every which way, and no one can stop it, like an explosion already in the air. No one but the Apache himself, or the soldier himself, not the prison warden or the shrink or the woman, can do it for him. It's not me or someone like me, no one from outside, but something deep inside himself. So in his world, it took a man just like him to begin the change, in one way or another, and he told the story of many people, which was his own singular story. He re-lived it as he told it, because he's a good story-teller, dark eyes flashing with humor. He pointed at the woman sitting on the porch smiling and listening.

"She shouted at me, 'Hey, Skin, come over here,' and I did. I walked across the street to where she was. What else could I do?" He shook his head and smiled at the Hunkpapa woman. "She's always been like that." He shook his head again, annoyed at how much she loved him. "She told me to go sit down with the old Apache. Him." He pointed at the older man with his chin, the husband, then with his finger. "Well, I looked at him, and he looked at me. And then I looked again. He just sat there, looking at me, smoking a cigarette." He stared and imitated the old Apache as he told the story, and we all laughed. We could see it because the old Apache is that way, plain and simple. He thinks and he waits and smokes sometimes, when he's not pissed off or talking circles around something that needs explaining from many directions, or remembering a moment in the jungles of Laos, or remembering something that took him out of this world into a much better place, somehow. The young Apache caught the mannerism perfectly, and we had to laugh because he became the older man for that second, a caricature and a character, and it was funny, like a snapshot of the same man at different ages, in different bodies.

"I looked at him, you know, but it wasn't him I was looking at." He paused to let that sink in. "It was me. I could see me in his eyes. No, it wasn't reflected. He wasn't judging me or telling me anything. He was just looking and smoking, holding the cigarette, just sitting there."

He paused again, nodding at me and smiling, shoulders back, stepping back and forth like a bear, grinning because he was describing the moment that changed his life, after all the prison and violence in and out of it, and he thought it was funny and even hilarious but deadly serious at the same time. He relished it, nurtured it, held it in his mouth and savored it, then went on, because it was delicious, that moment, and will always be.

"I mean, he didn't say shit, and he didn't do shit, and I thought, or maybe I thought, I don't know, because I wasn't doing a whole lot of thinking those days, 'this fucker is just looking at me, and you know what, it's okay. It's okay.'"

He paused, looking at both the old Apache and his wife, then added, "It was both of them, him and her. I'd be about to do some stupid shit, and there she'd be. Or I'd hear him, whether it was in person when I'd explain what I was going to do, or when I'd be out there somewhere far away, and I'd hear him ask, 'Are you sure you want to do this?' with no more judgment than there was the first day sitting there. He was just asking."

"So that's when I started. That's when it all began. That day," he said with finality and matter-of-fact passion, like the story was over. The most important part of it was over, to him, and then he clarified further, dropping down quieter. "I mean I began going back to the medicine," he said, "doing the work. And it's work, hard work, doing this. It's way easier to just shine it on, go your own way." He grinned. "But it ain't easier, not really. It just seems like it at first, and then you find yourself in the shit again, and it's that much harder to get out. You gotta do the work, and you know what?" He smiled, looking to both sides then back at me, like in confidentiality, "It's fun."

I don't have any idea when someone told him about Sand Creek or anything about the blood war of his own people. I don't have any idea about when he heard the old stories, and the newer hidden ones either, the stuff that's happened since he was born, or when he began to know the history that formed him, and it really only matters as he learned why it came down the way it did and how he saw himself, or what was important to see coming down the line that's put on everyone, all of us, the line of obedience to something so dysfunctional it boggles any mind that opens its sleepy eye on a groggy and confused morning. He was lucky in a deeply strange and twisted way despite it all, because he burst out of it saying, "No fucking way," to the whole world, in the worst way possible. He did this even though he may have had no idea of the origins, no sense of the antecedents that swim through all of us unaccounted for, those militant psychoses that are still "all present or accounted for, sir (or ma'am)", the ones that filter through the air like dust motes and molecules of memory creeping through our cells.

"And once you've started on it," he kept going, "and you get it, I mean really get it," he grinned, "There's no turning around, no going back. I mean, what for? Why would anyone want to go back there?"

What's back there anyway, not in time but in that place we dread to live in alone, where there is no accountability but plenty of vaguely defined malice floating around and through us? When I stop to watch the floaters carefully, I see there are many answers, and all of them are the sources of my traveling through as much time as I can reach in my life. It's the same old list of things we keep having to face, no matter what, until we learn how to carry them rightly, gently and with the respect they deserve, for our own good. Circling around again and again like on a merry-go-round, there are images like Chivington without remorse, without having uttered the name of his Soule. And blindness that stays on a person's face, buries the world around us, puts young men and women in prison, and silences the voices of children. There is Columbine, Colorado; ICBMs parading through its streets, and dead children. There is the disdain in the eyes that creates thoughtless murder. And dullness. There is the heroism of Custer on a movie poster, and the isolation of Hitler as a lone madman spouting from the pedant's lips. There is the silent and barely visible genocide of eighty-five thousand Mayan, trembling in the quiet shadow of Chivington's sword a hundred and twenty years later just down the road from modern California. There is silence and wondering on Indigenous country faces walking down an asphalt road, a Columbus Day parade in downtown Denver, and street fights on the sidewalks of inner cities, with epithets thrown like grenades, and grenades thrown like epithets. There is the Trail of Tears, always and for all of us.

Who can deal with all of this alone? I can't, and I listen intently to the young Apache's story because it contains what I need for my own strength too.

"I'm free now," the young Apache said, "in all this work and with these people, and that's where I want to be. Here. It's that simple." He holds all of it in his strong hands now by choice, and that's the important thing, the choice he makes. It's more than just him now because he's listened and is listening still.

I smiled to hear his story. I could picture him spending a long hour shoveling snow off the stones in Colorado, chipping away hard ice before he could build the fire, and I laughed at the welcome feeling coming across my chest again, like emerging into the sun after months in a winter cave, hibernating. I'd been too long in the harder side of things. His freedom and his obligation to that freedom made the day, his eyes reflecting my original time with a good knowing smile shared across generations. Because of him, and the old Apache and his wife, and all those connected to the day and the ceremony, the sound of the silver Chevy truck purred like manna working its way down from the sky when I left. It works that way, revelations, stories, and motor sounds. I drove away into the dark night and comforting stars, stars so soft I could smell their fragrance in the breeze coming through the open window. I drove south, and to the north, I could hear his black Harley flinging him down the highway with a roar, the bad man bringing it all back home.

GOING TO WATER

42

Monkeys bawled and screeched in the dark jungle in the distance around us, a warm and humid moon overseeing it all like the big eye of an annoyed and long-suffering mother. The king reclined on his dais and drank his tea, slowly approaching death, while I sat next to him on a chair. He was demanding even in his last days, used to being seen as next to Creation itself, almost like the human child of an unidentifiable and unshaped source of the whole world. At least that was the story, but in the eyes of his servants, I could see something else, something wandering through faces that no longer believed. Maybe they never had, or maybe they had left a childhood of belief behind in a lifetime of frightened servitude.

This king reminded me again that it was a sad work for me most times, going across the world to administer the herbs and be with people like him, but I knew it was necessary, and the cry of Little Rain in my ears kept me going. The thickness of these people's vision was like walking through tar on a prehistoric landscape, and I had to remind myself that changing things was not about each villain's revelation. It was not that simple, but it was true that as leaders, they were collections and representations, so this one king was important too, no matter how pathetic. He was important, and he was afraid, surrounded by those who obeyed him, but who did so in silent disdain, a lonely place for a monarch. When the priests he knew surrounded his bedside on the pyramid's flat stone top, hands held up to the night sky, voices reassuring him, he believed his divinity would conquer the indirect eyes of the servants, but when the priests filed back down to chat about the next steps of ruling, and walk in procession across the green courtyard below, the servants' turned-away faces held sway, and he was alone again. The stars that had been his exalted parents moments before became cold pinpoints of light in a jaguar's night sky.

This conversation with the king was almost a ritual for me, a litany, but each man or woman's voice and eyes brought the process away from being rote, away from being like a mass sung by a dullard priest whose religion had become merely political, his childhood fervor for the feeling of God in his skin forgotten in the aisles of interpretations and laws, the vast libraries of sins, all the ways of missing the mark. No, I could not fall to that because, I kept reminding myself, I'd seen my own face in each of theirs. Their choices were mine too, like the old Apache and the young Apache were each other, and I reminded myself over and over in my travels that each fallen leader who actually saw what had been done, even in some small proportion, created a veritable explosion across the imagination, not of himself alone, but of how we all perceive what is possible. Again, this fact was my litany, not so much the words, and it burned itself across my mind as I listened to the king whine like the old bloodthirsty colonel.

"I don't know," he said. "I don't know anymore when I look at the stars. The monkeys howl like they want my blood, and I think they'll cross the plazas and climb the walls to tear me apart, and my servants will not chase them away."

But the monkeys knew better. Generations of killing them when they scaled the stone sides had been planted in their skulls. Only the very adventurous and rash youngsters would attempt it late at night when there were no sentinels guarding the holy spots, and even then they moved silently, eyes darting back and forth for a lance that might come quickly out of the darkness. The elder monkeys watched from distant tree branches, shaking their heads when disaster did strike, impaling those who didn't listen.

I smiled. "They won't come get you. They know better by now."

Fighting laughter, I thought of the theory from up in the future, that a hundred monkeys in a room with a hundred typewriters could write a sacred book in a hundred chunks of however time was measured by the people around them. It was one hundred days or one hundred years, some number that made the poetic equation ring possible. Then in a vaguely related exploration of how the mind might really work, more scientific experiments and patient observations proved indeed that monkeys on one island learned a mechanical skill very mysteriously, without any direct contact from monkeys on another island, monkeys who had learned a specific mechanical skill either on their own or from people teaching them. Here even more men and women in white lab coats and puzzled expressions stood and discussed it at length. It was like tropical birds had flown from one island to another with monkey-blueprinting somehow holding to their plumes, and when a curious monkey picked up a fallen feather and waved it into a bright morning sky, the ideas from a distant monkey fell out and sifted down into his brain, like dust falling into the eyes. This comical and simple memory is what my thoughts did to me as I prepared the liquid for the king. I wanted to tell him the story but thought it would be too cruel to make him laugh or think more deeply about monkeys in a future he couldn't conceive. Besides, even in the future people had forgotten that story quickly and no longer talked about it or what it could possibly mean when they really needed to ponder it, during the time they taught their children how to track missiles and fire rockets and lasers with games bought in huge concrete block shopping malls. Each person had become independent by then, and Independence Day had become an explosion from a long list: Vietnam, the Philippines, California, Panama, the Black Hills of South Dakota, North Carolina and Georgia. There were echoes in the mind like shells from offshore naval batteries, but few heard them or thought about the ships that bobbed up and down in the sea like huge toys.

"They know," I repeated. "The monkeys know. And you're safe. They won't come up here." He was relieved, and he sighed deeply.

A small and beautiful servant walked quietly to the king and filled his cup with warm liquid, and he waved her off with a habitual gesture when she was done pouring. The monkeys were quiet during her presence, creating a lull even in their distant sounds, so the only sound we heard was the liquid falling into liquid, a soft and increasing pitch of water on water until it abruptly broke off into jungle silence again. The king looked at me as I unwrapped the leather around the gourd vial. Working the words out from deep inside, he spoke slowly.

"Do you think I am divine?" he asked.

There was a general down in the Philippines who was famous for commanding his troops to spare no male ten years or older. Smith was his name, a good common name for a common attitude, for when I listened to the soldiers of his time talk about what they were doing down there, it was "shooting niggers." "Got me another one." It was for their own freedom and their own good, the leaders argued. There were many ways to say it, and countless justifications. The twentieth century had dawned, if I can use that hopeful verb for such a horrible time in that particularly burning place, and almost all of the generals were veterans of the Indian Wars back home, and they waged a scorched earth policy. The blacks of America had been freed, ostensibly, and there were even regiments of them fighting there too, and I wondered if they were "shooting niggers" too, but I doubted it. The black American press said the islands should be allowed their own ways, but the soldiers were soldiers, not deciders, and they said so contritely as they did their jobs. And afterward, some stayed and married and began something beautiful, but first was the war, on its terms. The "goo-goos" was another name for the Indigenous people from all the tribes stuffed together into primitive slots in the saviors' minds, those still extolling Manifest Destiny, and maybe this name made its way through time to become the "gooks" of Vietnam, because naming is such a deep part of it all. Smith was very clear with me when I sat with him.

"They are a primitive people with no morals whatever. They are a cruel people, an inferior people, and they need to be chastised in every way. There must be no quarter, because they only understand destruction." There was not a bit of regret in his voice, and one of his senators said it even more plainly, behind the safety of his broad oak desk.

"There will be markets here for American goods, and this is the doorway to China, a vast market we must tap." It's an attitude, and one must admire the senator who speaks the truth, however despicable and commercial and bloodless.

I sat with both of these men, and with privates and sergeants too of all races in the conquering forces, for some of the Macabebe scouts working with the Americans had gone into the worst depths in themselves as well, into frenzies of torture and behavior gone out of control in a brutal war years long. And many Indigenous fighters had lost themselves too from grief and fury, as we keep seeing, so I sat with men on both sides in order to make the changes of thought. But in all my listening to the soldiers and senators who fought and who promoted this infamy, never did I hear anyone say the actual words, "This is their land." Oh, there were many back on Turtle Island who said it was wrong, that it was a war of empire, it's true. But strangely, they were the same men who'd forgotten the very same point about us Indigenous here, that this is our land and not theirs, but even that brand of contradictory patriot was labeled treasonous in a strange trick of historical logic, and they spoke to no avail despite their moral eloquence. The war proceeded, and another million Indigenous people died, but somewhere else this time around, not Indians of the Americas.

"I want you to see something," I said to the king, and I called the servant girl back over with my arm. She came carefully, stopping several feet away from us. "Come closer," I gestured with my hand, and when she was within my reach, I grasped her small strong arm in my hand, gently pulling.

"Come sit here," I said, patting the bench the king rested upon.

She shook her head vehemently and tried to pull away, but her pulling was only a gesture, not a struggle. Her curiosity and interest in me, another woman so close to the king without any dire results, was drawing her to us. She'd been watching from the shadows, and now her body was following her mind, an inevitable direction. I smiled to her, nodding at the king, and she and I acknowledged the man's impotence together, and this connection freed her emotions, broke through the servant's visage. As she got closer to him, her scorn and anger began to flash through her, but she kept it down, and it shook her body. She shook for all her suffering people. Her hands touched her skirt and thighs nervously, then she folded her arms to subdue them, but they wouldn't be stilled, and they moved back and forth, up and down over her body looking for a place to rest. I still held her arm above the elbow, and I gently pushed her to sit next to the king, who stared transfixed, open-mouthed.

"Ask her if you are divine. Don't ask me," I encouraged. "Ask her." Without his priests, he was like a child left alone without his mother or father, and though his old knees were swollen with arthritis, his hands withered and lined, his face was young and growing younger as he moved closer to the next world. I nodded to him and smiled. "Go ahead. Ask her, and look at her."

She looked up at me, and followed my lead to look into his face, something she'd never been allowed to do. It took great courage. Watching her and him together, I knew it would be days before his body faltered and failed him, before he would leave it, but I dropped the herbs into his mouth anyway. It had come to this method and pace for me because there was so much work to be done. I'd seen that some people would take it and move with it, let the stream carry them through all the images of their lives, and that they would be courageous, real soldiers and kings and queens, not propped up figures dispensing death until the last second of breath. Some would listen, and some would not, and even though the chances of surrender were greater at the last moment, much good could also happen even days before, maybe even weeks before, because the imminent face of mortality was always a powerful and unavoidable force in their decisions, a wall they must come up against, so I shifted my timing and went for the most I could do on any visit to any continent or time. I was like a factory worker on an assembly line, but never too fast, and always with the key listening. The young girl became a helper on this night, and she seemed to realize this, so she sat carefully and solidly by the king and bent over to look into his eyes. He seemed to see her, to recognize that she was a real woman for the first time, even though he might have had her sex at his whim, but that was different, with her head to the side and away. She didn't matter but to satisfy him, so she wasn't real. But now she was real, no matter their history together. Death encouraged him to speak to one who had known him long, death the equalizer, if he could only listen to its voice.

"Do you?" he started, then stopped and blinked, looked away into the night sky, and slowly brought his eyes back to hers, shocked at their darkness. "Do you think I am divine?"

His question broke open her face like a dam, and all her life's training welled up furiously on her mouth as it opened to speak, but she did not speak. She held it, because there was too much boiled up in there to

say in words, but she let it move across her expressions. First came outrage, like flames burning through
a plain of dry grass, then it was gone, tapering away,
even the smoke clearing away into a wind of cruel
irony. How could he ask whether what had been
beaten into her and raped into her was true or not?
Him? How could the divine doubt his own divinity?
She asked these things of herself. Her hands wanted to
strangle him, but they touched her own throat instead,
as if to silence her own voice again out of long habit,
for he was still king, even though he was lying help-
lessly next to her on a night like no other, hot and
humid and new, with some kind of promise on the
air. Then the sadness came, always a deep lake under
the fires of anger, impotence and despair. Her own
father had been proud and had not capitulated like so
many others, and he had taught her something else
about people, something much older and wiser about
people in the jungles among rain and trees, and how
they sang to each other, and how the people would
wake up once again to this kinder way of life. So he
had been sacrificed to the gods of the sullen and arrogant priests, and she had become servant and slave
to the king. She had entered her lake of sadness as a
small child, and now she remembered her father's and
mother's eyes, and she cried, but not for long, because
she'd been made hard by the rest of her life. There
was little room for tears in her manner of survival,
and now here was this man lying before her asking
her something that suddenly became absurd to her,
ludicrous, and she almost burst into laughter so strong

she had to turn away from his pleading eyes, and she held that scornful laughter away too, held it close to her breast and watched him.

But it was not done between them, and he reached a frail hand onto her arm, touching her for the last time. He didn't speak, but his question was between them, a huge thing waiting to be held, turned around in the hands and heart and answered.

Slowly, she turned her eyes to his again and took a deep breath, letting it out across his face without even thinking about it. She had arrived somewhere a long time ago, and her mother and father were with her in a thatched-roof hut on the edge of the city near the long fields that poured over the jungle, razing it, killing it. She dared to breathe on him, and his eyes started as he smelled her human breath, his cheeks shaking, then he breathed her in through his nostrils and stared at her, waiting. He breathed her in, but he did not take anything away from her anymore. She would not allow it ever again from anyone.

"No," she shook her head, "You are not divine." Her voice was clear and beautiful when it finally came out of her throat into the night.

He was not afraid of her words, but seemed to welcome them, and in a moment he saw all those who had fallen under his reign, not by name or face or even by number, but like pale fallen corn stalks in a wind of rule, all laid down in one direction, and he was relieved to say it, to repeat her words, and to say what he had done, if only in his silent, swollen mind, because it was true. It was simply true. He was a king who brought great suffering, and he said that. He still held her eyes, but he saw the fields and the people, and when she spoke, he breathed out fully into the night.

"All of this," she said, opening her free arm to the expanse of jungle and sky, "All of this is divine. Not you."

Pol Pot told me it was his lesser officers who killed millions of his own people, not him. "I didn't know. It grew beyond my control," he said, and when he was asked by the nations of the world to be accountable, he died suddenly in a cloak of mystery, without resolution. "They lied to me," he said, "my own people lied to me," but some said he took poison instead of admission, and I had given him the medicine and left, another king among many, another of the wrong kind of warrior ravaging land and ideas and people. I gave him Grandmother's green drops and listened to him ramble on about what people said about him, about the slaughter, his words jumping around like flies on something already dead, looking for where they could plant their eggs and multiply. I like to think the herbs found their way to the center of his being, but I kept moving, so I can't say with any kind of authority whether it was his shame that made him take the poison or not. I like to think so, but nothing is certain in these doings. I became like a whirr of wind then, crossing the world, circling like the gyres in the seas, brushing up against continents and people, building and building everywhere I went, and even though I often didn't know the outcome with this person or that, I came to feel it didn't immediately matter. It became a matter of percentages, for I'd been immersed in these troubled centuries long enough that I began to understand their style, the numbers game, and I had to play the odds. I had to see it that way, and to keep moving. Pol Pot was only one stubborn man, but he was a big fish, so I gave him a big dose, like the king, because the two of them bridged a vast and uncountable number of children's dreams, like a swath of cloth draped over the world's edge, going back and back into time, and where the darkness burst into even the slightest glow, dreams changed and began aligning themselves with something very old that was aching to emerge again, and that would not be stifled.

After this, one spring night in my hurried travels, I came across the Atsugewi elder again, as he answered a young mixedblood woman's question under florescent lights in a big square conference room in his native land of California. "Have we gone past the point of no return in our destruction of the world?" she asked. This was a big question to many in the room, and they leaned forward in their blue plastic chairs for his answer. It was a question even many little children had on their minds, very little ones whose chubby hands gathered discarded sandwich bags on the local forests' paths in panic and concern, and it echoed across science and art and politics like a trumpet call, like taps in the quiet evening or, hopefully, more like morning reveille.

The elder looked over the head of the young woman into the lights in the back of the room, thinking, remembering the old instructions to respect, and how different they were from the new imported instructions to exploit, as he observed these crucial differences of approach. He gazed into her eyes for a long time before he spoke, but he was letting the answer build before it became words, like he always does, not so much searching for something he doesn't know, but letting it gather into the momentum it should have in order to find its rightful place in the air.

"No," he said firmly but quietly. "It's not too late. The internal balance has not been destroyed." He paused again. "Anything can happen, and it is happening now, as we speak." He looked at her, then at the others. He did not say how to change it. That was up to them. "We must love the world, and we must sing in the morning light. That is all I know," he said. Then he paused still again. "I don't know much of anything else," he said, and laughed. "That's our job." Then he smiled at the girl, "You will sing that love song." His eyes sparkled. "Maybe you will sing it tomorrow." She leaned back in surprise, a grin on her young face.

I heard his gravelly laughter from very close that evening, then from far away on the next day, and then late one evening days later when it suddenly shot by me like a comet, like lightning bolts gathered toward a purpose beyond the dark horizon. This was his work, his job, words that fly and live forever, what he'd been given by his grandfather and grandmother and uncles, and the love he spoke of reached out everywhere. I smiled to myself, and then I hesitated, listening. There would be many consequences of this love on both sides of things, and I could feel them gathering in the air around us like a monsoon squall.

GOING TO WATER

43

Cold wind swirled through the giant gum trees lining
the green valley. It drove in off the ocean and spun the
fresh spring apple blossoms high into the air, thinning
the crops for fall with petulance, warning, and delight.
The witch stood in the middle of a long expanse of
grass dotted with golden poppies and new blue lupine,
hands on his suit of shiny silk. It glistened in bright
sunlight. He waited while the wind roared, staring
straight ahead. Behind him and to the sides were his
servants and soldiers, spread out as though in a line-
battle of centuries before. It was 2013, and he had come
to settle with me, and this would be no California
Indigenous line-battle, no balancing intended, not in
his mind. It would go on past the injury of one man or
woman, and there would be no sustaining the family
of the injured by the injurer, no feasting a season later
by the village of the injured. There was no leveling of
responsibility in the witch boy's mind, no civility or
mercy. He wanted it all. I walked alone toward him
through the grass, then stopped when I could see his
eyes at a safe distance.

"The painter girl is ours now," he shouted through the wind in triumph and blame, as though it was my fault that Little Rain had to be abducted. The wind caught his voice and spread it through the air to me in pieces. The butt of a silver pistol jutted from his suit pocket, duly noted. I calculated and scanned, but I could find no evidence of Little Rain's presence there, and the witch nodded as if in answer to my thoughts. The ghost of Magda Goebbels stepped forward out of a forming haze at his signal, her strong hand gripping the child's arm, who also emerged from the haze, staring. What was on Magda's face? Triumph? Unspeakable pain? She held Little Rain's arm above the right wrist, her painting arm, and the girl looked at me across the bending green grass. Buds were just beginning to form at the tips, and the blades were not yet sharp, the shafts still soft and tender. Little Rain was in shock, looking at me and the land and people all around her, but she was present too. She knew these people, and she painted the world, so she waited her chance and held back, unresisting the woman's power over her. She bent like the grass in the wind.

The witch took a step forward, motioning me to come and talk. Alone, I thought about it a moment, then headed forward. There was no choice. We walked toward each other, the bright air throwing my hair around me, in front of my eyes then away, blinding me from his glaring eyes then opening them to me again as we drew closer. I was grateful for the moments between, moments to think and see. His soldiers were ephemeral, yet I knew their power no matter what. Magda gripped Little Rain after all, suddenly no less corporeal than the child was. They had gone back to get her, to rip her from her village and bring her here, to show both of us their power and breadth of influence, but we knew this power already, though not the form it could take until now. But when I thought about it, it made sense. How they had gotten past Grandfather and Grandmother was another question, and I worried for a split second. I walked slowly, in pace with the witch, gripping the handle of the fiber knife in my pocket. The witch's slender hand hovered nearer and nearer the silver pistol as we came closer together. I saw it was the same gun from the mesa years before, the one that took the young mother's life. I calculated and watched, and then we stopped directly in front of each other.

I had never been so close to him, not even in the Vatican or hiding in the bush from him when he became the beast on that rainy night. We were almost nose to nose, and his smell revolted me, like foul chemicals, nothing natural, nothing of wood smoke and sweat, but more of polish and well-groomed death. Even in the harsh wind, his hair only lifted from its perfection here and there, and his buffed nails gleamed in the afternoon sun, right above the pistol grip. He spoke first, in control.

"I warned you once before, at the Berghof. You should have joined me then, like I wanted." He smiled without showing his teeth, a thin smile. "Now it's too late for you."

I gave him no expression to judge where it might go, or when. I simply waited and looked into his eyes, red veins snaking through the whites of them, shining black pupils that shifted in intensity like the wind, changing and restless yet persistent, not giving anything away, a promise of his continuance right there, present like the pistol and the memory of the shot behind me on the mesa, the woman falling face down in the yellow dirt. They would cut off her hands. This is who stood before me. I waited. He had to gloat, but he was afraid even then, for there is finally no permanent confidence in his manner of power because it has an end, a bigger gun, a faster mind or fists waiting out there somewhere, so it is never sated and is always hungry and afraid. In his deepest fear he is most dangerous, like right now. He had to say more to assure his place in the moment, little things to prove himself to me, to himself, and to everyone there, to make it all as he saw it.

"I will destroy you all," he said almost in a song, "though I am one of you. I am one of you and yet I am not. I was born only as a potential within you and our people, nothing more, a possibility you balanced out with your stories, and you held me down, even inside yourselves, and then the others came and I realized my true sources and their power, where I came from and where I belonged, and I grew in another era without your influence holding me down, and now I will destroy all of you, in the most essential ways. In more ways than you can count." He talked like this, and I was surprised, though I don't know why. Why wouldn't his sophistication or complication of thought and justification follow the complications of the evolution and digression so monumentally at play in the world right now?

Time seemed to freeze on the chill wind, in the roar and sway of the eucalyptus towering over the valley, and though he was afraid in his bluster, he was not hurried, and there was much he wanted to say, little things to catalogue his having won. He settled in, inviting me to sit, and I lowered myself onto my knees in the grass slowly opposite him, and we sat, him cross-legged, right hand in front of the pistol, me on my knees and leaning back on my feet, my hand in my pocket on the knife handle. I could stand in an instant and strike, and so could he from his position, but with the slightest bit more effort. He thought the pistol would make up for that difference, would be the compensation, but that could be his mistake if it came to violence. The grass swayed back and forth, laid down in the heavy gusts, then rose up around us, swirling green, a whirring rustling song. He wanted to lay out the details

"These are little things to some, but you know they are not little." He began his story quietly but firmly. He had been thinking it all over, watching, no simple beast raging over the world, but a cunning man, and more than a man, an impulse beneath every empire there ever was, an impulse like expansion and contraction, like the saying, "as above, so below," like electronic wave lengths, high and low, like pulsation, like the coming of fall and the death of leaves. And he had details, small things that were indicators of how far it had come.

"There are so many things to say," he began his chant, "so many ways to tear you apart, so many things you already know that you must hear again and again, even in your dreams." He studied me for a reaction, and settled in further. "I will continue to pit you against each other today, now in your remnants, and you will fight over pennies and who belongs to which piece of land you will never get back, not that way, not separated the way you think you should be. You will argue about who is an Indian and who is not, as you do now all across this land, and you will ask the masters to help you do this, even though they began that defining of blood to get what they wanted from you, and you will fight and fight, and the masters will laugh at you behind closed doors, pretending to your face that they would help if you would only, only just get along, but you cannot, alas, and it makes them so sad as they count their gold." He smiled, watching a truth of this time, one huge and powerful truth that is simply a newer kind of killing, a killing of the mind, one coming from the same kind of lust it always has. "And you will be right in your anger," he held up a finger, "you will be right in that, but not in where you throw it," he smiled again, "and this you will not see, and where you do not see, this is where I am waiting, and your blindness will make you mine." He looked steadily at me as he spoke, intoning like in a Mass, his eyes not leaving mine, though he must have thought I would not attack him, not with Little Rain in the madwoman's frenzied grip. But he was not certain.

His story was right, without a shred of doubt, for the scattering had done its job, the Indigenous Diaspora thorough and profound, and we reeled from it. The Indigenous who dis-enrolled their own from tribes they were born into proved it, a strange concept the opposite of what we knew over time was working for all of us, and you only had to look now in order to see the aberration, in so many corners of Turtle Island it made the head swim. Children who had not been born yet would never be able to claim their birthright or genes, dead to a huge part of themselves before they'd even come into the world, still another kind of killing of the unborn and the community. Men beat their wives and children, rising up out of whiskey bottles like monstrous spectral genies of destruction, no wishes present but the one that the raging man would disappear in the blink of the woman's eye, but that wish would not be granted. Mothers walked away from their children for a silver needle in the arm to quiet their pain, but only more pain ensued, for them and for the children left trying to make sense out of what contradicted the genetic memory alive even in their young eyes, knowing without a doubt what their lives should be, what it should be because it is simply natural, nothing complicated, simply what a mother is.

But destruction is complicated. It's ball bearings and brads, nails and gun-powder in a pressure cooker on a holiday city street, exploding in a celebrating crowd. It's a long slow explosion too, a national thing, expansive like the long-standing doctrine of discovery and the written right to control everything in its path, but it's out of control, ball bearings searching unerr-ingly for hearts in inner-cities and corners of quiet reservations. And it's international too, and when the citizens of Turtle Island hear the explosion and the screams in their own streets, they wonder instantly at the source, outside or inside their borders. They do not know, but they feel in their bones somewhere that it is never extraneous and is always connected, maybe to an exploded hospital or mosque or wedding party, some kind of historical collateral damage, no matter the depth of denial they live. We are the children of the addict now, all of us, but despite everything, we know it is the mother's job to love us, and she would deny us only if she is stark raving mad or deeply sick. We know this, and we look around frantically for help, and when we look closely enough, we find it.

The shattering did not destroy everyone, you see, not then and not now, not by a long shot despite the witch boy's mounds and mounds of evidence, evi-dence that could roll off his tongue continuously for days and days. The people still know who they are, even when they don't know what it means and can-not live many forms of what they imagine life could have been during my original time, or what it could be now. Though the blood is mixed and the land torn out under from them, there are millions who still know, and who continue searching through the wreckage of their traditions and lives and communities. Like countless families have done, the mixedblood pro-fessor's great grandmother, grandfather and mother have held the line, on the very line of their red blood for as long as he can remember, and for as long as he can imagine from family stories and neatly written poems in the back of the old tattered family bible, never a drinker or user in the lot, but hard-working people loving their children and teaching them that our way will never die, call it whatever you will. There was seldom a Christian in their family either, despite the presence of the Bible, but always believers in life, always proud even in their outrage and sorrow. Yes, they worked the corn plantations of Oklahoma and Texas, and though they were never a moneyed bunch, they always gave and provided the best they could for all those around them. In the last years of his life, the grandfather raised and fed and cared for nine foster kids chewed up and spit out by this society, long after his first family had grown and gone out into the world. He raised them on a subsistence farm in the foothills of the Sierra Nevada range, a farm he bought for five thousand dollars with saved alcohol and cigarette coupons from WW2, and that farm was stolen from him over time, piece by piece, by the good-old-boy city fathers who patted him on the back just before he died, robbing him with a fountain pen, not a six-gun, as the song goes. But he held the line even then. He held strong. And what do you call that in your smugness, Mister Witch Boy?

I smiled at him, and he was afraid, eyes narrowing in his own calculation, wondering what I was thinking. But he knew as well as I did what I saw and thought. He knew the Indigenous picking up guns in Oaxaca, meeting in the mountains and walking strong on long marches of tens of thousands to the cities, Indigenous and their Latino allies demanding to be seen. He knew them throughout the Americas, finally refusing to accept the brutality anymore, and he listened to the debates about whether it was falling from the right way of living to pick up an AK-47 and protect a village from storm troopers. Could an Indigenous soldier fight without hatred? Is that the question? Can anyone? Can a woman fight out of love, laying precious life on the line to stop a monster from devouring her children's lives? The witch-boy knew the answer because he saw this in the real world, and this too frightened him, another face of power rising up through a people just like all those who fought on Turtle Island until they were simply too tired of fighting, until the battle had to go inside, for a million reasons, for their very survival. Is this another face of inclusivity, slamming a loaded magazine into a steel rifle from another continent, and is finally giving up the blood war so the children may sing another day long from now still another face of the same thing? Is walking away from the battle at the right moment the kind of resistance that is needed? Are we including life and pride and survival on both counts, bending like the wind-blown grass into what is needed for the time? The question for the witch-boy is huge, for it shows the adaptability of people who know themselves and what they must do in order to continue. It eliminates the simplicity of his impulse and his drive to have the people simply lie down in the false comfort of his inevitability. He is uneasy with this manner of complication, so he watched me think and know, and then he continued, but there was an edge, a dangerous edge.

"We will train the painter now," he said, his voice like raspy steel, with emphasis on the word "we."

"No you won't," I said back quietly, instantly, without room for thought or doubt. It was fact, nothing more to me. Cold, one might say from the outside, but there is a difference between fact and coldness. One simply is, while the other rides emotion, and here in this moment there was no room for emotion, only for seeing.

He liked this manner of confrontation, with so many of his powerful people behind him, yet his elemental position of living on fear still shuddered through him, sparking his anger, and I liked this turn of events, even though I had no idea of where it might go, because his anger was a clear weakness. Behind him, Little Rain looked at me over the tips of the moving grass. She was strong now, no longer in shock. The witch-boy's story had not worked on her, and she felt my refusal, but he pressed forward.

"You speak this way to me now? In this situation?" He leaned back and chuckled, still angry, but it was not as controlled as he wanted it to be, and a stream of spit tripped over his tongue up into the corner of his mouth, running down toward his chin. He wiped it away with the back of his pistol hand involuntarily, and as the hand moved away from his face in the air level with his mouth, he suddenly realized his vulnerability, the forgotten distance from hand to gun, the tiny amount of extra time it would take to draw down and fire, so he dropped his hand quickly, but in this whole dance he betrayed himself, showed his weakness still again.

"I only see what will happen," I said, "and what will not happen. And you will not have the child." I saw this without knowing why, so I spoke it purely to help make it so, and then I let his anger tumble over me like water off a duck's back, but I still realized I was alone, Little Rain was captured, and his power was growing with time. I waited and watched, strong at first, and then the first hints of confusion came seeping in on the back of my aloneness, splinters darting through like tiny sharp fingers of threatening light in a dark and comforting womb.

GOING TO WATER

44

While the witch catalogued events and people and ideas with his voice, each particular thing he said perched on the tip of a volcano, an iceberg dropping miles down into the sea, a big eye on top of the pyramid, and underneath the image he drew of the fat camouflaged paramilitary belly overhanging a webbed pistol belt in the Amazon, his history breathed a thousand worse pictures into me, memories of his influence everywhere. Gradually I grew sad, and I fought the sadness, but it stayed. It tugged me down into itself like quicksand. I knew my rage would come next, and in growing fear of it, I listened to the sadness singing in me, listened closely because the struggle against it was causing me to go deeper into it. I thought that maybe, just maybe, if I listened to the sadness and surrendered to it, then there would be a brief moment of having to hold my breath, surrounded by heavy wet sand on my spirit, and then I would fall out into another universe beyond, that it had a bottom and would not be endless but an avenue to another reality. I remembered an old Tsalagi woman who once taught me to put up a shield of love with my mind, gold light in the shape of the cowcatcher on the old steam trains crossing the Wild West. This worked for her, she told me, and I put up that shield, but the sadness still surrounded me. Maybe I'd thought of it too late.

I looked away from the witch-boy as he catalogued his power and accomplishments, realizing he was working on me in another way, forgetting the pistol or thinking it no longer needed, drawing me into his world with his droning voice and the images he knew would course through my mind, like a child's dreams after a horror movie, unexplained blood across a doorway, a rice paper screen or golden tatami, the red stain on a curved bright sword. His line of villains hovered, wavered in front of me like heat waves rising from broad green jungle plants in wartime, like fingers of steam from something boiling, people coming in and out of density, flesh and spirit. Little Rain disappeared from view now and again, then emerged from behind the woman who held her, eyes looking up into the sky, at me, then away, as if drifting in a dream of her own. Reality slipped away from me, and my heart trembled, shaking in my chest, fluttering across my veins with a shudder, and I thought of Sweet Hunter and my son. I felt them drifting away, drifting out of my reach, looking at me searchingly as I stared, motionless as they slowly vanished. I closed my eyes tightly, searching, but there was no difference, only more darkness surrounding the faces and guns and burning villages I saw, people running down the face of an exploding volcano, red hot lava rising up over the lip of the caldera.

It was both slow and sudden, where in one moment I knew everything he was doing, and then in the next I knew nothing. I thought if I listened to the sadness I would find something freeing, but I found only more sadness, and I was still more and more afraid of the rage that lingered there like a rattler, the righteous anger, because I knew where it could take me, where it had taken me with the Nazis. Eyes still squeezed closed, I imagined Little Rain, her hand pouring sand by the pond back home, the people watching her. Then I saw her floating alone beneath the surface of the pond, her face and eyes open to the submerged cleft in the rock where the water flowed down and out, an opening in the shape of Moon's round mouth, where the water flowed into the circle, then under the earth and through the stones until it surfaced above the town and dropped snakelike down through the valley. She felt the water come from behind her easily, surrounding her, pulling everything bad from her, filling her with all she needed, then filtering down through the earth, away and away. She looked at me, but I could not hear her thoughts and the cool water surrounded her face quietly, the sky silver and silent against the pond's surface above her.

I knew it was illusion and imagination and sound, but it was a surrounding and I was alone, and Little Rain was captured, and I couldn't find the way through, not yet. I squeezed my eyes shut even tighter, and deep red lines shot in circles from the perimeters of my vision, my heart still fluttering, my hands unmoving, one before me on my thigh, the other in my pocket, loosely gripping the knife, which now seemed lifeless and impotent. One moment I'd been in full strength, the next second in danger even within myself, one moment loving, the next fearfully lost, and I careened against the walls of my dark mind like a child in a runaway boxcar on a mountain railway, back and forth. It was more than history, more than separation from those who needed me and who I needed, more than what he was doing to me and to everyone he could touch. It was something he had tapped into that was seemingly eternal and undeniable, and he brought me into hovering on its edge, like at the top of a whirlpool. I looked over the edge of it and heard voices from somewhere speaking out of a mountain climber's advice when you're scared, "Don't look down," but I did anyway, and he was right in his warnings, again the mundane and profound melting into one thing, simple lessons expanding into one sentence that can save a life or cause it to give up, surrender into the whirlpool. "Don't look down." Piercing sadness. What is that? Where can this go?

And then my eyes were pulled open. A red-tailed hawk's high scream arced above me, and the first thing I saw was her shadow across the green grass to my side, once, then again in the arc of a tighter circle. Her scream had opened my eyes, pulled my lids open with brown talons of sound. I saw the witch out of the corner of my eye, still in front of me, but I had opened my eyes into looking away, and I heard him listing and chanting his world thickly, steadily, prisons of words coming out of his mouth forming people and actions, shouts of hatred and slamming doors, gun-shots, nuzzling cruelty, all of it like the airplane engine popping away in the near distance. The second time the shadow came around I looked up, and the young hawk looked down at me, dropping lower, cocking her head at me and dipping a wing. I whistled up at her between my teeth involuntarily and she pulled away and screamed in reply, pumped her wings hard, then drifted in a long quick line down the valley to the oaks beyond.

As she disappeared, I came back. As her shadow vanished into the broad oak grove, my body began filling again, and my reappearing synchronized with her disappearance seamlessly. The gift was given, and now it was up to me to work with it, to find what to do with it, reality against illusion, illusion against real-ity, with me sitting in the center of an hourglass sur-rounded by waving green grass, but I was struggling to just see it, just to know the slender stalks were real.

As I came back, the witch increased his numbing chant. I met his eyes again and they were glazed over but for pinpoints in the very center that had latched onto me. He saw all my movements, my hand in my pocket by the grey fiber knife, the blade that now breathed life again. I took a deep breath slowly, for I had barely been breathing all this time, and the oxy-gen gave wind to my mind, my imagination sparkling alive like an engine on a cold morning, a bear shaking snow off himself coming out of hibernation, raising his snout into cool spring air, and the wind still roared in the gum trees high above. The breath filled my chest and ran down my legs into my feet, where they lay pressed into the damp soil beneath crushed grass. I let it out suddenly, the witch's pinpoint gaze stuck on me hard and demanding, sure in what he'd accomplished, his voice still pouring all it could into the valley, the specters vibrating behind him. Little Rain struggled in the woman's grasp but stood up halfway when she saw the second breath pour into me, and her standing pulled her captor into an angle of harsh resistance. I took my eyes off the witch and gathered the girl in with my seeing. I didn't care what he might do; my body was becoming a spring again, with the flesh and muscles of a predator, but I could still not see where it might go. I only knew that this man, this beast who had once been a boy of our own kind, would not, could not and must not have the painter of the world, no matter what it might cost.

I took a third breath, exhaled clear into the oak grove in the distance where the hawk had vanished, then slowly took a fourth breath, held it a moment and let it out suddenly, and when I did, it flew out in the sound of a long warbling cry that felt like something that had been waiting forever for this moment to release it. It blew the haze off the witch's eyes and stopped his voice in an instant. He grabbed the butt of the pistol with his right hand but still held it in his pocket, not quite poised to shoot because something stopped him, and he stared as it emerged, suddenly.

It was something behind me. I could see it with my senses, its presence but not its form, and it was strong and intense. The witch jumped to his feet, rocking back on one leg in preparation to fight, drawing the pistol out as he stood, and raising it, but he did not level it at me or at what was behind me. Something else was happening inside him. He held the gun in his cocked right arm, muzzle pointing skyward, the chrome reflecting a shivering bar of sunlight across his smoothly groomed face. Was he inviting me to the first move? If so, why? He stared straight behind me, to my left side, but I still did not dare take my eyes off him. Still ready for anything, I slowly rocked forward and stood, very slowly so as not to startle him into leveling his gun and firing. His words trailed off in the wind and disappeared, and what was behind me grew in power, and suddenly there was still another presence, to my right and behind now, and the witch's eyes expanded their peripheral vision, for he was a practiced hunter and he keened to the action, as though mentally counting the rounds in his pistol. Now there were three enemies he could see before him, and six rounds in his heavy revolver. The wind calmed, watching the confrontation on the valley floor, and the grass turned gentle circles as the air changed, circles like in a dance for planting, the green grass watching it unfold.

Then the witch nodded his head slowly with meaning, once, and in another layer of breath the soldiers behind him stepped forward and steadily became stronger and stronger, until I could hear their feet pressing the ground, one foot then another. And their breath came. I could hear their breath. I recognized many of them, but there were just as many others I had never seen, and I saw the fresh zealotry of their conversion, of their turning and choosing to join him. He had been even busier than me, centuries ahead of me. I could see his promises swimming in their eyes, and the pleasure of the kill on their hands, whatever kind of killing it might be. He smiled then, the first real mobile expression since he'd begun his requiem and his song of "man as a fallen creature" had laid its cornucopia of proof out in the open air around us. His spell waned, fell away, and now he had to resort to raw power and numbers, so he summoned his soldiers and they obeyed. He looked at me as he smiled and snapped the fingers of his left hand, the one without the pistol, which still raised its muzzle sniffing the cool air, and still more of his soldiers appeared. He grinned, then looked back at them, confident of his growing superiority and strength, the way he counted it, and in that moment I spun in a half circle from the waist, feet still planted firmly, and I saw the men who were behind me.

The Apache had been the first to appear, his eyes chilled and steady on the witch, and I saw why the witch had jumped up and stepped back, raising the pistol, and I saw too why he had not fired at the man. There was too much war on his body to kill and not enough bullets in the witch's gun to stop him, and the witch knew this as surely as he knew the feel of the rabbit's warm fur on his bare feet, the fur of the rabbit's body he danced upon in the meadow so long ago. The Apache glowered at Pol Pot, who had stepped forward as he appeared, as though in a memory he could not name but knew was present in them both, the memory of old enemies, but the Cambodian held his distance and glanced to his sides for power from those beside him. The Apache simply waited, and a thin Asian woman appeared in front of him from long ago, a once-pretty woman weighed and lined with unrequited sorrow. She had come with her question and its purpose. "Were you in Cambodia?" She waited intensely for his answer. "Yes I was," he said, and she was quick then. "Did you kill a lot of Khmer Rouge?" "Yes I did," he said, looking at her without expression, and she said, "Good," then turned and walked away. But she stopped mid-step some yards away, as though she'd forgotten something in distraction, like car keys, or why she was standing where she was, and she turned and looked back at him. "Thank you," she said, and he nodded. But a river rolled down his face now because he was so old, his face lined like hers, and there was no gladness or wild thrill in any of this, just memories and the huge change they'd brought to his life, piled on top of centuries of this very same horrible confrontation. She saw this and it completed something in her, and when Pol Pot saw this too, he stepped back and was afraid. The Apache was tired, here again, with nothing left to lose but his life.

The second man was the young Apache, and no one heard the roar of his bike, but it shone in the far background where the dirt road tapered into the field at the opening to the valley. Maybe it had been there forever, glistening like him, like a sword out of its scabbard, and he looked at the witch with excitement, a kind of rekindled enjoyment of fighting everything wrong in the world, and the witch smiled, thinking he had the younger man within his influence, on the edge of conversion, falling into the whirlpool of hatred and scorn, but the young Apache smiled and opened his hands palms outward toward the witch, raising his eyebrows. He smiled and the witch recoiled, and here was another man in flesh and blood it would do no good to shoot, for he'd already died and been born again, been lost and then found, and in some way nothing mattered to him but to do the right thing, and when the young Apache saw Little Rain held down by the Nazi mother, he tilted his head toward the witch and widened his eyes. He saw his own daughter in the painter's face, the girl who listened to the wind, and nothing more needed to be said.

It went like this, and the whole line of them watched. The new converts chafed at the bit, anxious to feel the heat of battle they had no real idea about, like the armchair generals sitting at tables over a cup of coffee saying, "We gotta go there and kick some Haji ass," knowing they'd never get out the door of Bea's Diner or Denny's or the halls of Congress or some politburo somewhere. But even they realized some part of this battle was over simply by the appearance of these two seasoned warriors. Something had shifted because I was not a lone woman anymore, and even the time-mellowed and simmering adrenaline of these two men sobered everyone there. I remembered the Cheyenne man quietly singing as Custer lay dying on that hilltop, remembering for a strange

349

reason I couldn't quite find as I felt the Apaches standing there. And then the Cheyenne was simply present, both trembling hands on the earth, and I listened to his song rising. It was a finishing song, a closing and a thanking, and it seemed to drive the witch's whole line into a frantic haste in themselves, agitating them, except for a few hardened fighters. They all wanted to tear into us, but they were afraid and frenzied, turning back and forth in themselves and toward each other, wanting to strike out in frustration. But the witch-boy held them in check, turning in a circle toward them, turning his back to us and facing all of them. They calmed, settling down in their anger and feeding off it, chewing on it, and the witch waved one man forward with a grin, Joseph Goebbels.

45

Goebbels stepped toward me smiling, and as he did so, the rest of the witch-boy's line moved too, and in this unified motion, like a wave, they blended into one mass of power, like an ocean wave surging back out away from a cliff's face to meet a wave coming in, cresting and spraying its violence high into the air, and the watchers suck in their breath involuntarily.

I stepped back quickly, five, ten steps in rapid succession as the line joined together, and I realized with a shock that the witch was no longer their leader, not at all, and that there was no leader and never had been. Not him, not Goebbels, not Adi. I suddenly saw the dream a grizzled old man once told me, about when he was young during a time of intense manipulation by the priesthoods and war, when he ached to know who the leader was behind all the suffering. In his dream, he traveled through long hallways of polished stone walls, fighting his way past powerful guards, racing through doors and up winding stairs to the top. He was fighting to solve the people's grief through his discovery and exposure of the deceptions controlling their world. He'd see who was running it all, and in this he would be free, and from there he could free others, even if he couldn't destroy the man then and there. Finally, he tore through the final door, and across a bare room there was a white archway with a golden curtain waving lazily in a breeze from an open window. He stopped a moment, realizing the enormity of his accomplishment and his task, then he strode across the room in one breath and with a sweep of his arm tore back the veil, his knife poised and heart ready. But there was no one there. It was empty.

The witch's people had all come forward but for the Nazi mother gripping Little Rain by the arm. Still in unison and with new purpose, they began to form a semi-circle around the Apaches and me, with the witch-boy at the center, but his face was no longer concerned with me alone. He was bent and focused on something much larger than me, something about us they wanted to engulf right now, and as they moved toward us, bringing in the ends of their line like an anemone's slow gathering mouth, we stepped still further backward, close together. The witch-boy's eyes took us in, but he moved in a trance, a present, visceral and expressionless trance. The talk was over between us, and it was time for him to finish the job with us before something else happened he could not control. The Apaches had come from a very real place in his world and mine, and he knew precisely where, so he began the surge of attack before more help could come. Only Goebbels stared directly at me, the smile of triumph fixed on his face like a medieval painting, certain in his drive and resolve and twisted sexual nature;

it was an unnatural smile that chilled my spine. But I was not daunted by it. The line curved around us slowly and we gathered our power together, waiting for the right moment to explode, and in this, we kept our prayer strong and steady. It coursed between us as individual prayers first, born in each of our times and worlds, our individual needs to survive in our three different worlds, but then the three meshed into one prayer, where our worlds became the same and we needed each other, for certainly this is the truth of our freedom and our obligation, coming together to form lives so much bigger than our own. I felt the power rise in the two warriors and it frightened me, shook my body to the center of my bones, for I am not a warrior but something different than that, something of it yet not, and the stark smell of their readiness expanded out like a circle of white hot fire surrounding us. I saw Goebbels' face blanch in recognition of what he faced, for this fire was made of things beyond his death, a fire of purification in which he could not survive at all, not on his terms or any terms at all. There would be no Hell, no joy in damnation even, but a complete removal from existence. He saw this, and he hesitated in his twisted desire of conquering me on any terms available to him, and when he hesitated, all the others stopped too, tied together in one mass. Even his old master Adi hesitated, who'd already been where Goebbels had been, who had seen his fate as the instrument of the power brokers who would rule unconditionally, accepted it, and defied responsibility for it. They had seen the place of defeat together where they could commiserate and find company in transcending their holy and tragic victimhood, but this kind of killing would be different, without glory of any kind. They hesitated, then they gathered again and surged forward.

But the moments of hesitation had done their job. They'd opened a small window of time, just enough to let more of the world through and into the valley. A breath of wind bore down on us from behind, from the east, as though from something flying, but there was nothing in the sky but pure fading blue, for the first touches of evening had begun to come upon us. The eucalyptus still shown yellow-green in the late afternoon sun, and the higher edges of the field to the north still glowed bright emerald, but the place where we stood wrapped itself in the beginnings of shadow. Everything was still very light, but it would not last long, and change was moving quick lavender shadows through the grass quietly but steadily.

The first to come through was Will, walking in his roper's gait toward us with one hand in his pocket, his hat tilted on his head, a thick rope slung over one shoulder. He looked directly at me, then collected the whole opposing line in his stare, and came back to settle on my eyes. He nodded, and I nodded in reply. He said nothing, but when he stopped walking he planted his feet and waited. He confronted no one, but in those eyes his clarity stood firm without an ounce of humor, and he would not budge, like a rock of seeing. He was there for me and for everything he saw as true, and it filled my heart to see him, for I was afraid.

Then Johnny came, holding a beaded white eagle feather, blue and red and yellow beads shining in the waning light. He walked slowly, at first scanning the line as though they were players before a game, sizing them up, light in his expression, almost nonchalant. But then he stopped, only twenty feet from the general who had killed so many in his homeland, and he too waited. It was not a game. Standing there, he became the Samurai his family had once been, long before they had been exiled by the emperor's clans because they would not give up their Christian faith, the whole clan exiled because of their choice to believe what they wanted. In the Philippines, they mingled with each other's blood until they found their ways into the Indigenous people, loving and blending there, becoming them over time, but they didn't forget who they were in their histories, and now the ancestral Samurai faced the general who saw his people as less than human, less than animals, and he stood firm with a Dineh brother's eagle feather in his hand, an Indigenous gift to an Indigenous exile and rebel man, standing strong in all of who he was. He would not be swayed anymore than Will would, and he stared at the general, who returned his stare in hatred, a hatred that ate away at his own knowing who he was in all that scorn. Did he know his history and how he had become that which destroyed our ancestors? No, because he worked for the ancient purveyors of the westward movement, without a moment's reflection or soul, and he thought nothing of the sea's great borders once they'd gone clear to California. He just kept

355

on going and kept on killing, exchanging his horse for a ship, getting off on a distant shore and continuing that brutal thinking which made him who he was. But now he was caught in this valley and in his inevitable death again, caught even more than ever, and Johnny was free, and they faced each other as evening promised something to everyone, each to his own desire.

Then the Mayan slave came, and she faced the king who found himself once again on the wrong side of the line, but he went along with it still again, too weak to fight the forces that would always seduce and use him, sold out on his power over her flesh and will simply because she was everything alive and free, sold out until he saw her spirit would not be penetrated. Not then, and especially not now. She would not bend. Then Betty came, and she stood next to Will, but a full step forward of him, and she pointed at the German mother holding Little Rain, as though to demand of her that she do what she knew was right and natural and release her. And then the young mother on the yellow mesa came too, whole and strong and trying to understand everything in her death, all that had happened in her lifetime, and she too fixed her life and power on Little Rain's captor with a vengeance, and she spied Eva too, so she looked back and forth in incredulity between the crazy mother and Eva, as though asking, "What are you doing?" in a voice that tore at the insides of her skull, but she was speechless, silent and blazing.

Grandfather Tree came too, dropping down from behind the gum trees and stomping across the valley from the south, and I cried out to see him. He glared at the witch's lines and pointed his strong arms like a Celt screaming a warning to the Roman soldiers in their ships offshore, an invitation to die gorily, and my heart leapt in joy, no matter the outcome of this day, because somewhere in the back of my mind I'd felt something had happened to him and Grandmother, and I worried, for how else could Little Rain have been captured? Then Grandmother came down the hill from the north, and the witches stared at her too, wild in her hair lit red by the falling sun, and with the two of them coming at once, the witch and his people saw that they were set upon from all directions, our line in the east, these two old ones from south and north, and now only the west remained at their backs. Some looked back behind them, but they could see nothing other than darkness forming under the thick canopy of oaks where the hawk had flown. They peered into the shadows, but the shadows were still, revealing nothing.

Grandmother held up both her hands as she walked in big strides, palms toward the witches, and scolded them mercilessly with a withering shaming, but with understanding too, because she knew the temptations they'd fallen to, being so close to those same levels of power in her own work and life. But even though she gave them compassion, her under-standing of them as living people drove her admonitions even deeper into them, for she knew the nature of their choices as individuals, as me and you, and that man and this woman, with names, and the nature of when they made their choice and why, and she would not compromise with what they had done. She didn't need to say the shame she threw at them. It was written across every fiber of her timeless and lithe presence as she moved rapidly in a line across their path, stopping them all in their tracks.

"Let the girl go," she demanded to all of them at once, nearly screaming.

No one replied, but they hunkered down and moved closer together quickly, and the witch and Goebbels reached out and brought the mother and Little Rain close to them, the mother's face twisted in anger that spit everywhere around her. She was like a dervish in one second, cursing, then silent and powerful as an ox the next, gripping the child's arm and dragging her along with her to the line. Little Rain submitted to the tall woman, and her face was eerily calm as she was pulled closer to them and to us. She held herself as though she knew something we didn't, but the building and tension of it steeled us even more in our resolve, and frightened us all as the witch-boy slowly raised the chrome pistol to the side of her head, scanning the entire line of us angrily.

We were now almost as many as them, in a strange dance of balance, and they were frightened too. The Anishinaabe woman and her grandmothers were there, the sons and cousins from out of the boats, and the young stone carver George, and many others all watching. But the balance was not in numbers, a simple way of seeing, for there were still more of them than us, but we kept our strength, and the prayer between the Apaches and me reached out to where each and every one of us standing together picked it up, making it singular and unified at once, and we all felt it in our breath as it happened to us. Then the Atsugewi elder rolled in slowly from the east in his wheelchair, and the line parted to let him move to the front. His mouth was open from the labor of pulling himself across the field, and from what he saw in front of him as well, and he looked at Little Rain as though she were the last and most important person on Earth.

"I will kill her," the witch declared plainly, in his dark unity of method and ultimate purpose, all the enemy faces masked over in a practiced cold they knew well, like ice on the ground, like waking in the morning to see first frost, and it shocks the mind and feet that walk into it.

"And when I do kill her, this confrontation will be over. And when it is over, you will see where the truth really lies." But he was done talking now with those sharp words, and he looked into each one of us, spilling his spirit over into each of us through our eyes, another technique of his practiced from one century to the next. Each of us turned from him and followed the Atsugewi elder's riveted gaze to Little Rain, and when we saw her strength, we turned back again and allowed the witch's attack on us without resistance. We could not know what would happen, so we could not move. We could only see that we didn't know, and that the silver pistol was familiar with its job, weighing heavily in a willing hand that could pull the trigger in a split second. But the witch too had a larger task in his mind, his history, and his heart, something she could only be one part of, for she was only one life. But she was the painter of life, so if he could have her, then he would have us all eventually. That was his thinking, but if he could not have her, then she must die, must be sacrificed for his greater cause because she had too much power. His people all knew this manner of being and thinking, and they waited for the hammer to fall.

But the little painter was not afraid. She held her captor's eyes, kneeled in the grass, and looked upward. She looked at Eva, then back to Eva's friend Magda, the crazed woman holding her in a powerful grip, then at the witch-boy and all of them distanced out behind those people right in front of her, all with the same expression of sadness and willingness and excitement, a strange acceptance of the worst world imaginable. As she kneeled, her free hand slid into the fine earth of a mole's surfacing door, a raised mound trail meandering across the valley floor from days before, and when the mole had gotten to this spot, he raised his head up through the opening to breathe, rest, and look into the spring sky with eyes that could only feel the sun and light, and not see. All around his craning brown neck the fine soil of his work steamed in the sun, and then he went back down, leaving the small mound to dry behind him. Little Rain kneeled down into this and filled her hand with it, and it felt warm and dry and good to her, Earth she would one day gladly become part of again. She pled with the mother holding her, silently in the only way she knew, with her dark eyes, and the woman faltered, young faces darting before her mind, and she turned away, but she couldn't stay away from what she'd done, for there was nowhere else to look, nowhere to go with the cold barrel glistening against the child's black hair in front of her now, where the skin of her temple went under the hair in tenderness and youth and promise. Magda had taken the medicine and seen. She looked back and saw her sons and daughters again, and then Eva looked too, and they both felt Grandmother standing there remembering all the births she had given in her time, all the births she'd brought not only from herself but from so many of the town's women that she knew every single person of that village as an infant, had held every one of them in her arms. She stood in this remembering clearly, like a halo around her, a shining circle of experience, and no one could see outside of her vision, separated, but we all had to include it, all of us on both sides of this willing inhabitance, this elemental choice.

The women on the other side faltered still again, another layer deeper as they saw Grandmother's life open before them, and when they did, the men came in and shored them up because they had to have the women too or nothing would further, so the trigger had to wait another precious moment before it fell, to provide time enough to bring them all back to the fold, back into the seduction, and they tried as hard as they could, promising the women that they held the ultimate power in the grip of the pistol, and they strained to make that moment as pregnant with their control as they could, but unity is not their strength. It's only a misuse of the greater truth they deny, a façade and a place they go to when they need enough truth to make things work for themselves, so it scatters easily because it's not real. It did not work for Magda, nor for Eva, nor for many others who had taken the medicine and seen a glimpse of what they'd done, and in that millisecond of their recognition, Little Rain moved.

And she moved like Rain, her name; she swept upward in an effortless swelling breeze, in one smooth rise of mercy and grace, coming to her full height. As she rose, she cast the smooth soil out of her free hand in an arc of dark mist over the hand that held her, and where the fine grains drifted down onto the harsh skin, the fingers and hand instantly opened and disappeared and she was freed. The witch-boy opened his mouth in shock, and in that moment, she cast the dust over the gun and it too began to come apart. The witch pulled the trigger, aiming now in panic at the center of her slender chest where she stood facing him squarely, but too much of the pistol's strength had disappeared for it to work, and he pulled and pulled at nothing real while Little Rain looked at him and at them all, her painter's arm raised. The mother who'd held her so angrily dropped to her knees, and tears burst out of her eyes, her face crimson in shame. Little Rain leaned forward and spread her arm out toward her, trailing fine brown sand over the woman, a soft earthen veil falling through the air effortlessly, and she disappeared completely, her eyes finally brimming over with gratitude and realization, holding Little Rain's eyes as long as she could in her leaving, so the girl would know, really know how deeply Magda knew she was released. At the same moment, Eva too vanished, simply left to go somewhere else no one could imagine, somewhere hidden away in her awakening dream beside a beautiful lake, but not here, not here, because it was over now, now again after death and this resurgence in the spirit world, and the others looked at themselves too as they began to dissipate in a chain of connection to the mole's fine dust, subterranean soil covering them with its magical life. Where Goebbels touched his wife's disappearing soft shoulder, he too became undone, and because the witch-boy had also been touched where he sought to hold the woman and Little Rain, he started to unravel in himself as well.

I wanted to know how he felt when I first saw his face twist in awareness of what was happening to his army, so I stepped toward him. He turned this way and that, mouth open as in a scream, but no sound issued from him. He flung his arms in the air around his body as though gathering big sheaves of wheat, trying with futile yet powerful circles to hold all his army together with his own muscles as the men and women came apart. I wanted to jump inside of him to see to the core of his early choices in our forests, his forbidden joy at the kill, because I wanted to track his reasons, to understand, to find some key that led him to this culmination so many centuries later. If I could see into him now, then I might know. But he was not the leader, not the leader, I had to remind myself, and when I remembered the old story of how he came to be this way and saw him as a boy with his strong bow and the big buck rabbit steaming out its life before him on the grass, I saw the ill wind circling him, and the moments in which he remembered the teaching, right there in front of him as sure as the dying creature at his feet. I saw him resist the wind as he remembered the story, and smell that wind in hesitance, and then he simply leaned back and took it in, cast his resistance away in a second and breathed it in and filled himself with it. There was no reason to it, and when I saw this, I knew I could never understand why he had done this, why he'd become part of this, and when I tried to open my heart to grasping his choice I tilted over into becoming another woman, simply by proximity, someone I did not like, someone I could not accept no matter the promise wafting through the air in front of me. I saw the pollution of my immersion into his world even to try to understand, and I had to step back and clasp my hand over my heart with so much strength that if I hadn't, it would have ripped itself out of my chest and flown away with him. And now his outrage was a mountain of flame inside him, red-hot and scorching, pouring from him, and he reached out for me in frustration, but it was too late. All these centuries of labor had brought him to this moment with me, and he wanted to swallow me whole, tear me apart with his strong hands, but now he saw once again that he could not do this, and his fury knew no bounds as he reached toward me and tried in vain to gather his vanishing army at the same time, all while trying to hold himself together where the painter's dust had penetrated his illusion of flesh and made him impotent.

Then out of the darkening azure evening, for the sun had not stopped falling during all of this confrontation, but watched steadily with a fiery eye, a gentle wind arose from the west, carrying a sound. A child's high voice rode the wind down the valley from the dark oak grove, my son's voice. The witch-boy turned to stare as the sound reached its fingers into us quickly, surrounding us all. The sound called out high and pure in rhythm, and the wind turned warm and ran between the legs of the people on the syllables, "hoko te ya, hey ya ha," and as the song grew in volume, coming closer and closer and ever more a part of the wind, the wind increased into a flurry of movement and sound, wrapping itself around the very worst and most powerful people in the army first, then all the rest of them too, old and new, and with a sudden surge it swept them all away save the witch boy, who stood in obstinate defiance in a pool of the last vestiges of wind and song. It circled his feet and calves, reaching up and climbing all around him, but he would not be moved, not by anyone's choice but his own. But the wind was strong and defiant too, only different, not rigid, but bending like the grass it swirled around his knees, insistent and gentle, like the power of water, seeking, always seeking the path of least resistance, never stopping. It gathered around him where the dust had erased parts of him, pulling, lifting, and it circled up his back and over his shoulders to his neck, and his veins bulged as he squeezed his eyes together then opened them wide, glaring at all of us, and then, with a supreme effort, collecting millennia of power into one moment, he burst free.

The song spread flat on the ground where he'd stood, like a low fog, gentle, unresisting, steadily moving as though watching unperturbed, and the witch-boy spread his wings and rose above us in an instant, violently shattering apart his image of the man and soaring into the beast he knew would save him, always save him. Shards of blue silk floated down through the air as his dark wings spread free and beat the air, and his muscles flexed in the evening sky, reveling in their freedom. He spun on his sharp talons, vertical in the sky, then lay out horizontal and glared down at us. He beat his wings in a circle around us, searching for a weakness, a place to attack, but there was none. The song rose up turquoise into the air toward him, then over us, and the breath it had been while low to the ground rose into a breeze once more as it lifted above our heads gently toward the circling beast. He flew higher, circling wider, then he dipped down toward us suddenly, opening his mouth to threaten us from the high position he held, but the sound that flew down toward us was flat, a scream bent out of shape and weak, as powerless as an old crow's complaint, and it bounced off the blue song, away and powerless. So he spun in the air and turned skyward and flew without looking back. We watched until he was a tiny black dot in the sky, and then he disappeared.

GOING TO WATER

46

Is it cowardice to want to hide away from the world, or intelligence? I was tired, worn down from being out there fighting what the world had become, despite the fact that it was my clear mission to do it. It's true I was buoyed by all those who did their very best to take care of everything precious and fragile, yet I still had to escape, get back into the time in which I would find return greetings on almost every person walking my way on the trails of the town and in the forests. There would be smiles or faces of concern, stopping a moment to talk about what lay on the other side of the hill that day, the birds calling to each other overhead in a wide v-shape going north, and how it felt to stand beneath them and listen to the season change. Direct connections between people would not be work or struggle, no averted eyes, and I needed this in every cell of my body and mind.

I woke early on the first morning with Sweet Hunter's arm under my neck. He lay on his back watching early morning light touch the dry dirt doorway of the house. I nestled into him and looked up into the rafters, watching the morning shadows move through the carefully laid branches. Unole heard our movement and crawled over to tuck himself into the robes with us, laying his smiling face on my shoulder. I was surrounded by my two men, and Sweet Hunter turned to rest his cheek on my shoulder, both their legs wrapping under me and holding me up in the soft morning air, their limbs under and around me, poking rough knees and toes into the muscles of my thighs and calves. Our feet mingled and danced together, and we laughed. I smiled at my husband, then looked into my son's sparkling bright eyes. Nothing was more powerful than this, nothing worth more than his looking straight into me with that clarity, and I thought of his song, how simple it was to him, a plain matter of being, an open asking from an innocent and beautiful mind, nothing curved or bent around the insanity I'd been immersed in outside our time. I wanted our lives to be like this forever, for him, and I laughed to feel his laugh and his gentle kiss on my shoulder.

It's not that he is without pain or fear. He's heard the stories around the fire of how men and women fall away into themselves, away from themselves, and he's seen bits and pieces of it around him even in our world, for it's not perfect, no ideal. And he's heard of things beyond the town and our woods that carry existential danger, so he's not an innocent young boy who has been spared any kind of suffering at all. I see it in his eyes, and I know what fear he has lived through because of my traveling and being away from him. He's part of me, an umbilical cord reaching through us into the whole world through all of time, and nothing could ever change that, so he knows what I go through and feel, even though he might not understand. There is so much there in our joining that I sometimes know without doubt that he is me, that we are each other. What does he feel when I come home and disappear into the ceremony and the woods and the streams for days to cleanse myself, even before greeting him? He knows I'm back, but he sees that I can't come to him, so he knows I am not safe wherever it is I've come from. He feels it in his stomach and heart, and his mind spins with it. He contemplates on what is so strong in my life that I cannot be with him when I'm home. This is a huge thing inside of him. But he doesn't ask me directly. He leaves it to me because when I finally do meet him, he sees my hunger for him, sweeping him into my arms and holding him as though it were the first time and the last time, all of our life together in this tight embrace between mother and son. He doesn't ask me because he sees that I'm back from something he can't fully fathom yet and may not want to, not yet. And because nothing has ever been held back from him, ever, and because he's suffered under no lie, ever, he knows he can ask when it's time for him, when he wants to know, and he will get everything he asks for. He has freedom and dignity, between us, and in his young freedom he chooses to sparkle into my face in the morning and fill me with life. That's his will and desire, and his choice is my home. Here I am fully alive, and here I find my deepest freedom once again.

The next evening I talked with Grandmother and Grandpa Tree, and they told me what happened. Little

Rain had foreseen the witch-boy coming in her painting, and she'd held the two of them back away from protecting her, holding her hands out in front of her toward them as they geared for battle, like holding back an animal with insistent patience. The witch and his army approached through the woods, but she subdued her two powerful protectors. Grandmother saw that Little Rain had wanted to meet the enemies all in one place somewhere far from the town, so she had let them take her to another time. Even as young as she was, she protected the people first, Grandmother told me, shaking her head in admiration with a serious smile, filled with pride. She said the little girl had known we would all gather together to protect her because that was the way it had to happen. "She wanted to see them all in one place because they had come into her in pieces of time, in fragments, as though from everywhere, and the fragments made her feel their power was everywhere, coming from anywhere at any time, much bigger than her," Grandmother said, "and when she saw them all together, she wasn't afraid anymore. She saw their fear and their source, and was not afraid anymore. It was not the same anymore, and they were not coming from her completely unknown mind. She could see them when they gathered, where their imaginations stopped and hers began. She saw their limits." Grandpa Tree punched his open left hand with his big right fist, grinning at the hard slapping sound echoing off the trees and rocks, then clenched both fists in the air before going back to tend his fire. They were proud, and something profound had shifted for them. They told me to go rest, to hide away and curl into my family, and I did that, but I listened first. I listened to them begin to talk about the little painter and what she'd done with a sweep of her arm and the mole's dust, but they only told a little, just enough for that day. They'd keep this story to themselves in their secret forest hideouts, hideouts almost all the people knew about but stayed away from out of respect, respect and the smallest amount of fear, for no one ever forgot these two lived another way. Everyone loved them, but with a healthy dose of awe, just enough to give them all the room they wanted to live their boundless lives. It was an agreement that suited everyone, especially them. I took their advice and went home with thoughts of what it could all mean, though I could not really know, not yet. It was still sorting itself in my mind.

Sweet Hunter took us hunting the next day, but we only tracked and observed because everyone already had plenty to eat. He knew all the animal families well and told us which mother had given birth how many times, and he pointed each of them out to Unole and me from our hidden places behind heavily laden berry bushes and thick shrubs. But the animals knew this stalking game too, and they watched us watching them as we listened to Sweet Hunter, and all of us danced our thoughts together across the meadow, talking into one another's minds, human to animal and back, and I realized with a start I'd almost forgotten this simple thing too, so immersed I'd been in that other way of seeing. I shook my head sharply, as though clearing cobwebs from my eyes, and Unole looked at me curiously, so I smiled at him and held a finger to my lips as we watched a small family of young deer stepping gingerly across the forest floor, moving steadily forward but with big eyes trained on us. They could see my newness, my coming home fresh again from a different world, and they spoke to me, "Did you forget?" they asked, voices echoing in my mind. "You're a curious one," they said, and when I smiled back at them, they looked away and paid us no mind anymore, finally satisfied with my presence, and that I was real, that I could hear them. Blue Jays called back and forth across the open spaces between high branches, and we let the sun move slowly across the sky, as it should be. We let ourselves dream together, and we let the dream grow and expand and become nothing different than the world that lay before us. This was the healing and the promise come together, what we have always known was ours.

As I leaned back and watched clouds move beyond the trees above me, I thought of the Atsug- ewi elder, who had almost died recently. It was just before the time of the confrontation in the valley. He told me his spirit had emptied out one day. He lay in a white hospital bed, in an intensive care unit full of beeping machines and tubes and doctors, unable to eat or hold anything the yellow-gowned nurses struggled to get into him, and he went away, falling down into nothing. He put his fist on his stomach as he told me, "There was nothing here, nothing left," he said, "and then I fell into a dream, almost gone." He took a breath. "But then I dreamed." He swallowed, looked out the window into a glassy white sky and continued. "Everyone came. All the people who ever gave me anything good," he paused, "anything positive." He turned back to me and continued quickly. "They came. My grandmother came, and my great-grandmother, and my great-great grandmother, standing there looking at me." He looked at me and named people, writers and artists and leaders and friends and children who tried to make some kind of sense to tell other people, or just to speak out what they felt, what was churning inside of them. Young women and old women walked into his dream. The quiet young woman about to have a baby on the other side of town came, the one who always wore the white bone arrowhead necklace he'd made for her. "I realized they'd all come to give me strength. Me. They'd come to give me life." He pointed at himself, smiled and clenched his fists, looking up at me. "So here I am."

The question for me has always been this: "How long can I endure, both out there and back home where it is safe?" It's true that when I am home I turn away from everything else, grateful that there is such a place, but at the same time the outside world calls me, not so much beckoning but needing, like a lost dog whining in the dark. I don't want it in, but once the doors open, it is hard to get them closed again, like window shutters in a hard wind. I can lean against them with all my might, but just as soon as I turn away, they fly open again. They're plantation shutters on plantation houses from Louisiana to Hawaii to Maori land, shutters on adobe Mission walls in the Santa Ana wind, El Diablo, and they have to be attended to.

Little Rain had been waiting for me, and she smiled broadly when I walked into the clearing, her face echoing Grandpa Tree's smile of strength, but on her it was a gentle strength, nothing of the rough power he carried with every step. She sat on her knees at the pond's edge near where the water sucked down into a sub-surface opening, the mouth that swallowed the ripples gently down into the stomach of the earth before sending it along the deeper arteries that would eventually surface to feed the valley below. Her hair was wet from going into the water, and her single set of small footprints led to where she sat. The painting arched out in a circle before her. Her eyes were so clear I thought she would speak out to me, finally revealing a voice I'd only heard as a cry, but she made no sound, nothing from this collected young girl who sat before me now, and the silence was her doing, and it was all right. Perfect. She gestured to the painting with her face, and I looked into it.

It was our town, just as she'd painted it before, but with nothing of her nightmares rising up out of the sand, no beasts or mushroom clouds or monstrous faces with wings and talons. Smoke rose from several fires, and people sat in circles around them. A bright sun shone on one side, a moon and stars on the other, and people walked freely in both directions on all the trails. Corn fields rose up the gentle slope of the south-facing hillside, brown silk bursting up out of thick ears near harvest time. Peace permeated the painting, and there was a blank circle in the center, where the face of a reclining figure would be, with a gentle rain cloud hovering above it, slanted lines falling directly down to touch the circle's edge, and she directed me to watch as the circle filled in under her steady, constantly moving hand.

The emerging figure was me, and I was lying on my side watching everything around me, legs stretched out in relaxation, resting on one elbow, hands gently clasped together. A young man stood behind me in the falling rain, and an old man sat to the side near me, a bow and quiver resting on the ground beside him, as Little Rain filled in the circle with a calm smile. I recognized the hair, the shape of my face, but not the face itself as she formed it with the sand. It was heavily lined, my eyes peering out from deep leathery folds of skin, not worry lines but lines of extremely advanced age. Looking down at the sand, I was suddenly afraid, as though I was dying with my life unfinished, and she stopped painting for a moment, looked up at me, and gestured back again. She touched my arm with her free hand, patting it with a smile, as if to tell me everything was all right, that we'd soon arrive somewhere good, somewhere we'd always looked forward to seeing, and my fear was only because I didn't even know we were traveling. I'd forgotten, I guessed, and she comforted me reassuringly, leaving her hand on my arm. It was warm and strong, and I was very old then.

On the fourth morning, I woke to find newly made boots outside our door, a pair for each of the three of us. All three pair had a shining circle of iridescent shell from the western ocean sewn at the outside top, and when the sun hit the shell it revealed glints of blue and green and orange, rainbow colors caught in glistening abalone. Little Rain's mother had made them, plain elk skin without anything but the crowning shell, strong boots for everyday wear, and when she saw us wearing them that day, she beamed with gratitude, and we did the same. These same boots were in the painting Little Rain had done, and none of this surprised me because the way in which the world had tilted over was leaving, and Earth was coming back to the way it liked to be. Little Rain gave me the world I longed for, in exchange, I guess might be the way she saw it, and when she painted me old, she found me old, foretold my future and allayed the fears that had penetrated me. I would grow old here, I knew this now, inside the dream I wanted to live, with my son and my man and the family I had grown out of, the family that would continue long after I'd gone, and she had shown me this. I had gone out of this world for her and for all the children she was one face of, but I'd paid a price too, and she saw it. She saw it and painted me back home where I belonged, and I could not have done it without her, not anymore, for our lives had merged more than anything I ever could have imagined, and she was my sister now, my exquisite and beautiful young sister, and we were home together in the center of the world.

EPILOGUE

The days were long though they were growing short with the coming of fall, and soon they passed into weeks and months and winter was upon us, one and then another. Snow fell steadily, silencing the forest softly, and when her parents came to get me I was not surprised. I wrapped myself in fur and followed them to the pond. The painting was crusted over, a few days old. They had not missed her, nor worried, for she'd taken to living in the woods in a small shelter Grandpa had built for her of brown hides over branches, but it was empty now, the coals of her fire cold and iced over with a silver glaze. She was strong now, so they'd let her go, grateful for her life and all she gave, and everyone greeted her with a smile. She stood tall even in her tiny stature as she moved back and forth from the woods to the village, but now she was gone.

I squatted over the sand, the pond white with hard ice, for it was a cold winter, one that drove us inside for days, huddling beside the fires. The circle of the painting was open at the top, like an orange had burst out from the inside, shards of the skin opening outward as from an explosion. He had come back, as we knew he must, but we hadn't known how it would happen or how long it would take. It never goes away, never completely vanishes, but waits inside us until it sees the time again, and the place where it might surface. Little Rain had seen it and gone to meet it. There was a sea, island nations in turmoil, with soldiers in long carved boats, low in the water at the circle's bottom, like the bottom of the world. They held off an armada of steel battle-ships with wooden spears and tips made of whale bone. Just below the waist of the world, people adorned in body paint and wearing bright feathers stood in front of huge yellow tractors and shouted in a language the drivers had never known, and their mouths fell open in astonishment. Above this, in the middle of the earth, tall men and women with great long metal stakes drove them into the ground, and the ground cried out through fissures opening out from the points of impact, steam from deep beneath the surface rising around the dark human figures, who drove and drove their stakes downward. At the top of the world, men and women wrapped in fur with round brown faces stood holding car-bines in front of ice-breakers and helicopters. Beneath it all, etched inside the whole of Earth's surface, like a molten hot core, a young woman crouched in readiness, watching for her moment, and when it was time she flew upward and outward, bursting out of the top, flying into the stars to see where she must begin.

I have never understood just how the magic works, just that it does. I had searched for days, then weeks, then beyond measuring time, everywhere the painting led me, but I could not find her, and so I wandered everywhere, listen-ing and walking, calling out for her. I saw all the places in her painting, but she was nowhere to be found, though all the images I'd seen in the frozen sand came alive and set me back inside myself in awe. I searched and searched and asked the people she'd painted, but no one knew her, no one had seen her. Then one cold morning in a northern Asian country, I walked along a vast sea's shoreline lined with ice. Ships lay moored in the distance under a grey-white sky, oil tankers and freighters sitting high in the water, faint tendrils of smoke rising from their boilers. It was a strange place, desolate, a grey rock roadway crunching under my feet, and I wondered how listening and searching for her had brought me to this place. Everywhere I'd gone I'd seen confrontation and strife, a war between worlds, something deep in our possibilities wasted, and I felt that all I'd done was meaningless, lost in time, stuck away in a box invisible to all the generations of people before and after me. I walked along the road forlorn and waiting, still calling but fading like the landscape I trudged through, and then I heard a distant sound. A rise in the road hid the source of the sound, but it was music, color flashing across a bleak picture, red and gold and green on a huge white canvas. The hill was slight, but I was tired, and the sound drew me slowly to the top. Looking down, not far, just twenty paces away, I saw them, a group of blue-uniformed school children sitting on their carefully wrapped books on the icy ground. It was a bus stop with a faded yellow sign, and they were all singing together in perfect unison. The song was beautiful, rising on white breath that steamed from their open mouths as they sang freely. They became aware of me standing there, and they turned toward me as one body, like a flock of birds turning in the sky. They sang to me, and there in the middle I saw her, the girl with a face in the shape of a heart, and she smiled.

GLOSSARY

Adi: Eva Braun's pet name for Adolf Hitler, leader of Germany's Third Reich, in power from 1933 until his death in 1945, generally held to be at the center of the Holocaust in Europe.

Amherst, Jeffrey: The British commander who, in 1763, during the war against Pontiac, is famous for approving the distribution of smallpox-contaminated blankets to the Native community, demonstrating willingness to use any ". . . method that can serve to Extirpate this Execrable Race." Amherst, MA, is named after him.

Berghof: The Bavarian mountain retreat purchased by Adolf Hitler from the sales of *Mein Kampf* in 1933. It was used as one of his main headquarters up to and during WWII, received many prestigious visitors, and was the seat of much of his planning.

Black Kettle: A leader of the Southern Cheyenne during the Sand Creek massacre, he had declared a truce, and was camped peacefully on the reservation when attacked, famously flying an American flag from his lodge. He and his wife survived and were killed four years later on the Washita by Custer's attack there.

Boarding Schools, American Indian: The term for militarily-structured schools in the U.S. formed to eliminate Indigenous cultures, replacing them with Euro-American culture in children. While efforts to "educate" Indigenous away from their own cultural values date from the 1600's, a concentrated effort existed from the late 1800's into the 1970's. Data emerging from current research into practices in these schools confirms the extreme trauma of "stories" told within the Indigenous community today. While Canada has formally apologized for its "schools," the U.S. has yet to acknowledge their effects.

Braun, Eva: Hitler's companion prior to and during the war. She was married to him just hours before their mutual suicide in Berlin in 1945, and was thirty-three at the time of her death.

Buffalo Soldiers: Comprising four regiments of "Colored Troops" formed in 1866, these cavalry and infantrymen served during the westward expansion and in the Spanish-American war.

Chivington, John: The American leader of a Colorado militia that attacked Black Kettle's camp at Sand Creek in 1864, despite their raising a white flag and being known to be at truce. Women, children, and elders were the vast majority of those killed, with extensive mutilations marking the barbarity of the attack.

Cochise: Leader of the Chiricahua Apache in the mid to late 1800's, whose son Taza died during a negotiating trip to Washington, D.C., in 1876, two years after Cochise's death.

Custer, George Armstrong: The U.S. Army general who famously led his men to defeat at the Little Big Horn in 1876, notorious in the history of the Indian Wars for his brashness as a soldier, and for his dehumanization of Indigenous people, which was common to the time.

Dineh: More commonly known as Navajo.

Dog Soldiers: A society within the Cheyenne nation, famous for its resistance to American expansion in the mid to late nineteenth century.

Goebbels, Joseph: The Reich Minister of Public Enlightenment and Propaganda from 1933 to 1945, Goebbels is thought by many to be one of Hitler's most influential and closest supporters. He was involved in the Nazi Party beginning in 1923, and committed suicide the morning after Hitler and Eva Braun did, in Berlin in 1945.

Goebbels, Magda: The wife of Joseph Goebbels, who took part in the deaths of the couple's six children in 1945, along with Martin Bormann.

Pol Pot: The leader of Cambodia from 1975-1979, his dictatorship is thought to have caused the death of 1-3 million people, approximately twenty-five percent of his country.

Rogers, Will and Betty: One of the best-known worldwide celebrities of the 1920's and 1930's, Will was "the Cherokee Kid," a humorist, columnist, movie star, and political satirist. He was a confidant of several U.S. presidents, and found an open door with world leaders everywhere. A fine man by all accounts, his wife Betty was, by his declaration, the center of his life.

Smith, Jacob H: Famous for ordering his troops to "Kill everyone over ten," the American general was court-martialed and reprimanded for his attitude, but was not officially punished. He is quoted directly in this novel, representing the connection between racism and expansionism at the time.

Soule, Silas: Captain in the Colorado Cavalry, this honorable soldier refused John Chivington's orders to attack Black Kettle's camp in 1864, then testified about the atrocities that took place, and was soon after assassinated in Denver. Many feel he was killed for testifying, directly at the behest of Chivington.

Tsalagi: More commonly known as Cherokee.

Note: These very brief descriptions are for those readers not at all familiar with the names or events used, and the author invites further research to gain a more comprehensive picture of who (or what) they were, and why they figure as characters or are mentioned in the novel. They are all people, or places, that have lived in the author's imagination for many decades, and their steady lifelong presence is the reason for their inclusion in the story.

ACKNOWLEDGMENTS

I thank my wife Heidrun Hoffmann for her love, and her solid and deep support throughout this process; my son Rico Rushworth for his reading acumen and enthusiasm as the sentences formed; Harold Dick Jr. for his steadfast listening ear, advice, true friendship, and honest and thoughtful counsel; Marita Hacker for her part in "hearing" the story alive; Victoria Devereaux, for her long friendship, true inspiration, and heartfelt work; Kristi Moya for her vision and belief; Dr. Darryl "Babe" Wilson for his inspiration and counsel; Bobby Cruz, for the fine tellings; and all those involved with Ho-dah-ten, for their stories, faith, and strength. All of these people helped make this story happen.

In addition, I'd like to thank those who read this book during its process and gave me the value of their insights: Valerie Klokow, for her intensive and personal feedback; Terry Whitebeach, for going above and beyond, and always inspiring me; Alison McGregor, for her belief; Jessica Hadden, for listening so closely; Carolye Kuchta, for her poetic sensibility; Shirley Ancheta, for listening from the heart; David Sullivan, for clear early comments; Diana and Kellogg Fleming, for poignant observations and encouragement; Johannes

Oehlmann, for steady commentary and insight; Martin Scanlon, for close reading and encouragement; Laurence Dang, for her startling viewpoints; Dr. Deborah Joy, for key thoughts of encouragement; and Ashley Crawford, for her amazingly beautiful words.

A special thanks to Justin Maxon, who contributed his art and vision in presenting the image of this book to the reading world. And to Joan Keyes, of Dovetail Publishing Services, for her professionalism, friendship, and advice.

In addition, as I wrote this book, particular friends and family members whose lives and art I admire floated in the wings, and I wrote with them in mind. They helped create what it became, so I thank them too: my mother Vivian Sherman; my grandparents Ed and Alta Stanley; my father William Rushworth; my friend Jeff Tagami; my son Will, my daughter-in-law Kana Soga, and my grandson Kai Rushworth; my step-mother Dorothy Downing; my sister Khalila Janis Alldis; my niece Jemila Alldis; Dave Pendleton; Saul Ramos; Martin Rizzo; Marcy Alancraig; Ann-Marie Sayers; Jacquie Ramos; Stephan Malacek; Diane and George Pettinger; and Bradley and Alecia Harger.

I also thank my friend Martin Simpson from the depths of my heart for making the music that has always inspired me so very completely.

Finally, I thank those many friends and artists for which there is not enough space to name, for your influence, support and friendship over time.

Stan Rushworth, 2013

BIOGRAPHY

Stan Rushworth was born in 1944 in Southern California; grew up primarily in the foothills of the Sierra Nevada; served in the Far East as an Army volunteer from 1962 through 1965; attended San Francisco State University, where he received a Master's degree in Language Arts; lived and worked in Guatemala in the 1970's; lived and worked in Hawaii in the 1980's; and has taught Native American literature and English for the last two decades at Cabrillo College, in Aptos, California. He is of Tsalagi, English, and Irish heritage. *Going to Water: The Journal of Beginning Rain,* is his second book. The first is *Sam Woods American Healing,* published by Station Hill Literary Editions (A Talking Leaves book), Barrytown, New York, 1992, and is currently available through Talking Leaves Press, Freedom, California.